The Spitfire Sisters

Margaret Dickinson, a *Sunday Times* top ten best-seller, was born and brought up in Lincolnshire and, until very recently, lived in Skegness where she raised her family. Her ambition to be a writer began early and she had her first novel published at the age of twenty-five. She has now written over twenty-five novels – set mostly in her home county but also in Nottinghamshire, Derbyshire and South Yorkshire. *The Spitfire Sisters* is the third in the Maitland trilogy, after *The Poppy Girls* and *The Brooklands Girls*.

Margaret Dickinson

The Spitfire Sisters

PAN BOOKS

First published 2020 by Macmillan

This paperback edition first published 2020 by Pan Books
an imprint of Pan Macmillan
The Smithson, 6 Briset Street, London EC1M 5NR
Associated companies throughout the world
www.panmacmillan.com

ISBN 978-1-5290-1847-9

Copyright © Margaret Dickinson 2020

1 3 5 7 9 8 6 4 2

A CIP catalogue record for this book is available from the British Library.

Typeset in Sabon by Palimpsest Book Production Ltd, Falkirk, Stirlingshire
Printed and bound by CPI Group (UK) Ltd, Croydon, CR0 4YY

Visit www.panmacmillan.com to read more about all our books
and to buy them. You will also find features, author interviews and
news of any author events, and you can sign up for e-newsletters
so that you're always first to hear about our new releases.

For all my family and friends for their love, encouragement and help through many years.

Acknowledgements

I wish to pay tribute to Mike Hodgson, who sadly passed away in October 2018. Mike, the founder of Thorpe Camp Visitor Centre at Tattershall Thorpe in Lincolnshire, acted as a guide on our coach trip to Belgium in 2016. His depth of knowledge about both world wars was remarkable and he generously shared his expertise with us all and continued to answer my many questions even after the trip. I am honoured to have known him and am sincerely grateful for all his help.

As always, this is a work of fiction; the characters and plot line are all created from my imagination and any resemblance to real people is coincidental.

I am very grateful to James and Claire Birch, of Doddington Hall near Lincoln, for allowing me to use their beautiful home as the setting and inspiration for this story, and also to the members of their team, who have been so helpful with my research over the last three years whilst I have been writing the Maitland Trilogy.

My love and grateful thanks to the members of

my family who have helped in various ways: Charles, Hilary, Alex and Matthew for taking us to Brooklands Museum and to Kew Gardens and for their help with my research there; and to Helen for reading the first draft.

Once again, my special thanks to my fantastic agent, Darley Anderson, and his team, to my wonderful editor, Trisha Jackson, and to everyone at Pan Macmillan.

Several sources have been valuable for research, most notably: *Brooklands: The Official Centenary History* by David Venables (Haynes, 2007); *A Spitfire Girl* by Mary Ellis, as told to Melody Foreman (Frontline Books, 2016); *Spitfire Girl* by Jackie Moggridge (Head of Zeus, 2014); *Spreading My Wings* by Diana Barnato Walker (Grub Street, 2003) and the Imperial War Museum at Duxford.

The Maitland Family

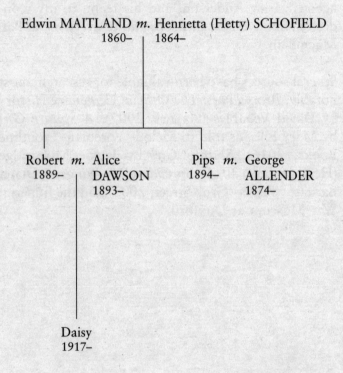

Edwin MAITLAND *m.* Henrietta (Hetty) SCHOFIELD
1860–   1864–

Robert *m.* Alice   Pips *m.* George
1889–   DAWSON   1894–   ALLENDER
         1893–   1874–

Daisy
1917–

The Dawson Family

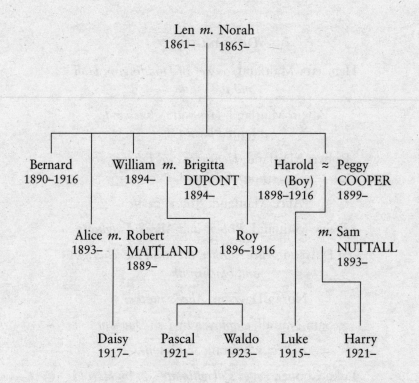

Cast of Characters

Charlie Cooper, *Peggy's father*

Betty Cooper, *Peggy's sister*

Clara Nuttall, *Sam's mother*

Conrad Everton, *a local GP who is in
partnership with Robert*

Florence Everton, *Conrad's wife*

LONDON AND WEYBRIDGE

Pips Allender, *Henrietta and Edwin's daughter,
Robert's sister and Daisy's aunt*

George Allender, *Pips's husband*

Milly Whittaker, *Pips's friend*

Paul Whittaker, *Milly's husband*

Mitch Hammond, *Pips's friend*

Johnny Hammond, *Mitch's nephew*

Jeff Pointer, *employed by Mitch at The Hammond
Flying School, based at Brooklands, near Weybridge*

BELGIUM

William Dawson, *Len and Norah's son,
and Alice's brother*

Brigitta, *William's wife*

Pascal and Waldo, *William and Brigitta's sons*

One

'You don't mind Daisy coming to stay with us during the Easter school holidays, do you?'

George Allender smiled at his wife. 'Of course not, Pips. I'm extremely fond of her.' His smile broadened. 'She reminds me more and more of you.' He chuckled. 'She resembles her mother in looks but you in character, without a doubt.'

Pips pulled a comical face. 'I don't think that's a compliment to Daisy – certainly not in my mother's estimation anyway.'

Pips and George had been married for almost two years, which George freely acknowledged had been the happiest two years of his life. They had been lovers for several years before that, but their marriage had been 'on hold' for several reasons, the most insurmountable at the time being the disapproval of George's daughter, Rebecca. But at last, the young woman had seen just how much the pair loved each other and had capitulated. Since then, Pips and Rebecca – not so far apart in age – had become good friends. She often stayed with them at their apartment in Clapham on her days off from her work as

1

a nurse at the London Hospital, even though she had her own living accommodation near the hospital. Although Pips and George now spent most of their time in London, they frequently visited Pips's family, the Maitlands, at Doddington Hall in Lincolnshire. Pips couldn't let many weeks go by without seeing the niece she adored and catching up with all the latest village gossip.

Pips pressed her hands together. 'Good. I must make arrangements to take her to Brooklands whilst she's here.'

George's smile faded a little. 'And for a flight in one of Mitch Hammond's aircraft, I suppose.'

'Of course. It's the highlight of a holiday with us.' She met her husband's gaze. 'But I won't break my promise. I won't take her racing or start to drive again myself. We'll just watch, as we always do. There'll be a race meeting on Easter Monday. We'll go then.'

George sighed inwardly and, not for the first time, struggled with his conscience. Before they'd been due to marry in December 1930, Pips had promised him that she would no longer race her car at Brooklands after their marriage, though she would continue to go flying there. During the very last race in which she'd taken part, she'd had an accident on the track that had left her unconscious for three days and it had meant that their wedding had been put off for a few months. She'd been nursed by Rebecca and that was when the girl had seen for herself her father's devotion to Pips. And his name had been the first Rebecca had heard Pips utter when she had begun to regain consciousness.

Despite her promise, George knew that Pips missed the excitement of racing. She was still an honorary member of a group of women who raced there – the Brooklands Girls, as they called themselves – but she met up with them now in a social capacity rather than as a participant alongside them on the track. Flying, however, was a different matter; she could not give up that, and, having gained her pilot's licence, she was able to take Daisy flying too. George, who suffered acute airsickness, would not go with her, but Daisy loved it and longed for the day when she too could learn to fly.

'So, we'll go up to Lincolnshire on Friday evening for the weekend – weather permitting – and arrange everything. It'll be something for us all to look forward to through the winter months. And besides, it's high time I beat my dear brother at chess again. I'll be losing my touch if I allow too many weeks to pass without challenging him.' She paused and then asked, 'Will you be able to take an extra day off from work so that we can make it a long weekend?'

George pulled a face. 'Last week I would have said "yes" without hesitation, but the news from Germany has put everyone in a bit of a flap. I'll have to see what I can do.'

George, a former major in the British Army, now worked in an advisory capacity at the War Office situated in a grand building on the corner of Horse Guards Avenue and Whitehall.

Pips frowned. 'News? What news?'

'Adolf Hitler becoming Chancellor.'

Pips stared at him in disbelief. 'The little corporal

who tried to seize power with Field Marshall Ludendorff in '24?'

George nodded. 'The end of '23, actually.'

'But I thought Hitler got sent to prison.'

George laughed wryly. 'He did, but it was no more than a slap on the wrist. He was released after only nine months.'

'And now he's been made Chancellor? I don't believe it.'

'Sadly, it's true.'

'We'll have to tell Robert at the weekend. I wonder if he knows.'

'I expect so. It's been in the papers and he follows the national and international news avidly. Just as I thought you did. I'm surprised you didn't know.'

Pips smiled and moved to him, putting her arms around his waist and lifting her face to be kissed. 'Why do I have to bother with the press when I have my very own handsome major to keep me informed?'

Now in his late fifties and twenty years older than Pips, who would be thirty-nine later in the year, George was still a distinguished-looking man; tall and straight-backed with dark hair that was only just beginning to grey at his temples, a neat moustache and dark blue eyes.

As he bent to kiss her, he marvelled yet again that this vibrant, strong-willed woman with her wonderful auburn hair and sparkling green eyes loved him and wondered, not for the first time, if he should release her from her promise and agree that she should race again. But now she no longer had a racing car of her own. To confirm her promise to George not to race,

4

she'd sold her beloved Bugatti. 'It's all smashed up anyway,' she'd said. 'I'll get Paul to do it up and sell it for me. I don't want to see it again.' Paul ran his own racing club, The Whittaker Racing Club, at Brooklands and was an expert mechanic.

Now Pips owned a four-seater Ford and, although it got her from A to B, she hadn't the same love for it as she'd had for her racing car. Pips drove expertly, but still a little too fast for George's liking.

On their journey to Lincolnshire that weekend, George clung onto the sides of his seat gallantly and said nothing. At Peterborough, Pips turned on to the quieter, rural roads and was obliged to lower her speed.

'You can stop hanging on now, darling,' she said merrily. 'I can't open her up on these roads.'

It was dark by the time they turned into the entrance to the hall and drove up the long drive-way, through the arch of the gatehouse to come to a halt outside the front door. Lights twinkled in welcome from several windows. Although Pips loved her life in the city with George, she always felt the thrill of coming home every time she saw, even through the darkness, the rectangular shape of the beautiful Elizabethan mansion that had been her family's home for generations. Her mother, Henrietta Maitland, had inherited the hall and its estate from her childless uncle and she had always been at the heart of the small village of Doddington. With one main street and lanes running from it into the surrounding countryside, the village lay five miles west of Lincoln, and Henrietta's estate provided employment for the locals, not only in the house itself but also in the gardens, parklands and on the farm too.

For many years, ever since he'd moved into the hall on his marriage to Henrietta Schofield, Edwin Maitland had been the local doctor, holding surgeries in a side room at the hall, but now he was retired and had handed over the running of the practice to his son, Robert.

As they climbed out of the car, Pips said, 'They do know we're coming. I telephoned to tell them . . .'

As if on cue, the front door opened and light flooded down the steps.

'Welcome home. Both of you.'

Pips's brother, Robert, stood at the top of the steps – a tall, straight-backed figure. His handsome face was in shadow, but, silhouetted against the light behind him, Pips could not help the familiar pang of regret when she saw the empty sleeve of his right arm tucked into his pocket. She ran lightly up the steps to hug him. George followed more slowly, tactfully holding out his left hand to shake his brother-in-law's.

'How are you, Robert?'

'We're all well, thank you. Come in out of the cold. Jake will bring your bags in. We didn't hold dinner back as you told us you might be rather late, but Mother has arranged something on a tray for you. We'll all sit in the parlour and we can talk whilst you eat.'

'Aunty Pips!' The gangly, fifteen-year-old girl came running down the long Great Hall and flung herself

6

into Pips's outstretched arms, followed more sedately by the rest of the family.

'Daisy, darling.'

Releasing herself from the excited girl's bear hug, Pips kissed her mother, father and her sister-in-law, Alice, but it was still Daisy who held her attention. 'Granny's got Cook to make you some sandwiches and Sarah will bring tea in now you're here. Oh, I've got so much to tell you.'

'Daisy, dear, do calm down,' Henrietta said, linking her arm through George's and leading the way to the parlour. 'Anyone would think you hadn't seen them for months.'

Daisy's blue eyes sparkled at her grandmother. 'It feels like that, Granny.'

Henrietta smiled indulgently. 'Well, yes, I can see that.'

Slim, with blue eyes and neat grey hair that was almost white now, Henrietta was normally very strict with what she considered 'unladylike' behaviour, but even she found it hard to be severe with Daisy for long. With black hair and dark blue eyes like her mother, Daisy was nothing like the quiet and reserved Alice in temperament. As everyone said, she was 'just like Pips'. She was still chattering when they sat down in the parlour and the maid brought in freshly made tea and coffee for them all. Henrietta poured whilst Alice handed round the cups. There was certainly no chance of 'children should be seen and not heard' when Daisy was around.

'Daddy lets me ride Samson on my own now, though I have to promise not to jump him yet.' She was referring to the biggest horse in the stables; the horse that Pips normally rode when she was at home.

'We'll go riding tomorrow morning,' Pips promised and then, with a mischievous twinkle, added, 'I'm surprised you haven't unearthed your father's motorcycle yet.'

Daisy pulled a face. 'Jake and I got it out and he cleaned it up but' – she glanced at her father with a cheeky grin – 'I've got to wait until the end of the year when I'll be sixteen.'

'We'll come for the birthdays as always,' Pips said, 'and see you ride it.'

Daisy's birthday fell on 1 December, three days before that of her cousin, Luke Cooper. Although Luke was two years older than Daisy, the two youngsters had always been close, both as cousins and as friends.

'I'm very surprised,' Pips said, 'that Luke hasn't wanted to ride it.'

There was a slight pause before Daisy replied airily, 'Oh, he has ridden it, Aunty Pips, several times.'

Two

As the family sat talking late into the night, all apart from Daisy, who had gone to bed, Pips said, 'Now, tell me all the news.'

Edwin smiled. 'Not much has happened since you were last here at Christmas, though there is quite a bit of illness in the village and the surrounding district.' He nodded towards his son. 'The usual winter ailments. Robert and Conrad are being kept very busy.' His eyes twinkled as he added, 'I can't say I'm sorry to be missing all the coughs and colds and influenzas. Retirement does have its compensations.'

Conrad Everton and his wife, Florence, had moved into the village almost four years earlier when he had taken up the post of junior doctor to Robert on Edwin's semi-retirement. They had fitted into the community very well. Conrad had served at the front as a doctor in the Great War and understood the occasional dark moods that Robert still suffered. Now, Edwin was more or less fully retired and only helped out in emergencies.

'Alice, how are your family?' Pips asked.

There was a great deal of history between the Maitland and Dawson families that bound them irrevocably together. Alice, once lady's maid to both Henrietta and Pips, had gone with her young mistress to the front in 1914 when Pips had insisted on accompanying her brother when he'd joined an independent flying ambulance corps to establish a post near the trenches to give much-needed first aid to the wounded as quickly as possible. But even amidst the horror, love had blossomed and Alice and Robert were now married. Alice had loved Robert in secret for years, but only during the time she had nursed him devotedly when he had lost his arm trying to bring wounded in from no-man's-land did he fall in love with her. Though his mother had been against the match at first, Alice was now loved dearly by all the family and also by the servants with whom she had once worked. It was Alice's own diplomatic and kind personality that had earned her a special place in the household.

In answer to Pips's question, Alice wrinkled her nose. 'Coping, I suppose, is the word, Pips. Just.'

There was a silence in the room whilst they all remembered the three Dawson brothers, who would never again come home, having been killed on the Somme within days of each other. The pain would never go away, even after over sixteen years. The whole country was still trying to come to terms with the devastating losses. Hardly a family had been untouched and many, like the Dawsons, lost several members of their family; of the young men who had returned, many were still living with the after-effects of life-changing injuries, like Robert.

'Mam,' Alice said, referring to her mother, Norah,

'misses Ma dreadfully. Dad does too, though he'd never admit it.'

Ma Dawson, Len's mother, had been regarded as the matriarch of the village. Though lacking in a formal education, she had been wise and everyone, young and old, had turned to her in times of trouble.

'We all miss her,' Pips murmured and her thoughts turned to another member of the Dawson family. 'And what about William?'

Alice sighed deeply. 'No change. Dad won't have his name spoken. Won't even allow Mam to have his picture displayed.'

William was regarded by Len Dawson as the black sheep of the family. When patriotic fervour had gripped the nation at the outbreak of the war, Bernard and Roy had volunteered at once. Even Harold, too young to enlist, had run away to sign up before his family could prevent it. But William had stubbornly refused to join them, insisting that he wanted to save lives, not take them. Instead, he had gone with Robert, Pips and Alice to join the ambulance corps as a stretcher bearer. Len had insisted that the family should disown him, refusing to recognize the young man's special kind of courage.

'I've had a letter from him,' Pips said. 'I've brought it with me to show to your mother, if I get the chance.'

Alice nodded. 'He writes regularly to me and I always share the letters with her, of course, but she's hungry for any news from him. He can't write directly to her, as you know.'

William had not returned to England after the war.

He had fallen in love with a Belgian nurse serving with the ambulance corps and had married her. They had lived with Brigitta's grandparents, who had brought her up. Recently, Pips had heard from William that the old couple had both died during the recent winter and their farm had passed to their granddaughter. William and Brigitta now had two sons, Pascal and Waldo; Norah's grandsons whom she had never seen.

'I wonder if your father will ever relent,' Pips murmured.

Alice said nothing, but merely shook her head sadly. It was Henrietta who spoke up. 'He's a very stubborn and foolish man. One day, I fear, he will have cause to regret his bigoted views. He is pinning all his hopes for the future on young Luke and it's a heavy burden for the boy to carry. Though I shouldn't call him a "boy" now. He is growing into a fine young man.'

Alice smiled lovingly as she thought about her nephew. 'I think he's taken over Ma's role of watching out for Mam and how my dad treats her.'

Luke was the illegitimate son of Harold Dawson, Alice's youngest brother, who had been killed before he could come home to marry his pregnant sweetheart. Although at first shocked, the whole village, led by Henrietta Maitland, had rallied round and supported the girl. As Henrietta had remarked to Peggy at the time, 'You're not the first to have a bairn out of wedlock, and I doubt very much you'll be the last.'

Now Peggy Cooper was happily married to Sam

Nuttall, one of the few young men to return home virtually unscathed from the war and who now worked for Len Dawson in his small village industry of carpenter, wheelwright and blacksmith.

'Does Luke still come here every Saturday to ride out with Daisy?'

'Oh yes. Never misses.' Alice chuckled.

'Then I'll see him tomorrow. We'll all go riding together.'

The day was cold and showery, but undeterred, Pips, George, Daisy and Luke set out towards the stables at the rear of the hall.

'No Harry today, Luke?' Pips asked.

Harry was Luke's half-brother, born to Peggy and Sam.

Luke grinned. 'Granddad didn't really want me to come here this early. We're supposed to work on a Saturday morning and then come riding with you in the afternoon.' The young man shrugged. 'But I just told him I was coming, so he insisted that Harry should stay and help him instead.'

Pips threw back her head and laughed. 'I bet that didn't suit Harry, but I expect he daren't stand up to Mr Dawson like you can.'

'It's high time Granddad retired. He's over seventy, you know.'

Pips nodded. 'He must be, but I've no doubt he's not quite ready to hand his life's work over to a seventeen-year-old.'

Luke grimaced. 'Maybe not, but he's always telling me it'll be mine one day. Not Sam's or Harry's, though

13

he's said there's a job for them there as long as they want it.'

'I've no doubt Sam will stay there, but what about Harry? Is it what he wants to do?'

'Not sure. I don't think he knows himself yet. He is only eleven.'

'I'll call and see your grandma later.'

The boy eyed her. He knew all about the letters from his uncle William, which Pips always shared with Norah. In a low voice he said, 'Best make it later this morning, Aunty Pips, if you can. Granddad will be at home this afternoon and all day tomorrow. He hardly ever works on Saturday afternoons and certainly never on Sundays.'

Pips nodded and said quietly, 'Thanks, Luke. We'll ride round past their cottage on our way back. You can bring my horse back here and I'll walk home.'

They entered the stable yard to see that Jake had already saddled up four horses.

'Morning, Miss Pips. All ready for you.'

'Hello, Jake, how are you?' Pips shook hands with the young man, who had been a member of staff at the hall for many years. Orphaned as a baby, Jake had run away from the boys' home for pauper children, operated by the Lincoln Union, where he had been brought up, to look for work. Henrietta had found the twelve-year-old sleeping rough and had taken pity on the skinny waif. His loyalty to Henrietta, who had given him employment and a home above the stables, was eternal.

'You ride Samson today, Aunty Pips,' Daisy said. 'He's your horse really.'

But Pips shook her head. 'No, Daisy, I want to see you riding him.'

Daisy's eyes shone. 'Can I try a jump, if you're with me?'

'Certainly not!' Pips said. 'What would your father say?' But unseen by anyone else Pips gave her niece a broad wink.

As they rode out into the countryside, through the fields belonging to the Maitlands, George breathed in the clear country air. 'I do miss riding when we're in London, I have to admit. I must do my best to come home with you more often, Pips.'

They rode side by side at walking pace, but as they were approaching a low hedge, Daisy suddenly spurred the big horse towards it.

'Oh, Aunty Pips . . .' From a young boy, Luke had always called her that name and even though he was already taller than she was, the courtesy title had stuck. He was even allowed to call Mrs Maitland 'Aunty Hetty', though Edwin was always 'Dr Maitland'. 'She shouldn't be—' He fell silent as they all watched Daisy heading towards the hedge. She sailed over it and landed on the other side. The other three rode sedately through the gate in the hedge and joined Daisy, who was grinning widely.

'I'm glad you were here, Aunty Pips,' Luke said wryly. 'Aunty Alice would have had my guts for garters if she'd fallen off.'

Pips rode up close to Daisy. 'Well done, Daisy, but I want you to promise me one thing. And you know in our family we never willingly break a promise.'

Daisy nodded.

'You must only jump when either your father or Jake is with you. It's not fair to put such a responsibility on Luke.'

'I don't think Jake will like it either and Daddy doesn't come riding very often.'

'In that case, then, you'll just have to wait until I come home.'

The girl pouted but said no more. She knew better than to argue with her aunt.

They rode back through the lanes until they paused outside the Dawsons' cottage. Pips slid from her mount and handed the reins to Luke. 'I won't be long. I'll be back in time for lunch.'

She walked round the side of the cottage, knocked on the back door, opened it and called, 'Hello, Mrs Dawson. Are you in?'

A voice called from the kitchen. 'Come in, Miss Pips.'

Closing the back door, Pips went through the scullery and into the kitchen where she found Norah sitting at the table, a cup of tea in front of her, whilst next to the range, in the chair that had once been Ma's, sat Bess Cooper, Luke's maternal grandmother.

'Nah then, Miss Pips,' Bess laughed raucously. 'O' course we should call you "Mrs Allender", but we just can't get used to it.'

'"Miss Pips" is just fine. How are you both?' Pips added, sitting down opposite Bess in the chair she knew was Len's.

'As well as we can be, y'know,' Bess said with a glance at Norah, who avoided meeting Pips's eyes.

'We've got two grandbairns each and they keep us going, don't they, Norah?' They had a mutual grandson in Luke, but Norah also had Daisy and Bess had Harry.

At last Norah lifted her head slowly and met Pips's gaze, guessing why Pips had called in. 'But I have two more grandchildren, don't I, Miss Pips?' Norah, though always energetic, was small and thin, with her grey hair pulled tightly back into a bun. She was only ever seen without her apron at church on Sundays. Her face was deeply etched with lines of sadness and, though she tried to smile, it never reached her eyes.

Pips nodded and pulled a letter from her pocket. She knew they were safe. She had seen Len at his workshop as they had passed it and she also knew that Bess was Norah's friend and confidante.

'This came to me in London last week.'

Norah read it swiftly and then a second time more slowly, drinking in the news of William and his family and committing the words to memory. It would not be safe for her to keep the letter even though she knew Pips would leave it with her if she asked. She passed the letter to Bess for her to read too before it was handed back to Pips.

'D'you know if William is still working in the cemeteries around where he lives?' Norah asked.

'Oh yes. And his boys help him too. And,' Pips added gently, 'he often goes to visit his brothers' graves.' She paused and then added, 'I think it's high time we had another trip to Belgium to see them. Would you come, Mrs Dawson?'

Norah's head shot up. 'It's good of you to ask me, but you know I can't, though . . .'

'Yes?'

'Luke might like to go. You could make the excuse you're taking him to see his father's grave again, like you did a few years back. Len might agree to that.'

Bess snorted with derision. 'I doubt it, Norah, duck, but Miss Pips can try.'

They talked for a while longer, but when she left, Pips turned back towards the workshop, in the opposite direction to her home.

Len was just packing away his tools for the day. 'Morning, Miss Pips,' he said politely, though there was a wariness in his eyes. The young woman from the hall didn't often seek him out.

'Mr Dawson,' Pips nodded acknowledgement, 'I wonder if you'd allow Luke to come to stay with us during the Easter holidays. Daisy will be coming and I thought I might arrange a trip abroad for them both. It'd be nice for Luke to visit his father's grave again and those of his uncles too.'

Len glared at her and flung down his heavy hammer. Stiffly, he said, 'If I thought that's all you meant to do, then I'd say "yes", but it isn't, is it? You'd take them to see – *him.*'

Pips stepped closer to him. 'Mr Dawson, the only lies I have ever told in my life were during the war to ease a soldier's passing, so I'm not going to start now by deceiving you. Of course I would want to take them to Belgium to see William. In fact, I'd like to take Mrs Dawson if—'

'Never! And you'll oblige me by not mentioning

18

that coward's name in my hearing. Oh, I'm not daft. I know Alice brings letters from him for Norah to read and' – he pointed an accusing finger at her – 'if I'm not much mistaken, so do you, but her seeing him again or communicating with him 'ersen, I won't have. You hear me?'

'Loud and clear, Mr Dawson.'

There was a long pause whilst they glared at one another, both determined not to be the first to glance away.

'So,' Pips said at last. 'What about Luke?'

'No, he can't go either and that's my final answer, so don't ask again.'

'Can't promise you that, Mr Dawson. He'll soon be old enough to make his own mind up. If he isn't already. And whilst we're on the subject of promises, didn't you say you'd get him a motorcycle when he was sixteen?'

Now Len looked uncomfortable. 'What if I did?'

'Well, he's already seventeen now and I don't see him riding one.' She was not about to tell tales on the young man, but it seemed that Len knew more about what went on in the village than they'd all thought.

'I don't see the need now,' Len smirked, 'seein' as how he gets to ride Master Robert's whenever he wants.'

At the end of February, the newspapers were full of the news of the German Reichstag burning down.

'This puts Hitler in an even stronger position,' Robert said to Pips on the telephone. 'I'm sure George will say the same thing, but it seems to me that this fire has been a stroke of luck for the Nazis, who are saying that it's arson by the Communists.'

'George says very little, but I do know the Nazis have arrested a young man whom they say is a Communist sympathizer.'

'Mm, I wonder. It's given the Nazis the chance to make more sweeping laws. They say that Goebbels, Hitler's propaganda chief, has virtually taken control of Germany's radio, and any newspaper or publication that criticizes Hitler's regime disappears very quickly.'

'One piece of information George did tell me was that the Nazis raided the Communist Party headquarters, and even though it had been abandoned several weeks before, they're saying they have found evidence of a plot.'

'Your little corporal is a dangerous man, Pips. I do worry about the grip he is getting on the German people.'

'They idolize him.'

'It's understandable, in a way; he has given them back their national pride and pulled the country back onto its feet. But I said at the time that the Versailles Treaty was far too stringent – that we'd suffer the consequences of their bitterness.'

'You did. You said we'd have more trouble. I think you were right.'

Robert sighed heavily. 'We'll just have to hope and pray that it doesn't escalate into another war.'

'Let's not think about it. I'm looking forward to having Daisy visit at Easter.'

'So is she.' He chuckled. 'I think her suitcase is half packed already.'

'Bless her. Give everyone my love. I'll ring again next week.'

Three

'I'll drive up on Thursday,' Pips told Alice over the telephone, the weekend before Easter. 'And Daisy and I will travel back on Good Friday. Then we'll all come up the following weekend to bring her home. Will that be all right?'

'Of course. But there's just one thing . . .' There was laughter in Alice's tone. 'You'll have to take Daisy riding on the Friday morning before you set off. She's been very good keeping her promise to you not to jump Samson when you're not here.'

'Of course I will.'

'By the way, are you going to Belgium?'

'Not this time. I thought we'd leave it until the summer holidays. We'll be able to stay longer then.'

'Then count me in, won't you? I'd love to see William and his family again and I'm sure Robert won't mind me going, unless, of course, we can persuade him to go too.'

Pips chuckled. 'Then you'd better start working on him now.'

The sisters-in-law laughed together as they ended the call with loving messages. They had always been very fond of each other even when Alice had been

Pips's lady's maid. They'd been friends even then rather than mistress and servant.

'Would you go to Belgium with us in the summer?' Pips asked George as they sat together over dinner.

'If I can get leave, then yes.'

'And will you come with us to Brooklands? I'm planning to take Daisy on Easter Monday.'

'Of course. I wouldn't dare let you go on your own. Not when Mitch Hammond is likely to be there.'

'Oh George. Can't you forget all that nonsense? He's a friend, that's all.'

'On your side maybe, but you know very well that the guy's in love with you. Has been, I suspect, ever since you rescued him from his crashed plane in no-man's-land.'

They exchanged a glance that was full of shared memories, both happy and sad.

'He's a playboy, George. He has a string of girl-friends and doesn't seem to want to settle down with any one of them.'

She was not about to tell George that Mitch had indeed once declared his love for her. That was one secret she could not share with anyone, not even with her husband. But it seemed that George was even more astute than she gave him credit for.

'That, my darling girl,' he said softly, 'is because he can't have *you*.'

'Oh phooey,' Pips muttered as she rose to clear away the dishes and serve the pudding.

*

'I do wish Granddad Dawson had let Luke come to London with me. I'm sure he'd love flying as much as I do and he'd love to see the racing – cars or motorcycles,' Daisy said as the three of them travelled from Waterloo to Weybridge Station, which was very close to the Brooklands track.

'You'll have to work on him,' George said. 'Your granddad, I mean. Luke'd be very welcome to come and stay with us.'

Daisy nodded. 'I will, but I don't think he'll let him go to Belgium with us again in the summer.'

'No. Sadly, I think you're right there. Will your father come, d'you think?'

Daisy pulled a face. 'Mummy and I are working on him. What about you, Uncle George? You'll come with us, won't you?'

'I – think so.' He smiled across at Pips. 'As long as I have your aunty at my side, I can face it.'

There was a pause as they watched the passing countryside until Daisy said, 'Will we see Aunty Milly today? I do like her. It was so nice of her to ask me to be her bridesmaid.'

Pips chuckled. 'She thought you did such a great job as mine.'

'Hasn't she got anyone else? I mean, I know you're her best friend, and all that, but I'd have thought . . .' Daisy's voice trailed away.

Pips shook her head. 'Milly is an only child and she doesn't seem to have any close family. I think she has a distant cousin living in Derbyshire, or is it Sheffield now? I forget. But the families don't keep in touch. And besides, she's very fond of you.'

'She looked so pretty on her wedding day, but you were beautiful,' Daisy added loyally.

Pips laughed. 'Kind of you to say so, but, yes, Milly made a lovely bride. She's got such big blue eyes and with her blond curls, she always looks just like a pretty china doll.'

'She's a bit scatty though, isn't she? Granny says she was what they called a "flapper" in the twenties. Were you one too?'

'For a while. It was Milly who introduced me to the wild parties and the merrymaking in London and, of course, it was she who took me to Brooklands.'

'But she doesn't race, does she?'

Pips shook her head. 'No, but she's an honorary "Brooklands Girl", like I am now.'

The Brooklands Girls were a group of women racers, who for many years had not been allowed to race under the auspices of the Brooklands Automobile Racing Club, but several private clubs who raced at the track, one of them being owned and operated by Milly's now-husband, Paul Whittaker, did allow women to race, either in all-women races or alongside men. Pips had raced with them during the 1920s.

As the train drew into the station, Pips chuckled. 'I quite understand how Milly must appear to you, but never forget what she did in the war.'

Solemnly, Daisy nodded. 'I won't, Aunty Pips. That's how you met, isn't it, when she came out to the front to help nurse the wounded?'

Pips nodded. 'She knew very little about nursing when she arrived, but if anyone could cheer up the injured, it was Milly Fortesque as she was then.'

'And now we must call her "Mrs Whittaker".'

'Oh, I think she'll be quite happy for you still to call her "Aunty Milly".'

Milly was there on the platform and, as George helped Pips and Daisy from the train, she ran forward, her arms outstretched. '*Dahlings!*'

She hugged them in turn and then linked her arm through Pips's. 'There's such a lot of excitement today. They've finished some repairs to the track just in time for today's meeting and – guess what? Sir Malcolm Campbell has brought his famous *Bluebird*, the car he drove to get the new World Land Speed Record at Daytona in February. He's going to demonstrate it on the outer circle but he won't race – or even go very fast – because of the track surface. But isn't it exciting just to *see* his car?'

'Is Uncle Paul racing?' Daisy asked.

'Yes. He's in two races, but doesn't expect to win. There's someone here with a Maserati that's just a little bit too good. Anyway, let's go to the clubhouse. The girls are all there. Muriel's racing later too. And Pattie.'

All Pips's friends greeted Daisy warmly and Paul hugged her hard.

'How's my favourite bridesmaid?'

Daisy laughed. 'Uncle Paul, I was your *only* bridesmaid.'

Milly's husband was a good-looking, fair-haired man with a firm jawline, an honest face and blue eyes that twinkled down at her. 'That doesn't stop you being my favourite.'

'Where's Uncle Mitch?' Daisy asked, looking round. 'I want to ask him if he'll take me flying whilst I'm here.'

'He'll arrange a flight for you, darling, I'm sure,' Milly said. 'He won't take you himself, as you well know, because he doesn't believe in flying – or teaching – family or close friends. But I'm sure Jeff will take you up.'

Jeff Pointer worked for Mitch as a pilot and instructor for The Hammond Flying School based at Brooklands and had taught Pips to fly.

Milly put her arm around Daisy's shoulders. 'Come on, darling, let's go and find him. He's around here somewhere.'

They found Jeff talking earnestly to Mitch at the far end of the room. Standing with them was a boy with the same dark brown eyes and black hair as Mitch, listening intently to their conversation.

'Johnny!' Daisy cried as they neared them. 'I wondered if you'd be here.'

The boy – or rather young man now, for he was two years older than Daisy – turned and his eyes lit up at the sight of her. He came towards her at once and his uncle Mitch and Jeff turned to look towards her too, though Daisy had eyes for no one but Johnny Hammond.

'Well, well, well. If it isn't the lovely Daisy Maitland.' Mitch Hammond came over to her and kissed her on both cheeks, whilst Jeff – a little more sedately – shook her hand in a very grown-up manner. Mitch smiled at her. 'And what brings you here, Daisy, as if I didn't know? Are you going to start racing, now that your aunt seems to have given up?'

Daisy smiled up at him. 'No, but I am going to fly one of your aeroplanes one day.'

Mitch's eyes widened, but he threw back his head and laughed aloud. 'Are you now? Well, if you're anything like your Aunty Pips, I've no doubt you will. Jeff will take you up. He's taking Johnny up during the school holidays. How long are you here for?'

'Just till next weekend.'

'Right, Jeff and I will sort something out and I'll give you a ring. We should be able to get in a couple of flights for you if your aunt will bring you down.'

Daisy's eyes shone. 'Thank you, Uncle Mitch,' she said politely.

'Now, it's time we were going out onto Members' Hill. The racing's about to start.'

'Come and say "hello" to Aunty Pips and Uncle George.'

Mitch squeezed her arm. 'I'll see them later, Daisy. I must get to the track now. I'm racing in the second race.'

As she watched him walk away, followed by Johnny and Jeff, Daisy whispered to Milly, 'Why doesn't he want to see Aunty Pips and Uncle George?'

Milly flapped her hand. 'Oh, I'll tell you sometime, but come along. We ought to be finding our places.'

Daisy was not to be put off quite so easily. 'But she saved his life, didn't she? She pulled him out of his crashed aircraft in the war and saved the photographs he'd been taking of enemy lines too. Daddy told me. So why—?'

'It's rather complicated, darling. Grown-up stuff.'

'But I'm grown up, Aunty Milly.' She grinned. 'Well, nearly, but there's something – well – funny because every time his name's mentioned, Uncle George gets very tight lipped and—' Suddenly, Daisy's eyes widened and her mouth formed a round 'o'. 'You – you don't mean that Mitch is in love with Aunty Pips?'

'Well – um – yes,' Milly said uncomfortably. 'I think he very well might be.'

'Ah, that would explain it, then.' Daisy sighed heavily. 'He is very nice, of course, but I do love Uncle George.'

Milly squeezed her arm. 'And so does your aunty, darling. Now, let's go and find somewhere to watch the racing. And mind, not a word about this to Pips and certainly not to George.'

'I promise. I can keep a secret, you know.'

Milly giggled deliciously. 'Better than I can, I hope. And you're just a little too sharp for your own good at times, Daisy Maitland. *Just* like your Aunty Pips.'

Four

Muriel Denton came fourth in the all-women's race, much to her disgust. Her disappointment was tempered a little by the fact that her friend, Pattie Henderson, won. Though fierce rivals on the track, outside a race they were all good friends and rooted for each other. 'Anyone but you,' she said, slapping Pattie on the back, 'and I'd've been spitting feathers.'

Pattie laughed. 'I only won because Pips doesn't race any more. If she'd been racing her Bugatti today, I'd have been lost in her exhaust fumes. Come on, let's get a drink and go and find her. I'm still hoping to persuade her to take up racing here again, though goodness knows why I'm bothering because she'll beat us hollow.'

'I don't think you'll manage it. She gave a promise to George that she wouldn't race any more after their marriage and Pips never breaks her promises.'

Pattie pursed her lips and glanced across to where their party of friends was standing on Members' Hill. 'Then it's George I have to work on, is it, to get him to release her from her promise?'

'You can try,' Muriel laughed, 'but I wouldn't hold your breath.'

A little later, Pattie, her racing over for the day, drew George aside. 'Dear George, I want to ask you something.'

He smiled down at her. He liked this dark-haired woman with warm brown eyes and a very firm handshake. In fact, he liked all of Pips's Brooklands friends. Even Mitch Hammond, in a way. George was forced to admit that his rival was a fine man; a courageous and daring man who'd flown with the Royal Flying Corps during the war as a reconnaissance pilot. Though he wasn't too sure just how much he could trust him around Pips. He had the reputation of being a lady's man, which Mitch himself seemed to delight in perpetuating.

'Now I wonder if I can guess what that might be?'

Pattie looked up at him, her eyes wide. '*Can* you?'

He sighed. 'You want me to persuade her to race again.'

'How did you know?'

'Because, my dear, I've been struggling with my conscience as to whether I ought to do just that. I know she misses it, but, you see, that accident she had frightened the life out of me. I couldn't bear to lose her.'

'Mm. I do see that. The rest of us aren't married, so it's not quite the same for us.'

'You have families though, who must worry about you.'

'Of course, but they all realize it's just something we have to do.'

'As I suppose I should for Pips,' he murmured. He

paused for a moment before asking, 'Are none of you married or engaged?'

'Not amongst our little group – the Brooklands Girls – no. Muriel was, of course, but her husband was killed on the Somme.'

After a slight pause, he asked softly, 'And you?'

There was a slightly longer pause before Pattie, her voice shaking a little, said, 'My fiancé was killed at Passchendaele and I haven't met anyone since who could even come close to him in my affections.'

'I'm sorry.'

'So,' she said briskly after a moment. 'What about it?'

'I'll think about it. I promise you that and – and maybe I'll talk to her. But, of course, she's still got her flying.'

'Yes, there's that,' Pattie said, but she didn't sound too enthusiastic. For her, flying could not even begin to match the thrill of racing round the Brooklands track.

They rejoined the others and, for the moment, the subject was put aside, if not entirely forgotten.

'Has Uncle Mitch telephoned yet?' Daisy asked impatiently at breakfast the following morning after George had left for the office.

Pips laughed. 'Give him a chance to get it arranged. I'm sure he won't forget, but until he does, what do you want to do today? Shopping? Sightseeing?'

'I'd love to go to Kew Gardens.'

Pips raised her eyebrows. 'Really? Why?'

Daisy chuckled. 'You know Granny has made Jake

head gardener. He has two boys from the village who've recently left school working under him and then Harry helps out at weekends and in the holidays when he's not working for Granddad Dawson.'

Pips nodded. 'Go on.'

'Jake has been reading everything he can get his hands on about gardening and he got a book about Kew Gardens.'

She seemed about to say more, but at that moment, the telephone shrilled and Daisy leapt up and then remembered that this was not her telephone to answer.

'Go on,' Pips laughed indulgently, 'you can answer it.' There was no missing the girl's excitement as she said, 'Hello, Uncle Mitch.' Then she listened carefully before saying, 'That's wonderful. Thank you *so* much. See you tomorrow.' There was a slight pause before she added, 'Will Johnny be with you?'

As she replaced the receiver carefully, she was grinning.

'So, when are we going?'

'Tomorrow afternoon and again on Friday afternoon – if that's all right with you.'

'Of course. But today, you want to go to Kew, do you?'

'Yes, please. Then I can tell Jake all about it.' With a mischievous grin, she added, 'And tomorrow we go flying.'

Daisy's excitement the following afternoon was palpable and infectious. Pips could fully understand it. She still got the same thrill when an aircraft under her control lifted into the air. It was the same nervous excitement lining up for a race on the Brooklands track, but now, she tried not to dwell on that. A promise was a promise and she would not break it. At least, she could still go flying.

'There's Uncle Mitch – and Johnny – with Mr Pointer.'

They were standing by the two-seater aircraft that was used for training.

Pips had lent Daisy her flying helmet and jacket, which, though a little large for her, would keep her warm in the cockpit.

'Ready, Daisy?' Jeff asked as they approached.

The girl's eyes shone. 'Yes, please, Mr Pointer.'

'Hey, none of the "mister" stuff, and I'm far too young to be "uncle" to anyone.' He wasn't, of course, but Daisy giggled as he added, 'It's Jeff. Now, are you sure you don't want to go up with your aunty? She has a full pilot's licence, you know.'

Daisy shook her head. 'No. I would like you to show me things and Aunty Pips says she's like Uncle Mitch. She won't try to teach a relative. She'll take me up, but only for a flight.'

Jeff nodded. 'I understand that. All right. Let's climb aboard, then.'

As they walked towards the two-seater biplane, Jeff said, 'This is an AVRO 504 built during the war. After the conflict, there were a great many for sale, so Mitch and I bought a couple. They make ideal training aircraft as well as being useful for taking folk up on pleasure flights.' He chuckled. 'We'll do anything anybody asks us – within reason. I've even been known to fly a banner across the sky for a mate of mine, who wanted an unusual way to propose to his girlfriend.'

Once they were both settled, Daisy in the front seat with Jeff behind her, he went through all the cockpit checks with her, before one of Jeff's mechanics shouted, 'Petrol on,' followed by two further instructions. Fascinated, Daisy listened, taking it all in.

Then the mechanic turned the propeller and shouted 'Contact!' to which Jeff replied 'Contact!' The mechanic swung the propeller forcefully and the engine fired. When Jeff waved his hand to signify that he was ready, the chocks set in front of each wheel were removed and Jeff began the take-off. The aircraft bumped along the grass and rose into the air. At once Daisy felt the thrill of being airborne as the aircraft climbed. Jeff levelled out and then began to turn. Now, if she looked to her left, Daisy could see the ground – to her right, the sky. She felt as if the world was spinning beneath her but, far from feeling nervous or nauseous, Daisy revelled in the new and exciting experience.

Now she understood why Aunty Pips loved flying. Oh, for the day when she'd be old enough to take lessons. But Jeff was already shouting instructions to her from the rear cockpit, explaining what each of the instruments in front of her was for. She took it all in, absorbing every word, every instruction, as he talked her through everything he was doing until she felt she could almost fly the plane right now.

Jeff must have felt her enthusiasm because suddenly he said, 'Have you got all that?'

'I think so,' Daisy shouted.

'Right, you have a go, but I'll take over again to land her.'

They were still waiting for her – Pips, Mitch and Johnny – when they landed.

'How was it?' Johnny was the first to ask.

'Magnificent! I can't wait for Friday.'

Jeff drew Mitch and Pips a little to one side. 'She has the makings of an excellent pilot.'

Pips's eyes widened. 'You've given her a lesson?'

Jeff held up his finger and thumb, a small space between them. 'Just a little one.' He glanced at Mitch. 'I did have my boss's permission.'

'Trouble is,' Pips glanced across at her niece, 'when she's old enough to start having proper lessons, she won't be down here enough for you to teach her.'

'Oh, I don't know,' Mitch said. 'There are the long summer holidays. We could do quite a lot in six weeks.'

Jeff nodded. 'She'll pick it up very quickly. I can see that already. As long as she can get the requisite number of flying hours in . . .'

'We'll see that she does,' Mitch said firmly. 'She's a great kid. I like Daisy, as I think' – he grinned at Pips – 'does my nephew.'

'What?' Pips's startled glance swivelled towards the two young people. 'Oh dear.'

Mitch frowned. 'You don't like him because of who he is?'

'What?' Pips said again. 'What d'you mean?'

'Because he's *my* nephew.'

36

For a brief moment, Pips stared at him and then burst out laughing. 'Heavens, no. It's not that. I think he's a lovely young man. It's just that' – her glance went again to Daisy – 'back home, there's Luke.'

'Luke? Oh yes, I remember. I met him when you were in hospital. But he's her cousin, surely.'

'Yes, but they've always been close friends since they were small. And then, of course, there's Harry too.'

'Harry?'

'Luke's half-brother. Since he was quite young, he's been declaring openly to anyone who'll listen that he's going to marry Daisy one day.'

'And what does Daisy say?'

'She just laughs. I don't think she takes him seriously.'

'Mm.' Mitch was thoughtful before saying slowly, 'Well, contrary to what you might think, Pips, despite the fact that he *looks* very like me, Johnny is nothing like me in character. I don't think he's going to be a lady's man or even a bit of a flirt. If he sets his mind on your Daisy, you can bet your life he'll be serious.'

'She's only fifteen, Mitch. I don't think her mother or father would be amused if she were to become romantically involved with anyone just yet. And my mother would have a fit.'

'I don't think you need worry. At the moment, Johnny's head is in the clouds. All he can think of is joining the RAF.'

'Perhaps that's just as well,' Pips murmured as she watched the two young people talking animatedly together; no doubt, she thought, all about flying!

Five

'I must say I like the sound of this new president they've got in America,' Robert said when Pips took Daisy back home. 'I think Roosevelt will be great.'

Pips nodded. 'He's got an uphill battle, though, if what the papers say about the financial crisis there is true. Frankly, I'm more worried about what's happening in Germany. Now Hitler has got such power, the boycott against Jewish businesses is escalating into violence.'

'It takes some believing, doesn't it, that people can act like that against their own countrymen?'

'I don't think they see them as that. That's the trouble.'

The brother and sister regarded each other solemnly. Where would it all end?

With no such dark thoughts to trouble her, Daisy couldn't wait to tell Luke and Harry about her trip and set off towards the village. 'Luke, you'd just love flying. I know you would.'

'What about me?' Harry piped up. 'Don't you think I'd love it too?'

Daisy smiled kindly at the eleven-year-old. 'I'm

sure you would, but I don't think your mam would let you go up just yet, do you?'

The youngster gave an exaggerated sigh. 'Why am I always being told that I'm not old enough to do *anything*? Can't ride your dad's motorcycle like Luke does. Can't go flying . . .'

'You will one day, I'm sure. But you do go riding,' Daisy reminded him gently.

Harry was at once contrite. He knew he should be grateful for the privilege the Maitland family afforded him and Luke. None of the other village kids had been invited to ride the ponies and horses in the stables at the hall every Saturday from the time they were old enough.

'Sorry, Daisy,' he muttered.

She linked her arm through his. 'You'll get there, Harry. Don't be in too much of a hurry to grow up. Enjoy your childhood, 'cos it'll not be long before you have to become a working man.'

'It's just – I feel left out sometimes,' he murmured, not wanting to sound like a crybaby.

'Oh now come on, we're always together. We're like the three musketeers. Anyway, I'm going to ask my dad if he'll take us to Skegness for the day. I've heard there's an airfield there where they operate pleasure flights. Perhaps we could go when Aunty Pips comes for a weekend. Your mam and dad might let you both go. You can only ask.'

It wasn't Peggy or Sam who refused to let Luke and Harry go with the Maitland family for a day out to Skegness to take a pleasure flight, but Len.

'Oh no, m'lad,' he said to Luke, 'you're not going off gallivanting like that. You'll get ideas above your station in life. Where d'you think I'm going to get the money for such things? Pleasure flights indeed! And if Sam thinks he'll treat both you and Harry, then I must be paying him too much. And before you say owt, I aren't having them at the hall paying for you either.'

'They did offer, Granddad.'

'No doubt they did but it's belittling me, that's what it is. You'd better put all that sort of nonsense out of your head, else I'll begin to think I'm not leaving my business in safe hands.' He wagged his finger in Luke's face. 'It's her I blame. Young Daisy. You can't ever keep up with her, lad, so don't think you can. You might be first cousins, but I can't help that. I didn't hold with yar Aunty Alice marrying Master Robert.' There was a pause before Len added, his tone softening just a little, 'I'll get you that motor-cycle I promised you, then you'll have no need to be beholden to them any more. How would that be, eh?'

'Thank you, Granddad,' Luke said with an outward meekness he wasn't feeling. Inside, he was raging. He had the distinct feeling that Len was trying to separate him and Daisy.

And to him, life without Daisy wouldn't be worth living.

'I can't go with you to Skegness,' Luke told Daisy, when he and Harry arrived at the hall as usual on the Saturday afternoon to go riding with Daisy. 'Neither of us can.'

'That's a shame. I expect your mam's worried about the flying, is she?'

Luke shook his head. He didn't like telling tales against any member of his family, but he wasn't going to allow his mam to be blamed for something that wasn't her fault. 'No, it's – me granddad.'

'Ah.' Daisy stared at him for a moment, tempted to say more, but then she realized just how much sway Len had over Luke. 'Never mind, then.'

'You'll still go though, won't you?'

'Probably not. The trip was mainly for you and Harry. Besides, I like to go and stay with Aunty Pips and go to Brooklands. You'd love that too, Luke. The racing. There are cars *and* motorcycles there as well as the flying.'

There was a pause before Luke blurted out, 'He's getting me that motorcycle he promised me ages ago.'

Daisy eyed him suspiciously and then glanced away. 'That's nice,' was all she could think of to say. She was shrewd enough to guess at Len's motives. 'Anyway, he's still letting you both come riding, so, let's go.'

But none of them enjoyed the afternoon as much as usual. A shadow seemed to hang over them; a shadow that was there but that they could not yet fully understand.

The following week, Len kept his promise and a second-hand motorcycle arrived at the workshop. Despite his niggling doubts about his grandfather's reasons, Luke couldn't help but be excited. But now, it was Robert who caused disappointment. He forbade Daisy to ride pillion.

'I want your solemn promise, Daisy. You're not to ride on the back of Luke's bike.'

Daisy, who had been expecting something of the sort, said impishly, 'But I could ride it myself? Would that be all right?'

'Certainly not,' Robert said sternly and then saw that his daughter was teasing him. 'You little rascal.' He put his arm around her. 'You stick to your horse riding and the occasional flight with Pips when you stay with her. All right?'

Daisy nodded. It wasn't quite 'all right' but, intuitively, she knew that now was not the right moment to announce that she wanted to learn to fly or even to admit that Jeff had already given her a couple of introductory lessons.

'Rebecca's coming to dinner on Thursday evening.'

George smiled. 'Lovely.'

George's daughter had been unwilling to accept that anyone could take the place of her mother, who had been ill for several years and had eventually taken her own life. Whilst George had been in the army and away in the war, it had fallen upon a young Rebecca to care for her mother. George had left the army after the armistice and had taken over the care of his wife whilst encouraging Rebecca to follow her own ambitions to become a nurse. George and Pips had first met at the front early in the war and he had fallen in love with her, but, being the officer and gentleman that he was, he had taken it no further except to tell her of his devotion to her and to give her a brooch in the shape of a poppy to remember him by. She still wore it every day fastened just below her left shoulder; she had even worn it on her wedding day. No one else, apart from Pips and George, knew the significance of the brooch and possibly many thought it was just Pips's way of remembering all those who had perished in the war. After his wife's death, George had seen a newspaper picture of Pips winning a race at Brooklands and he had attended a race meeting deliberately to seek her out. They had begun seeing each other often. At the time, Pips had been enjoying her life, living between London with Milly, partying, racing and flying at Brooklands, and her family home in Lincolnshire. She had been in no hurry to be tied down and with the added complication of Rebecca's attitude, marriage to George had been pushed further and further back. But since Rebecca had become more understanding, all was now well between the three of them.

'And,' Pips added now, her eyes twinkling with mischief, 'she's bringing the boyfriend.'

'Really? Good heavens! It must be getting serious, then. She's never wanted us to meet him before.'

'For that very reason, I suspect. She wants to be sure it's serious.'

'Mm.'

'Now, George, no playing the heavy-handed father asking him if his intentions are honourable.'

'Would I do a thing like that?'

'Yes, you would and you know you would. In fact, I'm going to ask Milly and Paul to come too. Milly will soon put a stop to any third-degree questioning.'

George chuckled. 'Dear Milly. If anyone can put the poor fellow at his ease, then it's her.'

'Oh, darling, of course we'll come,' Milly said when Pips telephoned her. 'How exciting. We knew she'd got a boyfriend, of course, but not how serious it is. He's a former patient from the London, isn't he?'

'Yes, she told me all about him quite early on – in fact, she first told me about him on our wedding day. It was very early days in the relationship then and she wasn't sure whether it would be frowned upon by the powers that be at the hospital.'

Milly giggled. 'Evidently not, then.'

'No, once he was fit and well and had left hospital, it was fine.'

'I can't wait to meet him. They must have been going out for about two years.'

'I suppose so.'

Milly gave an exaggerated sigh. 'Just like you and George. Not ones to rush into anything, are they, if it's taken this long for her to bring him to meet you?'

Pips chuckled and countered, 'You and Paul didn't exactly rush into it either, did you?'

'No, we were all having far too much fun in the twenties, weren't we?'

Pips forbore to add that their wild partying had been in an effort to forget the horrors of the war. Instead she said, 'Of course. But you will come, won't you?'

'Try and keep us away!'

Six

Matthew Jessop was a tall, lanky young man with a serious face, mousy hair and owl-like spectacles. But when he smiled, his blue eyes twinkled and his whole face lit up. He had a deep, soft voice and Pips warmed to him at once. He looked a few years older than Rebecca but he was gentle and courteous and his affection for her was obvious from the moment they met him.

'Make yourself at home and *please* don't feel we're giving you the third degree if we ask questions,' Pips laughed as she shook hands with him. 'Rebecca hasn't told us much about you.'

'And I'm well known for being nosey,' Milly giggled as, without ceremony, she moved forward and kissed the startled young man on both cheeks. As he stood back, he stared at her.

'Good heavens! Nurse Milly!'

Now it was Milly's turn to gape. 'I'm sorry, I . . .'

'Oh you won't remember me,' Matthew said, grinning broadly. 'I was just one of the many wounded soldiers you entertained with your wonderful impressions. But, of course, we *all* remembered you. I especially liked Marie Lloyd. Do say you'll do it again for me tonight?'

'Well . . .'

'Of course she will,' Pips said, as she linked her arm through his and led him into the sitting room. Rebecca smiled and shrugged at the sudden monopoly of her young man, hugged her father and followed the others into the room where Paul waited to greet them.

It was a merry dinner party, with Milly entertaining them with one or two of her clever impressions of music hall stars: Marie Lloyd – as Matthew had requested – and Vesta Tilly amongst them.

'There you are, Milly dear. Haven't I always told you that although you might not have had much nursing training,' Pips said, 'you were the one who kept their spirits up?'

'You most certainly did,' Matthew said gently. 'I'll go as far as to say that you gave us the will to live.'

Milly blushed as she murmured, 'That's awfully sweet of you, darling.'

As they sat together after her impromptu performance, Milly said, 'Tell us about yourself, Matthew.' She giggled. 'At least what is suitable for Rebecca's father to hear.' They all laughed, including George.

'I was called up and arrived in Belgium just after Passchendaele. I felt very guilty because I hadn't been there.'

'Don't be,' George said. 'It was a slaughter.'

'I was wounded the very first time I went into the trenches.' He grimaced. 'Not a very good soldier, was I?'

'Not your fault,' George spoke up again. 'Many

were killed on their first time at the front. Just be thankful it was only an injury from which you've obviously recovered. Did you have to go back?'

Matthew shook his head. 'No. My left leg was so badly smashed up, I was invalided out. At the time, the doctors told me I would never walk again, but I was determined to. I do have a limp and my leg is painful sometimes but other than that, I'm all in one piece.' He smiled. 'Well, apart from my appendix, that is. That's how I met Rebecca.'

'You were probably wounded when I'd gone home after my injury,' Pips murmured.

Matthew's bright blue eyes turned to her and a small frown creased his forehead. 'It must have been, because – I'm sorry – I don't remember you.'

Pips laughed. 'Nurses were ten a penny, Matthew, but not our Milly.'

'But I do remember the man who carried me from a shell hole in no-man's-land. A big man and so strong, he carried me in his arms whilst shells were still bursting all around us.'

'That sounds like William.'

'That *was* his name,' Matthew said excitedly. 'He carried me to the first-aid post and a lovely nurse – Bridget, I think her name was – took over. She spoke perfect English, but with a strong accent.'

'Brigitta,' Milly said. 'That'd be Brigitta. William married her and they still live out in Belgium – not far from Ypres.'

'I'm glad to hear he survived. He was a very brave young man.'

'I only wish his father thought so,' Pips said sadly.

'He disowned William when he refused to enlist alongside his brothers at the beginning of the war.'

Matthew stared at her as if he couldn't believe what he was hearing. 'More fool him, then. Sorry, that was said out of turn. I apologize.'

'Please don't. It's what we all think and the sorrow of it all is that he still won't forgive his son and welcome him home. It's very hard on William's mother.'

Briefly, Pips explained the relationship between the Maitland and Dawson families, ending, 'But we go out to see him and his family sometimes. In fact, it's high time we paid them another visit.'

'So, what do you do now in civvy street?' George asked.

'I'm following in my father's footsteps. I work at the Foreign Office.'

'Really? I'm attached to the War Office. It's a wonder we've never met. And your father? Is he still there? Might I know him?'

Matthew's face was bleak. 'My parents both died just after the war ended in the dreadful influenza epidemic. And, as I have no siblings, I'm rather on my own now.' He reached out and touched Rebecca's hand. 'That's why this wonderful girl is extra special to me. I know my parents would have loved her.' He looked straight at George. 'And that's why I hope you'll have no objection to us becoming engaged, sir.'

There was a moment's stunned silence around the table, then George stood up and held out his hand. In a voice that shook a little, he said, 'No objection at all, Matthew. I'm delighted.'

Milly jumped to her feet. 'Oh goody. I was so hoping the champagne I brought along – just in case – wasn't going to be wasted.'

'Well done, Milly,' Pips said. 'The perfect end to the evening.'

'There's only one problem as far as I can see,' George said after all their guests had left and he and Pips were getting ready for bed.

'What's that, darling?'

'It's quite probable that Rebecca won't be allowed to carry on nursing once she's married.'

'Maybe she'll want to have babies. She's still young enough. Or,' Pips went on, 'perhaps she could find some private nursing work, if she wanted to. I'm sure there are plenty of wealthy people who would employ a fully qualified nurse when they're ill, either short term or long term. I think she's done midwifery too, hasn't she? That could be very useful.'

'You know, Pips, you never fail to surprise me. You come up with the most wonderful ideas. That's exactly what she could do.'

Seven

The planned trip to Belgium took place during the last full week of July after Daisy had finished school for the summer term. George, Pips and Daisy travelled across the Channel and then into Belgium, hiring a car for Pips to drive. Although Robert had adamantly refused to go, Alice had hoped to join them, but at the last moment she had developed a heavy cold and had decided not to travel.

'I never did much driving when we were out here,' George admitted, as he sat beside Pips. 'I'm not confident of driving on the right-hand side.'

'Really?' Pips teased. 'And you a brave major in the British army?'

They exchanged a fond glance. Whenever they came back to Belgium it revived all sorts of memories for them.

In the back seat, Daisy was craning her neck to see out of the windows. 'I can't believe how flat it is. It's just like home, isn't it?'

'Very similar,' George agreed. They fell silent, each busy with their thoughts of previous occasions here. Only Daisy had happy memories of her first journey to see her cousins; for the others, who remembered earlier times, there were some very sad recollections.

After the flurry of their arrival at the farm near Lijssenthoek, Pips drew Brigitta aside and said, 'I'm so sorry that your grandparents are no longer here. They were a wonderful old couple.'

Brigitta smiled through sudden tears. 'They were both very ill last winter and died within a week of one another. It was a hard time for us, but I knew it was what they would both have wanted – to go almost together – and that was a comfort. They brought me up – I even used their surname – but they lived long enough to see their great-grandsons growing up to love the farm. It was their dearest wish to see it pass to them eventually. And, of course, it will.'

'They'll both inherit it, then?'

Brigitta nodded. 'It's all set out in my grandfather's will and there'll be no falling out. Already, they work very well together.'

Pips squeezed her arm. 'I'm so glad. It must be a great comfort to both you and William, especially after—' Pips broke off, not wanting to be tactless.

Brigitta, however, only smiled and said, 'How are the rest of William's family? Alice writes regularly, of course, but I know he'd like to hear all about the others from you. Even' – she smiled sadly – 'his father.'

The visit was a great success – a happy time for them all, though tinged with sadness at times. George and Pips went alone to visit his friend who lay at peace in a cemetery near Brandhoek and then all of them – even Pascal and Waldo – took a rare day off from the farm to travel to the Somme to visit the graves of William and Alice's three brothers.

'We wanted to bring Luke to see you again and to visit his dad's grave,' Daisy told William as they walked amongst the hundreds of white markers, 'but your father wouldn't let him come.'

'I'm sorry to hear that. I'd like to have seen him again.'

Daisy glanced up at him. 'When he's old enough to be able to do what he wants, he'll come to see you again, Uncle William. I know he will.'

'I wouldn't want him to be in trouble with his grandfather though, Daisy. Not on my account.' There was a pause before he asked, 'Is Luke happy working for him?'

'Oh yes. The business will be his one day. He's happy about that, though I just wish Granddad would let him do other things.' She went on to tell William about the proposed trip to Skegness to take both Luke and Harry flying. 'He put a stop to that too and Luke's just not quite old enough to go against him.' Impishly, she added, 'Not yet.'

'Daisy, you should warn Luke not to push him too far. His granddad can be a very stubborn old man, as you know. I wouldn't want Luke to lose his inheritance.'

Daisy laughed. 'You're right – about Granddad, I mean – but he's also not stupid. He's only got Luke to leave his business to because, of course, Harry is not his grandson as he's very fond of reminding him.'

William smiled at the young girl's confidence. 'Well, just make sure he's careful, Daisy. And now, here we are at Harold's grave. You can lay the flowers you've brought on Luke's behalf.'

Daisy laid the posy carefully and then stood up, looking down at the name on the marker. 'What was he like?'

'Harold?' William smiled. 'A young rascal in many ways. Running away when he was underage to join up in Newark so that his family couldn't stop him was just such an example. But you must always remind Luke that he would have come home and married Peggy if he could have done. I heard him say that when he was dying and I believed him. And now, let's go and find your other two uncles. They're buried a short distance from here. And then tomorrow we'll go into Ypres. Pips wants to see how the rebuilding is progressing.'

Pips, with George, William and Daisy beside her, stood looking up at Cloth Hall, which had once been a magnificent building in the heart of Ypres.

'I'm so glad they've decided to rebuild everything exactly as it was,' Pips said. 'It's going to be beautiful once again.'

'It looks like they're progressing very well with the tower and the western wing,' William said. 'They've done a lot more even since I was last here.'

Pips's glance roamed over the whole building. 'It'll take decades to complete it.'

'Now let me show you St George's church,' William said. 'It was completed a few years ago.'

'Oh, the one that's a memorial to the British and Commonwealth troops?' George said. 'Where is it?'

'Just across the road from the cathedral.'

They walked around the corner and, as they

walked past the cathedral, William said, 'This is finished now. The only change they made was that they rebuilt it with a pointed spire.' They walked on and crossed the road to the small church built on the opposite corner. 'Here we are. Now, as you know, there's a school here at St George's, but I think the children will be on holiday. The headmaster and teachers come from Britain and most of the pupils are the children of workers with the War Graves Commission, who live in the area. I'm told a lot of their school activities are rooted in British traditions.'

As Pips stepped into the quiet interior, she gasped. The walls were lined with plaques dedicated to regiments, associations and even to individuals. There were memorials in the stained-glass windows and on almost every seat was a hassock embroidered in cross stitch depicting the various badges of the different regiments who had served in the area.

Pips ran her fingers over the surface of one for the Sherwood Foresters and thought of Harold Dawson. 'I wish Alice had come with us. I must remind her when we get home to make one for the Lincolnshire Regiment and send it out to you, William.'

'That would be great. It's so good to see the people rebuilding their lives and to see Ypres rising from the ashes. It's – it's uplifting.'

Daisy was unusually quiet as she read the inscriptions on several of the plaques. 'There are so many,' she murmured.

William put his arm about her. The more he saw of her, the fonder he became of his niece.

'Tonight, we'll go to the Menin Gate service. It's very moving, but it's a good thing to do.'

'Yes,' Daisy said. 'I remember it. I'd like to go again. Oh, I do so wish Luke had been able to come with us.'

William squeezed her shoulders, but could think of nothing to say.

By the time they left, Daisy was firm friends with her Belgian cousins. The two boys had shown her all over the farm, had walked the fields with her, pointing out where crops were grown and which were left to pasture for grazing animals.

'You can tell our grandmother all about us,' Pascal said.

'And tell her,' Waldo added, 'that Father talks about her often and that we hope to meet her one day.'

'You will come and see us again, won't you, Daisy, and next time, do bring Luke? We'd like to get to know him better,' Pascal said. 'He's our cousin too.'

'It won't be for the lack of trying, I promise.'

Eight

'Aunty Alice, when is Daisy coming home?'

Seeing Luke's forlorn face, Alice said apologetically, 'She's staying with Pips for most of the summer holidays, Luke. Her father and I decided that, as she will have to buckle down and work extremely hard for her School Certificate this coming school year, she ought to be allowed some fun first. She loves to go flying with Pips – which we don't mind.' Alice smiled as she added, 'Though we have banned Pips from taking her motor racing other than to watch. There's no knowing what those two might get up to if we didn't set some rules. They're in Belgium at the moment, as you know, but they're back in London on Monday.' She touched his arm. 'I'm so sorry that your granddad wouldn't let you go with them. Daisy would have loved it and I know William and his family would've liked to have seen you again.'

Luke shrugged. 'Granddad doesn't believe in holidays. He says the Devil makes work for idle hands.'

Alice chuckled. She remembered her father's sayings so well from her own childhood. 'And he had another saying when any of us wanted to go to a party or the theatre in the city. "Always wanting pleasure," he'd grumble, but the boys would take me anyway. We'd even sneak Harold out of the house when he was still quite young and take him with us, if we could. We were often in trouble when we got home, but it was worth it.' Her face was pensive as she thought of happier times with the brothers she would never see again.

'Do you think that's what I should do? Just – go?'

'Oh now, don't involve me, Luke. But you are coming up for eighteen and although you're not legally of age until you're twenty-one, you are a working man; a very hardworking man. And you've – er – got a motorcycle now, haven't you? You don't have to ride Uncle Robert's any more, do you?'

Luke grinned at his aunt, then his smile faded. 'It's Grandma I worry about. I wouldn't want him to take it out on her.'

Alice wrinkled her forehead thoughtfully. Slowly, she said, 'I wouldn't just go off without saying anything. That would worry both of them. Be up front with him. Tell him you're going away for the weekend. Try it, Luke. You might be surprised.'

On the Friday evening, just before Daisy was due back to London from Belgium, as he helped Len and Sam close up the workshop for the night, Luke said, 'Granddad, I'd like to take next Saturday morning off. I want to go away for the weekend.'

Sam glanced up but said nothing. Luke had already discussed with his mother what he planned to do but, deliberately, he had not spoken to Sam about it.

'Oh aye,' Len growled. 'And what makes you think you can just take time off when you want? We've got that cartwheel to finish for Charlie.' Charlie Cooper was Luke's other grandfather and worked on the estate as Henrietta Maitland's farm manager.

Stubbornly, Luke met his grandfather's gaze. 'I'll work extra hard this week to get it done before I go.'

Luke was far too polite to turn up at Pips's home in London unannounced and uninvited. So he wrote to Daisy and asked if he might come down to see her over the August Bank Holiday weekend. The letter arrived on the Tuesday, the day after they returned from Belgium. Daisy rang her father at once.

'Daddy, can you get an urgent message to Luke for me? But don't let Granddad Dawson know.'

Robert chuckled. 'Devious schemes afoot, Daisy?'

'Something like that. I've had a letter from Luke. He wants to come down here on Friday night for the weekend. Pips says that's fine, so we need to let him know. He might not get the letter in time if I write. You could tell Peggy. She knows about it.'

'I'll ask Jake to go to their cottage and leave a message for Luke. Will that do?'

'Perfect. Thanks, Daddy. Oh, and can you tell Luke to ask if he can stay until Thursday or Friday of next week. We want to take him to the race meeting on August Bank Holiday Monday and then there's a motorcycle race meeting on Wednesday. Uncle Paul's arranged some motorcycle trials on Test Hill that day. Luke would love to see that and I'm sure it's high time he took a bit of holiday. I don't think he's had any since he started working for Granddad.

He's only had Saturday afternoons to go riding – and Sundays, of course.'

'Of course I will.' There was a slight pause before Robert asked, 'How was Belgium?'

'Wonderful. Sad, of course, seeing all those graves, but Aunty Pips said it was lovely to see how they're being so well cared for. William and his boys still look after those near where they live. And Ypres is being rebuilt just as it was before the war. It's going to be magnificent again. And we saw St George's church. Pips is going to ask Mummy to embroider a hassock to send out there. And, d'you know, they hold a service at eight o'clock every night at the Menin Gate when they sound the "Last Post"? Would you believe that?'

'Actually, I would. I wonder how long they'll go on doing that for?'

'I don't know, but it's a lovely thing to do, isn't it? Anyway, I'd better ring off. Love to everyone. Bye, Daddy.'

'Where's Luke?' Len greeted Sam harshly on the Saturday morning.

'He asked me to tell you that he's taking a few days off, probably until Thursday or Friday. He did ask you last week, Mr Dawson.'

'Aye, he did, but only for the Saturday and I said "no".' Len paused and then groused, 'Has he gone to Skegness with *them*? Because I forbade it and if he has—'

'I don't think so.'

'Then where has he gone?'

Luckily, Sam didn't know the full story. Jake had

delivered the message faithfully to Peggy, but she had been shrewd enough to censor it a little and had told Sam only the bare essentials.

'You can tell Mr Dawson that Luke's taking a few days off to try out his new motorcycle.'

'Where's he gone?' Sam had asked innocently.

'Best you don't know, love. It could put you in an awkward position. But, trust me, he'll be fine.'

So now Sam was able to say, quite truthfully, 'I really have no idea. From what Peg said, just riding around the countryside enjoying a bit of freedom on his motorcycle.'

Len glowered at him, grunted morosely and turned away. He didn't speak to Sam for the rest of the morning.

When Luke rang the bell of the apartment where Pips and George lived, the door was flung open and Daisy launched herself against him. 'I'm *so* glad you've come. We'll have such fun.'

She dragged him inside where both Pips and George greeted him.

'I'll come down and show you where to put your motorcycle,' George said.

A little later, when Luke had settled in, they all sat down to dinner. 'We're going into the city tomorrow and then on Sunday to Kew Gardens and then on Monday we're going to Brooklands,' Daisy told him. 'You'll love it.'

'Can you stay until after Wednesday?' Pips asked.

'Well, I'm going to. I'll just have to face Granddad when I get back.'

'Don't jeopardize your future, Luke,' George said solemnly.

Luke shook his head. 'I don't think I will, Major Allender, but even if Granddad sacks me, I'm a good carpenter now. I'd be able to get another job.'

'He won't sack you,' Daisy said confidently. 'Who else would he leave his business to?'

'Sam or even Harry.'

'But they're not related to him.'

'But William is,' Luke said quietly. 'And look how he treats him.'

There was silence round the table; no one could argue with him.

The weekend was an eye opener for the young man. Tied to the family business, working long days with no holidays and little free time except on Saturday afternoons and Sundays, when he was obliged to attend church with his family, Luke experienced a freedom and enjoyment he hadn't known existed. The sights of London astounded him; he couldn't believe his eyes at the magnificence of Buckingham Palace, St Paul's and Westminster Abbey – and standing in front of the Cenotaph moved him immensely.

On Sunday they visited Kew Gardens, but Bank Holiday Monday was the highlight of Luke's visit so far.

'Oh, isn't it hot!' Milly exclaimed, fanning her face vigorously as the friends met up at the track. 'Hello, Luke, how lovely to see you.' She giggled deliciously. 'Are you racing?'

He grinned at her. 'I wish. Aunty Pips is bringing me again on Wednesday to see the motorcycle racing. Cars are great, but . . .'

Milly linked her arm through his. 'But you just *love* motorcycles. Now, let's go and find something to drink, although I bet the bars will be crowded in this heat. Then we must watch the next race.' As she led the way, she called back over her shoulder. 'Pips, John Cobb has entered his new car. It promises to be absolutely thrilling.'

'Wow!' was all Luke could say as he stood on Members' Hill a little later and took in the sight around him.

The Byfleet Lightning Short Handicap race was almost *too* thrilling and could have ended in tragedy when Cobb, driving close to the top of the banking, passed another car. The crowd oohed and aahed as a near-disaster was only just averted. Although he almost touched wheels with the other car, he managed to remain on the track. He won the race, but in a second race he was heavily handicapped and could only manage fifth place.

'I thought he was going over the top,' Luke said to Pips.

'He would probably have been killed if he had,' she told him solemnly. 'I'm glad George wasn't here to see it today. It would only have confirmed his desire not to see me race again. Now, let's go to the bar. I need a drink after that.'

'You'll be lucky.' Luke grinned. 'Milly says that the bars in the public enclosures have run dry.'

'Oh phooey!'

As they met up in the clubhouse with the Brooklands Girls and other friends, Luke could not fail to feel the warmth of their welcome. Soon he was talking about motorcycles to Paul and Jeff.

'How about bringing your motorcycle here on Wednesday?' Paul suggested. 'I'll get you a pass to try it out on Test Hill.'

Luke's eyes gleamed. 'Really?'

'And I hear from Daisy that you'd love a flight?' Jeff said.

'I would – but it's expensive, isn't it?'

Jeff tapped the side of his nose. 'I'll have a word with Mitch. How about tomorrow?'

Luke nodded, hardly able to speak for excitement. At last he managed to say, 'That'd be great. I have to go home on Thursday and we're coming here on Wednesday for the motorcycle racing, so that would be perfect.'

The following day, Pips took Daisy and Luke to Brooklands again, where Mitch and Johnny were waiting to meet them.

The two young men shook hands, a little warily, Pips thought, but it seemed they were both making an effort. They fell into step as they walked towards the aircraft where Jeff was waiting for them.

'You'll love it,' Johnny told him. As they neared the aeroplane he shouted above the noise of the engine, 'You know Uncle Mitch, don't you? And I think you met Jeff yesterday.'

Luke nodded. Now he was near the aircraft, his excitement was fever pitch. Far from being nervous,

he couldn't wait to get into the aeroplane and experience all the joys that Daisy described so vividly.

As the aeroplane landed and taxied to a halt, Daisy
and Johnny ran across the grass to greet them. They
watched as Luke climbed down.

'So, how was it?' Daisy said as he came towards
them.

'Fantastic.' Luke grinned. 'It's just so – so *free* up
there, isn't it? You feel as if you're on top of the
world.'

Johnny laughed. 'You are. Sort of. I saw Jeff doing
a roll with you. Were you OK?'

Luke nodded. 'To be honest, when he told me
what he was going to do, I thought I'd be a bit
queasy, but no, I was fine. It was fun.'

'Then you're a flier, Luke. You ought to join the
RAF with me.'

Luke laughed. 'Well, if my granddad sacks me
when I get back, that's what I'll do.'

Daisy stepped between them and linked arms.
'Come on. Let's go and find something to eat. I'm
starving.'

Luke rode his motorcycle to Brooklands the following
day, whilst Pips and Daisy led the way in the car.

'I've got you a go on the hill,' Paul greeted them.
'You need to take your motorcycle over there, where
all the competitors are lining up.'

'Is it a competition, Uncle Paul?'

'Only an unofficial one, Daisy. The one with the
fastest time gets a small prize.'

'We'll go and stand on Members' Hill to watch you. Oh, there's Mitch and Johnny. Come on, Aunty Pips.'

'Daisy, I—' Luke began, but Daisy was already out of hearing distance. Luke's worried gaze followed her.

Oh dear, Pips thought. He's got the same look in his eyes as George has over Mitch! But aloud, all she said was, 'Good luck.' She squeezed his arm. 'You'll show 'em.'

And he did. As machine after machine roared up the steep hill, each one having three attempts, Luke's fastest time was placed second overall.

'That's brilliant,' Johnny told him when they all met up again. 'Only Petersen beat you and he's got a bigger engine than you have.'

'Thanks,' Luke said a little curtly and then, realizing that he might have sounded ungrateful, he tried to make conversation. After all, they were being very kind to him – even Johnny. 'Have you got a motorcycle?'

'No.' Johnny grinned. 'Afraid I'm all about flying.'

'You're joining the RAF?'

'Yup. I've already applied and will join next April when I'm eighteen.'

Inwardly, Luke smiled, but at Johnny's next words his heart sank.

'I'll be coming to Cranwell in Lincolnshire, so maybe I'll be able to come up and see you all. I might even invest in a motorcycle. I'll need something to get around.'

Luke's heart sank even further.

Nine

And so, the summer of 1933 was a glorious time for Daisy. Although she missed her family, in which she included Luke and Harry, there was so much going on in London that she scarcely had time to be homesick. Pips took her to see all the sights in the city and to Kew Gardens again. And at weekends, the three of them went further afield, often with Milly and Paul too. One particularly hot Sunday, they all motored down to the coast and wandered along the Dover cliffs. And, of course, they spent a lot of time at Brooklands. Sometimes, during the week, George was missing, but on those occasions, Jeff would take Daisy flying. And even though she was not yet sixteen, he began to give her proper flying lessons.

'Of course, we can't let you go solo yet, but no one else – not even Mitch or Pips – need know what we get up to up here,' he told her as they headed for the clouds once more. More and more, he let her take control of the aircraft, until she could even take off and land it smoothly.

'You're a natural, Daisy,' he told her. 'As soon as you're old enough, it won't take you very long to get your licence.'

'I can't wait.' Daisy grinned and thanked him

politely for all the lessons he'd given her. 'When will Johnny get his?'

'I think he's going into the RAF as soon as he turns eighteen next April, so they'll train him to their requirements. He's applying to be a pilot and I've no doubt he'll be accepted,' Jeff told her as they walked across the grass to where Pips, Mitch and Johnny were waiting for them.

As they neared them, Johnny fell into step beside Daisy, whilst the other three walked on ahead. 'How did it go?'

'Marvellous.'

'Jeff ought to hand the controls to you. Let you have a real go.'

'Perhaps he will one day,' Daisy said carefully.

Johnny chuckled. 'As if he hasn't already! You can't kid me, Daisy Maitland.' Then, seeing her startled face, he whispered, 'Don't worry, your secret's safe with me. But I'll tell you something, you must be good because Jeff is a hard taskmaster. He wouldn't let you have a go until he was sure of you.' He squeezed her arm. 'Well done, Daisy.'

To Luke's surprise, Len had said nothing on his return but he gave him so much work to do that there were no further thoughts of 'holidays'. When the new school year started, Daisy worked hard, only pausing in her studies to celebrate 'the birthdays' and Christmas with her family.

The weeks and months flew by and in April the following year, shortly after his eighteenth birthday, Johnny arrived at Cranwell as an officer cadet and began his training to be a pilot in an AVRO 504 – a Great War biplane.

'Only a few more hours' flying time and my instructor reckons I'll be able to go solo,' he told the Maitland family when they welcomed him to the hall on a weekend visit, after he had roared up the drive on his noisy second-hand motorcycle.

'He's a very handsome young man in his RAF uniform, isn't he?' Henrietta said to Pips as the three women and Daisy retired to the Brown Parlour whilst the menfolk lingered around the dining table to enjoy their port. 'No wonder you're smitten, Daisy.'

'Now, Mother, no matchmaking,' Pips laughed. 'She's only sixteen and still at school, working hard for her School Certificate. At least, I hope you are.'

She glanced at Daisy, who grinned. 'Of course I am, Aunty Pips. Daddy says I can stay on until I'm eighteen for my Higher and go to university if I want to.'

'And do you? Want to go to university, I mean?'

'I'd sooner go somewhere where I can do some sort of a course in estate management.'

'Oh!' Pips glanced at her mother, who was serenely pouring the coffee.

There was a pause as Henrietta handed the cups round. 'It's all been agreed. I think you know that Robert has always maintained that he didn't want to take over the running of the estate. His sole ambition has always been to be a doctor and though it was touch and go for a while after he was wounded, at last he's now back doing what he loves. So, with you happily established in London with George, there's only Daisy.' She glanced affectionately at her granddaughter. 'And, much to my delight – and relief, I might add – it seems that Daisy is as keen to take over as her father is *not*.'

'That's wonderful,' Pips said, genuinely delighted. It had been worrying her a little to think what was going to happen as her mother got older, though looking at her now – even though she had just turned seventy – Henrietta seemed as indefatigable as ever. She turned to Daisy. 'And are there such places – universities or colleges for agriculture?'

Daisy's eyes sparkled. 'I've been looking at one or two – though it's early days yet. I've got to get through all my exams first *and* find out if they take women.'

'Plenty of time,' Henrietta said and then added, 'Ah, now I think I hear the gentlemen coming. Ring the bell, Daisy dear, for Wainwright to bring fresh coffee.'

The following afternoon, Daisy said, 'Johnny, do you ride?'

'Ride? What – horses, you mean?'

'Yes. Luke, Harry and I go riding every Saturday afternoon. We have done ever since we were old enough.'

'Can't say I've ever tried it.'

'Will you give it a go?'

'As long as you promise me I won't fall off and break my leg – or, worse still, my arm. I don't want to jeopardize my RAF career.'

'We'll put you on Boxer, the most docile mount

69

we have in the stables. He's getting on a bit now, so he won't gallop off with you or try any jumps. Come on, let's get you kitted out. Daddy will have some jodhpurs and a hat you can borrow . . .'

Luke and Harry arrived promptly at two o'clock and the five of them, including Jake, who insisted he should accompany them as Johnny was a novice, set out through the grounds of the hall and into the farmland belonging to the Maitland estate.

Johnny was obviously nervous and clung onto the reins.

'Don't hang on so tightly,' Daisy warned him. 'The horse will feel your nervousness.'

They came to a stream and the horses splashed through, all except Boxer, who stepped into the water, stopped and then bent to drink.

'Aahh!'

As the others turned to watch, Johnny seemed to slide in slow motion from the horse's back and into the water.

'Oh no!' Daisy jumped down and waded through the shallows to reach him, whilst Luke could hardly hold back his mirth seeing his rival for Daisy's affections soaked to the skin and struggling to get up. Harry had no such inhibitions; he threw back his head and roared with laughter.

Daisy shot them an angry glance and helped Johnny to his feet. 'Are you hurt?'

Johnny was standing a little unsteadily, the water flowing around his ankles.

'Don't think so. Just my pride.' He glanced up and saw them laughing. For a brief moment, he frowned and then, realizing how foolish he must look, he too burst out laughing.

Jake turned his horse and came back through the stream. 'I'll go back with Master Hammond, Daisy, if you three want to go on.'

But Daisy glared at Luke and Harry, none too pleased with their unfeeling behaviour. 'No, it's all right, Jake. I'll go back,' she said curtly. 'You three go on.'

As if it was an order to all of them, she gathered the reins of her own mount and Boxer's. 'We'll walk back.'

'Oh, but I don't want—' Johnny began.

'You're soaked and my feet are wet. Come on. We're going.'

Now it was Johnny's turn to obey her and with an apologetic shrug towards the others, he turned and followed her up the bank of the stream.

As he watched them go, Luke, no longer laughing, murmured, 'I think we made a mistake there, Harry.'

As he walked back with Daisy towards the hall, Johnny said, 'I'm sorry I spoiled the afternoon, Daisy. I don't think riding a horse is quite my thing. I'm much safer in the cockpit of an aeroplane.'

'If you've never ridden before, it's not easy. I'm just thankful you're not hurt and that you were wearing some of Daddy's clothes. I wouldn't have wanted you to be in trouble because you'd ruined your smart uniform.'

Johnny laughed. 'No, I'd have been on a charge for sure.'

*

71

Back at the hall, changed and warm and dry, they sat together in the Brown Parlour, surrounded by family portraits that lined the panelled walls. It was cosy in front of the fire, which was always lit in the late afternoon except on the warmest of days, and they drank coffee laced with a little rum.

They talked for the rest of the afternoon, telling each other all about their lives and their ambitions.

'My father was killed in the war, as you know. So, for a while, there was only Mother and me until she found herself a boyfriend.' He grimaced. 'I'm afraid I don't get on too well with him, but Uncle Mitch has been a constant presence in my life. He's a great guy. I don't know what I'd've done without him.'

'It's funny he's never married. He's so handsome and well – just so *nice*.'

'I'm sure he's had plenty of chances.' He was quiet for a moment, regarding her steadily before saying softly, 'You do know that he's in love with your aunt, don't you?'

'Aunty Milly hinted as much some time back and I have noticed there's a bit of a frostiness between Uncle George and Uncle Mitch whenever they meet up.'

'But Uncle Mitch admires the major. He's told me so.'

'I think the respect is mutual, but . . .'

'Exactly. But . . .'

Johnny was thoughtful. Although Daisy was still young, he knew he already had feelings for her and it was obvious that her cousin, Luke, harboured those same sentiments. And as for Harry, he had already made it clear on their first meeting that he intended to marry Daisy one day, though she seemed to regard that as a bit of a joke from a twelve-year-old. Watching her now as she sat with her hands cupped round her coffee and gazing dreamily into the flames, Johnny wondered just who it was that commanded her thoughts. She was growing into a very beautiful young woman, but she was still only sixteen and he doubted that her parents would welcome the romantic attentions of a young airman.

'Daisy,' he said suddenly as an idea came to him, 'would you write to me?'

Startled from her daydreams, Daisy turned to him. 'I thought you RAF chaps did nothing else but fly and have parties in the pub. You won't have time for writing letters.'

He smiled. 'Not all the time. It can get a bit lonely.'

'But I won't have anything really interesting to write about. I've got to get my head down and work hard at school. My letters will be a bit boring.'

'Not at all. That's exactly what I want to hear. Just – everything you're doing.'

'Then of course I will.'

Now his smile widened into a grin.

Ten

In the summer of 1934, Daisy gained the highest possible result in all subjects in her School Certificate.

'How clever you are, darling,' Alice said, hugging her. 'Thank goodness you take after your father and your Aunty Pips.'

'Oh Mummy, don't say that. You're clever too.'

'Perhaps with my needle and thread, but I was never very good at school.'

'But you had to leave at twelve to go into service, didn't you?'

Alice nodded. 'There was no chance in my family of staying on any longer than the school-leaving age. Even the boys had to leave and go into my father's business, though William refused and came to work here at the hall.'

'Did he? I hadn't known that.' Daisy chuckled. 'He even stood up to Granddad before the war, then?'

'Yes, he did. But then there were Bernard and Roy to work alongside my father – and Harold too.'

'And now there's only Luke to carry it on.'

Alice pressed her lips together and nodded. 'But at least he was allowed to stay on long enough to do his School Certificate.'

'But not his Higher.'

Alice sighed. 'In your grandfather's estimation, he doesn't need it.'

'But what if he ever decides he wants to do something different?'

'I don't think he will, do you?'

'Probably not, but I really think Granddad should allow him to have some time off now and again. If he doesn't . . .' She left the words hanging in the air, but they both understood her unspoken meaning.

Johnny had become an infrequent, though regular, visitor to the hall, much to Luke's – and Harry's – disgust.

'What's he think he's doing?' the younger boy asked. 'Daisy belongs to us.'

Trying to be reasonable, Luke said, 'She's allowed to have other friends.'

'But not *boys*. What if he falls in love with her? What then?'

With an insight beyond his years Luke said, 'Harry, we can't monopolize her. If we try to, we'll drive her all the more towards him.'

'You think so?' The twelve-year-old couldn't yet quite understand his older brother's meaning. 'But he's always here.'

Luke laughed. 'Not really. It just seems like that to us, but don't forget, we're here all the time – and besides, I don't think he'll try going riding with us again, do you?'

Now Harry laughed too.

*

'So, have you been following the news about your little corporal?' Robert asked as he and Pips sat either side of the chess board set up in the drawing room on the first floor of the hall. The room, known as the Blue Drawing Room, was a long rectangle with windows looking out over the rear gardens. On either side of the white marble fireplace, ornate cabinets held Henrietta's precious china and at the far end of the room stood Alice's tapestry embroidery frame. Henrietta's bedroom walls were lined with fine tapestries and it was Alice's pride and joy to keep these in good repair. Now it was where she sat to work on a hassock to send out to William for the church in Ypres.

Pips had just brought Daisy home after a three-week stay with them in London and now she was enjoying a few days at home with her family; riding, seeing friends and beating Robert at chess.

Pips sighed. 'George says Hitler's trying to get very cosy with Mussolini. Evidently, he admires him and some of the news that is emerging is, frankly, terrifying. Anyone that voices the slightest criticism of him just – disappears.'

'And now Hindenburg has died, the way to total power for him seems to be clear.'

'He didn't waste any time, did he? Soon after the old man's death, Hitler announced that there would no longer be a president, and then he proclaimed himself Führer and Reich Chancellor. He also appointed himself as Supreme Commander of the German Armed Forces and demanded an oath of unconditional allegiance to him from officers and men alike.'

'Not to Germany?'

'No – to him personally. From what George has hinted, it seems that very soon Hitler will be in complete control of Germany.'

'It's frightening,' Robert murmured as he picked up a chess piece and moved it on the board. 'Anyway, let's forget about him. I need to concentrate if I'm to win this game. You've beaten me the last two times. I can't have that.'

Pips chuckled and moved a piece too. 'Check.'

In September, Daisy began her studies in the sixth form at school and, with the leaving age now set at fourteen, Harry had almost another two years to do – much to his disgust. He hated school and couldn't wait to begin working full time in Len's workshop. He was there whenever he could be; after school, Saturday mornings and during the school holidays. To everyone's surprise, Len granted both boys and Sam a full Saturday off once a month, though he reduced their wages accordingly. Sam, who couldn't afford to lose the money, decided not to take the offered extra free time. But for the boys it was a heaven-sent opportunity to spend a whole day with Daisy.

The families settled into a routine in both London and Doddington. For Pips and George, the highlight of the following year, 1935, was the wedding of Rebecca and Matthew in August. It was a very quiet affair; neither wanted a grand 'do' and there were few relatives on either side. Rebecca had not come to know the other members of the Maitland family, nor even the Brooklands set, and so it was a small party of twelve that attended the morning service in a church which Rebecca attended regularly near the hospital. Afterwards, they gathered in a local restaurant for lunch.

'It's a shame you're giving up your career,' Pips said, as they wished the couple every possible happiness.

'I'm not entirely. I took your advice and made some enquiries about private nursing. I'll be working part time helping an elderly lady quite near to where we'll be living.'

'That's wonderful. I'm so glad.'

Pips and George visited Lincolnshire often and always made sure they were there for the youngsters' birthdays at the beginning of December. Christmas, they had decided, should now be spent alternately between the Maitlands and Rebecca and Matthew, but they always travelled to Lincolnshire on Boxing Day to be there for Harry's birthday. They stayed on to raise a toast to the New Year, but the hopes of the villagers of Doddington for 1936, along with the rest of the country, were dashed. It was to be a year of sadness and disappointment for many. In January, King George V died and his eldest son, Edward, succeeded him. In March, Hitler openly defied the Treaty of Versailles and marched into the Rhineland, although he then offered a twenty-five-year peace guarantee.

'That won't be worth the paper it's written on,' Robert said gloomily. 'That is, if it is even written down.'

In the summer, Daisy passed her Higher School Certificate with the expected 'flying colours'.

'So,' Henrietta asked her as they sat around the dinner table celebrating Daisy's achievement with champagne. 'What are you going to do now?'

'I've been accepted into the Studley Horticulture and Agricultural College in Warwickshire.'

'Oh darling, how wonderful,' Alice said. 'That was your first choice, wasn't it?'

Daisy nodded. 'It was set up by Lady Daisy Warwick and it's an all-women's college.' Daisy grinned saucily. 'No distractions!'

The family all laughed, but then listened attentively as Daisy went on. 'You can do a three-year course for a Diploma in Horticulture, but two years ago they began a three-year degree course for a BSc in Horticulture. So, that's what I'm going to do.'

Henrietta frowned. 'That sounds all well and good, Daisy, but it's not exactly agriculture, is it? Will it be useful on the estate?'

Daisy grinned. 'Actually, in time I'd like to extend the horticultural side of things here, if you're agreeable, but the college has a farm and a dairy herd and offers a course in agriculture, so I'm going to do that alongside the degree course.'

Alice frowned. 'That sounds like an awful lot of hard work. Don't take on too much, Daisy.'

'She'll cope,' Robert said, confidently.

Word soon spread around the village – thanks to Bess Cooper – that Miss Daisy was going away to a grand college housed in a castle in Warwickshire.

*

'You'll be an awful long way away for weeks at a time,' Luke said dolefully. Daisy hadn't waited for the gossip to reach him, but had gone herself to the workshop to tell him.

'But once my course is finished, I'll be back here for good, won't I?'

'Yes, I suppose so.' A worried frown still creased his forehead.

'I'll write.'

Still, that didn't seem to wipe away his anxiety. 'You – you might meet – someone.'

Daisy laughed. 'I'm hoping I'll meet a lot of people and make some new friends. You wouldn't begrudge me that, would you?'

'Well, no.' Luke wriggled his shoulders, feeling foolish now. Two years older than Daisy, Luke now had definite romantic feelings for her. There were one or two girls in the village who'd made no secret of the fact that they'd like to 'walk out' with him, but his heart belonged to Daisy and he believed it always would. And then there was Harry. If he still persisted in his childhood declaration that he was going to marry Daisy one day, Luke could see a family feud looming. He stared at Daisy, trying to read her mind. She grinned back at him, her eyes as affectionate as ever, but he could detect no real romantic love blossoming there. Perhaps, he comforted himself, she was still a little young and her head was so filled with her upcoming college course. He'd just have to be patient. At least Johnny Hammond hadn't been posted anywhere near where she was going to be.

*

As Daisy planned her further education, Harry, too, left school. On the morning that he was due to start work as a full-time employee of Len's, he walked jauntily down the road towards the workshop. It felt good to be a working man now. No more 'little boy' jokes from Luke and at least he had a job to go to. Many of his contemporaries, who had left school that summer, had still not been able to find work. Times in many parts of the country were still hard, but here in Doddington, there was employment for everyone.

''Lo, Harry.'

Harry glanced around and saw Kitty Page swinging on the front gate of the cottage where she lived with her parents directly opposite Len's workshop.

'Hello, Kitty,' Harry said and sauntered across the road. 'I'm starting work this morning. Full time.'

'I know. Mam said. I've been watching for you comin'.'

Harry grinned at her. She was a pretty little thing with blond curls and bright blue eyes and about the same age as he was.

'Have you left school an' all?'

Kitty nodded. 'I've got an interview with Mrs Maitland at the hall tomorrow to be a kitchen maid.'

Harry grinned. 'Good luck, then. My Aunty Betty, my mam's sister, works there. She'll look out for you.'

'I've got summat for you.' Kitty held out a four-leafed clover, twirling it between her thumb and forefinger. 'To bring you luck.'

'Aw, thanks, Kitty. Wherever did you find it?'

'There's a patch of clover in the field just outside our back gate. I've found one there before.' That was

81

true, but she didn't tell him it had taken her hours of careful searching to find this one for him.

He fished in his pocket and pulled out a shiny, new leather wallet. 'Me dad bought me this for starting work. I'll keep it in here.'

'Wait a minute.' Kitty jumped down from the gate and ran up the path and into the cottage. She emerged a moment later with a piece of paper in her hand. 'Put it in this,' she said, folding the paper over. 'It'll keep it better. It'll be like flower pressing. Me mam showed me how to do it.'

Gently, he pushed the piece of paper, now with the clover laid flat inside its fold, into one of the compartments of his new wallet.

At that moment a roar from Len came from the other side of the road. 'Time you was at your work, boy. Never mind your flirtin'.'

With a swift grin at Kitty and a saucy wink, Harry turned and, hands in his pockets, strolled across the road.

'Morning, Mr Dawson. What are we doin' today, then?'

Len's only answer was a low growl and a baleful glare at Kitty, who waved and smiled prettily.

The night before she was due to travel to Studley, Daisy received a phone call.

'Daisy? It's Johnny. Just ringing you to wish you well for tomorrow – and guess what? I've been posted to Duxford. It's about a hundred and twenty miles from where you'll be, so I'll be able to get to see you on my motorcycle.'

'Johnny – that's marvellous.'

'I've got a seventy-two-hour pass next weekend, so I'll come and see you then.'

Daisy replaced the receiver thoughtfully. Some instinct told her not to mention Johnny's proposed visit to any of her family – and certainly not to Luke or Harry.

Eleven

Daisy's first letter home was full of enthusiasm for her life for the next three years:

> *Dear All*, she wrote, so that the letter would include everyone who would be interested.
>
> *This is a fabulous place. Fancy, I'm living in a castle! Everyone is lovely and I've already made a friend – Gill Portus. She's also doing the agricultural course alongside the degree, so we spend a lot of time together. She's from the Yorkshire Dales where her family have a farm, has a wicked sense of humour and is great fun!*
>
> *Not only are there extensive orchards and vegetable plots here, but greenhouses with grapes and such, so we're learning how and when to prune the different plants. There's a proper farm too with a dairy herd. I am learning to milk a cow! And make cheese. We've got chickens, geese, turkeys: oh, there's so much to learn. It's wonderful. Thank you so much for supporting me coming here. It's what I want to do for the rest of my life . . .*

Robert, in particular, grinned broadly when he read Daisy's letter.

'Lets you off the hook nicely, doesn't it?' Alice teased him.

'Absolutely,' he said. 'But it seems it's what she really wants to do.'

'There's no doubt about that, so you can stop feeling any guilt that you're pushing her into it.'

Robert guffawed. 'Push Daisy into anything? You must be joking. Now, who else will want to read her letters, apart from Mother and Father?'

Alice wrinkled her brow. 'Luke, of course, and Jake. He's so interested in all she's doing. Probably Harry, and I would think my mam and Peggy too.'

Robert chuckled. 'You've forgotten someone?'

'Have I?'

'Bess Cooper. She'd love to be able to share all Daisy's news with everyone.'

'As long as there's nothing private in the letters, then I don't see why not. All the village are so interested in what the next manager of the estate is going to do.'

'Can't blame them. Most of them get their livelihoods from the estate – in one way or another.' He was thoughtful for a moment before saying, 'You know, we ought to go down to see her in a few weeks' time. Jake could take us and then he could see what she's doing for himself.'

Alice beamed. 'I'd love that.'

*

'My goodness,' Gill said, 'who's the dishy RAF pilot who picked you up on his motorcycle yesterday afternoon and didn't bring you back until just after curfew? Mrs Gordon nearly had a fit when it got to ten past ten. You know what a stickler she is for the rules. I had an awful job persuading her not to report you.'

Gill's eyes twinkled and Daisy knew she was teasing her. Gill had bright red hair and green eyes. She was slim and energetic and was always the leader in any escapade.

'I'm an only child, so the family farm will pass to me,' Gill had told her when they had first become friends. 'Luckily, I like nothing better than plodding around in muddy wellingtons, ploughing or feeding the animals. What about you?'

Daisy had licked her lips and replied carefully, anxious not to alienate her newfound friend by appearing too grand. 'Um – much the same, actually. My grandmother inherited the – um – land, but my father has never been interested in running things. All he ever wanted to be was a doctor, following in *his* father's footsteps.'

They chatted amiably as they walked between classes, finding themselves attending lectures together and gradually learning more about each other.

'So, you still haven't answered my question. Who was he?'

'Johnny Hammond. His uncle's a friend of my aunt's.'

'Has he got any brothers? I'm not one to pinch another girl's chap, but oh, I could make a beeline for him.'

'He's not my boyfriend,' Daisy said and then wished she hadn't been so quick to deny it.

Gill threw back her head and laughed. 'Are you blind, Daisy Maitland? He's besotted with you.' She regarded her friend more thoughtfully. 'But then, you're so pretty that I expect you're so used to having all the young fellows you meet gazing at you with cow eyes.'

Colour flooded Daisy's cheeks, but she said nothing. She'd never really thought about it, but the way Johnny looked at her was exactly how Luke, and even Harry, regarded her.

Johnny had been her very first visitor, but towards the end of October, Jake drove Robert and Alice down to see her.

'I wish you could have met Gill,' Daisy said, as she showed them around the castle and its gardens, 'but she's working on the farm today and won't be back until after evening milking.'

Jake gazed around him. 'It's wonderful, Daisy. You'll have so many ideas when you come home.'

Daisy laughed. 'I'm here for three years, Jake. You'll have to hold the fort until then.'

He grinned at her. 'You mean your granny will, but I can't wait to try all the new ideas you'll have.' For a moment, his face was pensive and Daisy guessed he was a little envious that she had had the sort of chance that he could never have had. But, as if reminding himself just how lucky a scruffy little waif and stray had been to find Henrietta Maitland, his expression changed and he smiled down at her. 'You'll have to teach me everything you learn, Daisy.'

She put her arm through his and hugged it to her side. She loved Jake as a good friend. 'I will, Jake. I promise.'

As they parted, Robert said, 'I think your granny and grandpa would like to come down. Maybe in the spring when everything is starting to grow again.' He chuckled as he glanced at Jake, who was still gazing around him as if committing everything to memory. 'I'm sure Jake wouldn't mind bringing them.'

Daisy worked hard and, at the end of the first term, came out top of her course. Much to her relief, Gill was a close second.

'You must come and stay with us in the holidays,' Gill said, as they packed up ready to go home for the Christmas holidays. 'But bring your flannelette nighty. Winter can be a bit chilly up north. Eeh, what am I saying? You live not much further south than I do.'

Daisy smiled, thinking of the warm fires that her grandmother insisted were kept constantly burning through the long, cold days – and sometimes even nights – of winter. 'I'd love to,' she said, making a mental note to take her warmest clothes with her.

But an invitation to visit Yorkshire during the Christmas holidays was not forthcoming. Christmas at the hall was a merry affair, with the Dawsons, the Coopers and the Nuttalls invited to a buffet lunch as usual on Boxing Day, which was also Harry's birthday. Conrad Everton, the doctor who worked with Robert, and his wife Florence were included in the gathering too.

Bess Cooper, as jovial and loud as ever, sought Conrad out. 'I have to say, doctor, that when you came, we never thought you'd stay the course, but I must admit you and Master Robert make a good team. See, we'd had Dr Maitland' – Conrad knew she was referring to Edwin – 'for so long, we couldn't imagine anyone taking his place, except Master Robert, of course, and even then it took a while for the older ones to accept the little lad they'd known in short trousers becoming their doctor.' She laughed raucously. 'But you've done well and we've all taken to you.'

Conrad smiled modestly. 'Thank you, Mrs Cooper. I'm relieved to hear it as both my wife and I love it here.'

'He manages very well,' she said, nodding towards Robert on the other side of the Great Hall, 'but it took him a while to get back into it after the war.'

'Understandable,' Conrad murmured.

'Well, here's to you and your missus, young man.' Bess clinked her wineglass with him. 'And here's to 1937. Let's hope it's a good 'un.'

'I'll drink to that, Mrs Cooper.'

On the other side of the room, however, the talk between Robert and Pips was far more serious as they mulled over the events of the passing year.

'It's been a strange one, hasn't it?' Pips murmured. 'I never – in my wildest dreams – thought we'd have an abdication.'

There had been every sign that the new king would be sympathetic towards the ordinary working man. On his visit to Wales in November, he was moved by the plight of the unemployed there, which followed the Jarrow March to London in October, highlighting the sufferings of the jobless in the northeast. But at the beginning of December, the British newspapers broke their silence that the new king, loved by so many, was locked in a romance with a twice-divorced American woman. By 12 December, he had abdicated to marry the love of his life and the burden of monarchy fell upon his brother, George.

'He'll be a great king, you'll see,' Robert remarked confidently to Pips. 'He's even got a good name,' he teased his sister to which she replied with her usual 'Oh phooey.'

Being present for the young ones' birthdays wasn't quite so easy now with Daisy at college and George working, but alternate Christmases were sacrosanct. And this year, it was Lincolnshire's turn.

'You think so? Edward was the People's King. They don't know his brother so well.'

'Not yet. But he has a happy and settled family life. Give him time. He'll win them over.'

'I hope you're right,' Pips said, 'because I don't like the way things are shaping up in Europe again.'

'Nor do I. Since his victory over Abyssinia, Mussolini is now declaring that Italy has its empire. It's causing a lot of unrest and argument amongst governments and now we have a civil war in Spain.'

Pips sighed. 'They'll never learn, will they? You'd really think the whole world would have had enough of war, but no. What's this skirmish all about, then?'

Robert smiled. 'Hasn't George told you anything?

I'd have thought you'd know, better than any of us, what's going on.'

Pips grimaced. 'To be honest, Robert, George says very little about his work and I think it's better that way.'

'Surely he knows you well enough to know that you'd never ever repeat anything he told you.' Robert grinned. 'Not even to me.'

They laughed together. 'Quite. But if that's the way he feels, then I respect him. If I worked for the Government, or something terribly secret, then I'm sure I'd feel the same.'

'Fair enough. I'll just have to put up with what appears in the press, then.'

'You could ask him yourself.'

'I could,' Robert said thoughtfully, 'but I don't want to put him in an awkward position of having to refuse to tell me.'

Pips chuckled. 'I'm sure he's used to fending off nosy parkers.'

At that moment George appeared at Pips's elbow. 'What's all the laughter about? May I join in?'

'We were talking about you,' Pips teased.

George smiled. 'Oh dear!'

'Robert expected that I would know all about the political situation – especially about the Spanish Civil War – but I told him you don't tell me much about your work.'

George wrinkled his brow. 'It's not that I don't trust you, Pips. It's that I don't want you to be worried.'

Both Pips and Robert stared at him. 'Should I be?' she asked softly.

'There are – rumblings, shall we say – in Europe and in other parts of the world too, it has to be said. But our informers tell us that the little corporal in Germany is becoming more powerful by the day. Rumour has it that he wants to recover Germany's lost colonies. He's watching Mussolini's progress carefully.'

'And then, of course, there are all his new laws against the Jews,' Robert said. 'That has been in the press. There are some dreadful things going on.'

'He's virtually torn up the Versailles agreement.'

Robert grimaced. 'I said at the time I thought the terms were too stringent. It was bound to lead to resentment.'

'And it seems Adolf Hitler epitomizes that bitterness,' George said.

'You think the problems are going to escalate, George, don't you?'

Solemnly, he said, 'Sadly, Pips, I do.' He glanced across to where Daisy was joking with Luke and Harry. 'But God forbid that we should be plunged into another war, because it'll be those wonderful young people and their generation who will have to fight once again for our freedom.'

Twelve

Oblivious to the rumblings of unrest throughout the spring of 1937, Daisy continued her course at Studley. Johnny visited regularly, arriving on his motorcycle in a roar of exhaust fumes. She said nothing at home about their growing friendship, but one day towards the end of her second term, on a deceptively mild March day, Luke arrived unexpectedly on his motorcycle.

He parked his machine on the driveway next to another motorcycle and knocked on the door.

'Granddad gave me the day off.' He grinned at her and jerked his thumb over his shoulder. 'Nice motorcycle parked there. Whose is it?'

Daisy sighed inwardly, but managed to keep a welcoming smile plastered on her face. 'Come in, Luke. We've just had lunch, but I have to get back for a one-to-one with my tutor this afternoon.'

'Oh, sorry. I should've let you know I was coming. When will you be free?'

'About five, if you can stay that long.'

'Of course. No good coming all this way to—'

She led the way into the room where the students were allowed to entertain their visitors. Nearby was a small kitchen where they could make tea, coffee and snacks. Luke paused in the doorway as he scanned the room and saw who was sitting at the table.

'What's he doing here?' he muttered.

Daisy glanced back at him. 'Visiting – just like you. Come in. I want you to meet my friend, Gill.'

Reluctantly, Luke went into the room and shook hands with Gill, but the two young men only nodded curtly to each other.

'Hello, Luke,' Gill said. 'Pleased to meet you. Daisy's told me all about you and your brother, Harry.' She patted a seat at the side of her. 'Come and sit by me and tell me how things are on the farm.'

With another swift glance at Johnny, Luke sat down, whilst Daisy murmured, 'I'll make us some more tea.'

'I don't work on the estate,' Luke said. 'Not exactly. My granddad runs a small business in the village. Wheelwright, blacksmith and carpentry. But a lot of our work comes from Mrs Maitland's estate.'

Gill's eyes widened. 'Estate? Daisy didn't tell me it was an *estate*. I thought she just lived on a farm, like I do.'

'There is a farm, of course, but there are gardens, orchards and grounds around the hall.'

'The *hall*? She lives in a hall?'

Johnny, listening to the conversation, frowned but said nothing. Obviously, Daisy hadn't wanted her new friends to know about where she came from, but now Luke was truly letting the proverbial cat out of the bag.

Daisy came back into the room carrying a tray with four cups of freshly made tea and a plate of biscuits. Gill glanced up at her. 'You're a dark horse, Daisy Maitland. You didn't tell me you lived in a big house surrounded by gardens and grounds *and* a farm.' Then she grinned. 'Why ever didn't you say? Now I can't *wait* to visit.'

Daisy set the tray down carefully on the table and met her friend's gaze and drew in a deep breath. 'You're welcome any time.'

Luke looked contrite. 'I'm sorry, Dais. I didn't mean . . .'

Daisy merely shrugged. 'It's all right. We've already said we'll visit each other in the summer holidays. She'd have found out then. Besides,' now she smiled, 'from what Gill says, her dad's land is bigger than the area we actually farm.'

'But we don't live in a grand hall,' Gill laughed. 'Just a draughty old farmhouse that comes last on the list when it comes to spending money. But, d'you know what? I love it. Once I've finished this course, I'm off back home like a rat down a drainpipe and I don't intend to leave it again. I'll be ploughin' and sowin' and reapin' and hoein' and I'll be as happy a pig in muck. Aye, and we've got some of them, an' all.'

Johnny relaxed a little, but now he felt uncomfortable. Luke and Daisy had such a long history that he was beginning to think that perhaps there was a tacit understanding between them. He stood up. 'I'd better be getting back, Daisy. Don't want to be on a charge.'

'I'll see you out.'

'Cheerio, Gill,' Johnny said, giving her a little wave, but to Luke he only nodded again.

As he started his machine, Johnny smiled at Daisy, his eyes searching her face, vainly trying to find something in her eyes that would give him even a glimmer of hope. But, as always, there was her lovely smile and her eyes twinkled with her love of the life she had. Whether there could ever be a place for him in that life, he couldn't tell.

Now, he thought, I know exactly how Uncle Mitch feels about Pips.

When Daisy returned to the others, it was to find Gill, resting her elbows on the table, her chin cupped in her hands as she gazed at Luke with a rapt expression on her face whilst Luke was telling her about working for his grandfather alongside his stepfather and his half-brother.

Daisy picked up her books from the dresser. 'I'll be back in just over an hour.'

Luke glanced up and nodded, whilst Gill waved her hand airily. 'Don't rush, Daisy. I'll look after him. I'll make us a snack for when you get back.'

When Daisy returned just before five, it was to find Luke and Gill still sitting at the table, talking and laughing together.

'Oh sorry . . .' Gill leapt up. 'I meant to make a few sandwiches, but we got talking. I don't know where the time's gone. You sit down with Luke, Daisy.'

'We'll come into the kitchen so that you can talk to us too.'

Daisy and Luke, with a fresh pot of tea between them, sat at the small kitchen table and talked whilst Gill busied herself cutting bread, but Daisy could tell she was listening to their conversation.

'So, how's everyone at home?'

'Fine.'

'And Harry?'

'A pain, as usual, though I have to admit, he's shaping up at work quite nicely now he's full time. He works mostly with Sam in the blacksmith's at the moment, but he's going to learn the other side of it too.' Luke grinned. 'He's good at making coffins.'

Len was also the undertaker for Doddington and the nearby villages.

'And he gets on all right with Granddad?'

Luke pulled a face. 'Sort of. Granddad never lets him forget that he's not family and that the business will be mine one day – never his.'

'And what does Harry say to that?'

'You know how cheeky he is. He just says that I would never sack my half-brother and then Granddad says, "Don't be too sure about that," and so it goes on. It's a sort of banter between them, but there's this underlying truth behind it. It's just Granddad's way of keeping him in line, I suppose.' Luke sighed. 'But I wish he wouldn't keep reminding Harry that he's not *his* family. It makes me feel very awkward at times. After all, he is my half-brother and everyone else treats us equally, they always have done, but Granddad won't even get him a motorcycle like he

97

got me.' He grinned. 'Mind you, Harry can be quite determined when he wants to be. He's squirrelling away every spare bit of cash he earns. In two years' time, he says, he'll be able to come and see you on his own motorcycle.'

Daisy laughed. 'But I'll be home by then.'

Luke stared at her for a moment before saying slowly, 'Of course you will. I bet he hasn't thought of that.'

'Then don't spoil it for him. He idolizes you, Luke, and wants to emulate you. Let him save up and get his motorcycle.'

Thirteen

Pips's fears for the future only grew as 1937 progressed. Young men from all over the world, who saw themselves as some sort of crusaders, had joined the Spanish Civil War, some to fight on the side of the International Brigade against the rise of Fascism, whilst others fought for General Franco's Nationalists in order to halt the spread of Communism.

'Did you see that our government has warned that anyone enlisting in the Spanish war will face two years' imprisonment? Has George said anything?' Robert asked Pips when she visited at Easter.

Pips shook her head. 'You know he doesn't tell me much, but he's spending longer and longer hours at work. Sometimes, he doesn't get home until after midnight.'

'I'm not surprised. It's getting serious. Did you hear about the Mediterranean being mined?'

'Yes, one of our liners was damaged in February off the coast of Spain, wasn't it?'

Robert nodded solemnly. 'Luckily, it managed to get to the nearest harbour, but just think what that could mean to shipping in general.'

'At least we're building up our navy now. Do you

think this civil war is going to escalate and involve other countries?'

Robert shrugged, but could not answer her.

Pips forced a smile. 'Let's change the subject. Have you done today's crossword in the *Telegraph*?'

'Yes. In twenty minutes. You?'

'All but one. I just can't get it.'

'Which one?'

'Ten down. Five letters and the clue is "exasperated".'

Robert chuckled. He loved to get 'one up' on his clever sister. 'I thought that clue was one of the easiest.'

'Oh phooey to you,' Pips laughed. 'Go on, tell me the answer.'

'Heggs.'

'What? How do you get that?'

'Eggs – aspirated.'

There was a moment's silence as Pips digested the answer. 'Oh yes, dead easy,' she said sarcastically. 'Now, tell me about Daisy. I tried to ask her about college this morning but she was in such a hurry to go out riding. How's she getting on?'

Robert chuckled. 'Extremely well, as you might expect. Top of the class as usual. We've got her friend Gill coming to stay with us next week and then they'll go back to college together. We can't wait to meet her.'

'What about Johnny? Does he still visit?'

Robert laughed. 'Oh yes. You should see him and Luke together. They're like a couple of fighting cocks skirting round each other.'

'Oh dear. They don't actually fight, do they?'

'No, but I sometimes think they'd like to. The daft thing is that Daisy doesn't seem particularly interested in either of them in a romantic way. She's just concentrating on getting her degree.'

'She must notice it, though.'

'I'm sure she does. Perhaps she's rather enjoying the attention.'

Pips laughed. 'There is that.'

When the time came for Gill's visit, Jake drove Daisy to the station to meet her.

'Sorry about all the luggage,' Gill laughed as she helped Jake heft her suitcases and boxes into the back of the car. 'But we're going straight back to Studley from here, aren't we, so I've had to bring everything.'

'That's all right,' Daisy said, hugging her. 'Come on. I can't wait for you to meet everyone. Aunty Pips is still here, though Uncle George has had to go back to London.'

The Maitland family couldn't help but like Daisy's friend. She was wide-eyed with wonder at the hall and its lands. 'And you're going to inherit all this one day, Daisy? Oh my, I didn't realize I'd got such a grand friend.'

'I do hope that's not how we come across, Gill,' Henrietta chuckled.

Gill was thoughtful for a moment before saying candidly, 'Actually, no, you don't, although I expect the villagers treat you with the deference you deserve.'

Henrietta wrinkled her forehead thoughtfully,

trying to see her family through the eyes of a stranger. 'My family have always been at the heart of the village and all our employees are local. I'm pleased to say they feel able to come to us in times of trouble and we do our best to help.'

'We've got a sort of lord of the manor where we live – Mr Jeremy Hainsworth. We call him "Lord Bunny" because he's always out shooting rabbits on his land. I'm sorry to say, though, he's a bit aloof.' She grinned at Henrietta. 'I bet you're not.'

'Heavens, no!'

'There's one thing I'm working on, though. He owns an aeroplane and I've been pestering him to take me up in it.'

'You'll have to come and stay with us in London and we'll take you to Brooklands,' Pips said. She had stayed on especially to meet Daisy's friend.

'Oh, I'd love that. I know Daisy's having lessons.'

Henrietta's head shot up. 'Is she now? I didn't know that.'

'Oops. Sorry, Daisy, have I put my size six wellies right in it?'

But Daisy only laughed and shrugged. 'Granny knows I go flying when I'm with Aunty Pips. It's only a natural progression that I should want to learn to fly too.'

Henrietta gave an exaggerated sigh. 'Do you have to do everything your aunt does, Daisy?'

'Pretty much, Granny, yes.'

'Well, I'm glad you don't go car racing. That would worry me, though I don't suppose flying is *much* safer.'

Daisy wrinkled her forehead. 'Strangely, I've never taken to the racing. But flying – oh Granny – up there amongst the clouds, it's absolute heaven. You feel so free. Uncle Mitch says there's nothing like it.'

'I've no intention of finding out for myself, not at my advanced age, but I think I can understand what you're saying.' Henrietta rose from the dinner table. 'And now we'll retire to the parlour and you can tell me more about your father's farm, Gill. I'm really interested, and tomorrow Daisy can show you around our estate.'

As they left the Great Hall and moved to the parlour, Gill squeezed Daisy's arm and whispered. 'And the village too. I want to see Luke. And I absolutely must meet the one you call "the pain".'

'So, this is all going to be yours one day?' It was not Daisy to whom Gill was speaking, but Luke, as she stood in front of the workshops belonging to Len Dawson.

He grinned as he came to stand beside her, looking at his inheritance through her eyes. 'That's what me granddad says.'

Gill was quite serious as she said, 'I wish we had someone like you at home. We have to travel miles to a wheelwright and then to the blacksmith in the opposite direction. It's a real pain.' She smiled and turned towards him. 'And talking of "pains", where is he, then?'

Luke nodded to where sounds of hammering against an anvil came from the next-door workshop. 'Working with me stepdad, Sam. I'll get him.'

Moments later, a young man with curly fair hair and blue eyes, and the cheekiest grin Gill had ever seen, sauntered towards them. He was nothing like Luke, but then, Gill remembered, they were half-brothers, sharing a mother, but not a father.

'Hello, Dais, and you must be Gill,' he said, his eyes twinkling mischievously. 'We've been hearing a lot about you from Luke. I reckon you're getting your nose pushed out of joint with our Luke, Dais, but then, it's me you're goin' to marry, in't it?' He held out a grimy hand towards the newcomer.

Luke looked acutely embarrassed, but Gill only threw back her head and laughed as she took Harry's hand without a moment's hesitation whilst Daisy smiled and said, 'Not until the sun shines both sides of the hedge at once, Harry Nuttall.'

It was a Lincolnshire saying that meant 'never', but Harry didn't take her reply seriously. In fact, it seemed he never took anything very seriously.

As they walked home together, they met Kitty Page walking home after her day's work at the hall. Though some of the other staff lived in at the hall, Kitty still lived at home with her parents.

'Hello, Kitty.' Daisy smiled. 'How are you?'

'Very well, Miss Daisy, thank you.' The girl nodded a greeting to Gill.

'Are you enjoying working at the hall?'

'Oh yes, miss. Everyone's so kind.' She glanced further down the lane. 'Have you seen Harry?'

'Yes, he's still at work.'

'Oh good. I didn't want to miss him. Mrs Bentley's teaching me to cook when she's time and I've made

Harry a cake. Your granny knows about it, miss,' she added hurriedly.

'May we see?'

Kitty lifted the tea towel that covered the chocolate cake nestling in the bottom of her basket.

'That looks delicious. Lucky Harry.'

'Mrs Bentley made one for your afternoon tea, miss.'

'Then we'd better get home before we miss it. 'Bye for now, Kitty.'

As they walked on, Gill said, '*Are* you going to marry one of them, Daisy? Because I think you've got a rival for Harry's affections there.' Gill glanced back over her shoulder to see Kitty heading towards the blacksmith's workshop.

'Heavens, no, but it's been a long-standing joke between us. We're the very best of friends, of course. Always have been since we were kids, but Luke is my cousin. If anything, I look upon them both as my brothers.'

'They don't look very alike, do they?'

'Luke is like the Dawson family, but Harry has got the same curly fair hair as his mother, Peggy.'

'I think you'll find that beneath all that larking about, Harry is very serious.'

'Oh heck! I hope not. I wouldn't want him to break poor Kitty's heart. She's been following him around ever since she was a little kid. D'you really think he's serious about me?'

'I do, but what I don't know at this precise moment is just how serious Luke is about you.'

'Oh Lor'. I think the sooner we get back to college the better.'

Gill chuckled. 'But before you know it, you'll be back here permanently. Don't forget that and then there might be fireworks.'

Soon after the two girls returned to Studley for the summer term, Jake took Henrietta and Edwin to see them. The Maitland family had taken to Gill and Henrietta invited her to join them for 'luncheon', as she called it. Jake was a little overwhelmed eating in a restaurant, but Henrietta would not hear of him not joining them. 'You're part of our family, Jake.' Then she turned to Daisy. 'I'm very impressed with Studley. You made a wise choice, Daisy. Now what are we all going to eat . . . ?'

Both girls worked hard and came out with the highest marks in their group at the end of their first year at the college. During the summer holidays of 1937, the two girls spent a lot of time together, first at Gill's home, where Daisy met her parents. Bill Portus was a huge man, jovial and welcoming, with a round, florid face. His wife Mabel was small and thin, but Daisy couldn't remember ever having met anyone with quite so much energy. She was never still and hardly ever sat down to relax, yet she never seemed to get tired.

Every day, Gill and Daisy helped on the farm and in the evening sat talking to Gill's father about farming and their own hopes for the future. And then it was time to head to Lincolnshire and do much the same there. They ended their long holiday with a trip to London, where Pips took them both to Brooklands and Gill flew for the first time.

'There's no race meeting,' Pips told them as they took the train to Weybridge. 'But Mitch has arranged for you both to have flights with Jeff.'

He was waiting for them when they arrived and he took Daisy up first to give her an impromptu flying lesson. And then it was Gill's turn.

Daisy and Pips stood side by side as the aircraft took off and climbed higher and higher.

'She didn't seem nervous, did she?'

Daisy shook her head. 'Not much fazes Gill, Aunty Pips. Oh my!' Daisy giggled. 'He's looping the loop with her.'

'Oh dear. I do hope she'll be all right.'

'She'll love it. I promise you.'

And she did. When the aeroplane landed, Gill climbed out and came running towards them. '*Now* I know why you are always going on about it, Daisy. It's fantastic. Oh, I do wish Lord Bunny back home would let me fly his plane.'

'Maybe he will one day.'

Gill snorted. 'Highly unlikely. I've been asking him to take me up since I was about twelve.'

Pips, walking between them, linked arms with them and said, 'You can come down here whenever you can, Gill. Mitch will always arrange a flight for you.'

Gill nodded. She didn't like to say that she couldn't afford frequent trips and she was too proud to accept their charity. This one had been Pips's treat.

'Now, let's go and find Mitch in the clubhouse,' Pips said. 'I think Milly's here today somewhere.'

'Oh good. You'll like Aunty Milly, Gill,' Daisy said. 'She's a scream.'

Fourteen

They were all there; the Brooklands girls and their friends.

'Darling!' Milly threw her arms around Daisy. 'And who's this?' She smiled at Gill, who was at once captivated by the sweet-faced woman with curly blond hair and a merry laugh.

'This is my friend, Gill, from college, Aunty Milly.'

Milly kissed a startled Gill on both cheeks. 'Do you drive, Gill?'

'Er – only our tractor, Mrs, er . . .'

'Call me "Aunty Milly", like Daisy does, darling. Now, come along, let me introduce you to the gang . . .'

'So,' Mitch asked as they ended up sitting at a table with him. 'Did you enjoy your flight, Gill?'

Her green eyes shone. 'It was wonderful.'

'There's a chap who lives not far from Gill in Yorkshire, who has a plane,' Daisy put in.

'An aeroplane, Daisy. Always an aeroplane. Haven't we taught you better than that?'

Daisy grinned. 'Sorry, Uncle Mitch.'

'So, who's this chap, then?'

'Gill calls him "Lord Bunny", but he refuses to take her for a flight.'

'He's a sort of unofficial lord of the manor,' Gill put in. 'He owns a lot of land round where I live.'

'What's he got?'

'A Tiger Moth,' Gill said.

'Ah, a two-seater biplane,' Mitch said and then winked. 'That's handy. We've got one here, so I can show you over it and give you the low down, if you like, Gill. Maybe – if you can talk knowledgeably about his aeroplane and give him plenty of flannel – he'll take you up.'

Gill laughed. 'I doubt it. But anything's worth a try.'

'I don't suppose you got the chance to see the Vickers Spitfire on show at Eastleigh Aerodrome in March last year, did you?' Mitch said, when the girls paused for breath and he could get a word in.

Both girls turned towards him. 'Spitfire?' Gill repeated, whilst Daisy said, 'Aunty Milly's father's firm?'

Gill glanced at her. 'Aunty Milly's father builds aeroplanes?'

'His firm does.' Daisy nodded towards the building with the 'Vickers' name emblazoned on it.

'Does he *own* Vickers?'

Daisy glanced at Mitch. 'I – I'm not sure. Does he, Uncle Mitch?'

Mitch laughed and shook his head. 'Not exactly, but he's one of the founders and he's certainly one of the bigwigs in the company.'

'Spitfire,' Daisy murmured. 'That's a great name for an aeroplane, but it sounds rather – aggressive.'

'It's meant to be. It's a fighter aeroplane and at

this moment in time, the RAF's most powerful weapon.'

The girls glanced at each other and then stared at him. 'Uncle Mitch,' Daisy said quietly, 'is there something we're missing here?'

Suddenly, Mitch realized that perhaps their families didn't talk about the rumblings in Europe in front of the younger members. Swiftly, he grinned. 'I shouldn't think so for a minute. Not you two,' he said, trying to make his tone light. 'But our country – like any other – must keep its defences up to scratch. Now, let me go and get some drinks. I'm parched.'

The girls returned to college in September to start their second year at Studley, blithely unaware that their relatives were watching the newspapers and listening avidly to the news on the wireless.

'Have you read the papers, Pips?' Robert asked her on the first Saturday evening in October during their weekly telephone call to each other.

'Hitler and Mussolini getting so cosy at some sort of demonstration in Berlin this week, you mean?'

'Yes, that and at the recent Nazi party's annual rally in Nuremberg, Hitler was bleating on about needing more living space for Germany.'

'I don't like what Mussolini said about their plans not being aimed at other countries. Of course they are. How can you extend your borders unless you occupy other countries? And I don't think Hitler is going to stop at what he called reoccupying the Rhineland last year, do you?'

'Sadly, Pips,' Robert said solemnly, 'I don't. I think

Mussolini's conquest of Abyssinia has given the little corporal ideas; ideas that the rest of Europe – including us – won't like.' He paused and then added, 'What do George and Matthew say?'

'Not much, and I don't ask because I don't want to put either of them in an awkward position.'

'How very diplomatic of you, Pips. That's not a bit like you.'

Pips chuckled. 'No, it isn't, is it? But I do respect the fact that they mustn't talk about what they hear in the course of their work.'

'Point taken.'

'How's Daisy?'

'Fine. Working hard – they both are.'

'I do like her friend, Gill.'

'So do we. It'll be nice for them to keep in touch even after they finish college. Gill's not that far away in the Yorkshire Dales, is she?'

'Right, I'd better go. By the way, what's your time for today's crossword?'

'Fifteen minutes.'

'Oh phooey. It took me seventeen. Give my love to everyone. I'll ring again as usual next weekend and, in the meantime, I'll do my best to beat fifteen minutes.'

Life continued in much the same way in Doddington and on the Maitlands' estate, largely untroubled by the political manoeuvrings, but in March 1938, no one could ignore the news that Hitler had marched into Austria – the land of his birth.

'I can't understand why he met with no resistance.

The crowds were welcoming him,' Pips said as she and the Maitlands sat around the dinner table on Easter Sunday in April.

'Huh – he brought in supporters to cheer him, greeting him with the Fascist salute with cries of *"Heil Hitler!"*. I'm very much afraid that that is something we're going to hear a lot of from now on.'

'Is that why George isn't with you this time?' Henrietta asked.

'I think so. He works long hours now.'

'Does he tell you much?' Edwin asked and then added quickly, 'Not that we expect you to tell *us* anything.'

Pips shook her head. 'He says very little, Father, and Matthew even less, but they're both looking anxious. Rebecca says Matthew is working long hours at the Foreign Office too.'

'I have to admit,' Robert said slowly, 'I don't like it. Where is Hitler going to try next?'

'Pips, darling.'

'Hello, Milly,' Pips said as she answered the telephone to hear Milly's slightly breathless voice. 'Are you all right?'

'I'm fine, but I have some exciting news and you must tell Daisy and get her and her friend to come down to Brooklands a week on Saturday – the eighteenth of June.'

'But they're at college and they're probably in the middle of exams. There are always exams in June – so I understand.' There was an edge of sarcasm to her tone. Pips had not been allowed to go to university to study medicine as had her brother, Robert. And to this day a tiny bit of resentment still lingered.

'But they *must* come. Johnny and a few of his mates have got special leave to come down.'

'But why, Milly? You haven't said why.'

Milly's infectious giggle sounded down the wire. 'Oh, I haven't, have I? You know how Brooklands have an "At Home" meeting every so often?'

'Yes. They're very popular. We've been to one or two. Go on.'

'Well, sometimes, one of Daddy's test pilots, or one from Hawker, gives a display with one of their new aircraft still under production.'

'Ye-es,' Pips said slowly, wondering what was coming.

Triumphantly, Milly said, 'On the eighteenth, they're bringing a Spitfire from Eastleigh to give a display. You know that Supermarine, who make them, is a subsidiary of Vickers, don't you? Mitch and Paul are so terribly excited about it – Jeff too – and they're sure Daisy would be thrilled to see it.'

'I'm sure she would, but—'

'Oh, don't be a spoilsport, Pips. That's not like you. They won't be doing exams on a Saturday, surely. And you could fetch them on the Friday night. They could stay with you, couldn't they? If not, then—'

'Of course they could,' Pips interrupted. 'It's just that I don't want to take them away from their studies at an important time.' She paused, thinking quickly. 'I'll tell you what I'll do. I'll speak to Robert first. If

114

he thinks it would be all right, then I'll get in touch with Daisy. We've plenty of time to organize it.'

Milly giggled again. 'That's not like you, Pips. Asking permission to do something.'

Pips laughed with her. 'But not even I dare to jeopardize Daisy's studies.' Thank goodness, she was thinking, that Robert and Alice had been more forward-thinking than her own parents. Yet, even they seemed to have mellowed over the years and had encouraged Daisy's ambitions. Maybe, Pips thought shrewdly, it was because Daisy's course would help her to manage the estate better.

'I can understand that,' Milly was saying. 'But I think she ought at least to be told about it. If she found out later that we hadn't told her . . .'

'There is that, Milly.'

A little later, Pips rang her brother to ask for his thoughts. 'So, Robert, what do you think?'

'It's an excellent idea. A break from exams would do them both good.'

'But what about their revision?'

Robert chuckled. 'If they haven't done it by then, last-minute cramming isn't going to help and a break might be more beneficial.'

'Well, as long as I have your approval, I'll tell her and suggest that she and Gill come here for the weekend. A little longer, if they can.'

It wasn't easy to communicate with Daisy. Pips had to ring the office at Studley Castle and then wait whilst Daisy was found and brought to the telephone.

'Aunty Pips, is something wrong?'

'Far from it, Daisy.' Swiftly Pips explained why

she was telephoning, adding that Johnny and some of his RAF mates were going to be there.

'That sounds wonderful. Of course we'll come. I'm sure Gill would love to come too. We could both do with a break from exams and we haven't got any on the Friday or the Monday, so that would be perfect.' She paused and then asked, a little diffidently, which was unusual for Daisy, 'Aunty Pips, can I be cheeky?'

Pips laughed. 'Of course. When are you *not*?'

'Could I ask Luke and Harry to come? They'd both love it.'

'Of *course*. I should have thought of that myself.' Pips laughed. 'As long as Granddad Dawson will allow it.'

'I think they'll come anyway.'

Fifteen

'Dad,' Luke began as the family sat down to their supper. 'I hope this won't rebound on you, but I'm going down to London on Friday evening to stay with Aunty Pips and she's invited Harry to go too.'

Harry, sitting opposite, stared at him, his mouth open. 'Has she? Why?'

Luke grinned at him across the table. 'Because she's going to take us both to Brooklands to see a Spitfire flying.'

Harry's eyes sparkled. 'Really?'

'Yes, really?'

'What about Daisy?'

'She'll be there too. So will Gill. We'll all be staying at Aunty Pips's.'

'What about *him*?'

'Johnny? He'll be at Brooklands with some of his RAF mates, but not at Aunty Pips's.'

Harry pulled a face. 'Well, I suppose we can't stop him going there, can we?'

'No, it's a free country.'

Luke turned back to Sam. 'So, do you mind, Dad? I wouldn't want Granddad to take it out on you if we both go.' When Sam and Peggy had first got married, Luke had always called Sam by his Christian name, but over the years it had come naturally to the boy to call him 'Dad'.

Sam grinned. 'Don't even think about it, Luke. You go. Both of you. I half wish I could go with you.'

'Well, perhaps—'

Sam held up his hand. 'No, no, I'm only joking. I'll hold the fort here. You two go and enjoy yourselves. How are you going to get there? By train?'

Luke grinned. 'No, on my motorcycle. Harry will ride pillion.'

'Oh,' Peggy said. 'Do be careful, it's a long way.'

'We'll be fine, Mam. Don't worry.'

There was really nothing Len could do to stop them, though he grumbled and groused and made his feelings abundantly clear. 'Always wanting to go gallivanting.'

They set off after work on the Friday evening and sped down to London with Harry clinging onto Luke's waist. It was late when they arrived but both Pips and George were waiting up for them.

'The girls are here, but they've gone to bed,' Pips said in a low voice. 'They've both been working so hard, they're shattered. Now, come into the kitchen. I've made sandwiches for you.'

Everyone was up early the following morning and Pips listened to the non-stop chatter between the four youngsters as she cooked breakfast for everyone.

'Are we going down by train, Aunty Pips?' Daisy asked.

'No. George's car is a big one. You four will easily be able to squash into the back seat.'

At Brooklands they were met by Milly and Paul, who took them to the best viewpoint to watch the display.

Harry gazed around him in wonderment and asked all sorts of questions about the car and motorcycle racing and about the various flying schools that operated there.

'Uncle Mitch has a school here and Jeff Pointer works for him,' Daisy explained. 'He's an instructor. He taught Aunty Pips to fly and then me.'

'He took me up too,' Luke said.

'And me,' Gill put in.

'Can I get a flight whilst we're here, d'you think?'

'Don't be cheeky, Harry,' Luke said swiftly. 'Aunty Pips is doing enough for us.'

'Oh, she won't mind,' Daisy said airily. 'Though I don't think you'll get one today with the display on. But I'll ask Aunty Pips if we can come back tomorrow, if you like.'

'No, you'd better not, Dais,' Harry said. 'I wasn't thinking. I'd be in trouble back home if they knew I'd asked.'

'Hello, you lot,' a cheerful voice said behind them and Luke and Harry groaned inwardly, but they plastered smiles on their faces.

'Hello, Johnny.'

'It's great to see you all here. Hi, Daisy – Gill. We're in for a real treat. We're definitely going to see the Spitfire fly and we might see a Wellington, though whether one will fly, I don't know.'

'What's a Wellington?' Harry said before he thought not to show his ignorance.

But Johnny was not one to embarrass anyone and he said kindly, 'It's a bomber being made by Vickers at their factory here. Now, where's Aunty Pips? I've got a message for her from my uncle.'

'She's over there with Uncle George, Milly and Paul,' Daisy said, pointing.

'Ah, right. I must have a word. See you all later.'

'Not if we can help it,' Harry muttered, though only Luke heard him and cast him a warning glance.

They watched Johnny cross the grass to talk to Pips. They saw him gesticulating towards them and then Pips nodded. Johnny turned, grinned at them and gave them the thumbs-up sign.

'What's he up to?' Harry muttered.

'I don't know,' Luke murmured. 'But we're about to find out. Aunty Pips is coming over.'

Pips was smiling as she reached them. 'You're all in luck. Mitch has sent word that if we come back tomorrow, he'll treat you all to a free flight. Jeff will take you up one by one.'

The four young people glanced at each other. 'That's very generous of him,' Luke said. 'Is he sure?'

'There's one thing about Mitch Hammond, Luke. If he didn't mean it, he wouldn't offer. And Milly's also said that after the display today, her father has given permission for her to take us into the Vickers factory where you can see aeroplanes being built. Now, come along, let's ensure we've a good place to watch the display. I think it's about to start.'

The spectators were entranced by the Spitfire. They watched it performing amazing, acrobatic manoeuvres and listened to the sound of its engine.

'It sounds like a huge cat purring,' Harry said.

'What a wonderful aeroplane,' Luke muttered, his eyes shining. 'It'd be magnificent in aerial combat. I hope I get to fly one of those one day.'

Daisy sighed. 'Me too. Though I can't see it happening for a *girl*.'

'You never know. Maybe Uncle Mitch will buy one and let you have a go.'

Daisy chuckled. 'I think a Spitfire would be out of the reach of even Uncle Mitch's pocket.'

As the display ended, Milly rounded everyone up and led them towards the huge Vickers factory.

Stepping inside, they all gasped to see row upon row of the huge aircraft in various stages of production. They marvelled at the massive skeletal fuselages in the process of being covered with fabric.

'Now, that's what I call an aeroplane,' Harry said. 'That's what I'd like to fly.'

'But they're bombers, Harry,' Daisy said. 'You wouldn't want to drop bombs on people, would you?'

'If we were attacked or we go to war, I'd do anything to defend our country. Anything at all.' For once they could all see that Harry – the ebullient joker – was very serious.

'Let's hope that never happens,' Pips said. 'Now, come along, let's find something to eat.'

As she shepherded them towards the clubhouse, George and Milly fell behind. 'Does Pips realize how serious the situation is, George?' Milly asked.

'Of course she does, but, like the rest of the nation, we're trying to get on with our lives until something happens.'

'But behind the scenes we're getting prepared, aren't we?'

Solemnly, George nodded. 'I'm very much afraid, Milly dear, that it'll all become very necessary.'

Milly's glance went to the two young men walking with Daisy and Gill in front of them.

'And it'll all fall on their shoulders, won't it?'

Huskily, George said, 'I'm afraid so and even the girls will be involved.'

Milly nodded. 'I know, but at least the girls won't have to fly those aeroplanes we've just been watching because, magnificent though they are, let's be honest about it, in a war situation, they're nothing more than killing machines.'

George nodded solemnly and, not for the first time, he marvelled at Milly's intuition. As Pips had always said, there was a lot more to Milly than people gave her credit for.

'So, did you both have a good time?' Sam asked Harry and Luke when they returned home.

'Dad – it was wonderful.' Harry, his eyes shining, launched into a detailed account of all that they had seen and done. Smiling, Luke let him talk. It had all been so new and fascinating to Harry.

'And did you enjoy the flying?' Peggy asked.

'It was superb. *Now* I know what Daisy and Luke have been rabbiting on about, but I'd like to fly in one of the big bombers we saw.'

Peggy shuddered and glanced at Sam, who said slowly, 'I don't want to sound mean, Harry, old chap, but I hope you never get the chance.'

Far from taking offence, Harry nodded, solemnly. 'Yes, I know what you're saying, Dad, because if I did, then it would mean that we're at war.'

Sixteen

Despite a vague promise between England and France to defend Czechoslovakia, in September it was agreed that the Sudeten region of that country – a region mainly inhabited by German-speaking people – should be handed to Germany. On the last day of the month, the Prime Minister, Neville Chamberlain, arrived back from his talks in Munich waving a piece of paper which, he declared, bore Herr Hitler's signature and promised 'peace for our time'.

'And if you believe that,' Robert muttered morosely, 'you'll believe anything.'

In November, the vicious attacks on Jews, their synagogues and property – a night of violence throughout Germany that became known as Kristallnacht, the 'Night of Broken Glass' – made Robert confide in his sister, 'There's going to be a war, Pips. I can sense it.'

'I know,' she said sadly, 'so can I. Oh Robert, what is going to happen to our young ones?'

It was a question he could not answer.

The telephone rang whilst Pips and George were finishing a leisurely Saturday morning breakfast.

'Aunty Pips?'

'Hello, Daisy. Is everything all right?'

'Not really.' There was a pause before she added in a rush, 'I thought you'd like to know. Johnny rang me. Uncle Mitch has had an accident. He's in hospital.'

Pips felt as if she'd been thumped in the chest. 'What happened?'

'He was testing a car out at Brooklands which he and Jeff had been repairing. Something went wrong mechanically and he crashed into the wall.'

'Is he badly hurt?'

'Broken leg and concussion, Johnny said.'

'What hospital is he in?'

'The London.'

'I'll go and see him.'

'I thought you might.'

They spoke for a little longer before ringing off.

'I have to go to the hospital,' Pips said, as she sat down to finish eating her toast and marmalade.

George looked up, his face concerned. 'Why?'

'It's Mitch, he's been hurt in a car accident at Brooklands.'

Now George frowned. 'But I thought we were driving to the coast today. We won't get many more nice days for an outing. Can't it wait until tomorrow?'

Pips stared at him, not quite able to believe what she was hearing. 'No,' she snapped. 'It can't.'

George shrugged. 'Then I'll come with you.'

'No need. You enjoy your day.'

She rose from the table and hurried back to the bedroom to wash and dress. There had always been a wariness between George and Mitch, but this was the first time that George had shown real jealousy. She left the flat without speaking to him again and took a cab to the hospital.

'I can only allow you five minutes,' the ward sister said. 'He's not bad enough to be allowed visits outside the normal hours.'

'Thank goodness for that,' Pips said and then added, 'How badly hurt is he?'

'A bump on the head and a broken leg. He'll be in plaster for about six weeks, but after that he should be as good as new.'

Pips crept into the side ward. Mitch was propped up on pillows, his eyes closed. She moved to the side of the bed and looked down at him. His black hair was tousled and his face was paler than his normal weather-beaten appearance. As if feeling someone was standing beside the bed, Mitch opened his eyes. It took him a moment to focus and he swept his hand across his forehead. 'Pips? Am I dreaming?'

'No, it's me. I can't stay long, but I'll come back later during proper visiting hours.' She sat down at the side of the bed. 'How did this happen?'

Mitch shook his head slightly and then frowned as if the movement had hurt. 'Jeff and I bought an old banger to do up together, which we intended to race. I was testing her out on the track and something went wrong. I don't know what yet, but Jeff will find out.'

'Well, you won't be driving for a while. Is there anything you want bringing in?'

'I don't think so. I'm not thinking very clearly yet.

Johnny came in last night and brought my shaving tackle and a clean pair of pyjamas.'

'I'd better go now, but I'll come back this afternoon, though I expect that once word gets around, you'll have a stream of visitors, especially your string of girlfriends.'

She rose and leaned across the bed to kiss his forehead. As she drew back, the look of undisguised longing in his eyes startled her for a moment, but, recovering her composure, she patted his hand and said cheerfully, 'See you later. Be good.'

Now his brown eyes twinkled and he grinned. 'Can't be much else – unfortunately.'

But his gaze followed her as she left the room and, as the door closed behind her, he lay back against the pillows, closed his eyes and sighed.

'Why on earth are you going to see him this afternoon?'

'Because I was only allowed to see him for five minutes.'

'You don't need to go again today, surely. We still have time for a drive out somewhere.'

Pips glanced at George. 'We'll go out tomorrow. Mitch will have loads more visitors when word spreads. He won't need me to go then.'

George cast her a strange look, one that said, 'Do you really believe that?' Then he turned away and went into the bedroom to change. When he reappeared, he said, 'Unless you want me to come with you, I'll spend the afternoon with Rebecca, if she's free.'

'Don't you want to see him? He's *our* friend, not just mine.'

He moved close, put his forefinger under her chin and said quietly, 'My darling Pips, if you believe that, then you can believe anything. For a very clever woman, you can sometimes be surprisingly obtuse.' He kissed her lightly on the lips. 'I'll see you this evening.'

He left the room, leaving Pips staring at the closed door. Then she shrugged her shoulders, muttered, 'Oh phooey', and began her household chores before returning to the hospital in the afternoon.

As she had predicted, there were several people crowded into his room: Jeff, with an anxious look on his face, Muriel and Pattie with bunches of grapes and magazines – and Johnny.

'Well, I am popular all of a sudden. Almost worth breaking my leg for.'

He looked much better than when she had seen him that morning. He had more colour in his face and his hair was neatly combed; much more like the handsome Mitch she knew.

'You sit here, Pips,' Muriel said, moving from the chair at the side of the bed.

'No, no, sit still, Muriel. We'll probably get shooed out in a minute. Too many visitors at once and all that.'

'Just keep the noise down,' Mitch said, 'and maybe they'll leave us alone. We're hardly disturbing other patients.'

'Is this a private room?' Pattie asked.

'I've really no idea,' Mitch said, glancing round. 'But I certainly didn't ask for one.'

'Er – that was me,' Jeff said, seeming a little embarrassed. 'I felt so guilty that you'd had an accident in the car I'd been repairing.'

'We were both working on it,' Mitch said. 'No one's to blame. Have you found out what happened?'

Jeff shook his head. 'Not yet – not till I know you're all right. Well, as right as you can be. Mitch, I'm so sorry . . .'

Mitch held up his hand to silence him. 'Not another word. Just bring me in a bottle next time and keep wheeling the ladies in.'

Muriel laughed. 'Oh, there'll be a troop of those very soon, I promise you. We pulled rank to get here before the others, although' – she glanced archly at Pips – 'you made it to first place, like you often did. Thank goodness you're not racing any more.'

There was almost a party atmosphere in Mitch's hospital room, and because it was a private one none of the nursing staff interfered. At the end of visiting time, they said their farewells one by one, Pips being the last to leave with Johnny.

As she bent to kiss his cheek, Mitch caught hold of her hand. 'I don't want to be the cause of trouble between you and George, but do come again, if you can.'

'No trouble,' Pips said tartly. 'He's not my keeper.' She straightened up and smiled. 'I was going to ruffle your hair but as it's been combed so beautifully, I'd better not. Which pretty nurse did that for you?'

'The blonde one,' he said, with a saucy wink.

Pips chuckled. 'You never change – I'm pleased to

say. Right, Johnny, the bell went a few minutes ago. We'd better go.'

They walked down the corridor and out of the building together.

'I won't be able to get to see him until next weekend,' Johnny said. 'Will you be able to visit?'

'Of course, but I don't think he'll be short of visitors, Johnny.'

'Maybe not. But there are visitors – and visitors.'

'Have you time to come and have dinner with us?'

'That's kind of you, but no, thank you. I must call and see my mother before I go back to camp.' He paused and then asked, 'Has Uncle Mitch told you about her?'

'No, he's not mentioned her for years. Is she – ill?'

'No – far from it. She remarried some time back and now they're planning to emigrate to Australia.'

'Oh.' Pips couldn't think what to say. The young man was giving no indication as to how he was feeling about the news.

'So, I'm going to spend a few days with her before they leave next week.'

'Will they be selling the house?'

Johnny nodded.

'I'm sorry, Johnny. You'll miss them.'

'I'll miss my mother – but not him. We've never got on.'

'So – where will you go when you're on leave?'

'Uncle Mitch says I'm to look upon his place as my home.' He grinned. 'Both of them.' Mitch had a house in Weybridge, quite near to Brooklands, but he also had an apartment in London not far from where Pips and George lived.

'You'd always be welcome to stay with us, if you ever needed to.'

'That's kind of you, thank you. And now I must go. Mother will be waiting for me.' He kissed Pips on both cheeks and hurried away through the teeming crowds on the pavements.

'His recuperation seems to be taking a long time,' George remarked three weeks later. Mitch had been at his flat in London for just over a week and Pips had been visiting him every other day to help.

Pips forced herself to laugh. 'Don't be so grumpy, George, but you'll be pleased to know I'm taking him down to Weybridge at the weekend. He has a daily help there who will look after him.'

'I'll take him,' George said swiftly. 'My car's bigger than yours. He'll be more comfortable spreading out on the back seat.'

'We'll go together,' Pips said firmly, 'and then I can make sure Mrs Pearson knows what needs doing.'

George sighed inwardly, but when they called at Mitch's flat on the Saturday morning, he put on a display of solicitousness.

'Now, are you comfortable on the back seat, Mitch? Do you want a blanket? I'll drive carefully.'

'It's good of you to take me, George. I do appreciate it.'

'Don't mention it.'

George drove his recently acquired car sedately.

'Nice car,' Mitch said. 'Very comfortable.'

'It's a Humber. 1935 model, but she's been well looked after and not many miles on the clock. I need my own car to get to the office and back now that I work such odd hours and I thought a slightly larger one than Pips's Ford would allow us to take passengers in a little more comfort.'

'Well, like I say, I'm very grateful.'

The rest of the journey passed in silence, but Mrs Pearson was waiting at Mitch's house when they arrived.

'Everything's ready for you, Mr Hammond. Now, can you get upstairs or would you like a bed brought down? Mr Pointer has said he'll call by this afternoon and help me if needed. And I've seen old Josiah, who lives just up the road from me, about doing a bit of gardening for you, but he's not fit enough to be lugging beds downstairs. Now, come along in. I've got a meal all ready for the three of you.' Mrs Pearson chattered on as she led the way into the house. 'It's times like these when I miss my poor hubby. He was always on hand to give a hand, bless him. Now, come into the dining room and I'll serve lunch.'

Places were already set on the table and the small, rotund woman bustled between the kitchen and dining room, serving roast beef, Yorkshire pudding and three vegetables.

'There's apple crumble and custard for afters.'

Conversation as they ate was sparse, but George, trying to be polite, said, 'This is a nice house, Mitch. I'm surprised you don't spend more time down here.'

After lunch, Pips had a quiet word with Mrs Pearson as they washed up together in the kitchen.

'I've written my telephone number in the book on the hall table. Please let me know if there's anything he needs.'

'I will, Mrs Allender, but I think we'll be all right. Mr Pointer says he'll come every day and there are all the other Brooklands' folk who, no doubt, will be popping in.'

Though she said nothing more, Pips felt a pang of regret at obviously not being needed.

'Jeff,' Pips greeted him when he arrived in the early afternoon. She kissed him on both cheeks.

'How's my best ever pupil doing?' he teased.

'I'd've thought Daisy would have been a better pupil than I was.'

Jeff pulled a comical face. 'She certainly ranks a close second. Let's say you were equal, to save any arguments.'

'Oh, I don't mind playing second fiddle to my niece. I'm very proud of her.'

'How's she doing at college?'

'Very well. Come on through. They're in the sitting room.'

As they entered the room, George and Mitch were sitting near the window, deep in conversation, but when Pips and Jeff stepped into the room, they stopped talking abruptly.

As if to fill an awkward pause, Jeff held out his hand. 'Hello again, George. Good to see you. Am I going to get you flying yet?'

'Not a chance,' George said swiftly. 'Are you still working for Mitch?'

133

'At the moment, yes.' He glanced towards his friend and employer. 'But with all this uncertainty, neither of us knows how long our flying school will be needed if we are to be plunged into war again.'

'Probably even more so than in peace time. Another war won't be like the last one, you know. It'll be fought in the air.'

Mitch and Jeff glanced at each other and then both looked back to George.

'I know you can't tell us much, George – and we wouldn't expect you to – but is there a real threat of war?'

George took a moment before he answered carefully. 'I'm sure you follow the news avidly, as I think most people in the country are doing. All I can tell you is that we are making preparations just in case.'

'So, you didn't believe the Munich agreement either?' Mitch said bluntly.

George smiled. 'Officially – of course we did. Unofficially . . .' He shrugged his shoulders, but his action spoke volumes.

'So, Mitch, old chap, as soon as your leg's better, we'd better start putting our own plans into action, don't you think?'

'What? What are you going to do?' Pips asked.

The two men exchanged a glance before Mitch said airily, 'Oh, just offer our services to the authorities in any way we can be of help.'

As they drove home through the gathering dusk, Pips asked, 'George, what do you think they intend to do?'

'I've no idea, Pips. Something to do with flying, I've no doubt.'

'Like teaching young men who want to become pilots?'

'Something like that,' George said vaguely and Pips was left wondering just what he and Mitch had been discussing so earnestly when she and Jeff had entered the room. She had the distinct feeling that there was something neither of them was telling her.

Seventeen

Cocooned in the insular world of college, Daisy and Gill happily planned their Christmas holidays and looked forward to the final two terms.

'I can't believe we've done more than two years here,' Gill said. 'It's flown.'

Daisy nodded. 'Only two more terms and we're done.'

'But the exams come before that, don't forget.'

'Oh, you would have to spoil it.'

'You'll be all right.'

'So will you.'

They smiled at each other. Neither of them was conceited, but they both knew that if they were to fail, it didn't bode well for the rest of their year!

'And best of all, it's the year when Aunty Pips and Uncle George will be with us for Christmas and New Year. And I bet Granny will be planning extra celebrations because I couldn't get home for my twenty-first birthday at the beginning of the month.'

'We're not visiting each other this holiday, are we?'

Daisy shook her head. 'Too much revising to do. And the same goes for the Easter hols.'

Gill pulled a face. 'Shame, but I know you're right.'

'We'll make up for it in the summer, I promise.'
Gill wagged her finger. 'I'll hold you to that.'

Daisy was so busy during the holidays that she failed
to notice the serious faces of her older relatives, who
did their best to keep unsavoury news from her
anyway. And in the Dawson and Nuttall homes, there
was a tacit agreement that Luke and Harry should
be kept ignorant of the political unrest. Even Bess
Cooper kept her mouth firmly shut when the youngsters were around.

'I've never known my mother so quiet about what's
going on,' Peggy laughed.

'If all this trouble escalates into war,' Sam said
solemnly, 'it'll be our lads that'll have to go.'

Peggy's amusement faded and she bit her lip.
'Couldn't they get a – what is it called – an exemption because of the work they do?'

'They might. After all, all their work is allied to
agriculture, which was treated as a reserved occupation in the last war, but—' He hesitated before adding,
'They might not let both Luke *and* Harry get exemption.'

'But they work in different parts of Len's business,
don't they? Luke's in the wheelwright's workshop
and Harry's usually with you in the blacksmith's.'

'That's true, so they might both be all right.'

'Oh Sam, we're talking as if it's really going to
happen.'

'If Hitler tries anything else, Peggy love, I am
sorry to say I think it will. Chamberlain sold out
Czechoslovakia to him and that was once too often.

It caused a revolt amongst some of his own party members.'

'And what about the trouble in Spain?'

'I think it's almost at an end, with Franco victorious.'

Peggy sighed heavily. 'I don't understand it all. Why can't we all just live in peace, Sam? After all those poor boys we lost last time, why won't they learn?'

Sam put his arms around her and she leaned against his shoulder. 'It's all about gaining power. Look at Franco in Spain. All three of them – Franco, Mussolini and now Hitler – are hell-bent on becoming all-powerful dictators.'

In January, Franco's troops entered Barcelona, and by the end of February even the British Government recognized his possession of the greater part of Spain, which brought more disagreement in the House of Commons. When the President of Republican Spain resigned at the beginning of March, Franco's final victory seemed inevitable. But the greatest threat still came from Germany.

'We are now making four hundred aircraft a month for the RAF, but that's still only two thirds of what Germany are producing,' Pips told her family solemnly on a visit in March.

'It certainly looks as if they're up to something, doesn't it? Any other signs that we're starting to get prepared, Pips?'

'Air-raid shelters are being distributed to households in London in areas they think will be the most likely to be targeted. And there are discussions about the evacuation of children from cities, if hostilities should break out.'

'And does George really think they're likely to?' Edwin asked.

Pips drew breath, glanced around the table at her parents and Robert and Alice, knowing that what she now had to tell them would be devastating news. 'It will be in the papers tomorrow, but George said I could tell you this now. Hitler has marched into Prague.'

Four pairs of anxious eyes stared at her.

'I knew it,' Robert murmured. 'I thought all his posturing and promises that Germany had no more claims in Europe was a lie. Chamberlain should never have trusted him.'

'He meant well, Robert,' Pips defended the Prime Minister, 'but now, he's as shocked as the rest of us. He told the House that this is the first time that Hitler has occupied territory that is not inhabited by Germans.'

'So this time, you mean, there's no excuse for his occupation?'

'None.'

'I'm very much afraid, my dears,' Edwin said, twirling his wineglass between fingers that were not quite steady, 'that this might very well escalate into war.' He glanced at Pips. 'Has George – or Matthew – been able to tell you if the Government are planning any kind of pledge to other countries should they be attacked?' He shrugged and suggested, 'Like Poland, for example, or France? He seems to be intent on marching into the countries which border Germany.'

'Not in so many words, no, but like you he thinks the situation is very serious.'

'I expect they would bring in conscription a lot earlier than they did last time,' Alice said quietly. Her voice trembled as she asked, 'Will Luke and Harry be called up, d'you think? And – and what about Daisy? She'd be expected to do some sort of war work, wouldn't she?'

'When she finishes college in the summer,' Henrietta said firmly, 'she will be employed here on the estate and that will surely be regarded as important war work. The production of food will be paramount, if I'm not mistaken.'

'Quite right, Mother,' Robert said. 'Daisy will be fine and so will her friend Gill, but about Luke and Harry, well, I'm not so sure.'

At the end of March, Britain and France pledged to defend Poland against attack and by the middle of April, when Mussolini had occupied Albania, the British Prime Minister gave an assurance that Britain would go to the aid of Greece and Romania. France again gave its promise too. A few days later, Chamberlain also pledged to go to the aid of Holland, Denmark and Switzerland if they were attacked.

At the end of April, the British Government brought in the conscription of men aged twenty to twenty-two for military service.

'I won't allow it. I won't let Luke go!' Len shouted, jabbing at the newspaper and glaring at his wife as if it was all her fault.

'You've changed your tune since last time,' Norah said boldly. 'Learned ya lesson, 'ave ya?'

'That was different,' he growled. 'They didn't bring in conscription until much later in the last war. The lads went of their own accord. Volunteered like the brave men they were. But I won't have any government telling my grandson what to do.'

'He's twenty-three. It's not him they're talking about, and Harry's too young.'

'I aren't bothered about Harry. He's not mine.'

Norah said no more. Although Harry was not a blood relative, she'd always thought of him as another grandson.

And then her thoughts turned to the other two young men, who really were her grandsons: Pascal and Waldo. Would Belgium be attacked again this time? What would happen to them and would she ever see her son, William, again?

Whilst Britain quietly prepared, Germany and Italy signed a 'Pact of Steel' in May, a political and military alliance.

'We have agreements with France,' George told the Maitlands on a brief visit to Lincolnshire with Pips, 'but our approach to Russia doesn't seem to be meeting with enthusiasm. We suspect Stalin is seeking a closer alliance with Germany.'

'Really? That surprises me,' Robert said.

'Stalin's a bit of an unknown quantity at the moment.'

'Well, with the size of his country, I'd rather he was on our side.'

'Don't we all.' George's reply was heartfelt.

Eighteen

'I forbid it. You're not going and that's final. It's my last word on the subject.'

'Granddad, I don't want to go against you, but this is something I have to do,' Luke said quietly. 'I intend to volunteer for the RAF and I intend to go now before war is actually declared, because we all know it's coming, don't we?'

Len flung his lump hammer against the anvil with a loud clatter, making Luke wince. 'If you go,' Len said menacingly, 'there won't be a job for you to come back to, nor an inheritance. You know what happened to that coward of a son of mine, well, same'll happen to you. I'll change me will. I'll leave it all to Daisy. An' if she's daft enough to marry you – as some folks seem to think's on the cards – then I'll leave it to young Harry, even though he's not me own flesh and blood.'

Quietly, Luke said, 'Harry is going to volunteer for the RAF too – as soon as he's old enough.'

'Then it'll be on your head if owt happens to him, because he's only following you.'

Luke frowned. 'I can't understand your attitude. You disowned Uncle William because he *wouldn't* volunteer alongside his brothers, yet now I want to go, you're threatening me with the same. Why?'

'It were different then,' Len growled. 'All the young men were enlisting and anyone who didn't was branded a coward.'

'Uncle William wasn't a coward. He was a very brave man. He *chose* to go to the front as a stretcher-bearer, carrying wounded and dying in from the battlefield. He was there all the time – every day and through the night too. He didn't have a few days at the front and then go back behind the lines for a rest like the soldiers did. And he was there for four years doing that. Four – long – years.'

'But he didn't get killed like his brothers, did he? I bet he kept himself out of harm's way. I bet he only went to pick up the wounded when the guns had stopped.'

'That's not true and you know it's not. He went out to get Uncle Robert in when he lost his arm and he helped Aunty Pips fetch Mr Hammond in from his crashed aircraft when she got shot in the leg. The bullets must have still been flying then.'

'Aye, and it's her I blame for all this. She took you flying, didn't she, when you went AWOL the first time?' He narrowed his eyes as he glared at Luke. 'And I bet you've been again this time. I'll be having words with her, next time she's home.'

'She's got nothing to do with this. This is my own decision. I want to be a fighter pilot and, if I volunteer now, I've a good chance of being able to get what I want and not just be drafted anywhere.'

'More fool you, then,' Len growled and turned away. The conversation was at an end.

*

When all their examinations were finished, Daisy and Gill packed all their belongings, said goodbye to all their friends, hugged Mrs Gordon, who had been like a second mother to them, and thanked all their tutors.

'It's home, then,' Gill said, as they stood on the driveway and looked up at the castle where they had spent so much time.

'It's been a good three years,' Daisy said a little pensively, 'but I'm ready for home now, aren't you?'

'Can't wait,' Gill said, a broad grin on her face. 'At least we're lucky in that our parents – or granny, in your case – are willing to listen to all the ideas we've got. They're open to change, whereas one of the other students was telling me his father will never change.'

'He might find he has to, if what everyone is saying comes true.'

'That there's going to be a war, you mean?'

Daisy nodded. 'I think living here and working so hard, we've been missing what's actually been going on in the real world. But my dad will explain it all to me when I get home.'

'Mine, too. But I don't think we're going to like what they're going to tell us, Daisy.'

'We'll just have to cope with whatever's thrown at us, won't we? At least we'll be able to feel that we'll be doing something to help the war effort by providing food, if what Prof said is true.'

Gill's eyes gleamed. 'Like I said, I can't wait.' She paused and added, 'But you will keep in touch, won't you?'

'Of course.'

'Promise?'

Daisy linked her arm through her friend's as they walked to where Jake was waiting beside the car. 'Now I've learned to drive, I'm sure I'll be able to come up and see you sometimes.'

'Do they know yet that you've passed the driving test?'

Daisy shook her head. 'No, it's a surprise.'

'Are you going to race at Brooklands, then?'

Daisy shook her head. 'No, that's never interested me, but I shall carry on flying whenever I can.'

'I don't think you'll be able to, if there's a war on.'

Daisy stopped and turned horrified eyes towards her friend. 'Oh Gill, no. Don't say that. I couldn't *live* without being able to fly now and again.'

'I'm back!' Daisy flung her arms wide as Wainwright opened the front door.

'Good to see you, Miss Daisy. The family are all waiting for you in the parlour. Jake and I will see to your luggage.'

'Thank you, Mr Wainwright. Sorry there's rather a lot.'

'We'll cope, miss.' He smiled. 'Good to have you home.'

Daisy ran through the Great Hall, past the long table already set for dinner to celebrate her return.

'Here I am,' she said, opening the door into the Brown Parlour. Her parents and grandparents were there to greet her, but as she kissed each one in turn, she glanced around and asked, 'No Luke – or Harry? I thought you might have asked them to be here.'

'We did, darling,' Alice put her arm round Daisy, 'but I'm afraid there's a big row going on between Luke and my father. And even Harry's involved too.'

'Oh dear. What about?'

Alice glanced at Robert, but it was Henrietta who stood up and said, 'We'll tell you all we know over dinner, Daisy. Now, do you want to freshen up, because I think Cook is ready for Wainwright to serve?'

'I do, Granny, but you go in. I'll only be a couple of minutes . . .'

Moments later, as they all sat down and Wainwright began to serve their meal, Daisy said, 'Now, please tell me what's going on between Granddad and Luke.'

'Perhaps you'd better explain, Mother,' Alice said, turning towards Henrietta. 'You were the one Luke confided in.'

'I wouldn't expect you to break his confidence, Granny,' Daisy said swiftly. 'You know that.'

Henrietta inclined her head. 'No, of course I wouldn't, but he asked me to tell the rest of the family and specifically asked that I should tell you when you came home.'

'Oh dear. This sounds serious. Go on.'

'He wants – in fact, I think he's going to, no matter what anyone says – to join the RAF and become a fighter pilot.'

'How perfectly wonderful. The lucky thing!'

Henrietta eyed her granddaughter archly over the top of her spectacles with an amused smile. 'Mr

Dawson is blaming Philippa and you for introducing him to flying.'

Daisy wriggled her shoulders. 'Well, I can't deny that. When is Pips home again?'

'She's coming up this weekend,' Alice said. 'Mainly to see you, I think, but George won't be coming.' She hesitated and glanced at Robert who said, soberly, 'You do realize that we're on the brink of another war, don't you, Daisy?'

'I do now, Daddy, yes. But we were all so engrossed in our studies that we didn't take a lot of notice of the news, I'm ashamed to say.'

'Don't be, my dear. It's just as well you concentrated on what you had to do.' He smiled. 'We're all so very proud of you, Daisy. And I think' – he glanced at his mother – 'Granny has a surprise for you.'

Henrietta smiled. 'I've bought you a desk to stand next to mine in the room at the far side of the house that I use as an office. We'll work alongside each other.'

'Oh Granny!' Daisy's eyes filled with tears to think that her grandmother was so ready – eager almost – to involve her in the running of the estate. She jumped up from the table and rushed to hug her grandmother. 'We'll have such fun.'

'I don't know about "fun", my dear, because if this war does come, we're going to have to make a lot of changes.'

'I've got lots of ideas about that. We had a debate about it all and Prof told us what he thinks the Government are likely to demand from farmers.'

Henrietta's eyes twinkled. 'I shall look forward to hearing all about it. And we must include Charlie Cooper in some of our discussions. We mustn't leave the estate's farm manager out of our plans. I am sure he will have some useful ideas too.'

As Daisy sat down again, she said, 'And when Aunty Pips comes at the weekend, we'll go and see Granddad together about Luke.'

But Henrietta was shaking her head. 'I don't think you should, Daisy. It will be belittling Luke. He is a young man now and should fight his own battles.'

'I expect you're right, but we ought at least to let Luke know we're on his side.'

'I think he'll already know that,' Henrietta said, though her smile was a little sad to think what the young man was about to face.

Nineteen

'I don't think I have ever known such a stubborn, stupid man as Len Dawson,' Pips said. 'He just changes his thinking to suit himself. First, he disowns his son for *not* wanting to enlist, now he's going to disown Luke for *wanting* to join up. I don't understand the man, I really don't.'

'Granny says we shouldn't tackle Granddad. It'd be belittling Luke.'

'Mm, maybe she's right. But we must see Luke and tell him we're all on his side.'

'He'll be here tomorrow to go riding as usual.'

'Oh, so Mr Dawson hasn't stopped that yet, then?' Pips's tone was laced with sarcasm.

Daisy laughed. 'No, but I think he'd like to. I don't think he's ever been happy about the boys coming riding with us.'

'Or your close friendship with them.'

For a moment, Daisy was very still. She seemed about to say something, but then changed her mind. Instead, she said brightly, 'Well, he'll just have to lump it, because that's not ever going to change. And now, I must do another hour's work before dinner. I have some notes to write up. Granny and I went out this afternoon for a tour of the estate and I want to get it all down on paper before I forget all the things we discussed.'

Pips lowered her voice. 'How are you getting on, working with Granny?'

'Fantastic. We seem to be on the same wavelength, which is something of a miracle, considering the difference in our ages, wouldn't you say?'

'Your granny has always been forward-thinking. I'm not surprised and I expect your father is pleased it's all working out so well. He never wanted to take on the running of the estate.'

'Ecstatic, I think the word is.' Daisy grinned.

'And what about your friend, Gill? Are you keeping in touch with her?'

'We ring each other once a week. She's lucky too. Her father's just as go-ahead as Granny and prepared to listen to all Gill's ideas. She's hoping to come down at the end of August for a long weekend. Right, I must go. See you at dinner.'

Pips smiled as Daisy rushed from the room, eager to get back to her work.

As the family gathered in the parlour, apart from Daisy, who'd said she would join them at the table, Pips said, 'So, Mother, is it all working out from your point of view too? Daisy seems overjoyed to be working alongside you.'

'I couldn't be happier, Philippa.' Henrietta glanced a little reproachfully at Robert. 'I must admit I was very disappointed – and more than a little worried – that Robert has always been so adamant he didn't want to take it on. I know he would have done his best – and so would you, Philippa, if it had been necessary – but thank goodness for Daisy, is all I can say.'

'And so say all of us,' Robert said with heartfelt sincerity and the rest of the family laughed.

'It seems it really is what she wants to do,' Henrietta said, 'and she is *such* a clever girl. She has already come up with some remarkable ideas for us to increase production to help the war effort – if it becomes necessary.'

Everyone glanced towards Pips, not voicing the question that was on all their lips.

Pips sighed. 'All I can tell you is that you're right to be prepared.'

'We thought as much,' Edwin said quietly. He seemed about to say more, but the door to the parlour burst open and Daisy stood there, beaming. 'I've just had a telephone call. From my tutor. I – I got a First.'

For a moment there was a stunned silence in the room and then they all began to speak at once. Alice rushed to her to hug her, tears streaming down her face.

'Oh darling, how wonderful!'

'No more than I expected,' Robert said, teasingly, but they could all see the pride on his face, whilst Henrietta murmured, 'I told you she was clever, didn't I?'

'This calls for a real celebration,' Edwin said and, as the butler appeared in the doorway to announce that dinner was served, he added, 'Wainwright, fetch a bottle of champagne, would you, please?' His eyes twinkled as he added, 'And you can tell the others

Miss Daisy's good news and open another bottle for them.'

The butler gave a little bow and said, 'Thank you, sir, and I'm sure all the staff would join me in congratulating Miss Daisy.'

'Thank you, Mr Wainwright,' Daisy said, pink with delight. All her hard work had paid off.

'Did your tutor say anything about Gill?' Alice asked.

'Yes. The list has gone up on the notice board, so it's public knowledge. She got a First too.'

There were cries of delight from everyone.

'Oh, that's wonderful.'

'So nice that you've both got the same result.'

'What about everyone else?'

Daisy wriggled her shoulders, slightly embarrassed now. 'We were the only two to get Firsts in the whole year.'

'That's even more remarkable, Daisy,' Edwin said. 'Well done indeed.'

It was a happy family gathering which sat down to dinner, all thoughts of impending war pushed from their minds as they celebrated Daisy's success.

In August, when Pips held a small dinner party in their London home for Rebecca, Matthew and their dear friends, Milly and Paul, the talk around the table was serious.

'It's been in the papers,' Matthew said, 'so there's no harm in telling you. There's a squabble brewing over the Baltic Port of Danzig that could trigger a war. Germany are smuggling arms and military personnel into Danzig, already acting as if they are in command of it. Earlier this month in the House, the Prime Minister said that if Poland felt it had to use force against Germany, then Britain would be her ally.'

'But Danzig is what they call a Free City, isn't it?' Paul said.

Matthew nodded. 'There is the view that it is a German city, but the Poles are adamant that it must remain a Free City under the League of Nations directive.'

'It's the only way to the sea for the Poles, isn't it?'

'That's right and that's why Britain is backing the Poles.'

'Daddy's firm is certainly getting prepared for war,' Milly said solemnly. 'As you know, we're building Wellington bombers at Brooklands and there's a new factory nearing completion near Castle Bromwich Aerodrome. I understand they're experiencing a lot of problems there at the moment, but they hope to start producing Spitfires there soon as well as in Southampton.'

'Isn't all that top secret, Milly darling?' Pips said, but Milly only laughed and shrugged. 'Not really. Someone only needs a good pair of binoculars to see the testing going on at Brooklands.'

Now they all laughed. 'That's true.'

'Even though we and Hawker have the use of Brooklands for the production of military aircraft,' Milly went on, 'it's getting a bit crowded there, so, what you might not know is that a new Hawker satellite factory and aerodrome have been built at Langley.'

'At least,' George said quietly, 'we are getting prepared. My only worry is, is it going to be enough?'

Although everyone tried to carry on a normal life, the threat of war hung over the whole country and preparations continued.

During the last week in August, Gill came to stay for a long weekend at Doddington Hall, and now even Henrietta could not ban the talk of war around the dinner table.

'Have you heard the latest about Hitler and Stalin signing a non-aggression pact this week? Daddy was appalled,' Gill began, knowing that her hosts took an eager interest in world affairs. 'He thought they were the best of enemies.'

Edwin nodded. 'I agree with your father. I was shocked and I think Hitler will attack Poland in earnest any day now. I think he was just clearing the way.'

'Then we must be ready,' Gill said and glanced at Daisy. 'We've already ploughed up two meadows that we don't need for our herd of milkers. What about you?'

Daisy glanced at her grandmother, who gave a slight nod.

'We've all sorts of plans to put into action once it really kicks off. We haven't actually done anything yet, but we're well prepared. Granny and I spend hours touring the estate and then poring over maps and plans.' She smiled wistfully. 'If it wasn't so serious, it'd be great fun.'

'What about your farm workers? Daddy is so worried that we'll lose a lot of our men to the forces.'

'I'd've thought you might already have heard about this at college,' Edwin said. 'The Women's Land Army, which first appeared in 1917, was re-formed in June and recruitment is now under way.'

'D'you know, I think I did hear a whisper about it, but we were so busy with our exams everything else just went over our heads for a time, didn't it, Daisy?'

''Fraid so.'

'Well, your hard work certainly paid off,' Robert said. 'We're all so proud of you both.'

As they mounted the stairs to bed that evening, Gill whispered to Daisy, 'Can we go and see Luke tomorrow?'

'He'll be coming here to go riding as usual. Luke and Harry. We'll all go.'

Gill's eyes shone. 'Oh goody.' She paused before asking in a deliberately casual tone, 'Have you heard from Johnny lately?'

Daisy shook her head. 'He was coming last weekend, but telephoned to say that all leave had been cancelled.'

'Oh my! Then things really must be getting serious.'

It was a glorious afternoon and the four enjoyed their ride, though Luke seemed very quiet. As they left the stables, having each groomed the horse they had ridden, Luke said, 'There's something I want to tell all of you.'

'Let's go and sit in the orchard. It'll be shady there,' Daisy suggested.

Seated beneath the trees, Luke cleared his throat. 'I think you all know that I've been keen to join the RAF.' The other three nodded, but no one spoke. 'Well, I applied, had an interview a while back and—'

'Oh, so that's where you went,' Harry interrupted. 'I did wonder. Your granddad was in a right paddy the whole day . . .'

'Shh, Harry,' Daisy said. 'Go on, Luke.'

'I've been accepted to train as a fighter pilot, which is exactly what I wanted. I leave on Monday.'

'Good for you.' Harry grinned. 'And come early next year, I'll be following you.'

'You've kept that quiet,' Daisy said truculently. 'Why didn't you tell us?'

'I didn't want to say anything until I was sure I'd got in. There are all sorts of medical tests you have to pass – eyesight and all that – and I wanted to be sure. Sorry, Dais.'

'I can understand why you didn't broadcast it,' Gill said, 'but would you have said anything if you *hadn't* got in?'

'I expect so – eventually – but I would have been very disappointed.'

'Does your family know?'

'Mam and Dad have known all along, but Granddad and Grandma don't know yet. I'll tell them tomorrow morning.'

Harry threw back his head and laughed. 'Then we'd better watch out for fireworks over their cottage tomorrow.'

As the four of them returned to the house, Gill touched Luke's arm and they both hung back a little.

'I don't know if I'm speaking out of turn – I do know how close you and Daisy are, and, of course, I'll hear news of you from her – but . . .' Gill bit her lip, feeling suddenly hesitant.

Luke grinned. 'Of course I'll write to you. I was going to ask you the same thing.'

She looked into his eyes. 'Were you? Were you really?'

He nodded. 'It'll be good to get letters from friends. I am fully expecting the basic training will be a bit tough and, until I get to know a few of the chaps, a bit lonely. And then, I expect, we'll all get separated anyway and posted to different places. From what Johnny has told me, you can make friends easily, but it's best not to get too close to anyone in particular.'

Gill wrinkled her forehead. 'Yes, I expect he's right. I hadn't looked at it like that.' She paused and then added, 'Just keep me up to date with your address and I'll write every week to you.'

Luke's grin widened.

Twenty

'You young fool!' Len spat and thumped the table with his fist. 'Didn't I tell you what I'd do if you joined up?'

'Yes, Granddad, you did,' Luke said evenly, though he wasn't feeling calm inside. He didn't like upsetting any member of his family and he was particularly worried that Len would take out his anger on Norah. She was standing at the side of the table as she cleared away after breakfast, her anxious glance going from one to the other.

'You've changed your tune,' she said bitterly, for once in her life standing up to her husband.

Len shook his fist at her, but Norah didn't even flinch. She was angry and anger made her bold. 'Don't you shake your fist at me, Len Dawson. We've been married fifty years this year, in case you've forgotten – and I expect you have because you've never said owt. And in all that time, I've been a good wife to you and mother to your children. And I looked after your mam until she died. Not that I minded that, because she treated me a lot better than you've ever done.'

Norah paused for breath, but Len said not a word. He was staring at her, open-mouthed, wondering if she'd lost her reason. He'd heard it said that when some folks got older, their character changed and he wondered if this was happening to his meek wife.

He opened his mouth and then closed it again. Norah wasn't done yet, though her voice was a little calmer now. 'I've always done exactly what you told me to do, even siding with you when you encouraged the lads to go to war and, may God forgive me, I didn't even argue with you over William. He was no coward – I know that now – but I've always been too afraid to stand up to you. And now this. Luke wants to do his duty, but this time, you don't want him to go just because he's all you have left. It's always about you, isn't it, Len? What *you* want. Well, this time you've found someone who's standing up to you, and so am I, so if you think you can give me a good hiding after he's gone, you can think again, 'cos I'll pack me bags and be out of here.'

'Oh aye, and where would you go?' Len sneered.

'Bess Cooper's,' Norah said promptly. 'She's always said there's a bed for me at her house.'

'Been telling that gossip all our business, have ya?'

'I don't need to tell anyone. The whole village has known for years what ya like. Now, say "goodbye" to ya grandson and wish him well, why don't you? You've still got young Harry, at least at the moment, and there's always Sam.'

'I'll wish him nowt,' Len growled, and he stood up and stormed out of the cottage.

'Oh Gran, are you going to be all right? He'll not like you crossing him like that. I'm so afraid he'll take it out on you later,' Luke said.

Norah put her arms around him and laid her head against the young man's shoulder. Luke held her close. 'Don't you worry about me, love. Just take good care of yourself and come back to us safe and sound.'

His voice trembled as he said, 'I'll do me best, Gran.'

When he went back home to spend his final evening with his family, he told them what had happened, adding, 'Dad, keep an eye on me gran, won't you?'

Solemnly, Sam shook his stepson's hand and gave him his word.

Two days after Gill returned home, it was announced in the newspapers that the evacuation of children from cities and towns had begun. At once, the villagers, led by Henrietta's example, offered to take children from cities thought to be under the greatest threat.

'Why are children coming here to Lincoln?' Daisy asked. 'Surely Lincoln's industry will become a target, won't it?'

'More than likely,' Henrietta remarked briskly, 'but for the moment, they're coming to us, not going away from here.'

'Where are they coming from?'

'I don't know yet. I just know that our local billeting officer has asked for volunteers to take children arriving at the station. Oh, and by the way, Daisy, just so you know, I have been speaking to the headquarters of the Women's Voluntary Services and they have put me in touch with our local Rural District Organizer. They'll be wanting extra help.'

'Oh Granny, haven't you enough to do here?'

Henrietta smiled and put her head on one side. 'Not now you're here, dear.'

'But I'm supposed to be making life easier for you, not freeing up more time for you to undertake something else.'

'Nonsense, Daisy. I am quite fit and keeping active and busy holds the years back. And I shall enlist your Grandpa's help as well. High time he made himself useful again. He's enjoying the idle life a mite too much for my liking.'

Daisy giggled. 'Oh Granny, don't be so hard on him. He is almost eighty.'

'And I'm seventy-five, but that doesn't stop me wanting to do my bit.'

To that, Daisy had no answer.

Very few villagers owned a wireless set, apart from the Maitland family; Len refused to have one in the house, and Peggy and Sam felt they couldn't afford the luxury, as did both their parents. So it was that the Maitlands, the Dawsons, the Coopers and even the Nuttalls too – all connected by marriage now – gathered together in the Great Hall at just after eleven o'clock on the morning of Sunday, 3 September. To everyone's surprise, even Len had come. And this time the servants at the hall were there too. Only George was missing. He felt his place was in London at such a time.

'If it wasn't so serious,' Bess tried to raise a smile, 'it'd be just like our Boxing Day get-together.'

'I haven't put on quite the same spread, Mrs

161

Cooper,' Henrietta said, 'but there's tea, coffee and biscuits. Please help yourselves.'

When the Prime Minister's voice came over the airways, the gathering fell silent, their eyes all on the wireless set as if they were visualizing Mr Chamberlain sitting in the Cabinet Room at 10 Downing Street to deliver the sombre message.

As the broadcast ended, Edwin switched off the set and turned to glance around the room. 'So, that's it, then. We are at war once again and with the same enemy.'

'D'you know, sir,' Sam said respectfully, 'mebbe it ain't my place to say, but I don't think the last one ever really ended. I reckon we've just had a long truce and now they're determined to finish it. And this time, he's got Russia on his side.'

'For the moment, yes, he has,' Edwin replied, nodding.

Pips, home for the weekend, sat at one side of the long table, thoughtfully stirring her cup of tea. She glanced up and met her brother's gaze across the table. 'So, Robert,' she said softly, 'what are we going to do this time?'

Robert sighed. 'I don't think there's a lot I can do. No doubt you'll be driving an ambulance somewhere, though I hope this time you'll stay in this country. If they start bombing us, London will be a prime target. You'll be needed there.'

'I'll have to do something. I can't sit around doing nothing and I certainly won't see much of George. He's been coming home late from work for months now. He's almost grey with worry and tiredness. I expect it's only going to get worse for him and Paul now. And we mustn't forget Rebecca's Matthew at the Foreign Office.'

'You could always enlist Rebecca to go out in your ambulance with you.'

'She's already said she'll offer her services to the Red Cross.'

'They'd probably be glad of your services, too, even though you're not officially trained.'

'Some more tea, Mr Dawson?' Henrietta said. 'You, too, Mrs Dawson?'

'Thank you, Mrs Maitland,' Len said politely. The mistress of the hall and the surrounding lands was perhaps the only person for whom Len had real respect. 'I'd best be getting back. We've left young Harry holding the fort, because work does come in on a Sunday.' He nodded towards the wireless and then his eyes met Henrietta's calm gaze. 'No doubt you'll have heard that Luke's gone?'

'We have, yes.'

'I didn't want him to go,' he blurted out and now the other voices in the room fell silent. 'I know what you all think – that I was only too keen last time for my lads to go. *All* of them,' he added pointedly. 'And that I'm some kind of turncoat, saying the opposite now.'

'None of us want our children – or grandchildren – to go, Mr Dawson, but most of them will be called up anyway, eventually. No doubt Harry will have to go too at some stage.' Henrietta glanced towards Clara Nuttall, expecting an outburst of weeping from the woman. But surprisingly, though tears filled her eyes and the cup she held in her trembling hands rattled in its saucer, Clara said nothing.

'I reckon I could have got a – whatchamacallit – for both of them,' Len went on. 'Their occupations are allied to agriculture, now, aren't they? I reckon you could have helped me there, Mrs Maitland, if you'd had a mind to.' His tone was accusatory now. It was the boldest he'd ever addressed her.

'I'd have been only too happy to have tried, Mr Dawson, but the young men have to ask me themselves.'

'Oh Mrs Maitland . . .' Now Clara butted in. 'D'you mean you'll do it for Harry if he asks you?'

'I'd do my best to help, of course, in any way I could, but it must come from Harry himself.'

'Peggy,' Clara turned to her daughter-in-law, 'you ask Mrs Maitland. After all, they're both your boys.'

Peggy had been silent throughout the broadcast and even afterwards. She was standing next to Sam, leaning against him as if for support. Now she took a deep breath and straightened up. 'We all know what happens in a war, don't we?' Her glance took in everyone in the room. 'Of course I don't want my boys to go. I'd lock 'em in their bedroom and throw away the key, if I could, but I can't. We've brought both of them up to be good boys, to honour the memory of those we lost and now they've got to do their duty and fight once again for our freedom, because to give in and allow this monster Hitler to win would be to dishonour all those who gave their lives last time. Whatever the cost, as a family, as a community, as a nation, we have to pay it, because we have to win.'

Usually a shy woman, it was one of the longest speeches any of them had ever heard Peggy make and, even now, she hadn't finished.

'I know what an appalling loss you suffered last time, Mr Dawson, and I can understand you not wanting to lose your only grandson, but he has to go. He *has* to. And Harry will go too with our blessing, if he chooses to, even though it will break my heart. But I beg you, please, Mr Dawson, don't cut Luke off. Don't disown him.' As Len opened his mouth, she held up her hand to stop him. 'And before you say it, this isn't about him being the heir to your business. Not wanting to sound rude or ungrateful, but, right at this minute, I couldn't care less about that. It's just that I don't want to see any more family feuds.'

She fell silent at last and everyone in the room seemed to be holding their breath, waiting for Len to speak. Very quietly, he set his cup and saucer on the table, turned and left the room, letting himself out of the front door without speaking.

'He dun't give in, does he?' Bess muttered and then turned to Norah. 'I reckon you'd better come home with me and Charlie tonight, duck.'

'Mrs Cooper's right, isn't she?' Pips said, as the family sat down to dinner later that evening. 'Mr Dawson doesn't give in, but what I really can't understand is why he's saying exactly the opposite this time to what he said before.'

'I expect he's learned his lesson,' Edwin said drily, 'but he's not a man to admit he was ever wrong.'

'And what about Harry? Do you think he will go? He'll be eighteen in December.'

'Oh, he'll go,' Daisy said, before anyone else could answer Pips's question. She smiled wryly. 'He'll always follow Luke. And to be honest, if they allowed women to fly, I'd be going too.'

Twenty-One

The following morning when they met in the estate office, Henrietta said, 'You'll be far more useful here, Daisy, than becoming a waitress in the mess on some RAF or army camp, or working in a factory. We'll undoubtedly get an exemption for you, if it comes to it, because I'm sure that very shortly there are going to be demands from the Ministry of Agriculture for us all to grow more food and this is where we'll come in. We have a lot of land that can be utilized.' She laughed. 'Even the croquet lawn, if necessary.'

'Granny, do you think we should involve Jake more?'

'In what way?'

'With our plans. He's head gardener, so it's going to affect him if we extend his vegetable patch, as I'm sure we must.'

'But don't forget he's head groom too. He has a stable lad under him now and two boys in the gardens, but—'

'Then don't you think he should have a cottage on the estate now as befits his position instead of living above the stables?'

'I do indeed, Daisy.' Henrietta laughed. 'I ask him every year on the day we celebrate his birthday.'

'Midsummer Day, because no one knows his actual birthday – not even him.'

'Exactly, but his reply has always been the same and I expect it always will be.' She imitated Jake's broad Lincolnshire accent as she added, '"I likes living in the stables. I need to be near me 'osses."'

They laughed together, but it was done fondly when thinking about the man who had been part of their lives for many years – in fact, for the whole of Daisy's life and more.

'So,' Henrietta continued, 'let's start planning what we're going to do.'

They spent the rest of the morning happily poring over maps of the grounds and estate lands and making notes for the future. As the gong sounded for luncheon, Henrietta rolled up the maps. 'You know, I think we'll lose one or two of our workers to the war, especially the single young men.'

'I expect so, but there may be a few school leavers in the area looking for work and maybe one or two older men who'd be able to do the lighter jobs on a part-time basis, perhaps.'

'And then, of course, there'll be the land girls.'

Daisy giggled. 'If they arrive in droves, it'll cause a stir.'

'Alice, will you join Daisy and me in the office?' Henrietta said the next morning as they were all finishing breakfast. Robert had already disappeared to open the surgery and Edwin had retired behind his newspaper in the parlour. 'Daisy and I have several ideas we'd like to discuss with you.'

Alice's eyes widened. 'Me?'

'Yes, you, my dear.'

'But – but I don't know anything about running the estate. Surely, if you want another opinion, it should be Father or Robert.'

'This isn't about the estate as such, Alice. It's what I would like us to do to help the war effort that I wish us to discuss and who we can get to join us. I know you help Robert and Conrad with their paper-work, but I'm sure you could find a little time to help us, couldn't you? Would you just ask Sarah to bring some coffee into the office and I will explain everything?'

Still mystified, Alice shrugged, did as she was asked and then followed her mother-in-law and her daughter into the office.

When they were all seated, Henrietta stirred her coffee and murmured, 'I don't expect we'll be getting much more of this soon. They'll be starting all sorts of rationing.' Then she seemed to shake herself and bring her thoughts back to the matter in hand.

'First of all, I intend to set up a branch of the WVS here in the village. I've been in touch with our local organizer and she's all in favour of the idea.'

'There'll be one in Lincoln, won't there?'

'Very likely, but I want one here. One that I can run myself.'

Alice and Daisy did not dare glance at one another. 'Go on, Granny.'

'I also intend to offer my services as a billeting officer for the village. As we know, the evacuation of children and young mothers with babies has already begun. The first trainload of children arrived in Lincoln last week from Leeds, so I fully expect that very soon we shall be asked to take our share here in Doddington. And I am well placed to know who can take how many children, and so on, far better than an official from the city.'

'That's true, but you shouldn't be taking on so much, Mother.'

Henrietta smiled winningly. 'That's why I need your help – both of you. I want us all to join the WVS and I'm also going to ask Mrs Cooper, Mrs Nuttall, Peggy and, of course, Betty, who works here too. And then there's Kitty's mother, Mrs Page.' She paused for a moment before adding, 'What do you think about your mother, Alice? Would she join us, do you think?'

'I think she'd love to, but just whether my father would allow it, I'm not sure.'

'Mm. I'll have to see what I can do, then. Would they take an evacuee, d'you think?'

Now Alice shook her head. 'I don't think he'd agree to that.'

'He might have to. There's going to be such a thing as compulsory billeting. He might not have any choice.'

Alice smiled weakly. 'Mam would love having youngsters about the place again, but I'm not sure I'd want to put any children with him anyway.'

Henrietta laughed. 'There is that way of looking at it, Alice. Anyway, are you happy for me to approach the other ladies I've mentioned and to ask them to join us?'

'Of course,' Alice and Daisy chorused. Then Alice added, 'I think we should include Florence Everton, if you're agreeable. She and I have become good friends since she arrived.' Her face clouded for a moment. 'I think she misses being able to be useful in the community. Calls on her expertise as a midwife don't come very often in the village.'

'I'd've thought she and Conrad would have started their own family by now,' Henrietta remarked.

For a moment Alice looked uncomfortable and Henrietta, always astute, added, 'Ah, perhaps that is a subject best not gone into, is it, Alice?'

Alice bit her lip and nodded. Florence had confided in Alice that the greatest sadness in their lives was that she and Conrad could not have children. 'We've had all sorts of tests and nothing is wrong with either of us, but it just doesn't seem to be happening. But, please Alice, don't say anything to anyone. I don't want us to be the subject of gossip or of pity.'

Alice had given her promise and she would not break it even to members of her own family.

'So,' Henrietta went on now. 'We'll certainly include Mrs Everton in our group but we'll do it properly. Get them all to join the WVS and wear a uniform. That gives them a bit of authority.'

Alice and Daisy looked at each other and could no longer hide their laughter.

'What?' Henrietta glanced between them. 'What have I said?'

'Nothing, Granny. Honestly. I think we're both imagining Mrs Cooper strutting about the village in her uniform.'

Now Henrietta joined in their mirth just as a knock on the door came and Wainwright entered.

'Excuse me, Madam, but I wondered if you would have time to have a word with Kitty?'

'Of course, Wainwright. Please send her in.'

Kitty Page, who had been working at the hall since she'd left school, starting as a scullery maid, had by now been promoted to housemaid. She had grown into a very pretty seventeen-year-old, with her blond curls tucked neatly under her lace cap. Her apron, over her black housemaid's dress, was spotless and she bobbed a quick curtsy as she entered the room. It was not something that Henrietta had ever demanded of her staff, yet the girl always performed it of her own accord whenever she encountered her mistress or Edwin.

'Now, my dear, how can I help you?'

'I don't want to interrupt you, ma'am, but I would like your advice, please.' Henrietta inclined her head and the girl continued. 'I wouldn't want you to think I'm ungrateful for you giving me a job here. I love working here, but my mam says that next year, when I'm eighteen, I might be called upon to do war work . . .'

'And being my housemaid wouldn't be classed as helping the war effort, would it?' Henrietta finished for her.

Kitty nodded. 'So that's why she told me to see you to ask if you thought I should volunteer for something particular, so that I won't just get sent – well – anywhere. It's what Luke has done – chosen to enlist to be a fighter pilot – and Harry intends to volunteer for the RAF in January, after his eighteenth birthday.' Kitty's words came out in a rush now. 'He wants to fly bombers.' Her glance went to Daisy. 'He – he saw them being made at Brooklands, Miss Daisy, didn't he?'

'Yes,' Daisy was obliged to agree. 'Oh dear. I expect his parents blame me – and Aunty Pips – for taking him there and putting the idea into his head.'

'No – no, miss, they don't. They say we've all got to do our bit and if that's what Harry wants to do, then it's all right with them.' For a moment her voice trembled and there were tears in her eyes.

Softly, Alice said, 'You're very fond of Harry, aren't you, Kitty?'

The girl nodded and said simply, 'I've loved him for as long as I can remember, Miss Alice. I don't think he feels the same way about me, though he's always very kind to me, but then he is to everyone. And – I do know he's a bit of a flirt with all the girls.'

There was a short silence until Henrietta said briskly, 'So, have you thought of anything you'd like to do?'

Kitty took a deep breath. 'My dad' – Kitty's father had worked on the estate's farm all his working life and the family lived in one of the tied cottages situated in the village opposite Len Dawson's workshop – 'says that if some of the young men go from the farm, you might have to have land girls come here.'

'That's true.'

'So, I was wondering if I could become a land girl and work here on your farm?'

'I think,' Daisy put in, 'that if you were to apply to the Land Army, you'd have to go where they sent you, Kitty.' She glanced at her grandmother. 'But couldn't we employ her and then an exemption can be applied for?'

'Ye-es, I think we could. I'll look into it. I'll find out what the regulations are. Who actually has to apply and so on. Are you sure that's what you want to do, Kitty? Work on the land?'

'Oh yes, madam. I'm a country girl. I would hate to work in one of them factories in the city. But, of course, I'd go there if I had to.'

'Leave it with me, Kitty. I'll see what I can do. Now, can you do something for me?'

'Of course, ma'am.'

'I want you to take a message to several of the ladies in the village.' Henrietta ticked them off on her hand. 'Mrs Cooper, both Mrs Nuttalls, Mrs Dawson, Mrs Everton and your mother – and could you also find Betty Cooper and let her know too. Would you ask them if they could please come to the hall to see us tomorrow afternoon at three o'clock?'

Betty was Bess's daughter and sister to Peggy. After losing her sweetheart, Roy Dawson, at the Somme, she had never married. Now she worked at the hall as lady's maid to both Henrietta and Alice.

'Yes, ma'am. I'll just tell Mrs Warren and then I'll go right away.' The girl bobbed another curtsy and hurried out of the room to find Mrs Warren, who had been the family's housekeeper for a long time.

As the door closed behind her, Henrietta sighed.

'I think we are going to lose one or two of the younger members of our staff. Thank goodness Mrs Warren, Cook and Wainwright are all too old to be called up.'

'There's Jake,' Daisy reminded her. 'He's not too old, is he?'

Henrietta's smile widened. 'No, but I intend to make sure he gets an exemption too. We can't possibly manage without Jake.'

Twenty-Two

'So,' Pips smiled across her kitchen table at Mitch as she set a cup of coffee and a plate of biscuits in front of him, 'we'll be seeing a lot more of you, then.'

Mitch stirred his coffee thoughtfully. 'I'm not sure that would be a good idea.' Now he glanced up at her and deliberately met her gaze. 'I don't think old George would be happy about that.'

Pips groaned. 'Oh, not that old chestnut. For goodness' sake, Mitch. We're all friends. We're still part of the Brooklands crowd, even if there'll be no more racing for the duration. Is that why you're going to be at your apartment in London more now?'

'Apart from keeping my Lysander in good nick – just in case it can be useful – there's nothing much for me to do down at Weybridge. And, at the moment, Jeff's still there anyway.'

'What's he going to do? As regards the war effort, I mean.'

'Oho, Jeff has all sorts of contacts. He'll find something very useful to do, I can promise you that. But knowing him' – Mitch tapped the side of his nose – 'it'll be something very hush-hush.'

'I can well imagine you getting involved in something like that as well.'

Mitch laughed. 'Well, I'll be sure *not* to tell you if I do.'

They smiled at each other.

'So, in the meantime, until something more exciting turns up, you're going to be an air-raid warden in this area.'

'That's right.'

'You know, that's a very good cover for some clandestine work.'

'Pips, you're far too clever for your own good.' He set down his cup, picked up a biscuit and bit into it before saying, 'So, what are *you* going to do? Knowing you, I don't expect you're going to sit here twiddling your thumbs.'

'I'll do something, but at the moment, I don't quite know what.' She sighed. 'Maybe I should go back to Lincolnshire and help my mother. She is organizing everybody to be useful.'

Mitch chuckled and murmured, 'I wouldn't expect anything less, but I don't think that's quite you, is it?'

'Once the bombing starts – and it's bound to – I will probably offer my services to drive an ambulance here in London.'

Mitch frowned. 'I don't think George will like that.'

'George will have nothing to do with it,' Pips retorted.

Knowing her as he did, Mitch didn't doubt it for a second.

*

177

They were all seated around the long dining table in the Great Hall. Henrietta beamed at her daughter-in-law, her granddaughter and the seven women, which now included Betty Cooper too, who'd been invited to attend the meeting. 'Thank you for coming here this afternoon. It's very good of you.'

'Nah then, Mrs Maitland,' Bess said. 'Is this about having these kiddies from Leeds to live with us, because me an' my Charlie'll gladly take one or two. Ones that are related. You know, brothers and sisters – so that they're not split up.'

'Partly, Mrs Cooper, yes, but there's more to it than that.'

Swiftly, she explained her idea that they should all become founder members of the WVS branch she intended to open in the village.

'I want us to do it properly. The Women's Voluntary Services is going to be very important in this war. I have already obtained clearance from the headquarters of the organization and we shall be a recognized branch and have proper uniforms.'

Daisy took a surreptitious glance at Bess Cooper and was not disappointed to see a beam spreading across the woman's round face.

'Now,' Henrietta was saying, 'would you all like to join?'

There was a chorus of 'yes' around the table. Only Norah did not speak at once.

'I'd love to join you all,' she said hesitantly, 'but I'm not sure . . .'

'You leave that husband of yours to me, Norah,' Bess said. 'I'll have words with him.'

Norah's cheeks turned pink at the thought that her private business should be discussed in front of the other women. Then she sighed. There was no need for her to feel embarrassed; they had all known for years just how Len treated her. Perhaps this was something she really could do that would give her a feeling of self-worth. She glanced round the table at the women she considered to be her friends – even Mrs Maitland. She lifted her head and smiled. She'd do it. With their help, she'd defy Len and join them.

A little later, Bess walked back with Norah to the Dawsons' cottage. 'Put the kettle on, Norah duck. I'll just nip along the lane and have a word with Len.'

'Oh Bess, do be careful what you say.'

'I aren't going to have a row with him.' She laughed raucously. 'At least, not unless I have to.'

Moments later, she was standing outside Len's workshop. 'You there, Len?'

There was a pause before he appeared. ''Course I am. It's a working day, in't it? What d'you want, woman?'

'We've just been up to the hall . . .' Swiftly, she went on to explain what Mrs Maitland had asked them to do.'

For a moment Len was thoughtful. 'She'll not be wanting you all to go away from the village, will she? I don't want Norah gallivanting off.'

'I wouldn't think so, Len. It's the village she wants us to concentrate on.'

Again, there was a pause whilst Bess held her breath. 'Well,' Len said slowly at last, 'as long as my meals are ready on time and she does all her house-work, then, aye, she can join you.' Before Bess could say any more, he pointed at her. 'But one thing I won't have is strangers in my home. We're not taking any of these brats coming from God knows where.'

For once, Bess held her tongue. It was enough for the moment that she'd got his agreement to Norah joining them in the WVS. If the Dawsons were obliged to take evacuees, she'd leave that to Mrs Maitland to deal with. Her short walk back to Norah was triumphant. 'He's agreed, Norah. You can join us.'

'No! Really?'

'Yes, but he's adamant you're not having evacuees.'

Norah's face fell for a moment, but then she shrugged. 'Ah well, I expected as much. In fact, I didn't expect him to agree to the WVS bit. Thanks, Bess.'

'It's going to be hard work, Norah, but we'll have fun as well. And we'll all be doing our bit.'

It didn't take long for Henrietta to organize everything and by the second week in October, when the news-papers were full of the news that British troops had been sent to France, the newly formed Doddington Branch of the WVS had its uniforms and were meeting regularly to learn what their duties were to be. In the same week, the first evacuees arrived in the village. They were gathered in the church where Henrietta and her WVS ladies greeted them with food and drink and told them to sit down in the pews to await the arrival of the villagers who were to take them into their homes.

'Poor little mites,' Florence said, her gentle brown eyes filling with tears. 'They all look so white-faced and exhausted. I want to gather them all up and take them home.'

'I know what you mean,' Peggy said, standing beside her a little self-consciously in her new uniform. 'Which one will you choose?'

'Oh, I won't mind any of them,' Florence whispered. 'Probably the scruffiest, most peaky-faced one that looks in need of a good bath and a lot of love. The one that no one else wants.'

'Sam says I've to pick a good, strong boy that can help him in the garden.'

Their glances ran over the children who were sitting in rows and munching sandwiches.

'There's a boy at the back, Peggy, who looks a bit older than the rest. What about him?'

'I'll go and have a word. No good being dressed in this uniform if we can't pull rank now and again.'

The villagers were arriving now to make their choices and Florence shuddered. It was like a cattle market and she felt so sorry for all the children waiting to be picked.

Peggy approached the boy at the back of the room and sat down beside him. 'Hello. Where have you come from?'

The boy wiped his mouth with the back of his hand – a gesture that Peggy was always reprimanding Harry for. It endeared him to her at once.

'Leeds, Mrs. My mam reckoned I'd best come away, seein' as we're likely to be one of 'itler's targets. I wanted 'er to come, an' all, but she won't leave me

181

dad. He's in engineering. He can't leave.' The boy spoke in a broad Leeds accent that reminded Peggy of Daisy's friend, Gill.

'How old are you?'

'Twelve, Mrs, but I'm big for me age. I 'spect there'll be some as think I'm older than that, but I ain't.'

'What's your name?'

'Bernard Smiff, Mrs.'

Peggy stifled a gasp of surprise. It was the same name as one of the Dawson boys who'd never come back from the war. Not her sister's fiancé, Roy, but his brother.

'Well, Bernard Smith,' she said in a voice that was not quite steady now, 'would you like to come and stay with me and my husband? We've got two sons. Luke is in the RAF and there's Harry too. He's still at home at the moment, but he will be joining the RAF in January. What do you think?'

The boy regarded her solemnly. 'I fink I'd like that very much, Mrs. What's your name?'

'Mrs Nuttall. Now, you sit at the back here until I can take you home. I have to help with the others for now. But if anyone asks you, you're taken.'

The boy grinned and wiped his mouth again. 'Ta, Mrs Nuttall. Ta very much.'

The number of evacuees was thinning out rapidly. Under Henrietta's guidance, the villagers picked out the ones that would suit them the best or fit in with their family. At last, apart from Bernard, who was waiting for Peggy, there were only two little girls, standing at the side, clinging to each other.

'I think they're twins,' Florence whispered to Peggy. 'They look ever so much alike.'

'I think that's why no one's taken them. They didn't want two.'

'I think it's more likely because one of them has obviously been sick down her coat on the journey and the other has wet her knickers.' Her smile widened. 'Just what I was looking for. They're perfect for Conrad and me.'

Peggy glanced at her, but Florence wasn't joking. She smiled as she went towards the two little girls who couldn't be more than about four years old. 'Hello, you two. I was hoping you would be left – just for me. Come along, now. Let's go home.' She took the girls' hands, one on either side of her, and left the church, calling back over her shoulder, 'Tell Mrs Maitland for me, Peggy, will you, that I've taken the last two?'

Peggy walked to where Henrietta was sitting at the front of the church, ticking off all the names on her lists.

'That's all of them, Mrs Maitland. Mrs Everton has taken the last two little girls.'

Henrietta glanced up. 'But there's a boy still sitting at the back.'

'He's coming home with me.'

'Oh, right. What's his name?'

'Bernard Smith.'

'Ah yes, here he is.' She placed a tick against his name. 'And that's everyone. What a good day's work.'

Twenty-Three

'Thank you for coming, George. I wasn't sure if you would.'

'Why wouldn't I?'

George's manner was a little stiff. Mitch smiled ruefully.

'I think we both know why, George. We circle around each other like a couple of tomcats.'

George stared at him for a moment before saying, 'Mitch, I admire and respect you, but it's not – comfortable to know that you are in love with my wife.'

'Can't help it, old chap. Have been ever since she pulled me from my crashed aircraft in no-man's-land. George' – Mitch leaned across the table as if to emphasize his point and now he was deadly serious – 'I propagate the notion that I am a present-day Casanova deliberately. Yes, I do like the company of women and yes, I do have a few girlfriends, but I give you my solemn word that I would never do anything to hurt Pips and even if I were to *try* to come between you, that would hurt her – and you. And, though you might not believe me, I will return the compliment you have just paid me. Our feelings for each other are mutual. Let's just say the better man won the hand of the fair maiden. Now, let me order us both a drink and I'll tell you why I asked you to meet me.'

When they were settled in a secluded corner of the bar, Mitch said, 'I think you'll agree with me that this "phoney war" isn't going to last for ever. Although there have been a few skirmishes at sea, there has been no significant military action on land, even though we've sent men from the British Expeditionary Force into France. Hitler isn't going to be content with what he already has and then it will all kick off. When it does, George, I'm sure you know better than me, that we are going to be one of his prime targets. I think he will attack other countries first – probably Norway, Holland and, certainly, France and Belgium, for whom we hold such fond memories—' Mitch paused for a moment. 'And then he will get to us. When that happens, he's going to inflict a campaign of bombing upon us the like of which we have never seen.'

'I agree with everything you say,' George murmured, still mystified as to exactly why Mitch had wanted to meet him. As if reading his mind, Mitch said, 'I'm probably too old to rejoin the RAF – at least in an active position – but I want to be involved. And so does Jeff. I have my little aeroplane to put at the disposal of any department that needs it, either to fly myself or to be used by others. I thought you might have an idea of who I might contact to offer my services.'

'But I thought you'd volunteered to be an air-raid warden in our district. That's what Pips told me.'

'True, I have, but that's not going to be enough for either me or Jeff.'

George was thoughtful before he said slowly, 'There are one or two people I could put you in touch with – probably through Rebecca's husband, Matthew.'

Mitch smiled. 'I'd be very grateful, but there is also something else.'

'Oh?'

'Pips.'

'Ah.'

'Perhaps I'm breaking her confidence here, but I don't think so. You're bound to find out sooner or later anyway.'

'Go on.' Again George was tight-lipped. Was this something Pips had shared with Mitch and not with him?

'If – no doubt I should say when – we get bombing here in London, Pips intends to drive an ambulance.'

George gave an inward sigh of relief as he said, 'Yes, I do know about that. She's already approached Rebecca to introduce her to the authorities. The Red Cross, I think.'

'And – er – are you happy about that?'

'Of course not, but I can't think what to do to stop her.'

'Isn't there someone amongst your contacts who could find her some work – preferably somewhere out of London? I mean, surely the authorities are moving top secret stuff out of the city. She's a very clever woman. She'd be very good in that sort of work.'

George stared at Mitch. 'Now that is a very good suggestion. Thank you.'

A little later Mitch met up with Jeff.

'And did he buy it?' Jeff asked. 'All that stuff about you and me wanting to be put in touch with some of his contacts?'

'I think so. He didn't seem to suspect that we might already have all the contacts we need, but I had to ask him for help for myself – or rather us – so that I could then bring the conversation round to Pips.'

'And did you mention Bletchley Park?'

Mitch shook his head. 'No, only very indirectly. I just said that the authorities must be moving secret stuff out of London and that she might be able to help in that sort of work.'

'You devious bugger, Mitch! You really ought to be a spy.'

Mitch grinned. 'We might very well end up being just that, Jeff.' Then he sobered. 'I just hope my subterfuge works and he gets her out of London.'

'I think we're a bit long in the tooth for the spying malarkey,' Jeff said. 'Not physically agile enough now, but I think we can still make ourselves useful. But we're just going to have to be patient until things really start to hot up, then they'll be wanting the services of a couple of reprobates like us.'

Despite Mitch's protestations to the contrary, George was worried. He wanted to get Pips out of London, away from the bombing and – if he was perfectly honest with himself and he usually was – away from

Mitch Hammond. Mitch was going to be living in the city almost permanently now and, as an air-raid warden, he would be patrolling the area that included the block of apartments where George and Pips lived. It wasn't that he didn't trust Pips; he knew she would not be unfaithful to him and the fact that he actually liked Mitch made matters worse. He'd tried to dislike him, but he couldn't. He admired the man, but that didn't mean he liked the idea of Mitch dropping in to see Pips any time he liked for a cup of tea and a cosy chat. And now, Mitch had confirmed that Pips was serious about volunteering to drive an ambulance anywhere in London! He had to get her away. But where? And how? She wouldn't agree to go home to Lincolnshire; he'd tried that. She wanted to be useful. She *needed* to be useful in this war just like she had been in the last one. But his meeting with Mitch had put an idea into his head.

In his work at the War Office, George encountered a great many visitors to the department. He heard the whispers and the gossip and he was in a good position to sound out his colleagues for advice. And so, when he heard that the Government Code and Cypher School had been set up at Bletchley Park, he realized at once that this was what Pips could do, though he knew he would have to tread carefully. Somehow, he would have to let Pips come to the decision herself, but first he got in touch with one of the men who recruited people for the GC&CS at the Foreign Office. Because he worked at the War Office, and with Matthew's help too, George was able to obtain an appointment quite quickly. Sitting down in front of the tall, thin man with receding hair but sharp, intelligent eyes, he came straight to the point.

'My wife is an extremely clever woman and I think she would be an ideal candidate for Bletchley Park.'

'Really?' Michael Duncan sounded sceptical and George hid his smile.

'Of course, you would expect me to say that,' he said mildly and the man looked slightly sheepish. 'She and her brother are excellent chess players and they vie with each other to do the *Telegraph*'s crossword puzzles.' He paused for effect and added, almost casually, 'I think Pips's fastest time has been twelve minutes.'

'Twelve minutes! Good God – I can only manage fifteen.'

George smiled and inclined his head. 'I can't even get that close.'

Mr Duncan was thoughtful. 'Ask her to come and see me.'

'If you don't mind, I'd rather she didn't know I was involved.'

The man raised his eyebrows as George leaned forward. 'She drove an ambulance at the front in the last war and wants to drive again here – in London – in the bombing, because we're bound to get some sooner or later. I'll be blunt – I don't want her to and, besides, with her talents I think she could be of much more use at somewhere like Bletchley.' He held his breath whilst the man opposite him was deep in thought for a few moments.

'Then I'll write to her – I'll just say that her name

has come to my attention.' Mr Duncan smiled and his eyes twinkled over his spectacles. 'In my job, I don't have to say where my information comes from.'

George stood up and held out his hand. 'I'm extremely grateful.'

'Just leave your address with my secretary and your wife will receive a letter by the end of the week.'

'George, do you know anything about this?'

'What's that, my darling?'

'This letter from someone called Michael Duncan. He wants to see me at the Foreign Office. D'you know who he is and what it's about?'

George had rehearsed in his mind how to handle this very question when the letter arrived.

'Let me see.' He held out his hand for the letter. 'I've heard of him,' he said slowly as he read it, tacitly implying that he hadn't met him without actually lying. 'What does he do?'

'I'm not exactly sure. Some sort of recruitment for war work, I think, but how did he get hold of my name?'

'That, I can't tell you.'

'Can't – or won't, George?'

He smiled as he handed back the letter. 'Can't, darling.'

Pips frowned and muttered a sceptical, 'Mm, that probably amounts to the same thing.' She glanced down at the letter again and murmured, 'But I'll go and see him. It might be something interesting.'

Twenty-Four

'You know, you're all putting me to shame,' Edwin said at dinner one evening towards the end of October. He smiled benignly round the table at his family, peering over his spectacles at them, his eyes full of mischief. He was so proud of them all for their different contributions to life at the hall and in the village, not only in ordinary times, but now in war time they were all 'doing their bit', as the newspapers were exhorting everyone to do. Edwin still sported his colourful waistcoats that had been a source of amusement for his patients during his days as the local GP. 'My attire amuses the children and makes the old ladies smile,' he had always said. He had changed little over the years; he was still a little portly but was just as mild-mannered and kindly as he'd ever been. 'I feel I should do something,' he added.

'My dear, you're almost eighty,' Henrietta said. 'I don't want you overdoing it and making yourself ill.'

'What about you, Hetty, my love? You're seventy-five and yet, here you are, as energetic and involved as ever. I'm still fit and healthy, there must be *something* I can do.'

'I'm sure there will be, my dear,' Henrietta said,

191

'but it's early days yet. We're still in what everyone's calling the "phoney war". At the moment, the only things we can do are to house the evacuees and to make sure we're "digging for victory", as they're asking us.'

'And are all the children happily settled?'

'I don't know about "happily", Edwin, but everyone is doing their best to care for them and to make them feel wanted – at least in our village anyway.'

Edwin chuckled. 'Woe betide anyone who didn't on your watch, Hetty.'

'Poor little scraps,' Alice said. 'Florence was telling me that those little twin girls she took home with her were covered in head lice and she's had to buy new clothes for them. They didn't look so bad at first, but underneath their coats, they were virtually in rags.'

'Ah, well done, Alice, my dear. You've given me an idea,' Edwin said. 'That is something I could do.'

All eyes turned towards him as he smiled. 'I could visit all the homes where the children have been placed and give them a medical and see if there's anything they need. Would that be all right with you, Robert?'

'It would be ideal, Father. Conrad and I are both rather stretched at the moment. Now we're almost into November, we're starting to get the usual winter ills affecting the young and the very old and there's no knowing what infections will have come in with the evacuee children. Meaning no disrespect to them, poor things, but it's inevitable.'

Edwin beamed and nodded. 'I will keep you informed of anything I think you need to know and I'll ask Jake if he can drive me around when you're not using the car.'

'Jake is increasingly busy with the grounds,' Henrietta put in. 'Perhaps we should employ a driver for you and Robert now.'

'That's a very good idea, Hetty, my love. Leave that with me.'

'So now,' Alice said happily, 'we're all usefully employed in the war effort.'

'I've got an interview at the Foreign Office late this afternoon. Do you think Matthew has had something to do with this?'

'Darling, I really couldn't say.'

Pips arched her eyebrows quizzically, but said no more. Later that day, she made her way to the Foreign Office and was shown into Michael Duncan's office.

'Please sit down, Mrs Allender. It's good of you to come.'

'I'm intrigued,' Pips said, smiling.

The man rested his elbows on his desk and steepled his fingers. 'These interviews are very difficult because I am not allowed to tell you very much. All I can say is that you will be engaged on extremely important war work, but you can tell no one anything about it. You can't even tell your family where you will be. They can, however, write to you here, care of the Foreign Office.'

'Will I be in this country?'

'Yes, and not all that far away, actually. You would

get leave now and again and you would be able to go home, but because you will have to sign the Official Secrets Act, you can tell no one – absolutely no one – anything about the work you'd be doing.' He was repeating the same statement and this, more than anything, emphasized the nature of the work. Now Pips really was fascinated.

'Can I tell my husband? He works at the War Office. He knows how to keep secrets.'

'Absolutely not.'

She was silent for a moment before saying, 'Well, I would like to be considered for – whatever it is.'

'Then I would like you to do this crossword for me and I will time you. It's the sort that appears in the *Daily Telegraph*, although it's not one you will have seen before.'

Pips smiled inwardly as she took the newspaper and the pen he handed to her. As she bent her head and began to concentrate, she was aware that Michael Duncan had glanced at his watch to note the time. She worked swiftly and quietly as the minutes ticked by. When at last she looked up and laid the completed puzzle in front of him, he again looked at his watch.

'Thirteen and a half minutes, Mrs Allender. Well done.'

'Aren't you going to check my answers?'

He chuckled. 'I can see that you have completed the grid. It's unlikely to be incorrect if all the words fit with each other. Now, one last thing. Do you play chess?'

'Yes.'

'Then,' he rose from his chair behind his desk and

crossed to a small table near the window where a chessboard had been set up, 'may I challenge you to a game?'

'I'd be delighted,' Pips said and followed him across the room.

'You be black,' Michael said, as they sat down opposite each other. Pips hid her smile, wondering if this was a deliberate ploy on his part. They began to play and, after moving twice, Pips said, 'Checkmate.'

She glanced up to see Michael smiling broadly. He said, 'Fool's mate. Well done.'

'You gave me the opening to do that, didn't you?'

'Indeed I did and I was not disappointed.' He stood up and held out his hand.

'Welcome aboard, Mrs Allender. You will receive instructions within a few days, but we'll let you have Christmas with your family and start you in January. But remember, not a word to anyone, not even your nearest and dearest.'

She took his hand and shook it warmly. 'I understand.'

He laughed. 'I'm sure you don't – yet. But you will.'

That first Christmas of the war was a strange one for everyone throughout the country, though perhaps in Doddington it was the nearest to normal that they could make it – except that they had evacuee children in their midst. Several children had already been taken back home by their mothers when the anticipated bombing did not occur, despite Mrs Maitland's advice that they should stay in the countryside. But many still remained and it was for these children that the villagers tried to make Christmas extra special. Henrietta held her usual Boxing Day party, but with a difference. Now the Great Hall rang with the shouts and laughter of overexcited youngsters.

'You're running the risk of your precious china being broken, Mrs Maitland.' Bess cast her eyes around the cabinets which held china and glassware that had been handed down the generations.

'If Hitler sends his bombs this far, Mrs Cooper, they'll do far more damage than a few boisterous children can. It's good to see them enjoying themselves, when I expect they're missing their own families.'

'All your family's here,' Bess said, 'even Miss Pips and Mr George, but I don't see Dr Maitland.'

'Ah, Edwin has a very special part to play.' Henrietta's eyes twinkled. 'You'll see, Mrs Cooper.'

'Aye, well, they certainly look like they're having fun. In fact, I think we all are.' Then she chuckled. 'Except Len over there.'

They glanced across the room to where Len was standing with a glass in his hand, but a frown on his face.

Henrietta glanced around the room. 'There is one young man who doesn't seem to want to join in.'

Bess followed her glance. 'Aye. He's the lad staying with our Peggy and Sam. Bernard. He's a bit older than the rest. Maybe he thinks these games are a little beneath him.'

Henrietta chuckled. 'Well, they're not beneath my daughter and granddaughter. Oh look, they're starting a conga. Let's get out of the way, Mrs Cooper. I don't want to get caught up in that.'

The music from the gramophone blared loudly and Len's frown deepened. He sidled towards the door, and as he did so, he passed in front of the young boy.

'Bit rowdy for my taste,' he muttered. 'But aren't you joining in?'

The boy shook his head. 'Nah. I'd sooner be outside.'

Len glanced at him. 'In this weather?'

The boy nodded. 'I'm used to it.' He nodded towards the roaring fire in the huge fireplace. 'We don't have fires like that where I come from.'

'And where is that?'

'Leeds, mister.' The boy paused and then said, 'You're the feller that has the blacksmith's and that, aren't you?'

'I am.'

'I've been to watch Mr Nuttall once or twice. I'm staying with them. I reckon that's the sort of work I'd like to do when I leave school.' He nodded towards the window. 'I like it here in the countryside. Didn't think I would, but I do.'

'How old are you?'

'Twelve, nearly thirteen.'

'Aye, well, I started work when I was that age. What's your name?'

'Bernard Smiff.'

For a moment, Len was very still. Then, in a husky voice, he said, 'You're welcome to come and watch us at the workshop any time you want.'

*

Just before the party was due to end, Henrietta clapped her hands and, after a moment or two, the children fell silent, staring at her with round eyes. Were they in trouble? But all the lady of the big house said was, 'I hope you've all had a lovely time.'

'Yes, thank you, Mrs,' they chorused.

'Good. Now, just before you go, I have a special surprise. Harry – where are you?' She glanced around and spotted him. 'Come and stand by me, please.' Harry, a little embarrassed, moved towards her. He guessed what was about to happen. 'Daisy, will you and Pips turn the lights off?'

There were a few murmurs amongst some of the little ones, but Alice and Florence soon calmed them. 'Wait and see,' they whispered. The door at the far end of the hall opened and Kitty, Sarah and Mrs Warren entered the room, each bearing a big cake with candles. There were 'oohs' and 'aahs' from all the children.

'Now, we need to sing Happy Birthday to Harry. He was born here in this house on Boxing Day eighteen years ago.'

Harry actually blushed as everyone in the room sang to him. Then the cakes were cut and pieces handed around.

'They're making a right mess on your floor, Mrs Maitland,' Bess said.

'It'll clean,' Henrietta said and then clapped her hands again. 'Now, when you've finished your cake, I want you all to stand at the side of the room in a long line. There, that's it. Now, Daisy, will you see if our special visitor is ready? He may need a little help.'

Smiling broadly, Daisy left the room and a few moments later opened the door again to usher in a rotund figure with a long white beard, dressed in a red coat and hat.

'Ho, ho, ho,' Edwin boomed as he lugged a heavy sack into the room. Behind him, hardly able to contain her giggles, Daisy dragged in a second bulging sack.

'Now, children, line up and go in turn to speak to Father Christmas. He has a little present for each of you. The ones wrapped in pink paper are for the girls, the ones in blue for the boys.'

It took almost an hour for each child to receive a gift and then to sit on the floor to open it.

'By heck, Mrs Maitland, it must have cost you a pretty penny to buy them all.'

'By the look on their little faces, Mrs Cooper, it's money well spent.'

'Ah well, I can't deny that.' She glanced around, as if checking to see that everyone had a present. 'What about the lad over there, standing with Len? He hasn't been up.'

Edwin appeared to have one present left and he was holding it aloft. 'Bernard,' he boomed in his best Father Christmas voice, 'this must be for you.'

For a moment the boy didn't move until Len whispered, 'Go on, lad, don't spoil it for the little 'uns.'

Bernard accepted the gift with good grace and was rewarded by a huge wink from Father Christmas.

As the door closed behind the last small child to leave, there was only Bernard left. 'Can I help you to clear up, Mrs Maitland?'

'That's very kind of you. I'm sure we could use an extra pair of hands.' When everything had been cleared away, the floor swept and the room restored to order, Henrietta said, 'Thank you for your help, Bernard. Peggy and Sam will be here for a while helping in the kitchen so you're welcome to stay with us until they're ready to go home. Perhaps you'd like to go to the stables with Jake to feed the horses.'

'I would, Mrs. Thanks.'

'I saw you talking to Mr Dawson. Everything all right?'

Bernard frowned a little. 'He asked me what me name is and when I told him, he said I can go and watch him at work any time I want.'

Henrietta nodded and said slowly, 'Perhaps I should tell you: he had a son called Bernard who died in the last war. In fact, he lost three of his four sons in that conflict.'

'Oh. I'm sorry. Perhaps I shouldn't go.'

'If you want to, you go. Mr Dawson would not have made the offer if he didn't mean it. Believe me.'

''Lo, Harry.'

As the Nuttall family and Bernard left the hall and walked back to their cottage in the dusk of early evening, they heard footsteps behind them. Kitty caught up with them and fell into step alongside Harry, who was carrying the last remnants of one of the birthday cakes.

'Did you like your cakes? I helped Cook to make them.'

'Lovely. I'm going to wrap a piece up to take with me. I leave next Monday to join the RAF.'

'I know. Your mam told me.' Kitty walked along in silence for a while, but when they reached the point in the lane where Harry and his family turned towards their home, she blurted out, 'Harry, I've got summat else for you.' She held out a folded piece of paper. 'It's another four-leafed clover. I've pressed it properly this time so you can put it in your wallet.'

Harry laughed. 'You must have a right patch of 'em. Thanks, Kitty. I'll carry it always.'

They stood together for a moment, before Kitty leaned forward and planted a kiss on his cheek. Then she turned and ran down the lane leaving Harry grinning in the darkness.

Twenty-Five

'Darling, are you really sure you don't mind me undertaking this work? I don't know where I'm going to be, what I'm going to be doing or how often I'll be able to get home.' Pips laughed. 'And even when I do find out, I'm not going to be allowed to tell anyone – not even you, apparently.'

'My darling, I think it's absolutely perfect for you. I spend so much time away from home now, you need something of your own to do. I know that. We'll meet as often as we can.' George didn't like having secrets from his wife, but he was never going to admit to her that he had been instrumental in her being offered a place at Bletchley Park.

'Well, if you're sure. Right, I'd better go. I've a train to catch to – somewhere.'

'Take care of yourself, my love, and write to me.' He kissed her gently and when they drew back, she touched the brooch he had given her so many years ago that was always pinned to the lapel of whatever outfit she was wearing. 'This will keep me safe,' she said and her voice trembled a little.

'Guess what?' Gill's excited voice came crackling down the telephone wires.

'I couldn't begin to guess, Gill,' Daisy laughed. 'But it sounds like something good.'

'Lord Bunny is going to take me flying.'

'Never!'

'He is. He really is. I can hardly believe it myself.'

'Whatever made him change his mind?'

'The war, I suppose. Didn't you see the pictures in the papers of the first women pilots to join the ATA? There are eight of them at the moment, but I bet there'll soon be more joining.'

'The what?'

'The Air Transport Auxiliary.'

'No, I haven't heard of it.' Flying? There were women who were flying as part of the war effort? Why hadn't she known about it? Surely, Pips would have said something if she'd known. Unless, of course, her family were deliberately keeping it secret from her. Daisy's tone was tight as she added, 'Tell me.'

Gill launched into an explanation. 'It's been formed for pilots who aren't fit for some reason or other to fly in RAF combat, but they're perfectly capable of flying safely.' Gill's laughter echoed down the line. 'Mind you, they've already coined the nickname "Ancient and Tattered Airmen" for them.'

'But what are they going to do?'

'Ferry stuff about, maybe even abroad. Goods, equipment, personnel, I suppose, but mainly aircraft from the factories to airfields in this country.'

'New aircraft?'

'I suppose so.'

'So why has Lord Bunny suddenly decided to take you flying?'

'I showed him the paper and told him that it was something I'd like to do. So, he huffed and puffed for a bit, but then said he'd take me up in his Tiger Moth.'

'Right, then. I'm off down to Brooklands.'

'But it's closed for racing now, isn't it?'

'Yes, but something'll be going on there and I know just the person who'll know.'

'Aunty Pips, you mean?'

'No,' Daisy said carefully, not wanting to blame her beloved aunt for not telling her about this. Perhaps she hadn't heard of the ATA either. 'I was thinking more about Uncle Mitch. I'm sure he'll know something.'

'You could always ask Johnny,' Gill said archly.

'I could indeed.'

Daisy replaced the receiver thoughtfully. She was going to have to play this very carefully.

A little later, she sought out Henrietta. 'Granny, would you mind if I went down to see Pips at the weekend? She hasn't been able to get home much lately, partly because of George working such long hours. I know they were here at Christmas, but that was such a flying visit and I really would like to see what's going on at Kew Gardens too. Everything's ticking over nicely here, so would you mind if I went?'

'Of course not, as long as your mother and father are agreeable.'

Daisy smiled thinly and turned away. She didn't ever want to have arguments with her family, but she did wish they would stop treating her like a child. She was twenty-two after all.

Daisy had been so anxious to get to London that she hadn't even telephoned Pips to ask her if she could visit. She hadn't thought for a moment that Pips might not be there, but when she rang the bell, there was no reply. A neighbour, who recognized Daisy from previous visits, let her in through the main entrance and she sat on the floor outside the door to the apartment where Pips and George lived and waited. And waited. And waited.

When dusk fell and the city streets began to grow dark, she clambered to her feet, her legs stiff from having sat for so long, and picked up her small suitcase. She left the box of food, which the cab driver had been kind enough to carry up for her, sitting outside the door. If it got stolen, then she hoped it would be by someone who needed it more than they did.

'Good job I know where Aunty Milly lives,' she muttered, as she clattered back down the stairs and out into the street. Daisy took a cab to the apartment, which Milly's father had bought for her on her return from the front after the last war and where she now lived with her husband, Paul.

'*Dahling!*' Milly cried, when she opened the door and flung her arms wide in welcome. 'Whatever are you doing here?'

'Looking for Aunty Pips, but she's not at home. I've been waiting most of the afternoon.'

'Oh, you poor thing. You must be starving. Come in, come in. Let me take your case. You must stay with us.'

'That's kind of you, Aunty Milly, but why? Is she away?'

'Um – er – I don't know. I – um – thought she was with you all in Lincolnshire.'

'Aunty Milly,' Daisy said, feigning severity. 'You're not telling me the truth, are you?'

Milly was known for never being able to keep a secret for long. She would even say to her friends, 'Don't tell me any confidences, you know what I'm like.' Now, she wriggled her shoulders. 'I'd really rather you didn't ask me, Daisy dear.'

Daisy sighed. 'I don't want to put you in an awkward position, Aunty Milly, but can't you tell me *anything*?'

'Um – all I know is that she's away, but I honestly don't know where.' She brightened. 'George might be able to tell you more. He'll be here later. He comes round two or three times a week for dinner whilst – um – Pips is away. He and Paul talk about their work to one another, but not' – she giggled – 'in front of me.'

Daisy smiled as she followed Milly into one of the spare rooms. 'Now, you unpack, whilst I get dinner on the go and then, when George and Paul come home, we can eat together.'

'Where is Paul working now?'

'Oh, didn't you know? He's working at the War Office. Not in such a high-up position as George, of course, but in the same building.'

'So, he's not at Brooklands any more?'

Milly shook her head. 'No, none of them are. It's closed for racing. There's only aircraft production going on there now.'

'So, where's Uncle Mitch? I was hoping to find him. There's something I want to ask him.'

Milly's eyes widened. 'I really have no idea.' This time Daisy could tell that she was speaking the truth. 'We don't see much of him now. He's either at his home in Weybridge or here in London at his flat.'

'Ah,' Daisy said and there was a wealth of meaning behind the expression. Maybe, she thought, Uncle Paul will be able to tell me what I want to know.

The two men arrived home together and when they had greeted Daisy, George said, 'Have you telephoned home to say where you are? I think you should. They might be worried.'

'Use the telephone in the hallway, darling,' Milly said. 'Dinner will be ready in ten minutes now the boys are home.'

Daisy struggled to keep a straight face at hearing George referred to as a boy. He must be in his early sixties at least. Pips was forty-five and Daisy knew that George was a good few years older than his wife.

Moments later, she was speaking to her father. 'Daddy – I'm staying at Aunty Milly's. Aunty Pips is away.'

'Really? Where?'

'I don't know yet. I haven't had a chance to find out.'

'Doesn't Milly know?'

'Apparently not.'

There was a pause before Robert said, 'Curious. She didn't say anything at Christmas or when she rang as usual last week. Anyway, have a good weekend. Let me know when your train is due on Monday and Jake will meet you.'

Over dinner, the conversation centred on the Maitland family and life at the hall.

'So, Daisy, tell us everything you and your grandmother are doing.'

What had once seemed so exciting and useful to the young woman had now paled into insignificance beside the thought that she might be able to fly to help the war effort. But obediently, she launched into telling them all the changes that were taking place on the estate in an effort to help provide the country with food. 'I'd like to visit Kew whilst I'm here, if I could, to see what they're doing?'

'We can arrange that for you, Daisy,' Paul said. 'I understand it closed for a month when the hostilities started, so that all the valuable plants could be taken to a safer area in the country, but it's open again now and I believe they're working on areas to demonstrate how the general public can help in the "Dig for Victory" campaign.'

'That's exactly what I want to see.' There was a pause and Daisy ran her tongue around her lips. 'There is something else I wanted to ask you.' Carefully, she avoided mentioning Mitch. 'Do you remember my friend Gill – from Yorkshire?'

'The girl you were at college with? She came down here with you once, didn't she?' George said. 'Pips took her to Brooklands, if I remember. Go on.'

'She's told me that there's something called the Air Transport Auxiliary and that they have women pilots.'

The other three glanced at one another. There was no need for further explanation; they all knew of Daisy's love of flying.

Carefully, Paul said, 'Yes, I have heard of it. One of the girls Jeff taught to fly at Brooklands, just before war broke out, has joined.' He caught and held her gaze. 'Do I take it that you'd like to join?'

'Yes, I would.'

'Oh well, now, Daisy,' George began, 'I don't think—' He broke off and stared at her. 'Do your parents know that this is the real reason you've come down here?'

Never able to lie, Daisy sighed. 'No, Uncle George, they don't.'

George played with his spoon, twisting it round and round on the table, his gaze on it as if he were deep in thought.

'I want to talk to Aunty Pips. She'll understand.'

'I've no doubt she would,' he said softly.

'When will she be home?'

'I really couldn't say.'

Daisy cocked her head on one side. 'D'you mean you *can't* tell me or you *won't* tell me?'

He smiled wryly. 'A bit of both really, Daisy.'

'Uncle George, you are exasperating at times.'

'Look, Daisy, don't make it harder for your uncle,' Paul said. 'You're a clever and perceptive young woman. Why don't you write a letter to Pips and we'll make sure she gets it?'

Daisy stared at him, her mind working fast, but still she couldn't work out what Pips could possibly be doing.

'Actually, you can write to her directly,' George put in. 'Address it to Room Forty-Seven, The Foreign Office.'

'Is that where she is? Working for the Foreign Office?'

George hesitated, but all he would say was, 'They'll forward any letters. You can tell your family to write to her at that address too.'

'"Forward it"? Oh no . . .' Daisy's heart began to beat faster. Surely, surely Pips hadn't gone abroad on some secret mission. She swallowed hard and her voice was a little unsteady as she asked, 'Please be honest about one thing – that's all I ask. Is she in danger?'

George stared at her. 'No, Daisy, she is not. I give you my word. More than that, I can't tell you.'

'Darling,' Milly reached across the table to touch her hand, 'they'd tell you if they could. You must trust them, but George wouldn't let his beloved Pips be in any danger, you must know that.'

Daisy's voice was husky as she said, 'Yes, of course I do. But – you know what Aunty Pips is like. Maybe she's doing something that he couldn't stop. I mean – she hasn't gone back to France, has she?'

George's shake of the head was definite. 'No, she hasn't. I can promise you that.'

'But – but what am I to tell them back home?'

'I'd planned to tell them myself,' George said. 'In fact, Paul, if you can hold the fort at the office, I'll go back with Daisy on Monday and see them myself. It's hardly fair to leave it to her.'

Daisy laughed. 'Well, I can't tell them much, Uncle

George, can I? And you know what Granny is like. She'll wheedle it out of you.'

George's face was solemn as he said, 'Not this time, Daisy.'

Twenty-Six

The following morning, Milly and Daisy set off to visit Kew Gardens.

'There might not be a lot to see today, Daisy. The weather is so cold. You ought to come again in the spring. It's so much prettier then.'

'I thought Uncle George and Uncle Paul might come with us.'

'They've had to go into work, darling.'

'On a Saturday?'

'Sadly, the war doesn't stop because it's the weekend. But you'll see them tonight.'

That evening Paul said, 'Can you delay your return home until Tuesday, Daisy? There's someone I'd like you to meet who can give you advice about the ATA, if you're serious?'

'Oh, I am serious. That'd be great. Thank you.'

Daisy telephoned home to say that she would be arriving back home on Tuesday afternoon and that George would be with her.

'Philippa too?' Henrietta asked.

'No, 'fraid not.'

'Why?'

'Got to go, Granny, the line's awfully crackly. See you Tuesday . . .' And before Henrietta could

212

ask any more awkward questions, Daisy rang off.

The telephone stood on a small table in the hallway at the bottom of the main staircase. Henrietta replaced the receiver thoughtfully and returned to the parlour to face the rest of the family gathered together before dinner.

'That was a strange call from Daisy.'

Edwin looked up from his newspaper. 'Why? Is she all right?'

'I think so. She just said she'll be home on Tuesday afternoon and that George is coming with her. But not Philippa. When I asked why not, she just made some hurried excuse and rang off.'

'I shouldn't worry, Hetty, my love. If there was anything wrong, George or Milly would let us know.'

'Well, that's what is concerning me. Why is George coming on his own?'

'Pips has been ringing regularly as usual, hasn't she, Robert?' Edwin asked. Most weeks, she spoke to her brother and he relayed any messages to the other members of the family.

Robert frowned. 'Well, yes, but not at the same time every Sunday evening like she used to. It's sort of any time and on different days. I hadn't realized it until now. What do you think, Mother?'

'That we shall find out on Tuesday, my dear.'

'Daisy, I'd like you to meet Jane Miller,' Paul said. 'She's the young woman I was telling you about.'

'Oh, the one Jeff taught to fly.' Daisy smiled as she shook Jane's hand. 'And who's with the ATA now?'

The woman was a little older than she was, in her late twenties or early thirties, Daisy guessed. She had fair curly hair and hazel eyes. She was not exactly pretty, but when she smiled her whole face seemed to light up and her eyes twinkled friendliness.

'I'm pleased to meet you, Daisy. I hear you're interested in joining our little band. There aren't many of us at the moment, but we're hoping to recruit more very soon. I understand from Paul here that Jeff Pointer taught you to fly too and that you already have a pilot's licence.'

Daisy nodded.

'That'll help, although you will still have to undergo the ATA training.'

'Of course. I'd expect that.'

'Right, I'll see what I can do and let you know. Give me your address and telephone number, if you have one. I'll talk to Pauline Gower about you. She's the head of the women's branch of the ATA. She's the one who selects and tests recruits.'

When Daisy had written down the details for her, Jane said, 'Sorry to be in a rush, but I have to fly.' She laughed. 'Literally.'

'She's nice,' Daisy murmured to Paul as Jane hurried away.

'They all are. I know quite a few of the ATA girls. They're a merry bunch. You'd fit in well, Daisy.'

Jake met Daisy and George at the station and, when they arrived at the hall, the whole family were waiting for them in the parlour. As he walked through the door, George braced himself. He had spent a restless night rehearsing what he would say, yet now all his ideas fled from his mind. But the Maitlands were far too polite to bombard him with questions.

Tea and coffee were served and the usual greetings and enquiries about health were exchanged. When they had all been served, a silence descended on the room. Now they were waiting for him to speak. Now they expected an explanation.

George took a deep breath. 'I can't tell you very much. I'm sure you all understand why. Pips is away doing valuable war work. She *is* in this country and she is safe and well. I can't tell you more than that.' He glanced at Daisy. 'That was what Daisy wanted to know and what I expect is uppermost in your minds. There is an address you can write to – Daisy has it. You will hear from her and she will telephone you whenever she can, but please, don't ask her questions she won't be able to answer.'

'It seems all very cloak and dagger,' Edwin laughed, 'but we understand, George, and we won't embarrass you by firing questions at you – or her, I promise.'

Henrietta pursed her lips, as if physically trying to still the questions. At last she sighed. 'Of course we'll do as you ask, George, but will you promise me one thing?'

'I will if I can.'

'That if ever there is anything we really should know, you will be the one to tell us?'

'Yes, I promise you that.'

'Then I think we should all accept that Philippa

is doing what she feels she must' – Henrietta smiled wryly – 'as she has done before, and respect her decision.'

The atmosphere in the room seemed to relax, but it was Daisy who now caused a stir.

'Um – I wasn't completely honest about my trip to London.'

All eyes now turned to her; all except George's, for he knew what was coming.

'I'll just come straight out with it . . .'

'When did you ever *not*?' Robert murmured, only to be shushed by Alice.

'I want to join the ATA.'

The other members of the family – apart from George – glanced at each other mystified.

'Don't you mean the ATS?' Henrietta said.

'No, Granny. It's the Air Transport Auxiliary.'

'Flying!' Three voices spoke at once. Only Edwin and George remained silent, but they exchanged a glance.

'Is this because of Luke? Are you trying to follow his example?' Robert asked.

Daisy shook her head. 'No, if anything I'm to blame for *him* wanting to fly. And certainly, we're both to blame for Harry joining the RAF too. At least, that's what Granddad Dawson thinks.'

'But what about here?' Henrietta said. 'You're doing so well and we work wonderfully together. Aren't you happy here, Daisy? I thought it was what you wanted.'

'I do, Granny. One day, I will be quite content to take over running the estate from you, but not yet.'

'Well, I'll step down now, if that's what you want. You can have complete control.'

Daisy shook her head. 'No, Granny, that's not it at all. I love working alongside you. But – but this is something different. I ought to do my bit—'

'But you are. What can be more important than feeding the nation?'

'Ferrying aircraft from the factories to the airfields where the RAF pilots need them,' she answered promptly. 'That's what the ATA do and they're re-cruiting women pilots.'

They all stared at her again and Robert murmured, 'Well, Mother, I don't think even you can argue with that.'

'Is it dangerous?' Alice asked, her voice wavering.

'Not really,' George put in. 'The aircraft won't be armed and the women pilots won't be delivering aircraft abroad like the men do.'

There was a long silence whilst each member of the family struggled with their feelings before giving an answer. At last it was Edwin who said, 'Well, my dearest Daisy, we didn't stand in the way of your father or your aunt going to the front in 1914 and we won't stand in your way either, though of course we can't promise not to worry about you.'

Daisy glanced at her parents. Neither of them had spoken. They were looking at each other, holding hands tightly. Then they turned to face her. There were tears in Alice's eyes, but she said bravely, 'Of course you must go, Daisy, but, please, take care.'

*

Over dinner they all kept the topics of conversation to local matters, but they couldn't escape from the talk of the war for very long.

'D'you know, I feel as if I've been away for weeks instead of just for a weekend,' Daisy said. 'Has anyone heard from Harry yet?'

Henrietta shook her head. 'I ask Betty almost every day, but Peggy has heard nothing. He really is a little rascal not to write to his mother.'

Daisy laughed. 'I doubt he's much of a letter writer, Granny. He'll just turn up like a bad penny whenever he gets leave. How is Granddad Dawson coping without both of them?'

'Betty told me the other day that he's taken on two young lads from the village, one to work under him in the wheelwright's and the other with Sam in the blacksmith's shop. And do you remember the evacuee boy at the Boxing Day party? The one who's staying with Peggy and Sam and who stood at the side of the room for most of the time?'

'Yes. What about him?'

'Len got talking to him that day and ever since then, whenever he's not at school, he goes down to Len's workshop to watch them at work.'

'And Granddad doesn't mind?'

'Far from it. Betty says he encourages him.'

'Really? I thought he didn't want anything to do with the evacuees.'

'I think,' Henrietta said slowly, 'it's because he found out that the boy's name is Bernard.'

'Ah, that would explain it. And how are those little twin girls whom Mrs Everton took? Dear me, I really must get out into the village more. With being so busy here on the estate and now that the boys don't come riding any more on Saturdays, I seem so out of touch.'

Henrietta's face lit up. 'Oh Daisy, you should see them. Mrs Everton has worked wonders. They're well dressed and such pretty little girls. June and Joan, they're called.' Her face clouded for a moment. 'The only thing that worries me is that Mrs Everton is besotted with them. How she's going to be when they have to go back home, I daren't think.'

There was silence around the table for a few moments as they all finished eating.

'Uncle George,' Daisy asked, 'I know you can't say much, but can you tell me why on earth Russia invaded Finland at the end of November?'

'Stalin says he needs part of Finland to defend Leningrad. They thought it would be a walkover, but they reckoned without the Finns' ferocity.'

'And where do you think Hitler will turn his attention next, then?' Robert asked.

'Sorry, that's classified.'

'Fair enough.'

'I hope he won't go for poor little Belgium again. They had more than enough last time.'

Alice turned frightened eyes on Robert. 'Oh no! What will happen to William and his family if he does?'

*

As the women rose from the table, Henrietta said, 'I hope you've all enjoyed your dinner because rationing of certain foods has already come into force and I understand that meat will be added to the list next month. The Government is stopping all slaughtering whilst it sets up a control scheme. Now, Alice – Daisy – we'll go into the parlour. Join us when you're ready, gentlemen.'

As the door closed behind them, George said to Robert, 'May I have a private word with you in your consulting room?'

Robert glanced at him, for a moment startled by the request. 'Of course. Will you excuse us, please, Father?'

'Of course. In that case, I will join the ladies.'

George seemed to hesitate for a moment before saying, 'Perhaps it would be best if you came too.'

'Really?' Edwin frowned. 'Is there something wrong, my boy? Medically, I mean.'

'Oh no, nothing like that, but I think I should take you a little further into my confidence. I only asked for us to go into your consulting room because—'

At that moment, Wainwright appeared in the room and George waved his hand towards him as if to indicate why he needed more privacy.

'Ah, yes,' Edwin said, rising from his chair. 'I see. Wainwright, would you take the port and three glasses into Robert's consulting room, and then you can clear in here?'

'Very good, sir.'

When they were seated in the room and the door firmly closed, George said, 'First, I must impress upon you that this is top secret. You cannot tell anyone of this conversation – not even your wives. I suppose I really ought to get you to sign the Official

220

Secrets Act before I say any more.' He chuckled as he added, 'But I'll risk it. Have you heard of Bletchley Park?'

Edwin and Robert exchanged a puzzled look. 'No.'

When George paused, Robert said quietly, 'And that's where Pips is?'

'Yes. I recommended her for the work.'

Both men gaped at him. 'But you'll hardly see her for the duration of the war.'

A bleak look crossed George's face. 'I wasn't seeing much of her even when she was in London. Not recently anyway. She'll get time off and she'll come home then, or we'll meet up outside London. You see, there's another reason I put her name forward. London will be a prime target for Hitler's bombs. I wanted her safely out of the way.'

'But you'll still be there.'

George shrugged. 'As long as Pips is relatively safe.'

'It's always about Pips, isn't it?' Robert said softly. 'You always put her first.'

'Of course,' George said, as if it was the most natural thing in the world. To him, it was. 'I only wish I could think of some way to get Rebecca out of the city too, but I can't. She's determined to nurse and Matthew, well, of course he's in the same line of work as me, though at the Foreign Office. And we can't possibly leave.'

'Well, thank you for telling us,' Edwin said. 'Of course, we give you our solemn promise not to say anything to anyone else, but please ask Pips to keep in touch with us whenever she can.'

'And are you really all right about Daisy?' George asked.

'Yes – and no,' Robert said. 'Of course, I shall worry about her, but I'm proud of her too.' He glanced at his father. 'Now I know how Mother and Father felt in 1914 when Pips and I went to the front. But they didn't try to stop us and nor will I try to prevent Daisy from doing what she feels she must.'

'I feel responsible,' George said. 'After all, it was when she came to stay with us that she was introduced to flying.'

Edwin and Robert both laughed. 'Don't blame yourself, George. If anyone was to blame for that, as you put it, it was Pips. Now, shall we join the ladies?'

Twenty-Seven

'Have you heard anything from Pauline Gower?' Daisy asked on her weekly telephone call to Gill towards the end of the month.

'Not a thing. I'm thinking of writing to her myself.'

'So am I. Let's do that, Gill. It can't do any harm and she'll see how keen we are.'

'They might accept you because you already have a pilot's licence, but I've got nothing – yet.'

'How's it going with Lord Bunny?'

Daisy heard Gill's chuckle down the wire. 'Amazingly well. He's arranged for me to have flying lessons locally with someone who's a qualified instructor, so that I can get my licence. Dad's going to pay for the lessons. My mum and dad have been so good about it all. What about yours?'

'The same.'

'Your granny's not too mad at you for planning to leave her in the lurch?'

Daisy giggled. 'No, she understands.'

'So,' Gill said, as she ended the conversation, 'let's both write those letters.'

Several weeks passed and still they heard nothing. Gill completed her training and applied for her pilot's licence. 'Now, we can go together,' she told Daisy.

'*If* we ever hear anything,' was Daisy's morose reply.

'We'll just have to be patient. The poor woman is probably inundated with nutcases like us wanting to fly her precious aeroplanes.'

'Patience is *not* one of my virtues,' Daisy retorted and they ended the call in a fit of the giggles.

The whole country was shocked by Hitler's swift advance through Western Europe. In April, his army invaded Denmark and Norway.

Alice was tearful. 'What will happen to William and his family if Hitler invades Belgium? Will they be taken prisoner? I mean, we won't get any more letters now, will we? I won't hear anything.' William's letters had been spasmodic of late and now Alice realized that she would probably not receive any more.

Robert put his arm around her and held her close. 'We'll ask George if he can find out anything for us. Besides, the Germans can't take every Belgian prisoner.'

Her eyes swimming with tears, Alice looked up at him. 'But William's British. They'll think he's a spy, or something.'

'He's lived there since the end of the last war, darling. He has a Belgian wife and family. Try not to worry. I think William will be quite safe.'

On 10 May, a momentous day, the Dutch and Belgians fell to the German invaders and Winston Churchill became Prime Minister in Britain following Chamberlain's resignation. He faced an uphill task, one that would involve some difficult and heart-breaking decisions, but his bulldog attitude and his patriotic speeches inspired everyone.

'He's the man for the job, no doubt about that,' Robert said confidently when the news gave the Maitlands and all those around them hope for the future even though the war news only got worse.

'The Germans have reached Amiens on the Somme,' Robert said over the dinner table a few days later. His eyes met Alice's gaze, as they both remembered the horrors they had witnessed.

'Not again,' Alice whispered. 'What must the poor folk who live there be going through?'

'It doesn't bear thinking about,' Robert said solemnly.

'Now that *is* something else I could do,' Edwin said.

'No, you couldn't. Not at your age. Old men running about with guns and bayonets. Don't be ridiculous, Edwin.'

'But it would give me a bit of exercise, Hetty, my love. And Conrad will be on hand. He's going to be the captain, I think, because he served in the last war. And Sam is going to be his sergeant. I'll be well looked after, I promise you. And I do so want to be involved in something useful.'

Henrietta sighed and then asked, 'What about Robert? Is he going to join this – whatever they're calling it?'

'The LDV – the Local Defence Volunteers. Didn't you hear Anthony Eden's broadcast just over a week ago asking for men not serving in the forces to form such units all over the country? The newspapers say there has been a magnificent response. But no, Robert doesn't feel it's for him.' They were silent for a moment before Edwin added, 'He's going to offer his services as an air-raid warden in the village, though whether they'll accept him or not, I don't know.'

'Oh well, you must do what you want. But do be careful, Edwin. You are eighty now.'

'As everyone keeps reminding me,' he murmured wryly.

'Have you still not heard anything?' Daisy asked Gill over the telephone.

'No, but I've written again to Miss Gower and told her all about the flying lessons I've been having with a qualified instructor and that I've applied for my pilot's licence and that I expect to get it any time soon. I also reminded her about you – that we applied together and want to join together, if that's possible.'

Two days after this conversation, they both received letters inviting them to a flying test. They travelled to Hatfield Airfield together. They had both dressed conservatively, but smartly. They wanted to give the impression of being capable and committed. The first pilots in the women's branch of the ATA had been subject to some scepticism and even derision in the press. Even Lord Haw-Haw had made deroga- tory remarks about the women pilots of the ATA in his Nazi propaganda broadcasts. Daisy and Gill knew they had to be on their best behaviour – at least for now.

'Wow,' Gill muttered as they passed the security gates and looked around them. The airfield was alive with aeroplanes taking off and landing, with ground staff and engineers busy everywhere. They found the ATA offices in a small wooden hut behind the de Havilland aircraft factory and reported to the adjutant on duty. She gave them instructions and soon they were walking towards a Tiger Moth.

'Good old Lord Bunny. At least I know what I'm doing with this aircraft.'

'Me too.' Daisy grinned. 'Thanks to Uncle Mitch and Jeff. I've had a flight in the one Uncle Mitch has at Brooklands.'

'Our trouble is going to be that we haven't much experience on anything else.'

'I expect there'll still be some sort of ATA training if we get in. The woman Paul introduced me to said as much. Come on, let's go and find whoever's testing us and see which of us is going up first.'

The pilot testing them was probably in his early forties. He was tall and thin and smiled very little. But Daisy was not one to judge. In these difficult times, no one knew what unhappiness another person was coping with.

She climbed into the cockpit and prepared herself.

'Three circuits and landings,' the pilot said curtly through the speaking tube. How different he was from the calm, encouraging tones of Jeff Pointer, but Daisy straightened her shoulders, carried out all the checks she needed to do and took off smoothly. Once in the air, however, the aircraft swung from left to right and Daisy fought to bring it under control. Her first landing was bumpy – not at all what she had hoped to achieve. Her second and third take-offs and landings were better, though not as perfect as she would have liked. She just hoped they were good enough.

Gill went next and Daisy watched her from the ground. Her flights seemed to go much better.

As they walked back to the office, Daisy moaned, 'I made a right pig's ear of it. I don't think they'll pass me.'

'You've got more flying hours than me. That's my worry.'

They each had an interview with the Commander, though it was more like a friendly chat.

'We are developing our own training programme,' she told them. 'You start by ferrying light, single-engine aeroplanes. You will then be given further training and testing so that you can advance to other "classes" of more powerful aircraft at your own pace and on your own merits rather than by any set time. Once you are qualified to fly a particular "class", you are then given detailed ferry-pilot notes to enable you to fly similar aircraft within that class, but which you may not actually have flown before.'

Daisy nodded enthusiastically, but could hardly contain her excitement. 'How long will it take to graduate to flying Spitfires?'

The Commander smiled indulgently. 'Sadly, at present, women are not permitted to fly combat aircraft. But never fear, Miss Maitland, we are working on that.'

They returned home to wait for an agonizing week

until they were told that they had both passed the test. They were to be issued with passes and told to be fitted for a uniform. They were to report back to Hatfield in the middle of June.

'Aunty Milly wants to take us both to her Savile Row tailor to be fitted properly for a uniform. Her treat,' Daisy told Gill over the telephone. She giggled. 'She's heard some horrific tales of the girls not being fitted properly because the tailors are men and too embarrassed to measure them properly!'

'Oh, but I can't let Mrs Whittaker pay for my uniform.'

'Yes, you can. She says it's a gift to us both. We're to go as soon as we can and stay with her until they're made, which should be just in time for us to report back to Hatfield on the date we've been given. Oh, do say yes, Gill. We've got a war to win.'

Twenty-Eight

By the end of May, the news was even worse. British troops were surrounded by German forces, pushed back against the French coast after having fought valiantly to save towns like Calais and Boulogne. They were overwhelmed. Trapped by the advancing enemy around Dunkirk, the British army faced annihilation or capture. There was nowhere left to retreat except into the sea.

'They say in the papers that you can see the bombing and fires from our south coast,' Robert told the family.

'How are they going to rescue our boys?' Henrietta asked, but Robert could only shake his head sadly. He had no answer.

Flying over the beaches in an attempt to keep the Stukas at bay, Luke saw for himself the hordes of allied soldiers hiding in the sand dunes or just lying on the beaches as if they were resigned to their fate. But he also saw, a little further inland, fierce resistance from the British and their comrades, still trying to cover the retreat. To his horror, he saw lines of refugees amongst the fleeing soldiers being mown down by the enemy. No one was being spared – not even children. Time and again, he returned to England to refuel and go back. He had to do whatever he could to fight off the foe in the air. And then he saw it. Far below him, ploughing their way through the choppy seas, were dozens of ships and boats of all sizes – a veritable armada – crossing the Channel from Sheerness to Dunkirk. Able to get closer to the shore, they could pick up the soldiers and ferry them to the bigger ships waiting offshore. Pointing the nose of his Spitfire skywards, he went to work, seeking and finding enemy aircraft heading towards the beaches, trying to cut them off before they arrived. He could do nothing to help those below except to stop as many aircraft as he could from dive-bombing and shooting at the soldiers as they waded out into the water towards the first boats to arrive.

Operation Dynamo went on for several days. It had been hoped to rescue about forty-five thousand men, but by the end of the mission, a remarkable figure of over three hundred and thirty thousand men of the British Expeditionary Force, French and Belgian troops had been rescued. The British soldiers who had remained behind to hold back the enemy for as long as possible were taken prisoner, but they had fought bravely and with great sacrifice to help save their fellow soldiers. Even army doctors drew lots to see who should stay behind to tend the wounded. They, too, were likely to be taken prisoner.

'I've never seen anything like it,' Luke said as he discussed the events with his fellow airmen. 'If ever a potential tragedy was turned into a triumph, then that was it and we got to see it for ourselves.'

France fought on but on 10 June, Mussolini declared war on the Allies and four days later, German troops marched up the Champs-Élysées as Nazi swastikas flew from the Eiffel Tower and the Arc de Triomphe. Hitler danced with glee. Paris had fallen and thousands of refugees left the city heading south, only to be dive-bombed by enemy aircraft yet again. In an act of bitter revenge, Hitler sought the capitulation of France and demanded that they sign the surrender in the same train coach that had been used for the German surrender in 1918. By the end of the month, half of France was under occupation and on 1 July, Germany invaded the Channel Islands.

'That's the closest he's going to get,' Luke and his fellow pilots declared.

One of the most heartbreaking decisions the British Prime Minister would have to make – and there were to be many more – was the sinking of the French fleet on 3 July to prevent it falling into German hands. Marshal Pétain, the leader of Vichy France, broke ties with Britain because of this action and a few days later declared that France was a Fascist state.

'Father, have you seen this?' Robert asked, when they met at breakfast. 'German troops have landed on the Channel Islands – without opposition.'

Edwin stared at him for a moment. 'Now that surprises me. That it's without opposition, I mean.'

'It says here that they were thought too difficult to defend, but a lot of the residents have already been brought to the mainland together with livestock and crops.' Robert allowed himself a wry smile.

'Trying to make it as difficult for the invaders as possible, I expect.'

'Good,' Edwin said with asperity. 'Though I expect there'll be a lot who've had to stay.'

'Yes, let's hope it's not too bad for those left behind. But it brings our enemy a little bit too close for my liking.'

'Tiger Moths? Is that all we're going to be flying?' Daisy said in disgust. 'But I want to fly Spitfires.'

They had been at Hatfield for two weeks, sharing a room in a house only walking distance from the airfield. During that time all they'd been allowed to fly were Tiger Moths to different parts of the country. Daisy had even flown the open-cockpit aeroplane to Scotland on a rainy June day with three other pilots. She'd been numb with cold when they'd landed and the journey south hadn't been much better on a draughty, overcrowded train.

'And why do we have to fly with two or three others? Why can't we go on our own?'

'We have to fly within sight of the ground,' Gill reminded her calmly. 'Keep to our special routes to avoid barrage balloons, and so that we're easily identified as friendly aircraft by the ground defence. On our own, they might start taking potshots at us, if they think we're an enemy spy.'

'In a Tiger Moth?' Daisy said scathingly.

'It's probably exactly what they would use.' Gill laughed at her and then added, 'Cheer up, Daisy. I've got a bit of good news. It's been agreed that some of us are going to be sent to the Central Flying School at Upavon to fly single-engine trainers' – she paused for effect – 'used by the RAF to teach their pilots to fly fighter aeroplanes.'

Daisy stared at her. 'Why?'

'Because that will take us nearer to being able to fly other aircraft.'

'Spitfires?' Daisy's eyes lit up.

'Not immediately, but maybe one day. Daisy, you just have to realize that we've got to prove ourselves – doubly so, because we're women. Come on, we've got to go and pick up our chits for today's deliveries from the office. Let's toe the line and do everything we're asked to do and maybe – just maybe – we'll be amongst the first ones to be sent to Upavon.'

'Oh Mrs Maitland – do come in.' Norah held her back door wide open. 'Have you heard about the Channel Islands? He's getting a bit close for our liking, but Sam says we shouldn't worry 'cos Luke and the other RAF lads will keep him at bay. Have you come on WVS business?' Norah was quite chatty these days. She had found confidence through mixing with the other women in the village and she was no longer quite so in awe of Henrietta.

'Not really. I just came to see how you are, Mrs Dawson, and how you feel about Daisy having joined the ATA. She is your granddaughter as well as ours.'

'Come through. Bess, Peggy and Clara are here for a bit of a natter. We're just having a cuppa. Would you like one?'

'I would *love* a cup of tea. I've been traipsing around the village checking on all the evacuees. It's quite tiring, I must admit.' She smiled at Norah. The village women had become closer through their war work and whilst they were still respectful of Henrietta's position in their community, they all now looked upon her as a friend as well as someone they had always known they could turn to in times of trouble and, in these very turbulent times, they needed her to take the lead.

Having greeted the other women, Henrietta sat down and accepted the cup of tea gratefully. Each woman there was busily knitting as they chatted, their needles never slowing.

'We've been thinking of ways we could raise some money for a Spitfire fund,' Clara said. 'I've been reading about it in the papers. What with the cost of the last war and then the Depression, our government's coffers aren't exactly overflowing, so ordinary folks all over the country are starting to collect money to help build more Spitfires. And we can do our bit too. I've suggested having a jumble sale at the church. We could involve the other villages. Skellingthorpe, for one. Maybe even Nettleham and Saxilby. What do you think, Mrs Maitland?'

'That's an excellent idea, Mrs Nuttall. May I leave you to organize that and if you need Jake to collect from other places, you only have to ask?'

Clara beamed with importance.

'And how *is* Daisy?' Norah asked. 'She came to say "goodbye" to us all, but she wasn't able to tell us much about what she'll be doing. I expect she didn't really know herself then.'

'Enjoying every minute of her new life, apparently.

She telephones about once a week. She's still training, of course, but as both she and Gill already had a pilot's licence, I don't expect it will be long before they're ferrying aircraft around the country.'

'Is that what she'll be doing?' Bess asked.

Henrietta nodded. 'Collecting them from the factories and taking them to wherever they're needed. I believe they also sometimes have to fly aircraft that need overhauling or repairing.' Henrietta now glanced at Peggy. 'Have you heard from Luke recently? He hasn't been home on leave for ages.'

Peggy shook her head. 'Luke's not much of a letter writer and Harry's even worse.'

Henrietta sighed. 'I gathered as much. Poor Kitty is often in tears.'

'She comes to see me most days on the way home from the farm,' Peggy said. 'Just to see if there's any news.'

'She's a nice girl.'

'She is,' Peggy said. 'But you know what Harry is. He's not serious about any girl at the moment.'

'How's Bernard settling in with you?'

Peggy smiled. 'Wonderfully – though I don't see much of him. When he's not at school, he's at the workshop. Sam says he's already a good little worker for his age and he talks about nothing else when he's at home with us.' Peggy laughed. 'Poor Sam. I think he'd like to forget about work for a bit, but the lad's that keen to learn.'

'Years ago, when the school-leaving age was twelve, he would already be a working man,' Henrietta reminded them.

'What'll happen when Luke and Harry come back?' Clara asked, no doubt thinking of the future for both her son, Sam, and her grandson, Harry.

'By the time they come home, Clara, duck,' Bess said, 'war'll be over and all the evacuees'll go home.'

A silence hung over the room but no one wanted to be the one to voice what was in all of their minds. *If* Luke and Harry come back.

Twenty-Nine

A few days later, Luke came home on a seventy-two-hour leave, but there was no sign of Harry.

'D'you know what he's doing, Luke?' Sam asked. 'Because we never hear a word from him.'

'He's training to fly bombers, as far as I know.'

'Do you know where he is at the moment?'

Luke shook his head. 'No, but I'll try and find out for you, if I can.' He paused and then said, 'I'm being posted to the south coast. That's why I've got leave to come home. It – it might be a while before I see you again.'

He watched his parents as they glanced at each other and then looked back at him. 'You're not daft, either of you, so I'm not going to hide anything from you. You went through the last war, so you know better than us young ones just what war is all about and I think we're about to find out for ourselves. As you know, Italy declared war on the Allies in the middle of June and, a week later, Churchill announced that Britain fights on alone. It's thought – and I suppose I'm asking you not to discuss this with anyone else – that Germany intends the Luftwaffe to get control of the skies as a prelude to invading England.' He took a deep breath. 'So, if that is the case, there's only the RAF to stop them.'

Peggy gulped and covered her mouth with trembling fingers. She tried to stop her tears from flowing, but couldn't. Luke crossed the space between them and put his arms around her. 'You'd rather I was honest with you, wouldn't you?'

She nodded against his shoulder, but could not speak.

'I'm flying a Spitfire – the best little fighter aeroplane there is. I'm sure Daisy and her mates will soon be bringing them to us as they're made – though they're not allowed to fly Hurricanes and Spitfires yet. And all that's thanks to the collecting that the civilian population is doing. And then there's Harry waiting with his bomber. How can we possibly fail, Mam, with the Doddington gang out in force?'

Peggy tried to laugh, but it came out as a sob.

Sam gripped Luke's shoulder and said huskily, 'I'll look after her, Luke. You just take care of yourself. That's all we ask.'

Flying at the designated height above the ground, Daisy had no such worries. Her days were filled with delivering aircraft safely to their destination. Secretly, she was rather enjoying her war, but she would not have uttered such a thing to another soul, even though she was still flying the draughty Tiger Moths to wherever they were needed. But in a week or so's time, she and Gill were to go to Upavon for further training. Maybe then . . .

She landed at Duxford, taxied to where she was

directed and climbed out, taking the hand an RAF pilot held out to her. As she jumped to the ground, she looked up into his face.

'Good Lord. You!'

Johnny grinned at her. 'You've no idea how many ferry pilots I've greeted over the past fortnight hoping it would be you. Come on. I'll take you to the mess and get you a slap-up meal.'

Daisy glanced at her watch. 'Is the Fox Moth here yet? Gill's piloting it today.'

The Fox Moth, still an open-cockpit aircraft, had an enclosed cabin below that could carry four passengers. It was used as a taxi to pick up pilots so that they could return to base all the more quickly to deliver more aircraft. Today, Gill was piloting the taxi.

Johnny glanced about him. 'I don't think so. I haven't seen it. Anyway, aren't there more pilots to come in yet, for it to collect?'

Daisy grinned. 'Yes, at least two that I know of, so "Lead on, McDuff".'

'Oh my! Bacon, eggs, sausages, fried bread *and* mushrooms. You certainly know how to spoil a girl, Johnny Hammond.'

'How's the rationing affecting your family?'

'Not too badly, I think. 'Course, living in the country, things are a little easier for us. Everyone in the village is digging up their flower borders and planting more vegetables.'

'Ah yes, "Dig for Victory". Is your grandmother coping without you?'

'Granny will always cope, Johnny, but, yes, she's doing fine. She's got a lot more to do with all the Ministry of Agriculture directives coming through regularly, but she still finds time to lead the local branch of the WVS, though Mummy helps her a lot with that.'

'And what about Luke? Do you hear from him?'

'Now and again. Did you know Harry's joined the RAF too?'

'Really?'

Daisy nodded. 'I've no idea where either of them are, though I do know Luke's been posted down south somewhere.'

'Right,' Johnny said vaguely. He was quiet for a few moments, watching her eat. As she cleared the plate and laid down her knife and fork, he said, 'Daisy, are you delivering a lot to airfields in the south?'

'All over the country really, but, yes, now that you mention it, we do take a lot to southern aerodromes. Why do you ask?'

He leaned closer and lowered his voice. 'We're doing a lot of flying over France now – since the Dunkirk evacuation – and we can see for ourselves that the German Luftwaffe is gathering on the French coast. Everyone here is pretty sure they're going to try to get control of the skies prior to a land invasion and there're only us fighter pilots – and our bombers – to prevent an invasion because, despite all his posturing, I believe that's what Hitler intends.'

'I agree. I never did believe his "peace" moves. He wants to dominate the whole world.' She was quiet for a moment before muttering, 'God help us all, if he ever gets here.'

Johnny reached across the table and clasped her hand. 'It's up to us to stop it, Daisy. Me, Luke, Harry and the rest. And you too, Daisy. You and your fellow ferry pilots. You've got to keep bringing us the aircraft we need.'

'We will – if only they'll let us loose on the aircraft you *really* need. The Hurricanes and Spitfires.'

Johnny sighed. 'I know – and they really ought to let you fly those too. But just think of it this way. At least by flying the other types of aircraft, you're freeing up the men to fly the combat aircraft.'

Daisy pulled a face. 'I suppose so,' she agreed reluctantly.

'Where are you based? Maybe I can come over to see you when I get leave?'

'Still at Hatfield at the moment.'

His face lit up. 'Why, that's no distance. Not on my motorcycle. Look . . .' He fished in his pocket for a scrap of paper and a stubby pencil. 'Here's a telephone number you can ring when you know you're going to be off duty. I'll do my best to wangle some leave.'

As Daisy tucked the paper into her pocket, Johnny said, 'You look awfully smart in that uniform. It suits you.'

As they left the mess hall, Daisy looked up towards the noise of a Fox Moth coming in to land. 'There's my taxi.'

'Have you any more deliveries today?'

'Yes, one to Tangmere.'

As the Fox Moth's pilot climbed out, took off her helmet and shook out her hair, Daisy said, 'Here's Gill.'

'Hey, you two,' Gill called out cheerily. 'Was this planned?'

'No,' they chorused.

'Well, it should have been,' Gill chuckled.

'I didn't know he'd be here,' Daisy protested, but she was laughing as she said it.

A little sheepishly, Johnny said, 'But I've been watching out for weeks, hoping she'd make a delivery here.'

Gill stepped between them and linked arms. 'Right, I'm gagging for a cuppa. Are the other two girls here yet?'

'One is. Violet – but there's no sign of Ivy,' Johnny said.

'I know Violet, but I don't think I've met Ivy,' Daisy added.

'She's new. Only arrived yesterday straight from training.' Gill glanced worriedly at the sky. 'I hope she's all right.'

'She'll be fine. It's not as if it's bad weather for her first delivery, is it?'

'Mm.' Gill paused and then, with a final glance at the sky, said, 'Right, let's go and find that tea whilst we wait.'

Violet joined them at their table and the four chatted amiably for over an hour until Gill said, 'I'd better ring our ops manager and ask what I ought to do. No good delaying any longer.'

'I think that'd be a good idea,' Daisy said. 'I've

got another delivery to make this afternoon and you know we have to land before dark. It'll probably mean I'll have to stay overnight.'

'Go to the office, Gill. They'll let you ring from there,' Johnny said. He turned back to Daisy. 'You'll have to bring an aircraft here late one afternoon and stay the night, Daisy.'

'We have to do as we're told, don't we, Violet?' Daisy said primly, but her eyes were sparkling as she said it.

'I haven't known you and Gill long, but I get the distinct feeling that that's not always the case.' Violet got up. 'I'm just going to powder my nose. Won't be a minute.'

As the girl moved away, Daisy said, 'By the way, I haven't asked you how Uncle Mitch is?'

'He's fine. Got himself involved with fire watching in London. And – don't tell a soul, Daisy – but he and Jeff have got involved in something highly secretive.'

'Really? A bit like Aunty Pips, then. No one knows exactly where she is or what she's doing.' Daisy laughed. 'She's not allowed to tell anyone – not even George, by the sound of it, though I expect he knows more than he's letting on.' She paused and then added, 'Has Uncle Mitch got a girlfriend?'

'Dozens of them, I expect, knowing my uncle, but no one special.' He put his head on one side. 'I think you know why, don't you?'

Daisy opened her mouth, about to say something, when Gill returned. Her face was white and her eyes wide. At once, Daisy said, 'What is it?'

'Ivy crashed on take-off.'

'Oh no! Is she . . . ?'

'In hospital. Critically injured, but still alive. At the moment.' Gill bit her lip. 'They don't think it was her fault, but something went wrong with the aircraft and, probably because of her inexperience, she didn't know how to handle it.'

'That's awful.'

Violet returned at that moment. When they told her, her eyes filled with tears. 'She'd become my closest friend. We joined on the same day, went through training together and then she followed me to Hatfield.'

'Come on, we'd better get back. By the way, Daisy, someone else has done your second delivery.'

'You all right to fly, Gill?' Johnny asked.

Gill looked at him a little disdainfully. Her voice was tight as she said, 'Perfectly, thank you. We're professionals, just like you are. If one of your mates gets shot down, you don't give up, do you?'

'Gill, he didn't mean . . .'

At once, her face softened. 'Sorry, Johnny, I know you meant well, but we have to carry on – just like you do.'

'I apologize, Gill. But don't believe all you hear about us. One of our lads got shot down last week. His aircraft went down in flames. There was no hope and his closest mate, who saw it happen, hasn't flown since. He's on sick leave at the moment. So, we're not as tough as they make out. As they *have* to make out. Come on, I'll walk you to your aeroplane.'

As they neared the aircraft, Johnny took Daisy's

arm and held her back for a moment. He hugged her hard, not caring who might see, and whispered. 'Do take care of yourself, Daisy Maitland.'

She hugged him in return and said, in a voice that shook a little, 'You too, Johnny Hammond.'

Gill flew the aircraft perfectly and they landed safely back at base, but all three girls probably breathed a sigh of relief. Daisy certainly did. A pall of sadness and an unusual silence hung over the base and when Gill and Daisy returned to their billet, neither of them felt like talking, so they had supper and went to the room they shared.

They were soon in bed, but Daisy was sure neither of them was going to sleep well that night.

I just hope, she thought, *that they don't hear about the crash at home.*

Thirty

'Robert,' Alice said, her eyes wide with anxiety, 'I haven't heard anything from William for weeks.'

'Sadly, darling, I don't think you will. Sending letters out of an occupied country must be virtually impossible.'

'And there's been no telephone call from Pips or from Daisy recently and no one has any idea where Luke or Harry are now.'

'Luke will be a bit busy, I'm afraid, if he's down south now. And I have no doubt Daisy is, too, for the same reason, though she won't be in danger like Luke will be. He'll soon be fighting the Luftwaffe over the south of England – if he isn't already – and Daisy will be delivering all sorts of planes to the airfields, though as I understand it, only non-combat aircraft.' He forbore to add 'up to now'. Alice looked terrified already. Robert put his arm around her. 'I do have a number I can ring to leave a message for Daisy. Would you like me to do that?'

'Oh please, Robert. I – I just want to know she's all right, that's all.'

Later that day, Robert managed to get through to the offices at Hatfield where a member of staff assured him that Daisy was safe and well. 'She's not here at the moment, but I will tell her you rang,' was all the woman was able to say.

The telephone at the hall shrilled just as Robert and Alice were mounting the stairs to go to bed.

'Oh!' Alice said, startled. 'I hate telephone calls late at night. I always think it's going to be bad news.' She ran lightly down the stairs and reached the phone before Robert had even turned round.

'Hello – hello—'

'Mummy – it's me. I'm so sorry I haven't called recently. We've been so busy. I've had to stay away a couple of nights this week and it's difficult asking to use telephones for private calls.'

'I understand, darling. I just wanted to know if you're all right, that's all.'

'I'm fine and so's Gill. She's beside me, waiting to ring her parents too. Is everyone your end well?'

'Yes, but a bit anxious, as you might guess. Daisy – do you know where Luke is? We've heard nothing from him.'

'No, sorry, I don't. I did bump into Johnny not long ago, so maybe I'll see Luke some time. I'll let you know if I do.'

'We're all trying to busy ourselves with war work, but it's so hard, not hearing for weeks on end.'

'I know, Mummy. Look, I've got to go, but I'll try to write or ring you more often. I promise.'

Alice replaced the receiver slowly, reluctant to break the connection. 'She's all right, Robert, but she doesn't seem to know where Luke is. She's seen Johnny though.'

She climbed back up the stairs.

'Did she say where she'd met Johnny?'

Alice shook her head. 'No, I expect it was at one of the airfields. Maybe she's not supposed to say.'

'Probably not. Now, come on, let's get to bed. Perhaps you'll sleep a little better tonight at least.'

Two days after their telephone calls home, Gill, Daisy and two other ferry pilots were due to take Tiger Moths to Tangmere on the south coast. They would be picked up by the Anson, a much larger taxi aircraft that could carry more pilots. Daisy and Gill were not yet qualified to fly it, though they hoped that after their sojourn at Upavon, they would be.

As Daisy taxied to a halt at Tangmere, Gill came running towards her, impatient for her to climb down. 'He's here. I've found him.'

'Who?'

'Luke, of course.'

'Really?'

'Yes, come on. We're all in the mess hall. We were waiting for you.'

'It'll have to be quick. We ought to get back. The Anson should be here any minute.'

'Oh, you've time for a quick cuppa.' Gill grasped Daisy's arm and almost dragged her towards where the other two ferry girls were sitting, surrounded by a gaggle of RAF pilots. The air was filled with laughter and they appeared to have not a care in the world. Seeing them, no one would have guessed that the previous day they had lost two of their fellow fighter pilots or that at any moment the bell that called them to their aircraft and into the air might jangle.

'Hey, Dais.' Luke rose at once and came towards her, arms outstretched. He kissed her on both cheeks in cousinly fashion and then led her to a chair. 'I'll get you some tea. Biscuit?'

'Please.'

As he moved away, Gill said, 'I've been asking about him at every aerodrome I've been to in the south for weeks, but today I struck lucky.'

'You're lucky they told you. I've been asking too, but all I get is a blank stare, as if I'm some sort of spy.'

'It's been a bit like that too for me, but today when I asked at the office, as I've been doing, I got my delivery chit signed by a fresh-faced young feller, who didn't look much more than twelve, bless him. He hesitated and then said, "Wait a minute, miss." Well, it was a lot longer than a minute. It must have been getting on for fifteen, because I was about to give up and go in search of a cuppa whilst I waited for the other two and you to arrive, when back he came with Luke in tow.'

Daisy lowered her voice. 'He looks exhausted.'

'They all do, if you look behind all the ribbing and the laughter, which sounds a bit forced to me.'

'Understandable, I suppose,' Daisy murmured. 'Does he know where Harry is?'

'I haven't asked him yet,' Gill said, just as Luke came back with tea and a plate of biscuits. He sat down between them, but it was to Daisy he turned to ask, 'How's everyone at home?'

'Fine. Coping really well, though they're all worried about you.' She punched him lightly on the arm. 'It seems you haven't written in weeks.'

Luke gave a weak smile. 'It's difficult to know what to say, Dais.'

'I know, but they all want to hear that you're all right. Give my granny a ring sometimes. She'll always deliver a message.'

'Trouble is,' he said softly, 'you're only all right at the moment you're writing or telephoning. The very next time you go up . . .' His voice faded away. Then, more strongly, he added, 'I will keep in touch more, I promise.'

'And I'll phone home tonight and ask Daddy to give them messages from you. By the way, d'you know where Harry is?'

Luke grinned. 'Last I heard, he was still at training school. He'll have an awful lot of tests and examinations to get through before he gets his wings. Of course, now we're in a war situation, the courses have been shortened. No doubt, he's still finding time to take a different WAAF out every night.'

They laughed easily together, but at that moment the door swung open and a squadron leader shouted, 'Scramble!' at the same moment as a bell began to ring loudly.

The pilots leapt up and rushed for the door, spilling tea and overturning chairs, grabbing their jackets and flying helmets. Within seconds, only Daisy and her fellow ferry pilots were left.

'We'd better get going, too,' Daisy said, looking towards Angela, the pilot of the Anson, who had just arrived and had sat down with a cup of tea. She was a far more experienced pilot than they were and was trained to fly the larger aircraft. But the young WAAF who'd come out from behind the counter said, 'No need to rush, miss. They won't let you go until they're all airborne.'

'Of course. I didn't think.'

'Let's go outside anyway and wave them off,' Gill said.

Outside the five young women – Daisy, Gill, Angela and the other two ferry pilots – stood watching as aircraft after aircraft took off. The squadron climbed until they were specks in the clouds.

'Right, we'll see if we can go,' Angela said.

They were given clearance and took off, but the Hurricanes and Spitfires were no longer anywhere to be seen.

Gill sat in the seat nearest to Daisy. They were flying in line with the coastline before turning north when Gill suddenly said, 'Oh look, over there to the left. Over the sea.'

'Black smoke,' Daisy said grimly. 'I bet they've been bombing our shipping in the Channel. That's where our fighters will have gone.'

Gill was still craning her neck and now she was looking through a small pair of binoculars. 'Look, over there in the far distance. Our lads have found their fighters. There's a dog fight going on.'

'We're getting out of here,' Angela said firmly and she put the Anson on track towards home. After a moment, she asked, 'Did you see any aircraft go down?'

'No. But there were bombers and their fighters as well as ours.'

'We'd better go to some kind of debrief when we get back,' Angela said. 'We must tell them what we saw, even if I get hauled over the coals for going slightly off course. But you didn't see any go down, did you?' she asked again.

'No, but I wish we could have tootled around up here for a bit longer and watched the fun.'

Daisy frowned. 'Fun?'

'Yup. That's what Luke and the other lads call it. So, we've got to do the same, Daisy.'

Daisy said nothing. She was wondering just what she was going to tell her father when she made the promised phone call that evening.

Thirty-One

From the time the enemy had attacked the ships in the Channel, the battle in the air intensified, and when, in August, the Luftwaffe attacked the airfields in the south of England, the Battle of Britain, as Churchill had foretold in June, was at its height. It was rumoured that Goering had said that the RAF would be defeated within a month, clearing the way for Operation Sea Lion, Hitler's planned invasion of the British Isles in September. As the battles raged and there was an urgent need for more aircraft, Daisy and Gill, along with a few other pilots, were sent to Upavon for what was called a conversion course on Miles Masters and Airspeed Oxfords.

'My goodness,' Daisy said, when they landed after their first two hours. 'These aircraft are a bit different. More controls and more checks to do.'

'But faster.' Gill grinned. 'We're getting there, Daisy. We're really getting closer to our dream.'

When their training was successfully completed, they returned to the Hatfield Ferry Pool and now their daily chits contained Oxfords to be taken north for training RAF pilots. Now, too, Daisy and Gill were qualified to fly the Anson. More and more, the taxi aeroplanes were used so that the ferry pilots could deliver more aircraft in a day. Although the ATA women were not allowed to fly after darkness fell and had only a map and a compass to guide them – there was no radio contact with the ground – with the lighter days of summer they were often working until long into the evening, returning to their digs near Hatfield Airfield exhausted, but elated that they were at last doing useful war work.

If only they were allowed to fly Spitfires! It was Daisy's last thought before she went to sleep at night and the first thing she thought about when she awoke next morning.

Early in September, Gill said, 'Daisy, have you heard? Brooklands was bombed yesterday at lunchtime.'

Daisy stared at Gill, her eyes wide with fright. 'Oh no. They must be turning their attention to aircraft construction sites as well as the airfields. I must telephone—' She stopped. Who could she telephone? Who would know?

Aunty Milly! Aunty Milly always knew what was happening, even though she always declared she didn't want to be told secrets.

'Ask the adj in the office. She'll let you telephone. Just tell her it's where you learned to fly and you have friends still there.'

Minutes later, Daisy was listening to the ringing tone going on and on. She replaced the receiver, more worried than ever. There had been reports of bombing in London during August; she prayed that Milly was all right.

'If her place had been hit,' Gill said reasonably, 'the telephone wouldn't be working.'

Daisy chewed her lip worriedly. 'Who else can I ring?'

'What about your uncle at the War Office?'

'Oh, I daren't ring there.'

'What about Uncle Mitch? You've got his number in London, haven't you?'

'Well, yes, but it's him I'm worried about. Him and Jeff. If they're at Brooklands . . .' Her voice faded away.

'Try him,' Gill urged. 'I can see you're really worried.'

Mitch answered almost immediately. 'Daisy? Are you all right? Something wrong?'

'No – not here. I was worried about you – and Jeff. We've heard Brooklands has been bombed. Is it bad?'

'Pretty bad this time, yes. But Jeff's OK. We're both here in London now. Most of the time anyway.'

'You said "this time". Has it been bombed before?'

'Yes, in July. Just small bombs that missed their target, but this time, it's bad. Over eighty workers at the Vickers factory have been killed and hundreds injured.'

'Is – is Milly's father all right?'

'Yes, he is. He was there, but only got cuts and bruises. He's devastated, of course. He treats all his workers like family.'

'Has Aunty Milly gone down there? Because there's no answer from her; I tried ringing her first.'

'Yes, she's in Weybridge with her family. I think

she might stay there for a while. The bombing in London has already started and it's going to get worse, Daisy.'

'Thank goodness Aunty Pips is away.'

'Most of the time anyway.' Mitch couldn't hide the anxious tone that crept into his voice. 'She comes home every now and again. She was here last weekend.'

Daisy sighed heavily. 'Oh dear.' There was a pause before she asked, 'What about the aircraft production at Brooklands?'

'Vickers expect to be up and running again within twenty-four hours, though production will be slower than normal. Understandably.'

'Can you give me Milly's telephone number at her parents' house? They wouldn't mind, would they?'

'Of course not. Have you got a pen?'

Daisy chuckled down the line. 'I don't need one. I'll remember it.'

'Sorry, I was forgetting.' He laughed with her. Daisy's mind was as sharp and clever as her aunt's.

Two days later, when they went to collect their delivery chits, Daisy said, 'Oh look, I've got Tangmere again. Delivering an Oxford.'

'And I've got an Oxford too – for Duxford.' Gill bit her lip. 'Daisy, would you swap? Unless, of course, you're desperate to see Luke . . .'

'I don't mind, but we'd better get permission. They need to know exactly who's going where.'

Gill's face brightened. 'Sure you don't mind? I mean . . .'

'Of course I don't. Give him my love, though, won't you?'

As they walked towards their respective aircraft, Daisy was smiling. In her hand she now held a chit that took her to Duxford, where Johnny was stationed. It couldn't have been a better swap and now she also had a Tiger Moth to pick up from there to take to the maintenance unit at Henlow. It would probably mean an overnight stay somewhere but she didn't mind that if it meant she could spend an hour or so with Johnny.

'You know, we're incredibly lucky that neither of them have been posted elsewhere yet,' Gill remarked.

Daisy agreed. 'Whole squadrons get moved too as well as individuals. I expect it'll happen eventually, but let's make the most of it whilst they're still where we can see them sometimes.'

As they parted, Daisy hugged her. 'Take care, Gill. See you later.'

Johnny was there waiting when she landed and taxied towards the place where she had to park the aircraft. He ran towards her to help her. As she jumped down, he put his arms around her, hugged her and swung her round.

'You've got to stay the night.'

'Here? Why?'

'The aircraft you've to take on to Henlow isn't ready. They can't get it started.'

Daisy pulled a face. 'I don't like the sound of that.'

'They're working on it, but it's obviously a bit dodgy, as you're taking it to a maintenance unit anyway,' Johnny said breezily. 'But you'd better telephone your office and explain. Don't want you on the carpet when you get back.'

'I'd better find out what's wrong first.'

'Oh, all right. My mate Jimmy's working on it. I'll take you over.'

A few moments later, Daisy was greeting a ginger-haired, freckle-faced aircraft mechanic.

'So you're the famous Daisy.' He grinned, giving Johnny a sly wink. 'I won't shake hands. I'm covered in grease trying to get this Moth of yours fixed.'

'What's wrong with it?'

'Don't know yet,' he said cheerfully, 'but I should have it ready by tomorrow . . .' He glanced at Johnny and then added, 'Or the day after.'

Daisy bit her lip. 'If it's likely to take as long as that, they might want to send the Anson for me.'

'Aw, come on, Daisy,' Johnny said. 'Surely you could have at least one night here? I've got a forty-eight. I thought we'd go dancing tonight. Several of the lads have arranged transport into London. Do say you will, Daisy.'

'There's bombing going on there now. Hadn't you heard?'

Johnny shrugged. 'They dropped a few in August, I grant you, but it's not every night. We'll just have to find a shelter if there's an air raid. Look, Daisy . . .' Suddenly, he was serious. 'The RAF lads are up almost every day in what Churchill calls the Battle of Britain. It started in July and already we're in September and it's still going on. Even our superiors recognize that we need a break now and again. Please, Daisy, say you'll come with us.'

She stared at him, seeing the tiredness in his eyes, the weariness of facing danger – even death – day after day. Of course they needed a bit of fun; anything to take their mind off the war in the air, even if only for a few brief hours.

'I'll telephone first,' she said firmly. She was loving her time in the ATA and didn't want to risk being on a charge or, worse still, grounded.

Her superior officer took the news calmly. 'It happens, Daisy, and we don't want you flying an aircraft that's suspect. We know it's going for a major overhaul, but we've been told it's airworthy for you to take it there. Just make sure they get it right before you fly. Ring me again tomorrow and let me know the progress.'

Daisy was smiling as she turned back to Johnny. 'It's OK, I can stay tonight at least.'

His grin seemed to stretch from ear to ear.

It was a merry party of RAF airmen who hired a bus to take them to London that evening. Several WAAFs had been invited too.

'If there's an air raid, Daisy, we must make a beeline for the nearest shelter. The place we're going to, which Ron has organized' – Johnny nodded towards one of his fellow airmen sitting on the back seat of the bus, his arm around a blond-haired girl wearing bright red lipstick but still in her WAAF uniform – 'is quite near one of the tube stations. Did you know folks are using the Underground for shelters?'

Daisy shook her head. 'Do you think the bombing in London will get worse?'

'Our lads try to get up before they get there, but we can't bring them all down. More's the pity. Still, let's forget about the war, Daisy. Just for tonight, eh?'

His arm crept around her shoulders and, smiling, Daisy snuggled against him. 'Yes, let's.'

The dance hall was packed with men – and some women – in service uniform.

'At least I don't feel out of place,' Daisy murmured, as Johnny put his arm around her and led her into a waltz.

'You look very smart and you should be very proud of what you're doing. We all know it can't be easy. I was appalled when I heard that you don't even have a radio on board.'

'No, just maps and a compass.' She laughed. 'It's all right until you get into fog or low cloud. Then it can be a bit hairy.'

'I bet. D'you get lost often?'

'Not often, no, but it does happen. The biggest danger then is either getting out over the sea or running out of fuel or getting tangled up in barrage balloons. I carry a list of airfields in the vicinity of where I'm going – just in case.'

His arm tightened around her. 'Well, I hope our base is on your list.'

'Of course it is,' she whispered against his ear.

As the waltz ended the band struck up a Charleston.

'Can you do this?' Daisy asked. 'Milly taught me years ago.'

'She taught me too. Come on, let's show 'em how it's done.'

261

The floor was almost clear with only four couples left, expertly executing the fast and furious Charleston. They swivelled in perfect synchronicity, then Johnny threw her around his waist and then up into the air to loud cheers from the onlookers, who stood at the side of the floor clapping in time to the music. As the music came to an end, the breathless dancers sat down to rapturous applause. Then they took to the floor again to a more sedate tango.

'Let's sit the next one out,' Johnny said, as the dance ended. 'Wait here. I'll get us some drinks.'

Daisy watched him as he threaded his way around the edge of the dance floor, noticing that he drew admiring glances from several girls. She couldn't blame them; he really was a good-looking young man and the smart blue uniform only added to his undoubted attraction. One girl even approached him, smiling and swaying her hips.

But he's mine, she wanted to shout. The realization hit her with a jolt. She was in love with Johnny Hammond. Her palms felt clammy and her heart beat even faster than when she had been dancing. She felt herself blushing and hoped she could control it by the time he came back. She watched as the girl touched his arm, jealousy rising in her like bile, but Johnny only smiled and gestured over his shoulder to where Daisy was sitting. The girl grimaced and appeared to say something, but then she patted his shoulder and turned away. Johnny continued on his way to the bar.

He'd paid for the drinks and was about to pick them up when the wail of an air-raid siren sounded.

The band stopped playing at once and the MC took the microphone. 'Ladies and gentlemen,' he began, but his instructions were lost in the cacophony of noise. However, it seemed that the people there knew the drill, as they began to file towards the exits.

'Daisy, Daisy!' Johnny was shouting as he pushed his way through the throng. He grabbed her hand and pulled her towards the door and out into the street.

'Isn't there a basement or something here?' she gasped.

'No, we must get to the Underground. Uncle Mitch told me it's the safest place. It's not far . . .'

When they stepped into the street, they were greeted by the terrific noise not only of sirens now, but also of the drone of bombers overhead. Bombs were already falling a few streets away, great crashes followed by fires. Incendiaries scattered in the middle of the road as they ran, hand in hand, along the pavement.

'Here's the entrance. Oh heck, there's a queue already. Quick, let's wait in this doorway until we can get down.'

An air-raid warden was marshalling the people down the steps into the Underground station. 'Come on, you two,' he shouted, catching sight of them huddled in the doorway. 'Can't have our brave RAF lads getting caught.'

A little boy of four or five was standing near the entrance, crying. Johnny paused and bent down. 'You lost your mum?'

The child hiccupped, grimy tears streaking his face, and nodded.

'Come on, old chap. Come down with us. Daisy, tell the warden that we've got a lost little boy and that we're taking him down with us.' As he picked him up, he said, 'What's your name, little man?'

The tears stopped momentarily. 'Alfie.'

'Well, Alfie, you come with me and Daisy down here where we'll be safe and the warden will keep an eye out for your mum.' He pointed down the stairs. 'Did she go down there?' The child nodded again.

'Let's go and find her, then. Daisy, hold onto my jacket. I don't want to lose you.'

As they descended, the sound of the bombing lessened a little, but now there was a different noise; that of hundreds of Londoners trying to find safety.

They stood to one side on the bottom step for a moment, whilst others pushed past them. 'Can you see anyone who seems to be looking for a child, Daisy?'

Daisy glanced about her, peering through the gloom. 'No, but there are so many people. Even if she's down here, we might not find her.'

'Let's keep him with us at least until the air raid's over.'

They found a place by the wall and a family lent them a blanket to sit on.

'That's so kind, thank you.'

'Anything to help our lads.' The man grinned and poured them a cup of tea from a flask. 'If you don't mind sharin' – hadn't time to bring the best china.

I'm Ted, by the way.' He handed the mug over and Daisy and Johnny drank gratefully.

'The missus has got some juice for the kids. Your little lad like some, would he?'

'I'm sure he would, but he's not ours. We found him lost at the entrance and thought the best thing to do would be to bring him down here with us. We could hardly leave him up there.'

'Poor little feller. I bet his mum's out of her mind with worry. It's so easy to get separated when everyone's rushing for the shelter, 'specially if you've got more than one to keep hold of.' The man stood up and looked about him. 'Can't see anyone, but we'll keep an eye out. Now, little feller, you drink this.'

The child drank thirstily and then his head lolled against Johnny's shoulder and he fell asleep. Johnny put his arms around him and rocked him gently, whilst Daisy snuggled up to Johnny's other shoulder.

'Is this what Uncle Mitch does? He's an air-raid warden, isn't he?'

'Yes. Somewhere in Clapham near where he has a flat. He's not far from where your aunt lives, I think.'

'She's not there very often now, though I think she goes home on her days off.' Daisy yawned. Johnny released one arm from holding the child and put it around her. She snuggled closer and, despite the noise and the closeness of so many people, she too fell asleep.

Ted nodded towards her. 'Your girlfriend, is she?'

Johnny smiled in the half-light. 'I'm working on it,' he murmured.

The man laughed. 'Pretty girl. Don't leave it too long, mate, or someone else'll snap her up.'

If they haven't already, Johnny thought, thinking of Luke.

Ted was speaking again, determined to keep a conversation going. 'I know what you do, mate, but I don't recognize her uniform. What is it?'

'She's in the Air Transport Auxiliary. She ferries aircraft about the country mainly from the factories to the airfields.'

Ted's mouth dropped open. 'You're kidding me! A young lass like that flying Spitfires and the like. No!'

'Not Spitfires yet. Though she can't wait to fly them.'

'Get away. Well, I've heard it all now.' He turned to his wife. 'You hear that, Mabel? This lass 'ere flies all sorts of planes, taking 'em to the likes of this young feller for him to keep Hitler at bay.' In his enthusiasm, the man hadn't quite got it right, but Johnny didn't bother to correct him. He, if no one else, was confident that it wouldn't be long before Daisy and the other ATA girls were flying Hurricanes and Spitfires, to say nothing of Wellingtons.

Johnny glanced up to the roof of the tunnel they were sitting in. 'I should be up there now, trying to stop his bombers.'

'You can't fly twenty-four hours a day, young feller. Even you've got to get a break now and again. Now,' he wagged his finger, 'if you'll take a bit of advice from me, get a ring on this lass's finger before you miss your chance, 'cos I'll tell you now, if I was thirty years younger—' His remark earned him a sharp dig in the ribs from Mabel, but he only laughed and winked broadly at Johnny.

'D'you know, Ted? I think I will.'

'Don't think about it, lad, do it!'

Thirty-Two

The air raid lasted over an hour, during which time Johnny sat with the child cradled in his right arm and his left arm around Daisy, ignoring the stiffness in his shoulder that her weight was causing him. He would have borne any cramp for a week if it meant he could hold Daisy close.

As the all-clear sounded, she stirred and the child, too, woke up and began to whimper again when he found he was in the arms of a stranger. People began to move, picking up their belongings and heading towards the stairs.

'Alfie! Alfie!' They heard her voice echoing down the platform long before they could see her.

'Mum!' The child shouted so loud that Johnny felt his right ear tingle.

'Alfie – where are you?'

Then they saw her, thrusting her way through and dragging two other children with her.

Daisy waved. 'Over here. He's here . . .' And Alfie cried out again. And then she was in front of them, reaching out for her boy and clasping him to her, whilst Alfie wound his arms around her neck and clung to her, still crying, but now with relief and thankfulness.

'Oh, thank you, thank you for looking after him. Gawd bless you. I thought he was holding onto me coat. It wasn't till I got to the bottom of the steps that I realized he'd let go. And then, I couldn't find him. I've been so terrified he was still up top.'

'We'll help you. Here, Daisy, you take the little girl's hand and we'll make sure you all get up the stairs safely. Do you live far from here?'

'No, just round the corner. This is the safest place to come, but it's always crowded.'

As they parted at the top of the steps, Johnny asked, 'Are you sure you'll be all right now?'

'We will and thanks again.'

Johnny and Daisy walked back to the dance hall, only to find some of their friends looking forlorn.

'The bus has been damaged in the raid. God knows how we're going to get back to camp. Phil has rung the adjutant. He's hopping mad, but I don't think we can get back tonight, so we're all going to find a hotel. What about you two?'

Johnny glanced down at Daisy. 'Shall we do the same?'

'I think we'll have to. It's a bit late to descend on Aunty Milly or Uncle Mitch, isn't it?'

Johnny laughed. 'Maybe, but I don't think they'll be asleep. That's if Aunty Milly is even here. No, you're right. We'll find somewhere to stay.'

In a small but clean and friendly hotel, Johnny found them a twin room and they slept chastely only three feet apart, both yearning to be in each other's arms, but not saying a word.

With alternative transport arranged, they all returned to camp.

'I think I'll have to report for duty, Daisy,' Johnny said, when they alighted from the bus bringing them back to Duxford. 'Even though I've still got another few hours left. After last night's escapade, I don't think I'd better push my luck.'

'No, and I'd better see if my aircraft is ready.'

'Oh, it will be,' Johnny said swiftly, without stopping to think what he was saying.

'Have you seen Jimmy?'

'Er – well, no, not exactly.'

'Johnny,' she said warningly, 'what's going on?'

'Erm – I've a confession to make.'

Daisy pretended to adopt a serious expression, but could hardly suppress her giggles. 'Go on.'

'I – um – got my mate to say that there was something wrong with the Moth so that you'd be forced to stay the night.'

She stared at him and then could contain her laughter no longer. 'How did you know it would be me coming?'

'I didn't. We just arranged that if I brought a girl to see him, it'd be you.'

'You could have got us both on a charge and the poor aircraft fitter as well.'

'Not really,' Johnny said smiling, relieved to see that she was not angry with him. 'No one ever argues with an aircraft fitter. If they say an aeroplane can't fly, then it can't fly. Even Air Chief Marshal Lord Dowding wouldn't dare argue with Jimmy.'

Impulsively, he took her hands into his. He had

no idea when he might see her again. 'Look, Daisy, you must know how I feel about you. Just tell me one thing. Have I a chance or are you really going to marry Luke – or even Harry, like he's always saying?'

For a moment, Daisy stood completely still, her heart hammering so loudly in her chest that she was sure he must hear it. For a moment, she couldn't speak.

At last, huskily, she said, 'No, I don't know how you feel about me. You've never said.'

'I thought women knew these things. Daisy Maitland, I have been in love with you for years, probably since the very first time I met you. Only I thought you and Luke—'

Daisy's eyes were shining and she was shaking her head vigorously. 'No, there's nothing like that between me and Luke – at least not on my side anyway. Nor with Harry. I love them both dearly – they're like the brothers I never had – but marry them, heavens, no!'

'Oh Daisy, Daisy.' He pulled her into his arms and there, on the windswept airfield, not caring who saw them, he kissed her soundly.

'And if that gets me on a charge,' he murmured against her lips as, at last, they broke apart, 'then it was worth it.'

Although she desperately wanted to stay longer now, Daisy was obliged to take off. She circled once, waving to Johnny on the airfield below, and then set course for Henlow. After that, she knew she would have to return to Hatfield and somehow, sometime very soon, she would have to try to get a delivery to Tangmere to see Luke if she could.

This was something she must tell him herself.

On the same day that Daisy was flying to Duxford, and, as it turned out, into Johnny's arms, Gill was landing at Tangmere.

As she taxied to a halt and climbed down, she asked the fitter, 'D'you know if Luke Cooper is here?'

'He was earlier, miss. Try the mess.'

She knew where it was, but hesitated at the door. This was the airmen's domain.

'Looking for someone, miss?' a friendly voice spoke behind her. She turned swiftly but her heart sank. It wasn't Luke.

'I – er – um – yes. Luke Cooper. D'you know him?'

'I think he's in here playing cards and probably losing all his money. Come on in.'

He held open the door for her and she stepped inside. Several faces turned in her direction and began to smile, but there was only one who stood up quickly, his chair falling over behind him.

'Gill! What a lovely surprise.' Luke came towards her. 'How long can you stay?'

'Only till the Anson picks me up.'

'Is Daisy flying that today?'

Gill felt her heart sink. It was Daisy – always Daisy – he wanted to see. As if rubbing salt in the wound, he said, 'Where is she today?'

'Gone to Duxford.'

'Ah. She might see Johnny.' He paused and then

asked, 'Is there anything between them, d'you know? I think you'd know if anyone would.'

'I . . .' Tears choked her throat but she held them back and said bravely, 'I really don't know, Luke.'

'I really want to see her – to talk to her. Sooner rather than later. Perhaps you'd tell her that for me, would you? Maybe I can come over on my motorcycle some time.'

Gill sighed deep inside herself. It looked as if she had no chance with Luke, yet she knew now that she had been in love with him for months, maybe even years, since she had first met him when he'd been visiting Daisy at Studley.

You see, she told herself sharply, it's always been Daisy. It's obvious now that he wants to see her to make sure there's nothing going on between her and Johnny. Why do you go on torturing yourself over someone you obviously can't have?

She forced a bright smile on her face. 'What have you been doing recently?'

Luke pulled a face. 'Same as usual. Still trying to keep control of the skies over Britain and to prevent enemy bombers getting through.' For a moment his face was bleak. Gill wanted to touch his arm, but she gripped her hand into a fist to prevent it reaching out to him. Instead she said, 'You're one of those whom Churchill calls "The Few". You should all be very proud. You're the ones standing between us and being invaded.'

He nodded, but did not meet her gaze.

'It's – not easy,' he murmured. 'It's all we can think about just now. Your personal life goes on hold.'

A little later, as he walked with her to where the Anson waited, Gill pressed her lips together to stop herself blurting out all that she so dearly wanted to say to him because now she knew she could never tell him just how very much she loved him.

Back at Hatfield eventually, Daisy sought out Gill.

'Have you seen Gill?' she asked Violet.

'She's on a delivery up north somewhere. Won't be back till tomorrow.'

Daisy didn't see Gill for three days. She continued her own deliveries and their paths didn't cross until the fourth day, not even at the billet they shared.

'There you are,' she said, finding Gill sitting at a table, a cup of coffee in front of her, stirring it absent-mindedly and staring into the far distance. She jumped at the sound of Daisy's voice. 'If I didn't know better, I'd've thought you were avoiding me.'

Gill smiled weakly and dropped her gaze, now looking intently into her coffee.

'Don't tell me you've got sugar in that. You're stirring it to death.' Daisy cocked her head on one side. 'What's up, Gill? Have you had some bad news?'

'No. I – um . . . No.'

'There's something wrong. Come on, you can tell me whatever it is.'

Gill shook her head and got up suddenly from the table, almost knocking her coffee over.

'Sorry. I've got to go. I'll – see you later.'

Daisy watched her friend rush from the room. She was puzzled. There was definitely something troubling Gill, but Daisy couldn't understand what it could possibly be that she felt unable to confide in her closest friend. With a sigh Daisy collected and ate her evening meal and then, yawning – it had been a long four days – walked the short distance to their digs. Gill was already in bed, lying on her side facing the wall and curled up into the foetal position, making it obvious that she didn't want to talk. With a sigh, Daisy quietly got ready for bed. She was tired and sleep would not be long in coming, but just as she drifted off, she was sure she heard a muffled sob from the other bed.

Thirty-Three

At the end of September, after a fortnight of solid flying operations, Luke was due leave and, deciding to use his precious petrol allowance, he travelled to Lincolnshire on his motorcycle. He needed to talk to Sam and his mother, if no one else at this point. They would keep his secret and he was sure they would understand too.

'This is a lovely surprise,' Peggy said, beaming, scuttling around her kitchen to get him something to eat.

'Don't go to any trouble, Mam.'

'Trouble! It isn't trouble to look after my boy. That's what mothers do, Luke.'

He grinned sheepishly and allowed her to fuss over him. After all the weeks and months of worry, he knew it was what she needed to do.

'Dad and Bernard will be home soon and then we can have a proper tea.'

'How's everyone?'

'We're all fine, really. Times are difficult – I don't need to tell you that – but in general, we're all faring pretty well.' Her face sobered. 'We hear that London is suffering dreadfully under the bombing.'

'They are. It's so tough for civilians. They just have

to sit there and take it. They can't do anything. At least we can get into our Spitfires and chase the buggers. Sorry, Mam.'

She smiled and gestured with her hand, indicating that she understood.

'No – bad news yet?' Luke asked. Several young men from the village were serving in the forces.

Peggy shook her head as if to put aside that question; it was something she didn't like to think about when both her sons were flying.

'Most of the men have joined the Local Defence Volunteers, only they've changed the name now to the Home Guard. Dr Everton is the captain and your dad is his sergeant. Dr Maitland, senior, that is, is just a member of the platoon. Evidently he didn't want to take on any responsibility, but he's enjoying being a part of it. And Mrs Maitland has got all us women working for the WVS.' She laughed. 'Even Granny Nuttall.'

Luke grinned. 'Not taken to her bed this time, then?'

Clara Nuttall was a legend in the village for taking to her bed every time something catastrophic happened in her life. The first time had been when her only son, Sam, had enlisted in the Great War. On that occasion, it had been Henrietta and old Ma Dawson who had prised her out of her bed. The second time – that Luke knew of – was when Sam had married Peggy, when she was pregnant with his baby. Clara had not wanted him to marry a girl who already had one illegitimate child and was now expecting another. That time it had been Pips to the rescue.

'Not even when Harry went?' Luke asked with a chuckle. Harry was Clara's blood grandson whereas Luke was not, though everyone always treated the boys equally, apart from Len Dawson, who never seemed to tire of pointing out that Harry was not his blood relative.

'Surprisingly, no, but, yet again, I think Mrs Maitland helped there, either deliberately or inadvertently – I'm not sure which. She'd already signed Clara up to WVS work.'

'Aunty Hetty's a wonderful woman,' Luke murmured, wondering how the Maitlands would react to his news when they eventually heard about it. The last thing he wanted was to lose their friendship and respect.

'She's been so good to your Aunty Betty, you know. She's got a job there as personal maid to both Mrs Maitland and Alice for the rest of her life.' Peggy's face sobered. 'She wouldn't have much of a life if it wasn't for them.'

Betty's fiancé, Roy Dawson, had been killed on the Somme with his other two brothers, Bernard, and Luke's father, Harold.

'I've been so lucky to have Sam. There weren't enough men to go round after we lost so many in the last war. There are a lot of spinsters from that generation and your Aunty Betty is one of them.'

Luke forbore to say that the very same thing might happen again this time round.

'And he's been a good dad to you, hasn't he?' Peggy went on, knowing nothing of Luke's sober thoughts.

'He has indeed. I couldn't have asked for a better stepfather, Mam, so don't you ever worry about that.'

'I don't, Luke. I can see with me own eyes just how fond you are of each other. He'll be that pleased to see you home. It's just a shame Harry's not here too.'

'Has he been home recently?'

'A couple of weeks back. I think he's still training to be a bomber pilot, though he doesn't tell us a lot.' She set a steaming cup of tea in front of him and two buttered scones. 'There, that'll tide you over till tea's ready.' She bent towards him, her eyes sparkling with fun. 'He didn't stay long. We reckon he's got a girlfriend.'

Luke, with a piece of scone halfway to his mouth, paused and stared at her. 'A – a girlfriend?'

Peggy nodded. 'He couldn't stop talking about a WAAF called Lucy, who works where he's stationed. And he only stopped the one night with us, even though we knew he had three days' leave.'

'But – I thought . . .'

She sat down on the opposite side of the table. 'Yes, I know what you're going to say. Daisy. All that about him going to marry Daisy one day was obviously childish nonsense. I think it was to try to compete with you. After all, it's always been *you* and Daisy, hasn't it? And now, you must excuse me while I get the tea on. You sit by the fire and read the paper. Sam and Bernard will be home soon and then we can all have tea together and a nice chat.'

As Luke settled himself into one of the armchairs, he sighed. Chat they certainly would, but whether it was going to be 'nice' remained to be seen.

At Hatfield, the ferry pilots were busy. All types of aircraft were needed all over the country and, during the daylight hours, the men, and the girls too, felt as if they were flying non-stop. Daisy and Gill hardly saw each other, but Daisy still had the feeling that Gill was doing her best to avoid her.

'D'you know what's wrong with Gill?' Daisy asked Violet, who had become their closest friend amongst the other ATA women, as they walked to the airfield. Violet rented a room in a house close to where Daisy and Gill lived and they often walked into work together. But this morning, Gill had risen and disappeared before Daisy had woken up.

'Not a clue,' Violet replied cheerily, 'though, now you mention it, she does seem a bit glum. D'you want me to have a word?'

Daisy shook her head. 'She'll tell us in her own good time. I can't think what it can be. If it was bad news from home, I'm sure she wouldn't keep that from us.'

'And she'd be asking for leave to go home on a visit, surely.'

'You'd think so,' Daisy murmured. 'Ah well, we'd better go and get today's chits.'

As the two girls neared the office, they saw Gill already walking across the grass towards her first delivery.

'Lucky thing!' Daisy said a few minutes later. 'She's

got a Miles Master and I've got a Tiger Moth. The end of September is getting far too cold for open cockpits. Never mind. It's to Tangmere. I might see my cousin, Luke.' Silently, she thought, *I hope so. There's a very difficult conversation I have to have with him – and sooner rather than later.*

She landed smoothly at Tangmere and taxied to a halt. She glanced around. No sign of Luke, but then he didn't know she was coming. There was no shortage of willing young airmen to help her down and escort her to the office and then to the mess, where they plied her with cups of tea and cakes.

'Is Luke around?' she asked one of his friends.

'No,' Tommy said. 'He's on three days' leave. Gone up north, I think. Isn't that where his home is?'

Daisy nodded, disappointed that she would not have the chance to see him on this trip. If she had a problem to sort out, Daisy always liked to get it over and done with. But there was nothing she could do. He wasn't here. Their conversation would have to wait.

'Mrs Nuttall,' Bernard said politely, as they finished eating, 'may I go out for about an hour? Some of the lads are playing football.'

'Of course, Bernard, but be sure to be home before it gets dark.'

After tea, when Peggy had washed the dishes and sat down in front of the fire where her menfolk were already toasting their toes, Luke took a deep breath, 'There's something I need to tell you and it's not easy.'

Peggy and Sam exchanged a glance.

'Best get it off your chest, then, Luke,' Sam said gently.

'It's about Daisy – and me.'

Peggy gave a startled gasp and covered her mouth. 'Oh Luke, no. She's not – she's not . . .'

He frowned. 'What, Mam?'

'You haven't got her – in the family way, have you?'

His face cleared. 'Heavens, no!'

'You want to marry her, then?' Sam put in.

Luke held on to his patience. He wished they wouldn't keep interrupting with ideas of their own, but just let him get on with telling them what his dilemma really was.

'Well, no, but I wondered if the family – hers as well as mine – are expecting us to marry one day.' He looked towards Peggy. 'You hinted at it earlier.'

'Yes. You've always been so close, ever since you were little, and although you're first cousins, it's not against the law and the Maitlands have never said they'd be against it.'

'Yes, we are close. She's like my sister and I love her dearly, but not – as a wife.'

They stared at him, glanced at each other and then turned their gaze back to him. 'Does Daisy know this?'

Luke bit his lip and shook his head. 'No, but I need to talk to her. You see, I've fallen in love with someone else.'

*

On her return, Daisy had the opportunity to corner her friend.

'Gill, what *is* the matter, because there's obviously something. Have I done something to offend you?'

'Of course not.'

'Then what is it? We're friends, aren't we? The best of friends, I thought. Whatever it is, I won't be shocked. I'll stand by you.'

Gill stared at her and then her usual sense of humour reasserted itself for a brief moment. 'I'm not pregnant, if that's what you're thinking.'

'Actually, that never entered my mind. But something's bothering you, I can see it is. Are your parents all right? You've not had bad news from home, have you?'

'No, they're fine. The land girls they've got are doing a superb job.' She pulled a face. 'They're hardly noticing I'm not there.'

'And you're feeling these girls are usurping your position?'

Now Gill actually laughed, but it had a forced quality to it. 'No, no one can replace a daughter, now can they?'

'Knowing your parents, I wouldn't have thought so.' Daisy paused, but Gill was avoiding direct eye contact again. Daisy sighed. 'If you don't want to tell me, dearest Gill, so be it, but just remember I am always your friend and always here for you.'

Gill nodded and turned away, but not before Daisy had seen tears welling in her eyes.

Thirty-Four

Early in October, Pips was at home in London on four days' leave and, to her delight, George had managed to have some time off from work too.

'Shall we go up to Lincolnshire?' she said as they lay in bed together, their arms round each other.

'If you don't mind, no. I've seen so little of you recently, I want you all to myself, though I do wonder if we should get out of London. What Churchill called the Battle of Britain seems to be on the wane. The Luftwaffe have not gained control of the skies, but now they've started a vicious bombing campaign against the big cities, London, of course, being a prime target.'

'We'll be fine.' She snuggled closer. 'We'll just dash to the nearest shelter, as soon as we hear the sirens. That's all.'

'Just as long as you promise me that's what you'll do if I'm not here.'

'I promise, but I thought you said you'd got four days off too.'

He chuckled. 'Allegedly, but you know I can always get called in.'

'We'll have the first two days all to ourselves and do just what we please, which probably won't be very much, but the night before I'm due back, we'll have Rebecca and Matthew over to dinner, if they're both free. It's ages since I've seen them.'

'I'd like that,' George murmured and turned over to kiss her.

The proposed dinner party took place the night before Pips had to report back to Bletchley Park for duty. She did not, of course, talk about her work there; she wasn't actually sure if Rebecca even knew exactly where she was when she was not in London. Both George and Matthew knew, of course, but because their own work was so highly sensitive, they knew not to talk about anything to do with what any of them were doing. The only person who could talk freely about her work was Rebecca.

'I'm working at a first-aid post and I'm on duty whenever there's an air raid, which, sadly, are becoming more frequent nowadays. And before you ask, Daddy, we're in a fortified basement the Red Cross found for that very purpose. We're as safe as it's possible to be.'

George smiled. 'Good. I was just going to ask.'

'What about you two?' Pips glanced between her husband and Matthew.

'Well, for us,' George said, 'the roof spotters just let us know if the bombers are getting close and we all go down into the basement.'

'We just dive for the nearest shelter,' Matthew said. Then, changing the subject, he added, 'This really is an amazing dinner, Pips. I don't know how you've managed it with all the rationing and shortages.'

Pips chuckled. 'We're lucky. Every time we go home, my mother piles the car high with enough food to last us a month. All the villagers are helping one another and they've found the most ingenious ways of preserving food. You can't begin to imagine.' She laughed. 'Last time I was home, Norah Dawson was demonstrating to the other women at a WVS meeting how to use a hay box to cook. She was very proud of it.'

'However does that work?' Rebecca asked.

'You bring food to boiling point in a pot and then put it in a hay-filled box and it carries on cooking. Of course, it takes about three times as long to cook anything, but it does save on normal fuel. Norah said, "As long as it's ready for his dinner, Len doesn't know any different".'

They were lucky that evening; it was foggy and the bombers didn't come. It had been a merry dinner party, even though it was impossible to turn the conversation very far from the war, but it was probably the happiest time the four of them had spent together since the conflict had started.

'We must do this again and very soon,' Pips said, as she kissed both Rebecca and Matthew goodnight.

'We must. And don't worry about Dad, Pips. I'll keep an eye on him for you. I come round here as often as I can when he's not working.'

Pips squeezed her arm. 'Thank you.'

'I've got an Oxford to take to Tangmere,' Daisy told Gill. 'I hope Luke's there. I really need to talk to him.'

Gill looked at her for a moment and then turned away without a word. Daisy stared after her. 'Now what have I said?' she murmured. Then she shrugged and readied herself for her flight.

This time, when she landed, she saw Luke waiting for her. As soon as she came to a stop, he was there to help her down.

'I missed you last time I came. You'd gone home. So Tommy said.'

'Daisy, I need to talk to you.'

'That's funny, I want to talk to you too.'

'Let's go and find a quiet corner, then.'

'As soon as I've reported in.'

Daisy felt her insides quiver as they walked from the offices towards the mess, nervous about what he had to say to her and what she must say to him.

Once they were seated, she said, 'You fire first.' She smiled a little tremulously. 'As I hope you always do.'

'It's about us, Dais.'

Daisy stared at him, her eyes round. This was going to be much worse than she had expected. Surely, he wasn't going to propose . . . Oh dear.

He reached across the table and took both of her hands into his; hands that were now trembling.

'Daisy, you know how much I love you – oh dear, I'm not putting this very well, and I think our families have always wondered if – expected, perhaps – that one day we would marry, but Daisy – the last thing in the world I would want to do is to hurt you – but, you see, I don't love you in that way.' His words jumbled and, almost incoherent, he rushed on, regardless of the smile already beginning on her lips, knowing nothing of the nerves in her stomach settling down at his words. 'You see, I've fallen in love with someone else. Oh Dais, do say I haven't broken your heart. I couldn't bear to do that.'

'For goodness' sake, Luke, just stop a minute and let me get a word in edgeways. I love you too, but as my cousin – as a brother. I don't want to marry you. I never did.'

He stared at her. 'Then – then is it Harry?'

'No, it's not Harry either.'

'Thank goodness for that, then, because Mam thinks he's got a girlfriend. A WAAF where he's stationed.'

'I'm delighted to hear it, though I expect poor Kitty's upset if she's heard about it.'

Luke shrugged. 'She knows what he's like.' He paused and then added, 'You're not just saying you don't want to marry me to make me feel better?'

'No, Luke, I promise you I'm not. Do I look heartbroken?'

'Well, no, but you're good at hiding your feelings.'

'Not that good. There's just one thing. I want to know who the lucky lady is.'

For a moment, Luke looked shame-faced again, as he said softly, 'It's your friend. It's Gill. But she doesn't know yet. So, she may not feel the same about me – I know that – but I wanted to confide in you first. Get everything straight between us.'

Daisy stared at him and then began to laugh until the tears ran down her face.

'Oh Luke, you don't know how glad I am to

hear this, for all sorts of reasons. And now I'd better tell you what it was *I* was so worried about telling you . . .'

As they walked out to the Tiger Moth, she said, 'I really think you should try to see Gill as soon as possible. She's as miserable as sin and keeps avoiding me like the plague. Now, I think I know why that might be.'

'What?'

Daisy chuckled. 'I think she might very well be in love with you.'

'You do?'

'So, you really should try to see her very soon.'

'I'll come up the day after tomorrow. I've got a forty-eight-hour pass. But don't tell her.'

'Of course I won't, but please don't leave the poor girl in the state she's in right now any longer than you have to.'

'I won't.'

He came to watch her take off, waving until the last moment. Once in the air, Daisy circled once, waggling her wings in farewell. First, she had to deliver a Tiger Moth to Henlow, where she would be picked up by the Anson and flown back to Hatfield.

Again, Gill neatly avoided talking to Daisy, going to bed before she did and rising early before Daisy woke up.

The following day, Daisy had a long trip to Scotland and would be away for at least two nights. 'I just hope Luke gets over here before I'm back,' she muttered as the aircraft lifted into the sky.

Two days later, as dusk gathered around the

airfield, Daisy arrived back in Hatfield after a long and exhausting train journey. She trudged home to their billet, yawning with tiredness. As she neared the gate, the front door flew open and Gill ran down the path.

'Daisy, oh Daisy . . .' She enveloped Daisy in a bear hug.

Smiling, Daisy extricated herself. 'I presume Luke has been.'

'Yes, yes, he has. Oh Daisy . . .'

'Let's just get inside and you can tell me everything. I'm about out on my feet.'

'Oh sorry. Here, let me take your bag. I'll make you some tea.'

'So,' Daisy said, stifling another yawn, as Gill sat down opposite her moments later, cups of tea in front of them both. 'Everything's hunky-dory between you and Luke, then?'

'Yes, but are you sure you don't mind?'

'Of course not. I'm thrilled. You'll be my cousin-in-law, if there is such a thing.'

'But I thought you and him – that you were sort of promised to each other. Even he wasn't sure before he talked to you the other day. He said the families had always sort of taken it for granted that you two would get married one day.'

'Then our families should know better than to take either Luke or me for granted about anything.'

'Then you really don't mind?'

'I do not.'

They leaned across the table and hugged each other again before Gill said, 'Luke wouldn't tell me much about you, but he hinted that there was someone. So – is it Harry?'

'No,' Daisy said firmly. 'It isn't either Luke or Harry. I'm in love with Johnny Hammond.'

After her initial surprise, it was now Gill's turn to say, 'Well, you might have told me.'

Thirty-Five

Night after night enemy bombers visited London and other major cities, the ports and docks in the south and the industrial cities in the north, but Hitler had miscalculated the grit of the British and the tenacity of their inspirational leader. All attacks were devastating; all caused loss of life and property, but the one that perhaps angered the British people the most and left a legacy of bitterness was the destruction of Coventry Cathedral in November.

After a lot of persuasion from Paul, Milly reluctantly agreed to go and stay permanently with her parents near Weybridge until the worst of the bombing was over.

'But I should be *doing* something,' she'd protested.

'You will be. Hasn't your mother joined the local WVS? You can help her.' Paul had taken her into his arms and rested his chin on her blond head. 'Darling, just because you're not in the thick of it like last time, it doesn't mean you can't do something of value. The WVS do terrific work. Ask Pips. Her mother's the leading light in their branch.'

'I hardly ever see Pips,' Milly mourned.

'We'll see lots more of her and George when all this is over.'

'But when will it be over and will we win?'

'Of *course* we'll win. Never doubt that for a moment. And now, I really must go or my boss will have my guts for garters.'

Milly giggled. 'But your boss is George.'

'Exactly! And that's why I never take advantage. Now, pack your bags and go today. Promise?'

'I promise.'

'And whenever I get time off, I'll come down on the train to see you.'

'But you'll telephone every night, won't you?'

Now it was Paul's turn to give his promise.

'*Harry!* How lovely to see you.' Peggy hugged him hard. She stood back and tapped him lightly on the cheek. 'I should give you a smack for not writing.' She laughed delightedly. 'But I won't. I'll just make you suffer another hug.'

Harry submitted with good grace.

'How long have you got?'

'Only two days, Mam. I'm a fully fledged bomber pilot now and I've been posted to a place called Feltwell in Norfolk.' His grin widened. 'I'll be flying Wellingtons.'

Peggy felt a spasm of fear run through her, but she could see the delight on his face; it was what he wanted and she had to be glad for him. But with one son already flying fighter aircraft, it was a struggle to show delight at his news.

They sat together, drinking tea, whilst Peggy filled him in on all the local news.

'I'll take a walk down and meet Dad from work,

though I don't expect I'll get much of a welcome from old man Dawson.'

'Pop in and see Mrs Dawson on your way. She'd love to see you. She's always asking after you.' Peggy paused and then added coyly, 'And there's someone else who's always asking about you too. Kitty.'

Harry laughed. 'Aw, little Kitty.'

'Not so little now, Harry. She's blossomed into a very pretty girl.'

Harry's face sobered. 'I know, Mam, but she'll always be "little Kitty Page" to me. Besides, I can't – I daren't – get serious about anyone. It wouldn't be fair.'

'What about this WAAF we've been hearing about?'

Harry gave a bark of laughter. 'Which one, Mam?'

'Oh you! There was one called Lucy, wasn't there?'

Harry wrinkled his forehead. 'Oh yes, so there was. That was ages ago. There've been at least three since then.'

Peggy bit her lip. 'There is something I ought to tell you – unless, of course, you've heard already.'

'I don't know till you tell me. Go on.'

'It's about Luke – and Daisy.'

Harry raised his eyebrows. 'Don't tell me they're getting married. Not whilst the war's still on, surely.'

Peggy shook her head. 'No, on the contrary. Luke came home to tell us that he has fallen in love with someone else.'

'Good Lord! Now, I didn't expect that.' He frowned. 'Is Daisy heartbroken?'

Peggy laughed. 'No, she's – she's seeing a lot of Johnny Hammond.'

Harry sat very still for a moment before he began to smile. 'That's all right, then.'

'But what about you, Harry? You've always said you were going to marry Daisy one day.'

Harry guffawed loudly. 'Oh Mam, don't tell me you took all that kid's stuff seriously. It was only to wind Luke up. I really thought they'd end up together and you know me; anything Luke had, I wanted.' He shrugged. 'I do love Daisy dearly, but not in that way. Besides, I'm too much of a flirt to settle down yet. I'm having too much fun.'

When he walked down the lane to the Dawsons' cottage and then on to Len's workshop, his progress was slowed by men walking home from their labours in the fields or women hurrying home to cook tea, all wanting to shake hands with him, asking him what he was doing and wishing him well. Opposite the workshop, Kitty was leaning on the gate; she was a little too old to be seen swinging on it now.

''Lo, Harry.'

He smiled at her and crossed the lane to talk to her.

'Hello, Kitty. How are you?'

'I'm fine. I'm still working at the hall.'

'I know. Do you like it?'

'I love it, but I'm working in the gardens now with Jake. Mrs Maitland got me an exemption because we grow vegetables and fruit.'

'Is that better than being a housemaid?'

Kitty wrinkled her forehead, considering. 'In some

ways, yes. I like being out of doors, but winter's coming. It might not be so much fun then.' She stared at him as if drinking in the sight of him and committing his every feature to memory. He was so very handsome in his RAF uniform. 'What are you doing now?'

When he told her, she turned pale and her voice was unsteady as she said, 'I'd better go in. Mam's got tea on the table. Take care of yourself, Harry. Don't forget to carry the four-leafed clover with you.'

'I will, Kitty,' he began, but she was already halfway up the path, running to hide her tears and didn't hear his final two words. 'I promise.'

'We really shall have to start planning for Christmas, Norah duck,' Bess said.

'I know, but me heart's not in it this year. It was different last year. Not much had happened then and we all had hope that it'd soon be over, but now . . .' A great deal had happened since then that had left the country reeling.

'I know, but we've got to make the effort for our families and for the little kiddies here far from home. Think about them, Norah.'

Norah sighed. 'I wish Len would let us have an evacuee, but just because he lets Bernard come to the workshop, he thinks he's doing his bit.'

'So are you. You've got the WVS.'

'I know, but Len won't let me go out in the evening and the dark nights, just sitting and knitting, are so very long.'

'Let's start planning for Christmas, then. That'll

give you summat to do.' Bess laughed raucously. 'It'll take a lot of thinking about with all the rationing to cope with.'

It was a strange December for all of them. No one got home to celebrate the birthdays as they always had at the beginning of the month, nor at Christmas. The only merriment in Doddington came from entertaining the evacuee children and helping them not to feel too homesick. A few parents, invited by the people looking after their children, came for Christmas but whether that had been a good idea or not, no one could say, for having to part again brought more tears from children and parents alike. In London and other major cities, many spent Christmas Eve in air-raid shelters or in temporary accommodation, having been bombed out, their homes destroyed, their possessions lost.

Paul managed to get two days' leave and went down to Weybridge to be with Milly and her family.

'I'll cover for you,' George told him. 'Pips isn't coming home.'

'I'm sorry to hear that. What will you do?'

'Oh, hold the fort here. Rebecca has asked me to have Christmas lunch with them so I won't be alone on Christmas Day.'

As he walked home through the blackout, George wondered if he should have made some effort to go to Bletchley. Then at least he and Pips could have been together some of the time. Pips had been home the previous weekend and they had discussed it; she had drawn the short straw to be on duty all over Christmas and would be working long hours, so they had decided it would be better for George to spend time with Rebecca and Matthew.

'I'll be home at New Year though,' she'd said. 'So just make sure you get some time off then. Perhaps Paul will cover for you in return?'

He was thinking over all that had been said between them, when a voice came out of the darkness. 'George?'

'Mitch. What are you doing here?'

'My beat.' He chuckled. 'Or whatever the name is for my round as an air-raid warden.'

George took a deep breath and forced himself to be friendly. 'Have you time for a drink? I'm just on my way home.'

'Thanks, I don't mind if I do. I'm due a break and the bombing's not started yet.'

They walked the last few paces together and entered the apartment block where George and Pips lived. As George opened the door and they went inside, Mitch didn't bother to enquire if Pips was at home; he rather thought he would not have been invited if she had been there.

'Tea, coffee – or something stronger?'

'I'm still on duty. Coffee'd be great – if you have any.'

'Only the chicory stuff, but it's quite nice.'

'Don't let me stop you eating.'

'It's all right. I got something on my way home. I'm not much of a cook.'

'Are you managing all right whilst Pips is away?'

'In the main, yes. She comes home every two or three weeks, usually at a weekend. That's the best time for me to get time off too.'

'Over a year of war already and no sign of a let-up in the bombing, is there?'

George set a cup of coffee in front of Mitch and sat down on the opposite side of the small table in the kitchen. 'No, and I'm very sorry to say that I don't think there will be for a while. Hitler seems determined to break us.'

'He'll not manage it. He doesn't know us. You should see the folks that have been bombed out, George. They've lost everything, even family members sometimes, but they've got such fortitude, such strength of character, despite all they've suffered. They'll see it through, whatever it takes.'

They sat in silence until George said, 'Did you manage to make the contacts you were asking me about a while back?'

'Oh yes, that. Er – yes, thanks, I did.' Mitch was silent a moment, debating with himself. There couldn't be any harm in telling George.

'Have you heard of an organization called the Special Operations Executive?'

George stared at him. 'Yes, I have. Their head-quarters are in Baker Street now, I believe?'

Mitch nodded.

'Are you involved with them?'

'In a way. Jeff works there and I – um – help out if I can.'

'And your air-raid warden duties are a good cover?'

Mitch chuckled. 'Something like that, George, but I'm only involved on an ad-hoc basis. Usually with my little Lysander.'

'Is that still at Brooklands?'

Mitch nodded.

'I won't ask any more, Mitch, but all I can say is, good for you.'

As Mitch left to resume his duties, the two men shook hands, their mutual respect even greater than it had been.

Thirty-Six

Early in the New Year of 1941, the ATA suffered a grievous loss. Amy Johnson, so famous for her flying exploits and who had been ferrying aircraft for them, was lost. The aircraft she was flying was seen to go down in the Thames Estuary. Wreckage was found, but not Amy. Everyone at Hatfield was saddened by her loss. She had been well-liked amongst the girls and a 'celebrity' face which had brought credibility to the other women ferry pilots.

But Pauline Gower never gave up fighting for her girls to be able to fly all types of aircraft. By April, she had permission for the ATA women to fly obsolete operational aircraft, which now had other uses.

'It's even more important,' the Operations Manager, Mary Bryant, told them as she handed out the chits, which contained some unfamiliar names, 'that you study your ferry pilots' notes carefully.'

'Oh, I've got a Westland Lysander,' Daisy said gleefully. 'I've flown one of those. Uncle Mitch has one at Brooklands. He calls it his "Lizzie".'

'I understand that's its nickname.'

'Is it?' Daisy glanced up at Mary Bryant. 'I thought it was just Uncle Mitch's name for his aeroplane.'

'Evidently not. It's what the RAF boys called the Lysander. It still has a very valuable role,' Mary Bryant said. 'It's used for' – she stopped and then ended, rather lamely, Daisy thought – 'all sorts of things.' Mary turned away and busied herself handing out yet more chits for the day's deliveries.

The bombing of London, the southern counties and major cities in the north of the country continued right through the spring.

'Isn't it ever going to stop?' Milly moaned to Paul on one of his rare visits to Weybridge. 'I want to come home. I can do so much more in London.'

'But you're helping your mother with her war effort and your granny loves having you here, darling. Just hold on a little longer.'

But a devastating air raid in May almost broke even the steadfast reserve of the hardened Londoners. Over five hundred German bombers dropped incendiaries and high-explosive bombs through the night hours. The House of Commons was hit and Big Ben damaged. Westminster Abbey's square tower fell and St Paul's Cathedral, which had miraculously survived previous bombs, was hit again. High above the carnage Luke, Johnny and their fellow RAF fighter pilots chased the bombers and brought down twenty-nine enemy aircraft.

Patrolling his usual street, Mitch saw and heard the bombs falling. He watched in horror as the apartment block where George and Pips lived took a direct hit.

He began to run. All he could think of was George's

words: 'She comes home every two or three weeks, usually at a weekend.'

And tonight was Sunday, 11 May.

'Have you heard that the bombing was really bad in London last night? I hope your relatives are safe, Daisy,' Gill said.

'I expect they will be. Pips is away somewhere, though no one will say where and Uncle George will be in whatever shelter the War Office staff use.'

'What about Milly?'

'She's gone to her parents' home near Weybridge.' She paused, reflecting. 'There's only Uncle Mitch who might be in real danger. I know Johnny worries about him.'

'What about your folks at home? Will Lincoln get bombed, d'you think?'

Daisy hesitated. 'I rang home last night. Some bombs fell on the outskirts of Lincoln four nights ago, but nothing near us.'

'Dad thinks we should be OK out in the middle of the Yorkshire countryside, but you can never be complacent, can you? If they're on their way home and have got any bombs left they'll just chuck 'em out anywhere.'

'Presumably, Lincolnshire will be a prime target anyway because of all the airfields there.'

'Mm. Yorkshire's got a few too.'

The two young women were standing in line at the office waiting for their orders for the day.

'Right, come on, we're next. Where are we today?'

As they were handed their chits, they compared notes.

'Blimey,' Daisy said. 'I'm off up to Scotland. I'll be away for a night or two by the looks of it. A Tiger Moth.'

'That'll be a long, cold haul in an open cockpit, even though it's May. I'm just pootling around locally. I'll see you when I see you, then. Good luck.'

In Weybridge, Milly answered the telephone when Paul rang in the early afternoon instead of waiting until the evening as usual. At once, she knew something was wrong.

His voice was husky. 'Milly, darling. Are you with someone?'

'Yes, Mummy, Daddy and Granny. We've just had luncheon.'

'I have awful news, my darling. The apartment block where George and Pips live took a direct hit last night. George wasn't at work, so we are assuming he was at home, but he hadn't gone to the nearest shelter. We do know that. We don't know if Pips was there or not. They're still searching and I'm trying to get a message to her at – um – at where she works.'

'Has anyone let her parents know? Or Rebecca?'

'Matthew went back to his home this morning – he'd been working all night – but Rebecca wasn't there. He's still trying to find her. He thinks she must still be out somewhere helping the injured from last night's raid. It was appalling. Some are saying the worst ever and Rebecca could be anywhere.'

'Do you think I should go up to Lincolnshire? It's

an awful thing to tell them over the telephone. I could go by train or perhaps Daddy would let his chauffeur drive me there.'

'I'm sure he would. I think that's a good idea.' He paused and then added quietly, 'You know, Milly darling, I'm very proud of you. That's not an easy task to undertake. But Pips always said you had a lot more courage than anyone ever gave you credit for. Now I see it for myself.'

With further fond messages between the two of them and a last promise from Milly to telephone him as soon as she arrived at the hall, they disconnected. Milly's parents and grandmother knew Pips and George well and were very fond of them both. They did everything they could to help her as she packed quickly for the long journey north. Cook made up a hamper for her and Timson, the family's chauffeur. 'Obviously, you'll be staying at the hall, Milly, but what about Timson?'

'I'm sure the Maitlands will find him a bed. If not, he can always stay in the village or even in Lincoln. It's only three or four miles away. He can come back tomorrow, but I shall stay for a few days.'

In under an hour, she was on her way.

Mitch stood up and eased his aching back and gazed at the mound of rubble in front of him. It didn't seem to be getting any less, even though there were a dozen workers digging in an effort to see if anyone could still be alive. How could they be, he wondered, under all that lot? They'd been working for the rest of the night after the bomb fell, and all day, and now it was early evening on Monday. They'd already brought out two bodies, a man and a woman, but no one had been able to identify them. They weren't anyone Mitch knew. He knew in his heart it was hopeless, but he had to try. He had to keep on digging. He didn't even notice that his hands were bleeding, that his face and uniform were covered in dust or the fact that he hadn't eaten since the previous day. Locals provided a constant supply of tea to the rescuers, but no one had stopped to eat.

Somewhere under there could be his beloved Pips and he wasn't going to stop searching for her until all hope was gone.

'We'll have to stop in an hour or so, Mitch old man.' The senior air-raid warden put his hand on Mitch's shoulder. 'It'll be dusk and we can't put lights up, you know that.'

Mitch nodded and bent again. After ten minutes he heard a shout from the other side of the mound.

'Here – over here.'

Everyone scrambled towards where the voice came from.

'I've found a body. It's a man and he's dead, but I think there's someone else with him. I need help. Just two of you.'

'Please, let me,' Mitch almost begged. 'I might know him. My – friends live here.'

Sympathetic glances were cast his way as most of the rescuers stood back. Only one moved to Mitch's side. Gently they cleared away the remaining rubble covering the body and then wiped his face.

Mitch nodded. 'Yes,' he said huskily. 'It's George.'

'There's someone else, just a couple of feet away from him.'

They worked carefully, although there was hardly any hope that whoever it was could be still alive.

'It's a woman,' a voice said. 'Go carefully, boys.'

They lifted the lifeless form from the debris and laid her reverently on the ground. Hardly daring to look, Mitch knelt beside her and gently wiped her face. As her features became recognizable, a sob escaped his throat. Then he leaned forward and rested his face against her shoulder, no longer able to hold back the tears.

When Milly arrived at the hall that evening, the family were gathered in the parlour, as they always were, for a pre-dinner drink. Wainwright showed her in, knowing there was no need to ask if he might do so. Milly was always a welcome visitor at the hall.

'Mrs Whittaker, madam.'

'Milly, my dear . . .' At once Henrietta was on her feet. She was about to add 'what a nice surprise', but the look on the young woman's face and her unexpected arrival stilled the words on her lips.

'I had to come myself,' Milly blurted out, glancing around the room. 'I couldn't do it by telephone.' They were all there, so this would be easier. 'You must know about the awful bombing happening almost every night in London.'

'Of course.' Robert stood up and guided her to a chair. He could see, not only with a doctor's trained eye, but also with that of a friend, that Milly was very upset. 'Now tell us slowly whilst Mother pours you a drink.'

Henrietta bent to her task, but everyone noticed that her hand was shaking. For Milly to come all this way, unannounced, something must be terribly wrong.

Milly pulled off her gloves. 'Last night, there was a dreadful raid and – and the apartment block where Pips and George live' – she swallowed painfully – 'took a direct hit.'

They all stared at her. Robert sank back down into his chair. 'Were they definitely there? I mean, George often works late and Pips – well – Pips might not even have been in London.'

'Wouldn't they have gone to a shelter?' Alice asked.

'Not that we can find out.'

Robert looked towards his father. 'Have we a number to telephone Pips?'

Edwin shook his head. 'No, she always telephones us. George is our link, if we want a message passed to her.'

Henrietta had sat down again. 'So, no one knows where either Philippa or George were last night?'

'That's right.'

'So, they could have been anywhere. Away from London. Out somewhere in the city, perhaps, and taken shelter.' Henrietta was clutching at straws. She knew it, they all knew it, but could fully understand why. And she had a point. No one knew for sure yet whether they had been in the building at all.

'Is Paul there? At – at the site?'

'No, but there is someone we know there helping in the search.'

'Who?'

'Mitch Hammond.'

The telephone shrilled as they were about to sit down for dinner, even though no one felt like eating now.

'I'll go,' Robert said, starting to rise, but Milly forestalled him.

'No, please let me answer it. Paul promised to telephone so that I could – could relay any messages.'

Robert struggled for a moment and then realized that this was exactly why the kind-hearted young woman had travelled all this way. She hadn't wanted the family to receive bad news in an impersonal telephone call. He forced a smile and nodded.

Milly rushed to the telephone. She returned a few moments later – moments that seemed like hours to the anxious family.

'That was Paul. He's in touch with the site. They brought out two bodies earlier. A man and a woman, but they've not been identified yet.' She rushed on, 'But Paul says it can't be George or Pips because Mitch is there and he'd know.'

They tried to eat, they tried to make conversation, but both were impossible. They were all listening for the telephone to ring again.

Thirty-Seven

The telephone at the hall rang again a little before midnight just as the family were discussing whether or not they ought to go to bed.

'I'll stay up,' Milly had offered. 'I know Paul will ring as soon as he knows anything definite, whatever time it is. I can always wake you.'

'My dear girl, that is thoughtful of you,' Edwin said, 'but I doubt any of us will sleep anyway. Why don't we all have something to drink and perhaps a sandwich so we can let the staff go to bed. I know Wainwright is still hovering in the hall.'

'Yes, let's do that,' Henrietta began, but at that moment the telephone trilled again. Milly leapt up and hurried to it.

Eventually, after what once more seemed an age, she came back into the parlour. This time there were tears in her eyes, but she said swiftly, 'They've brought out two more – a man and a woman – and Mitch was able to identify them. One is George and the other is George's daughter, Rebecca. There's no sign of Pips, but they're still searching.'

'So, they still don't know that she's *not* there, do they?' Henrietta said.

'I'm sorry, they can't say for sure. Not yet. Paul

now thinks she might be at – her place of work. He's been trying to get in touch all afternoon and evening, but a lot of the telephone wires are down – as you might expect. We're lucky he's been able to get through here.'

'Of course, I hadn't thought of that,' Henrietta murmured, her face bleak with sadness. 'Poor George – and Rebecca.'

But their minds – quite naturally – were still filled with thoughts of their beloved Pips.

Alice rose. 'I'll go and get those drinks and sandwiches now and tell the staff to go to bed. What d'you want me to tell them about . . . ?' She waved her hand helplessly.

'All that we know, Alice dear. They have a right to know.'

She paused at the door. 'And what about Daisy? How are we going to get word to her?'

'I'd leave telling Daisy for the moment,' Robert said, 'until we have some definite news about Pips.'

Despite her face being numb with cold most of the time, Daisy had quite enjoyed the long trip north, stopping every so often to refuel and for the night at the nearest airfield when it grew dark. The evening spent in the company of lively RAF boys was filled with music and laughter.

'Now when, lovely lady, are you going to bring us Spitfires?' one of them asked her.

She grimaced. 'I only wish I knew.'

'They can't keep you away from them for ever.

We need the Spits up here as badly as anywhere else. Just get on to your boss, will you?'

'Believe me,' Daisy said, 'it's not for the lack of trying.'

When he left work just after midnight, Paul went to the bombed street in Clapham where George and Pips had lived. It was a foggy night and, thankfully, the bombers had not come again. As he neared the site, he heard a scrabbling sound. Slits of lights, like those used on cars in the blackout, illuminated a small patch where a man was still carefully sifting through the rubble.

'Mitch! Oh mate, are you still here?'

'I can't leave, Paul, till I know one way or the other.'

'You should get some rest and come back in the morning. You can't do much more tonight and there'll be more willing hands tomorrow – well, today now.'

'But what if she's still alive under there,' he said brokenly, 'and I leave her . . .'

Paul put his arm around Mitch's shoulders. 'If she's in there, Mitch, she won't be alive. She can't be.'

Gently, he led Mitch, now unresisting, away. He slumped against Paul who half led, half carried him towards his car. 'Come home with me and I'll bring you back first thing in the morning.'

As Paul opened the door and led the way into their darkened flat, Mitch said, 'Is Milly in bed? Does she know?'

'Milly's not here. She was in the country at her parents' place, but she's gone up to Lincolnshire to be with Pips's family. I telephone her if there's any news and she relays it to the family. It was her idea to go. She didn't want them to hear via an impersonal telephone call.'

Mitch tried to smile as he thought about Milly. 'She's a sweetheart,' he murmured. Gently, like a nurse, Paul helped Mitch out of his dirty clothes and into a hot bath. Then he made him sit at the kitchen table to eat a sandwich and drink some tea, before taking him to one of the spare bedrooms and tucking him into bed. The exhausted man was asleep almost immediately. Whilst he slept, Paul bathed and dressed his damaged hands. When he had finished, he stood looking down at him. 'My God, Mitch Hammond,' he murmured. 'How you do love that woman.'

Unable to sleep, the Maitland family all rose early and were still at the breakfast table when Milly answered the telephone. Coming back into the Great Hall, she shook her head. 'No more news, I'm afraid. Paul went there last night – to the site – and found Mitch still digging on his own in the dark. He took him back to our flat, but Mitch insisted on being taken back to the site this morning. Paul still can't get through to – um – where Pips works, so he's taking the day off and going to travel there himself. He'll let me know.'

In the village, folk were up early at the start of what they thought would be a normal day.

'Norah. *Norah!* You here?'

'I'm upstairs making the bed, Bess. What is it?'

'Bad news, duck. You'd better come down.'

Bess moved about Norah's kitchen, setting the kettle on the hob and placing cups and saucers on the table.

Norah opened the door leading from the stairs into the kitchen, her eyes fearful. 'What is it?' she asked again.

'The bombing in London on Sunday night was the worst they've known – and that's sayin' summat – and the flat where Miss Pips and her husband live took a direct hit. Our Betty came to tell us.'

Norah gasped, her eyes widening. 'Is she – are they . . . ?'

'Him and his daughter – they're dead – but they haven't found Miss Pips yet. If she was there . . .' She left the words hanging between them, but her meaning was clear.

Bletchley Park wasn't far from London. On arrival, Paul's War Office credentials were examined and he was taken to the main house and shown into a small room on the left-hand side of the main entrance.

'Someone will come to see you, sir. If you'd like to sit down.'

But he didn't sit down; he paced the floor restlessly. After what seemed an interminable wait, a woman appeared. 'I understand you are asking to see Mrs Allender?'

'Is she here?'

'What is it about?'

Paul held his frustration in check – but only just. 'I have some very bad news for her. Her husband was killed in an air raid the night before last and right at this moment I don't know if she was with him and hasn't been found yet. So, please, just tell me – is she here?'

The woman's face softened and at once she said, 'Yes, she is. She's been on a watch of nights, so she'll be in bed at this moment. Do you want me to tell her?'

'No,' Paul snapped, a little more sharply than he'd intended. At once, he said, 'I'm sorry, but I'd like to tell her myself. If you could organize that, I'd be very grateful.'

'Please wait here. I'll fetch her myself, but I'll have to go to her digs. They're not far away, but it may take a few minutes, if she is asleep.'

'I hate to wake her,' Paul murmured. 'But I think we should.'

'Of course.'

Again, he paced the room, looking first out of the front windows and then turning back to the fireplace. He couldn't settle; he hardly took in his surroundings. Twenty minutes later – the longest twenty minutes Paul could remember – the door opened and the woman came into the room, ushering Pips in.

'I'll just be outside,' she murmured and left, closing the door quietly behind her.

Pips came towards Paul, holding out her hands. She had dressed hastily and her hair was still tousled from sleep. 'It's bad news, isn't it?'

Paul took her hands and nodded. 'It's George' – Pips pulled in a sharp breath – 'and Rebecca.'

Pips gasped. 'Both of them?'

315

'I'm so sorry, yes.'

'How? The bombing?'

'Come, sit down.' Still holding her hands, he led her to a sofa and they sat down side by side.

'The night before last there was a very bad raid. Your block of apartments took a direct hit.'

'So, they hadn't gone to the shelter?' Her voice trembled and tears filled her eyes.

'No.' He paused and then added, gently, 'They were found together. I presume Rebecca must have been visiting him when they both had some time off.'

Pips nodded. 'She sometimes stayed the night if Matthew was working late. Does he know?'

'He will by now.'

'Has anyone told my family?' Pips wiped her tears, blew her nose and tried to concentrate on practical matters. The time for weeping would surely come, but for now she had to be strong.

'Milly's gone up there to be with them. They know about George and Rebecca but not that you're safe. None of us knew until this moment that you were here. I couldn't get through by telephone, but of course a lot of the lines are down because of the bombing. Miraculously, I can get through to Lincolnshire. Besides, I wanted to see you in person to break the news.'

Pips nodded. 'I'd better ring home. They'll let me telephone from here.'

For a moment, Pips leaned her face against Paul's shoulder and he put his arm around her. 'Poor George,' she whispered. 'My poor, darling George and Rebecca too. Matthew will be devastated.'

Paul held her close. One day, he decided, he would tell her about Mitch and his frantic search for her, but now was not the time.

Thirty-Eight

It was the middle of the afternoon by the time the telephone rang again at the hall. The family were all in the parlour; no one wanted to move very far from any news that might come. Conrad had taken over all the surgery duties and the home visits so that Robert could stay with his family until they heard some definite news. Milly rushed to answer it, leaving the door into the parlour open.

'Hello . . . ?' There was a pause and then a shriek. 'Pips – oh Pips, *dahling*. Wait, let me get your father.' But before she could move, they'd all risen and were hurrying into the hall. Edwin reached for the receiver, his voice husky as he said, 'Pips? Is that you?'

'Yes, it's me. I'm fine. I wasn't in London.'

'Thank God!' Edwin murmured, but then he cleared his throat. 'We're all so very sorry to hear about George and his daughter. If there's anything you need us to do, you must tell us. We could come down . . .'

'Thank you. I'll let you know. I'll keep in touch. Give my love to everyone—' Her voice broke and she rang off hastily. Edwin replaced the receiver slowly. 'I'm sorry,' he said, glancing at his wife. 'She's very upset.'

318

Henrietta nodded and murmured, 'Of course.'

Leading the way back into the parlour, she turned to Wainwright who was hovering in the doorway. 'Please tell all the staff that Miss Philippa is safe and then – would you bring us some fresh tea?'

The butler inclined his head and hurried away.

'I suppose I ought to be getting back,' Milly said, 'unless there's anything else I can do.' She smiled tremulously. 'I don't want to outstay my welcome.'

'My dear Milly,' Henrietta said, 'you could never do that. You've been an absolute angel – so kind and thoughtful to come all this way to be with us. We're very grateful.'

'At least stay until tomorrow morning,' Alice suggested. 'We don't want you travelling back when there might be more bombing.'

'That's kind of you. I will, but I want to get back to be there for Pips.'

'I thought you were staying in the country with your parents,' Alice said.

'I was, but I won't go back there straightaway, not until I've seen if Pips needs my help. Oh dear . . .' Suddenly Milly's face crumpled as the enormity of Pips's loss overwhelmed her.

Alice moved to her at once and put her arms about her. 'You've been so wonderfully brave for all of us.'

Milly pulled in a deep breath and dried her tears. 'George was such a dear man. Pips must be devastated. Paul will look after her, I know – he'll take her to our apartment – but I do want to get back to her as soon as I can. I mean, she'll have lost everything. All her belongings, apart from what she'd taken with her . . .' Her voice trailed away.

'Are you sure you don't want one of us to come with you?' Robert said.

Milly shook her head firmly. 'No, it would only cause us more worry if you were down in London too. The Blitz, as people are calling it, is dreadful.'

'We shall come for the funeral, of course, bombs or no bombs,' Henrietta said, adding, 'and, Robert, we really ought to try to get in touch with Daisy, now that we have definite news.'

'Yes. I'll telephone Hatfield. Leave that to me.'

Johnny heard the news from Mitch and at once rode over to Hatfield on his motorcycle.

'She's not here,' Gill greeted him. 'I don't think she'll be back until tomorrow at the earliest. They've got her delivering aircraft all over the place up north.' She eyed his worried expression. 'What is it?'

'It's George – her aunty Pips's husband. He's been killed in an air raid in London. His daughter too. I didn't want Daisy to hear it by chance before her family – or I – can tell her.'

'Oh no,' Gill breathed. 'How dreadful.' She thought for a moment and then said, 'Come with me. We'll go and see Mary Bryant. She'll know what to do for the best.'

Their operations manager was very understanding and sympathetic when Gill told her the news and added, 'Daisy was very close to them both.'

The woman picked up the telephone. 'I'll see what I can do to get her back here as soon as possible.'

'I could go and fetch her, if there's a taxi aeroplane free,' Gill offered.

'No need. I can get her deliveries altered to get her back down here. It's no real problem. Certainly not in the circumstances. Leave it with me. I'll let you know.' She smiled a little as she nodded towards Johnny's anxious face. 'Now, take this young man to get a cup of tea. He looks as if he could do with one.'

A little later, Mary Bryant received a telephone call from Robert. 'I'll make sure she's all right,' she promised him. 'She has friends waiting for her and her young man has arrived. He wanted to tell her himself before she heard by accident.'

At the hall, Robert replaced the telephone thoughtfully and then went in search of his wife.

'Alice, darling,' he asked softly, 'don't say anything to anyone else, but who would you describe as Daisy's "young man"?'

Alice gaped at him. 'Well,' she said slowly, 'I can only think of Luke really. Or, I suppose, Harry.'

'She's kept that quiet, the little minx. I wonder which one it is.'

'Probably Luke, if he's gone to her. He's the one with a motorcycle and besides, from what we've heard, Harry has a string of girlfriends.'

'Mm, and he'll leave a few broken hearts in the village.'

Alice smiled and touched her husband's arm. 'It's wartime, Robert. Let him have his fun.'

*

'Whatever are you doing here?' Daisy greeted Johnny as she alighted from the Miles Master she had brought back to Hatfield. Then, seeing his face, she breathed, 'Oh no! What is it?'

He took her arm and led her away from the aircraft, walking towards the office to check in, which she had to do regardless of what was happening in her personal life.

Swiftly, he explained. Tears flooded down her face and they stopped walking whilst he put his arms around her and held her close. As they resumed walking towards the buildings, she clung onto his arm and then, through her tears, she saw Gill hovering near the door.

'I'm so sorry, Daisy,' she said, hugging her. 'Is there anything we can do?'

'I don't know. I can't take it in.'

'The CO has said you can have compassionate leave, if you need it, and, of course, when you know when the funerals are . . .'

'I'll telephone Daddy. He'll know what's happening.'

'The CO said you could use her office.'

Daisy nodded. 'That's kind of her.'

'Daddy – it's me. I've heard the awful news. Johnny came to tell me. What ought I to do? Where's Aunty Pips? Ought I to go to her?'

'She's in London with Milly and Paul. They're looking after her.'

Daisy's voice trembled a little as she said, 'She might have been with him – with Uncle George.'

'We thought for a while she was, but Mitch was there helping in the rescue, so of course he knew it was poor Rebecca and not Pips.'

'Uncle Mitch? He was there?'

'Yes. Milly told us that he's an air-raid warden in the area where Pips and George lived. It was lucky, I suppose.'

After a little more conversation, Daisy replaced the receiver thoughtfully. Luck had nothing to do with it, she thought. She guessed that Mitch had chosen to patrol that area deliberately so that he could watch over Pips.

At the hall, Robert rang off and went to find Alice. 'Well, that solves that question.'

'Which one is that, darling?'

'The one the Operations Manager left us with when she referred to Daisy's "young man".'

'She's told you who it is?'

Despite the sadness in their hearts, Robert chuckled. 'Not that she realized she was doing so but, yes, she did. It was Johnny Hammond who went to tell her about George and Rebecca.'

Thirty-Nine

Pips had been staying with Milly and Paul for over a week. A joint funeral had been arranged in a church as near to where they lived as possible that was still undamaged by the bombing. They were to be buried side by side.

'George once told me that he didn't need to be taken to where his first wife is buried. I know this is what he would have wanted.' Her face was bleak. 'Bless him, he didn't expect to be buried at the same time as his daughter. It's so sad, isn't it?'

'Pips, darling . . .' Milly was on edge. 'There's something I have to ask you and I'm not finding it easy.'

'Oh phooey,' Pips said, finding some of her old spirit. 'You can talk to me about anything, Milly. You should know that by now.'

'All right – yes – but it's about Mitch, you see.'

Levelly, Pips said. 'What about him?'

'He – um – would like to come to the funeral, but he's not sure if you'd want him there.'

Pips stared at her. 'Of course I would. He's our friend.'

Milly relaxed visibly. 'Oh, that's all right, then. I'll send word to him.'

Puzzled, Pips said, 'Why would he think that?'

'Well, because . . .' Milly floundered again. 'He's always had this "thing" about you and . . .'

Pips actually laughed aloud. 'Oh, that nonsense. I thought all that was over long ago.' Her smile faded. 'Although I have to admit, George was always a little – what shall I say – wary, when Mitch was around. But from what I've heard, Mitch has a string of girlfriends.'

'Yes, he has, but, Pips, darling, he's never *married* one of them, now has he?'

The Maitland family insisted that they would come down to London to attend the joint funeral, though Pips begged them not to attend. 'The bombing is less now than it was – ironically since the night they were killed – but no one knows when it might start up again,' she said. Now she was telephoning home each evening. 'George wouldn't have wanted you to put yourselves in danger.'

'We'll stay at a hotel somewhere on the outskirts and get a taxi in,' Edwin said firmly. 'Can you recommend anywhere?'

'I'll ask Milly and we'll book you in. She and Paul know London so much better than even I do.'

'And book two extra rooms for Daisy and Johnny, won't you? Daisy rang here last night. They're coming.'

'What about Luke?'

'Daisy's been in touch with him, but he can't get leave as George isn't classed as a close relative.'

'Understandable, I suppose,' she murmured. 'All right, I'll do as you ask and let you know the details.'

The day of the funeral was foggy and damp but there was a large number of mourners.

'There was a huge piece in the paper about him and I think there are quite a few old army colleagues here as well as people he now works with,' Pips told her family as she met them outside the church. 'He was always well liked. In fact, six serving soldiers from his old regiment are acting as pall bearers and I've chosen his favourite hymns and music and Matthew's chosen the part of the service that will concentrate on Rebecca. Now, we'd better go in. We're sitting on the right-hand side, Matthew's friends on the left. Sadly, he has no family to support him. Father, Mother – will you sit either side of me?'

'Of course, my darling,' Edwin said, putting her hand through his arm, whilst Henrietta walked beside her.

It was a long service as both George and Rebecca were given a full service and glowing tributes were paid to both of them.

They emerged at last into the dank weather for the committal and then walked to a nearby pub where Pips had arranged for refreshments. Not everyone was able to stay; the army personnel excused themselves, citing pressure of duty, and only one or two of George's colleagues from the War Office stayed. Rebecca's nursing friends surrounded Matthew and one or two of his colleagues from the Foreign Office stayed too.

Fortified by the company of her family, Pips found she was able to speak to each and every one of those still present. She hugged Daisy and Johnny, acting as if he was already part of their family.

Watching, Robert raised his eyebrows and murmured to Alice, 'It looks as if we were right. They were holding hands throughout the service.'

'Not much escapes you, my darling, does it?' Alice murmured.

'Not where Daisy's concerned, no.'

At last Pips found herself facing Mitch.

'It was good of you to come,' she said simply. 'Thank you.' She reached out to take his hands into hers, but then noticed that both his hands were bandaged.

'Whatever happened to you?'

'Oh – er – nothing much,' he said awkwardly, trying to hide them behind his back.

'It doesn't look like "nothing much",' she began, but Mitch interrupted her.

'I'm so sorry about George, Pips. He was a fine soldier and an even better man.'

Pips felt the lump in her throat that had been threatening all day grow larger, but she was determined not to cry.

'He was,' she said huskily.

Mitch lingered for a few moments, but the silence between them now was strained. 'I must go,' he said. 'But if there's anything you need, Pips, Milly knows where to find me.'

'Oh Mitch, don't . . .' she began, but already he was hurrying away, weaving through the throng towards the door. As he reached it, however, an imperious voice stopped him. 'Mitch Hammond? I hope you weren't going without a word to me.'

He turned slowly. 'Mrs Maitland,' he murmured

and, unable to lie to this woman whom he admired so much, he said, quite truthfully, 'I'm afraid I must plead guilty to that. I – I'm not sure I should even be here.'

'Of course you should. You are a good friend to Pips.' Her piercing eyes seemed to read his thoughts as she added softly, 'I understand exactly how you feel – and why – but believe me, that is not entering Pips's head. Not today.'

'Of course not. I – wouldn't want it to.'

'Give it time, Mitch. She'll need all her friends over the next few weeks and months. Just be there for her.'

His voice cracked a little as he said, 'Always, Mrs Maitland. Always.'

Then he turned and left abruptly. Pips's mother was far too astute for his comfort.

Henrietta watched him go with narrowed eyes. 'Now,' she murmured to herself, 'I wonder just how he injured his hands so badly? And who, I wonder, could tell me?'

As several of the mourners began to leave, Henrietta sought out Paul. 'Is Philippa going home with you or coming up to Lincolnshire with us?'

He shook his head. 'She wants to get back to her work. She says it's the best thing for her.'

'Actually, knowing her as I do, I agree.' Henrietta glanced fondly across the room to where Milly and Pips were deep in conversation. 'Your wife has been wonderful, Paul. Everyone should have a friend like Milly. Tell me, do you know how Mitch came to damage his hands?'

'Um – yes, I do.'

'And?' she prompted.

He sighed. 'He'll kill me for telling you.'

'I doubt that. Go on.' Henrietta was not a woman to be denied an answer.

'He was one of the first on the scene that night. You know that he is an air-raid warden in that area?' She nodded and he went on. 'I found him still there after several hours, still searching the debris, tearing at it with his bare hands – almost like a madman.'

'Milly mentioned that he was still digging long after the other rescuers had left, but I hadn't realized why. He was searching for her,' Henrietta murmured softly. 'For Philippa. He thought she was under the rubble.'

Paul nodded then begged, 'Please don't tell her. He'd be mortified.'

'No, I understand. Today is not the time to be told something like that, but if she ever asks me about it, Paul, I will not lie to her.'

Solemnly, Paul said, 'I wouldn't expect you to, Mrs Maitland.'

The days and weeks following the funeral for George and his daughter were difficult for Pips, but work was her salvation. Being away from London helped and she was amongst people who, though they knew what had happened, had not known George and therefore were not a constant reminder.

She kept in touch with Matthew, but he too found that the demanding work at the Foreign Office was a blessing.

The weeks passed by and the shock and the acute pain of loss began to lessen, just a little. Pips, always an optimist, tried to think about all the wonderful times they'd shared and how blessed she'd been in the quiet peace of her marriage to George. She still wore the brooch he'd given her as a tribute to the gentle man who'd loved her so dearly. She buried herself in the work which, she now guessed, George, in his concern for her safety, had engineered for her. Once again, she had reason to be grateful for his love, for not only was she away from the dreadful bombing, but also she loved the work at Bletchley. It stretched her mind, was all-consuming and the world outside faded away. Now, more than ever, it was exactly what she needed.

Forty

'What does he think he's doing? It's madness,' Robert said, handing the morning paper over the breakfast table to his father.

Towards the end of June, the newspapers were full of Hitler's invasion of Russia.

'I don't like to think of him attacking yet more countries, poor devils.' Edwin sighed. 'Though, being entirely selfish, it might take the heat off us for a bit.'

'I'm not sure it will. I know the bombing in London has lessened, but now he's got control of airfields in northern France, he's systematically bombing ports and cities throughout Britain. D'you think he still intends to invade us too?'

Edwin shrugged. 'Who knows what a madman will do next, because that's what he is. But if he spreads himself too thinly, that'll be the end of him. It says here he's attacking Russia along an eighteen-hundred-mile front. How can you service the needs of troops along a line like that?'

'I expect he'll find a way,' Robert said grimly. 'Meanwhile, our youngsters will just have to keep on doing what they're doing.'

Finding themselves alone as they finished breakfast,

Edwin said quietly, 'I fear for them, Robert. I really do, especially Luke and Harry and Johnny, too, if we must now look upon him as a member of the family.' He paused and then added, 'Are you happy about that?'

Robert wrinkled his forehead. 'I'm not *un*happy about it, Father, but I worry about Daisy getting hurt. What Johnny does is so very dangerous.'

Edwin sighed heavily and folded up the newspaper as if to shut away any more bad news. 'I know, but all we can do is to be here for them if – God forbid – they should need us.'

'Daisy! *Daisy!*' Gill was running across the airfield towards her as Daisy climbed out of the Anson which had just brought her back to Hatfield. 'Guess what?'

It was Gill's usual greeting when she had a piece of news to impart. Daisy eyed her friend fondly. The girl reached her and was still hopping up and down in excitement, her eyes sparkling. 'You'll *never* guess.'

Daisy smiled and indulged her. 'I'm sure I won't. So – enlighten me.'

'You and me. We're going to be tested on flying' – she paused and pulled in a deep breath – 'Hurricanes.'

Daisy stared at her and her heart felt as if it leapt in her chest. 'What?'

'Hurricanes. We're going to be tested on Hurricanes. All of us, eventually. But five of us – including you and me – are going first. Now, before you say anything' – Gill held out her hand palm outwards as if to fend her off – 'I know it's not Spitfires, but Miss

Gower says we've just got to be patient.' Her grin widened. 'They'll be next.'

Daisy nodded thoughtfully. 'We're getting closer, but I won't be happy until I'm flying a Spit. Anyway, when's this happening?'

'Today. Right now, in fact. Come on.'

'I don't understand.'

'This test pilot has brought a Hurricane from our headquarters at White Waltham. Come *on*, Daisy. Hurry up, or we'll get left out.'

'But I've got to . . .' Daisy began, but already she was running alongside Gill to where a group of excited ATA women pilots were standing near a sleek little aircraft, glinting in the July sunshine.

'Right,' said the pilot who had brought the aeroplane to Hatfield. 'Who's first?'

Daisy felt a dig in her ribs. 'Go on,' Gill hissed. 'You've never stopped going on about flying Hurricanes and Spitfires, so get going.'

Daisy stepped forward and climbed up onto the wing and into the cockpit. After the pilot had gone through the checklist with her, she started the engine and taxied to the take-off point. Her heart was beating rapidly; she was so anxious not to make any serious mistakes. The future of the ATA girls being allowed to fly operational aircraft was, at this moment, on her shoulders, or rather beneath her guiding hands.

'Contact,' she shouted. Her take-off was smooth and she roared into the sky, the sound of the engine thrilling her.

It was a lovely little aircraft, so manoeuvrable that

Daisy was tempted to try a few aerobatics, but knew she mustn't. After a few circles over the airfield, she landed sedately – and perfectly – to allow Gill to climb in next.

'What a beautiful aeroplane,' she enthused when she landed and all five of the girls who had been lucky enough to be chosen agreed as, one by one, they took their flight.

'We're flying fighters,' Daisy murmured, as they watched the aircraft leave the airfield to return to White Waltham. 'We're actually flying fighter aircraft. Come on,' she linked her arms through Gill's and Violet's, 'let's go and celebrate.'

One bright sunny morning in August, Daisy's dream finally came true. As she stared at the delivery chit in her hand, her heart began to beat a little faster. 'Gill,' she whispered. 'I've got it. I've got my first Spitfire.'

'No!' Gill peered over her shoulder to see the words for herself. 'You lucky thing. Don't you realize, you've got *the* first Spitfire for our little group. I wonder when I'll get one.'

'I've to collect it from Castle Bromwich and take it to Duxford.'

'You double lucky thing,' Gill said and there was a definite trace of envy in her voice now. 'You might see Johnny. I can't seem to get a delivery to Tangmere for love nor money.'

But, for once, Daisy's mind was more on flying her first Spitfire than of meeting Johnny.

Gill walked out to the aircraft with her. 'Now,

don't forget to read your notes again and listen to the fitter. They often give us useful tips.'

Daisy smiled inwardly. Gill was doing her 'mother hen' bit.

It seemed appropriate, Daisy thought as she climbed up onto the wing, that she should be given her first Spitfire today. Only yesterday, she had received promotion to first officer and had been given an extra gold stripe.

She fitted perfectly into the close-fitting cockpit and fired up the Merlin engine which sounded so loud close to, but it was a beautiful sound and thrilled Daisy to the core. This was what she had always wanted. The aircraft was so easy to fly, the controls so responsive to her touch. She was in the air and reaching a speed of 250 mph almost before she realized it, climbing and circling with gentle touches on the stick.

Johnny was waiting for her when she landed, his arms outstretched as she climbed out of the cockpit and launched herself from the wing into his arms.

'Isn't she just magnificent? I don't ever want to fly anything else, but I don't expect I'll be that lucky.'

He kissed her soundly and then led her to the officers' mess. 'This calls for a celebration, but I'm afraid it'll only be tea or coffee.'

'Ooh coffee, please. It's in short supply where we are.'

As they sat together, surreptitiously holding hands, Johnny asked, 'So did it live up to expectations?'

'Beyond everything I'd dreamed it would be.' Her eyes were shining, her nerves still tingling with the thrill.

Johnny chuckled. 'I guessed as much. You *look* just like I *felt* the first time I flew a Spit.'

'You just feel so – so right in it. It seems to wrap itself around you like a glove and fly for you.'

'It's what you've wanted for so long. You were made to fly Spitfires, darling.' He paused and then asked tentatively, 'I don't suppose you're staying the night, are you?'

She shook her head. 'No, sorry. Violet's coming for me a bit later. She's got another pick-up first and then will come here.' She squeezed his hand. 'But I think I've got a couple of hours.'

'Daisy, Daisy – guess what?'

'I couldn't begin to guess.' Daisy smiled at her friend. She and Gill had grown even closer over the last few months. Gill had been a terrific support during the awful time after the bombing which had taken the lives of George and his daughter.

'You know that the Number Fifteen Ferry Pool at Hamble has become an all-women's pool. Well, we're being posted there!'

'Really? Just you and me? I'll be sorry to say goodbye to some of the others. We're quite a sister-hood now, aren't we?'

'No, there're quite a few of us going. Violet and . . .' She reeled off several names of the girls who regularly socialized together when the chance came, ending, 'And Mary Bryant is going too as our ops manager there. There's a lot of aircraft production around Southampton and they reckon we're going to be based there so we can get aircraft away from a vulnerable spot on the coast more quickly.' She put her head on one side teasingly as she added, 'All sorts of aircraft, but a big majority will be – Spitfires.'

'Oh, that's all right, then,' Daisy said happily. 'When do we go?'

'Next week.'

Forty-One

There had always been a celebration at the hall for Daisy's and Luke's birthdays which fell close to each other at the beginning of December. Boxing Day too had always been special, for Harry had been born there, arriving unexpectedly when the families were all gathered for Henrietta's annual party.

'I've got an idea,' Alice said, over breakfast one morning in October. 'I don't know if it will work, but we can only ask.'

'What's that, darling?'

'Wouldn't it be nice if we could get them all home together – Pips too – for "the birthdays". We could even ask Gill to come.'

'It's a brilliant idea, but perhaps Gill would want to use any precious leave to go home.'

'Like I said, we can only ask. Maybe she could come here for a day or so and then go on home.'

Miraculously, it seemed to all of them, Alice's idea worked and they all arrived at the hall on 30 November, the night before Daisy's birthday. Even Harry came home to his parents to join an early celebration for his birthday too, just in case he couldn't be at home this year for Boxing Day. Johnny and Gill had also been invited to join the family party.

It was the first time that either Luke or Harry had seen Pips since George's death and they took her aside to express their condolences. She hugged both of them.

'It was such a cruel irony,' Luke said, 'that after that night the constant bombing of London lessened. Of course, they're still coming over here, but they're targeting other cities and towns.'

'I think they're trying to hit industry now,' Harry said. 'Look how they went for Sheffield two nights in a row a year ago.'

'They think the first night when they hit the civilians of Sheffield was a mistake. They came back the next night to target the industrial quarter.'

'We don't think it was,' Harry said. He turned to Pips. 'I've been at Feltwell in Norfolk for a few months now. I'm involved in night-bombing offensives. The talk there is that everything Hitler and his cohorts do is quite deliberate.'

'I wouldn't be at all surprised,' Pips said tartly.

'So, what exactly are you doing, Aunty Pips?'

'Well, for a start, you can both stop calling me "Aunty". Two strapping lads like you calling me that makes me feel incredibly old – and I am determined not to be. George is the very last person who would have wanted me to wear widow's weeds for very long. In fact, he said as much when we first got married.'

'Because he was a bit older than you?'

'How very tactful you are, Luke.'

'He was years older than you,' Harry chirped up.

Pips laughed and gestured her head towards Harry,

'But I can't say the same about him.' She linked her arms through theirs and led them to the table where a wartime feast awaited them all. 'Though, I have to be truthful, Harry, you are right, but he was a lovely husband. We had a wonderful time whilst we were together and I will never – ever – regret marrying him. But we all have to move on. I expect both of you are finding that out when you lose fellow pilots. It doesn't mean you don't care, just that you have to cope. Now come on, tuck in. My mother and your families too must have been hoarding stuff for weeks to make this.'

'That's against the law, isn't it?' Harry said.

'In large quantities, yes, but not just to save up a few bits for special occasions – and your birthdays are certainly that.'

As they helped themselves to Spam sandwiches and a slice each of carrot flan, Luke said, 'You still haven't told us where you are and what you're doing, Pips.'

'I'm sorry, I'm not allowed to, but it is helping the war effort. That's all I can tell you.'

'Ho, ho, are you a spy?' Harry guffawed.

'Not exactly, but it is top secret, so I'm trusting you not to go telling anyone even that.'

'We won't,' the young men chorused, now completely serious.

'We're always getting it drummed into us that "careless talk costs lives",' Luke said and Harry added, 'And "Be like Dad, Keep Mum". I like that one.'

'And now I must circulate the room a bit. It's good to see you both. Stay safe, won't you?'

'You too, Pips.'

'I suppose,' Harry remarked as she walked away, 'we can't drop the "Aunty" from "Aunty Hetty"?'

'Lord, no. I wouldn't like to be in your shoes if you tried. That was a rare privilege granted to us when we were young.'

'She never seems to age, does she? She's as energetic as ever.'

'Who? Aunty Hetty?'

'Mm. Just look at her moving around the room, making sure everyone has got something to eat. How old must she be now?'

'Mid-seventies, I'd guess. At least.'

'What about Dr Maitland? He's beginning to look a bit older now.'

'Ah, now I do know that. Mam said he had his eightieth birthday last year, but they didn't celebrate it because of the war.'

'Well, I hope I'm as good as they are when I'm their age,' Harry said.

'Aye,' Luke said with feeling. 'If we survive to make old bones, Harry.'

On the other side of the room, Pips found Bess Cooper.

'Nah then, Miss Pips,' the older woman greeted her. 'We was right sorry to hear of your loss.'

'Thank you, Mrs Cooper, and thank you for your lovely letter. I did appreciate it.'

'I wish we could've supported you at the funeral.'

'I didn't expect it. It's a long way to come and not the safest of places at the moment.'

'No. Terrible, isn't it? All this bombing. Even

Lincoln got a bit of a pasting in May.' Her face was bleak as she added, 'And look at my two grandsons over there. Very smart in their uniforms, aren't they? But we're not daft, we know that every time they go up they might not come back.'

Pips sighed. 'Sadly, Mrs Cooper, I can't argue with that.' Pips glanced across the room towards Clara Nuttall. 'Mrs Nuttall seems to be coping better this time.'

'Oh, she's worried sick like the rest of us, but your mam forestalled her taking to her bed this time by enlisting her into the WVS. Clara feels she's doing summat worthwhile. It's what she needs. It's what we all need. We all need to keep busy and feel we're helping.'

'What about Mr and Mrs Dawson?' Pips gestured towards Norah and Len, who were now talking to Luke and Harry. 'I'm glad to see that he's at least speaking to them both.'

'He's not forgiven Luke exactly, but at least he hasn't disowned him like he did William.'

'And is he managing with his business?'

'Aye. Sam's there, of course, and they've taken on a couple of lads from the village, though they might have to go to war when they reach eighteen.'

'Still no change over William, then?'

Bess snorted derisively. 'I dun't reckon there ever will be. No one hears from him now, Miss Pips. It's to be expected, I suppose, now he's living in occupied territory, but it's breaking poor Norah's heart. It's the not knowing.'

'Don't say anything to her, Mrs Cooper. I wouldn't

want to raise her hopes, but I'll see if I can find out anything. Of course, poor George would have helped, but I still have contacts at both the War Office and the Foreign Office. I'll do what I can.'

'Thank you, Miss Pips, I know you will. And now' – she nodded towards where Luke and Harry were talking and laughing with Daisy, Johnny and Gill – 'you can tell me just what is going on with those youngsters over there, because there's summat. You mark my words.'

Pips stared at them. 'I really haven't a clue, Mrs Cooper. I haven't seen any of them lately. Only Daisy and Johnny at George's funeral—' She paused and then added thoughtfully, 'But whatever's going on, as you put it, they all seem to be happy about it.'

If Pips and Bess could have overheard the conversation between the youngsters, as they called them, they would soon have realized exactly what was happening.

'So, Luke, you're seeing Gill, are you?' Johnny was saying.

Luke and Gill smiled at each other. 'We are now that we know about you and Daisy.'

Now everyone turned to look at Harry. 'What about you, Harry?' Johnny said. 'Are you going to challenge me to a duel over Daisy?'

Harry laughed so loudly that several heads in the room turned to look at him. 'No, I wish the four of you every happiness.'

'But you've always said you were going to marry Daisy one day,' Luke said.

Harry laughed again. 'That was only because I

thought *you* were going to. What is it they call it now? Sibling rivalry? I didn't want to be outdone by my elder brother.'

Daisy chuckled. 'And there I was thinking I had two handsome young men vying for my hand.'

'Three,' Johnny murmured, taking her hand and raising it to his lips.

'Just one thing, Johnny Hammond,' Luke said and this time he was serious. 'You mind you take care of her. If you ever hurt our Daisy, you'll have both me and Harry to contend with.'

Harry grinned. 'And we might very well challenge you to a duel then.'

As they moved back to the table to gather another plateful of food each, Daisy slipped her arm through Harry's. 'Have you got a girlfriend somewhere, Harry?'

'Oh, dozens of 'em, Dais. "Safety in numbers" – that's my motto.'

Forty-Two

Whenever Daisy or Gill had leave, they got in touch with Johnny or Luke to see if they could get leave too. Sometimes it was Daisy and Johnny who could meet, sometimes Gill and Luke. On one very rare occasion the following March, all four of them managed to get a weekend off at the same time. They met in a London hotel, the two young men insisting that they should splash out and treat the girls. They dined at the hotel and then went dancing.

'We haven't got pretty dresses to wear,' Daisy moaned. 'We shall look so out of place in our uniforms.'

But when they arrived at the dance hall, they found nearly all the dancers were in uniform. When a Charleston struck up, there were only a few dancers left on the floor, Johnny and Daisy being one of the couples.

'I can't do this,' Gill said. 'Let's sit and watch them.'

When the music stopped, Johnny and Daisy were breathless but smiling, especially when they got a round of applause.

The evening ended with a slow, romantic waltz. As they walked back to the hotel, Daisy said, 'And we didn't even get an air raid.'

'I don't think we'd have heard it anyway,' Johnny said, pausing to kiss her. 'Oh Daisy, when will it all be over?'

She wound her arms round his neck. 'When we've sent Adolf packing, and now we've got America in the war, I'm sure it's not going to take so long.'

The whole world had been shocked by the sudden unprovoked attack by Japan on Pearl Harbor in the previous December, but at least Britain no longer stood alone.

'But in the meantime . . .' Daisy whispered.

In April 1942, Luke received promotion and was posted to RAF Hornchurch.

'You were so close to Hamble when you were at Tangmere,' Gill moaned.

'Nothing's too far on my motorbike to come and see you, darling. And you'll still be ferrying aircraft to us.' Luke had tried to cheer her up. 'Just be thankful it's not the north of Scotland.'

'Briefing in ten minutes, chaps,' Tim Millerchip shouted across the mess one morning in early May. Luke threw down his newspaper and followed his friend.

Close friendships were rare. It was hard enough to deal with the losses after each mission without losing a good mate, but Luke and Tim, who came from Yorkshire, had become friends. They socialized in the mess but whenever they had a proper leave – which wasn't often at the same time anyway – Tim would go home to see his parents, sister and girlfriend and Luke, too, would try to see Gill or visit

Lincolnshire. On duty, however, they often flew side by side and would watch out for each other as often as possible.

'Where to this time?' Luke asked him as they walked to the briefing room together.

'Rumour is that it's escort duty for bombers on a mission to an electric power plant in northern France, but we'll get details in a minute.'

At a quarter to three that afternoon, their squadron took off from Hornchurch to meet up with the bombers over Clacton. The bombers reached their target, but because of low cloud, they did not drop their bombs. They returned home and landed unscathed, but Luke's squadron was attacked by German fighters and suddenly the sky over northern France was filled with swooping aircraft and the noise of gunfire.

Luke felt a jolt and knew his aircraft had been hit. The engine burst into flames and the Spitfire, uncontrollable now, went into a steep dive. He must get out . . .

Daisy was flying a Spitfire to Duxford under a cloudy sky. She grinned to herself. If the cloud got worse, she might have to stay overnight. She just hoped Johnny would be there.

When she taxied to a halt, three airmen came running to help her. Johnny was not amongst them, but she recognized one of his friends, Martin.

'Hi, Daisy. Johnny's not here, but he should be back any time soon. Are you staying?' He grinned and winked at her. 'It's getting late and the weather's very murky.'

Daisy laughed. 'The Fox Tiger's supposed to be picking me up. If it arrives, then of course I'll have to go.'

'Come into the mess whilst you wait. We'll look after you until Johnny gets back. Does he know you were coming here today?'

Daisy shook her head. 'No. Usually we don't know where we're going until we get given our delivery chits each morning.'

The three of them kept her laughing helplessly for over an hour. There was no sign of Johnny or the Fox Moth as the weather turned worse. Rain clouds blew in and the day darkened.

'I'd better telephone Hamble to find out what's happening.'

When she was put through to the Operations Manager, Mary said, 'The taxi isn't coming. The weather's closed in here. Sorry, Daisy. You'll have to stay the night there.'

Daisy's heart leapt. Now she had official permission – no, more than that, an order – to stay. But at Mary's next words, her delight faded. 'By the way, Johnny's here. He had engine trouble over the Channel and decided to land here. His Spitfire is being checked out now.'

When Daisy returned to Martin and the others, her disappointment had turned into amusement at the irony of it. 'He's there and I'm here,' she told them. 'You couldn't plan it, could you?'

Martin laughed. 'Maybe he did.'

Remembering Johnny's earlier escapade, she thought it quite likely, but instead she pursed her mouth primly and said, 'Oh, I'm sure Johnny would never do something like that.'

'Come off it, Daisy. We'd all do it to see our girl-friends if we thought we could get away with it. Now, let's go and see if we can find you a bed for tonight and then we're taking you out to dinner. None of us are flying tonight.'

Very early the following morning, Daisy felt someone shaking her shoulder very gently. 'Daisy, Daisy, it's me.'

Sleepily, she held out her arms to him.

As Luke landed with a thump and rolled over, he felt as if the breath had been knocked out of his body, but he knew he must hide his parachute and himself as quickly as possible. Breathing hard, he gathered in the billowing silk. He looked about him. No sign of soldiers running towards him with guns pointing at him. Just a small herd of cows, lazily munching grass, eyed him with curiosity. In the far distance he saw the smoke billowing from his crashed Spitfire and prayed it had not landed on buildings. To his left was a copse. Bundling his parachute under his arm, he ran towards the trees. Only beneath their cover did he start to breathe more easily. He pushed the parachute into a thicket of bushes and then crept quietly to the edge of the wood. Where on earth was he? Driven off course in the dogfight, he could be anywhere in France or even Belgium.

He was thankful that his burning Spitfire had carried on flying for several miles after he had bailed out. He hoped that if the Germans searched around the crash site – as they undoubtedly would – they wouldn't think to come this far to look for the pilot.

He had a compass, but if he didn't even know where he was to start with, it wasn't a lot of use. If he was still somewhere near their target, he would need to head north-west to reach Calais or Dunkirk, but those towns would be heavily guarded. He wouldn't stand a chance travelling on his own. Unless he could meet up with a member of the Resistance who could direct him to an organized escape route, there wasn't much he could do other than surrender to the Germans and spend the rest of the war in a prison camp somewhere.

'Not an option,' he muttered.

He stood for several minutes beneath the shadow of the rustling trees, scanning the countryside. On this side of the copse the land sloped down into a shallow valley. At the bottom, he could see a farmhouse and people moving about the farmyard. But no one seemed to be coming to look for him. Perhaps they hadn't seen the parachute and where his plane had crashed was some distance away. He wondered if the cows in the field where he had landed belonged to the farmer. Perhaps he could approach him when he came to fetch them for milking. Born and brought up in the countryside, Luke knew the cows weren't yet ready to be milked, so he decided to use the time to reconnoitre the land from each side of the copse.

By the time the afternoon light was fading, Luke had found out that on the other three sides of the copse the land stretched away to the far distance with no sign of a village or even lone houses. The only dwelling he had seen was the farm in the valley below on the west side of the trees. He returned there and sat down, watching for signs of life. Then he heard a dog bark and saw a collie running up the slope, followed by a farmer carrying a stick. He swore softly. He hadn't reckoned on a dog being about, but then it stood to reason; farmers always had a dog or two. The animal seemed to be about to run straight past him to where the cows were, but suddenly it stopped and sniffed the air. It glanced back towards its master, who was plodding slowly up the slope. Then it came closer. Luke got up slowly and stood very still, but kept his gaze fixed firmly on the sheepdog. If it was going to attack him, he needed to be ready.

A shrill whistle halted the dog in its cautious approach. It listened for a moment, but then came on. The farmer came level with the dog and whistled again. Then he shouted, but the dog ignored him. It lay down only a few feet in front of Luke and stayed still, just like a well-trained sheepdog. But this time, Luke thought, wryly, he's herding a man. Luke was still standing beneath the shadows and could not be easily seen by the farmer. He held his breath, hoping the man would call the dog away, but instead the farmer with a muttered oath turned towards them.

There was no use in running away; the dog would follow him and then probably attack him and the last thing Luke wanted was to be bitten. As the farmer neared the dog, he bent to pat it and spoke in a language which Luke didn't understand. Then the farmer looked up and saw him. He gave a start and raised his stick, pointing it at Luke. He spoke again but because he didn't understand, Luke used the only universal language he knew. He raised his arms above his head in surrender.

The man gestured him to move forwards. With one eye on the dog, Luke moved out from beneath the trees. The animal was now standing docilely beside his master awaiting any instruction, but not moving. The farmer's glance raked Luke and then, suddenly, he smiled. 'RAF,' he said in a guttural voice.

'Yes, sir.'

In precise English, though with a strong accent, the farmer said, 'You were in that plane?'

He gestured with his head in the direction where Luke's Spitfire had crashed.

'Yes.'

The farmer glanced about him. 'Parachute?'

'I've hidden it in the bushes,' Luke said slowly and clearly.

The farmer nodded. 'Later, I will burn it.'

Did this mean the man was going to help him? The farmer's next words confirmed Luke's hopes. 'You must stay here. Too dangerous . . .' He gestured towards his farm. 'I will bring you food and clothes. We must burn your uniform too. Tonight, I will get in touch with someone who can help you.'

Carefully, Luke lowered his arms.

'You are very kind, but I wouldn't want to put you in danger.'

The man shrugged. 'We are glad to help the British. They helped us last time and again this time.' There was bitterness in the tone and Luke felt sympathy for the man and all his compatriots whose country had been invaded for a second time in only twenty-five years. 'Now, I must get my cows. Carry on as normal. Stay hidden. Sometimes patrols come by.' He turned and moved away, calling to his dog. He did not look back. If anyone had been watching, they could not have seen Luke beneath the trees, only a farmer and his dog.

As darkness came, Luke moved back to the edge of the copse, watching for any movement from the farmhouse below. He wasn't quite sure whether he trusted the farmer. Perhaps he would bring a German patrol and Luke would be captured. But right at this moment, Luke had no choice but to stay where he was and take his chances. He didn't know where he was and to set off blindly in an occupied country with no help was madness.

He would just have to put his faith in the farmer and his dog and wait until nightfall.

Forty-Three

Back at Hornchurch at the debriefing it was discovered that Luke was one of the missing fighter pilots. Each returning Spitfire pilot was asked what they had seen.

'Last time I saw Luke,' Tim reported, 'he was being chased by a Focke-Wolf.'

'In which direction?'

'North-west, I think.'

'And you didn't see him hit? Or go down?'

Tim shook his head. 'I was a bit busy myself.'

'Quite,' the officer debriefing the crews murmured. 'So, he could have come down in northwestern France or even just into Belgium. Is that right?'

'Yes, sir, I think so.'

'Very well. We'll see what intelligence can tell us, but I'd better inform the CO. He likes to tell the families before they hear anything from another source. Do you know any of his family?'

'Only his girlfriend. She's an ATA pilot. She some-times comes here to deliver aircraft.'

'Ah, yes, now you mention it, I've seen them together. Well, Millerchip, not a word to anyone until the CO's had time to get in touch with his immediate family. I see we have a telephone number for him. Will that be his parents?'

Tim shook his head. 'No, sir. He lives in a small village in Lincolnshire and that number is the hall. A family called Maitland live there, I think. Luke's related to them by marriage, but it's not his home.'

'But he's given this number as a contact number in case of – well, in a case like this.'

'Yes, sir.'

'Thank you, Millerchip. That will be all.'

As darkness shrouded the airfield and there was no sign of a damaged Spitfire limping home, the CO decided he must make the telephone calls – or write letters – to the loved ones of the pilots who had not returned. In due course, the parents would receive an official notification from the War Office, but he liked to send a more personal message before then. He regarded all his pilots as being in his care and he felt the loss of each and every one.

He sighed as he picked up the receiver of the telephone on his desk and asked the operator to put through a call to Lincolnshire.

'I'll get it, Wainwright,' Robert said, rising from the dinner table. 'It'll probably be for me anyway and we've all finished.'

As he picked up the receiver the rest of his family went into the parlour, apart from Alice, who, sensing bad news at this late hour, followed him to the telephone.

'What is it?' Alice asked at once as he replaced the receiver.

His face solemn, his eyes anxious, Robert turned to her and put his arm about her shoulders. 'It was

Luke's CO. Luke was escorting bombers on a mission to northern France. He's – he's not come back.'

Alice stared up at him. 'Oh no! Is there – is there no hope?'

'There's always hope, my darling. No one saw him go down, so they don't know if he bailed out. Or he might have had to land if his aircraft was damaged or he ran out of fuel. There are all sorts of possibilities, so at the moment he's just posted as "missing".'

'Is it usual to telephone?'

'I'm not sure. The CO – he seemed a very caring man – said he liked to get a personal message to relatives before the official telegram or letter arrived.'

'He must have a very difficult job.'

'He must. I wouldn't want it.'

'So, what do we do?'

'I'll go and tell Peggy and Sam right away.'

'Would you like me to come with you?'

'Yes, I would. We'll get Jake to take us in the car. It's dark now and there's no moon. But let's tell Mother and Father first.'

Henrietta and Edwin were saddened by the news. 'Tell Peggy and Sam to let us know if there's anything we can do,' Henrietta said as Robert and Alice left.

'I'm afraid we've bad news, Jake,' Robert told him as they climbed into the car. 'Luke has been reported missing, somewhere over France, we think.'

'That's terrible, I'm so sorry.' Jake had received an official exemption from serving in the forces because of his valuable work on the land, but it didn't stop him feeling guilty every time bad news came to the district. This time it was even closer to home.

'Don't say anything to anyone until there's been time for all his family to hear.'

'Not a word, Master Robert.'

He drew the car to a halt outside the cottage where Sam and Peggy lived.

'Are you coming in with us, Jake?'

'No, Master Robert. If you don't mind, I'll wait here.'

'We might be some time.'

'I'll be fine.'

When Sam opened the door to find both Robert and Alice there, he knew at once that something had happened for them both to call this late in the evening. 'Come in. Peggy's in the kitchen. You go into the front room. I'll get her.'

'It's all right. We'll come with you.'

As Sam ushered them into the kitchen, Peggy looked up, stared at their solemn faces for a brief moment and then tears filled her eyes.

'Which one of them?' she whispered before Robert could speak. 'Tell me quickly.'

Robert took her hand. 'Sit down, Peggy love. It's Luke. He's been posted missing over France.'

As his words filtered into her shocked brain, she murmured, 'Missing? Not – not killed?'

'No. None of his fellow pilots saw his plane go down so they don't actually know what happened. Not yet.'

'And they'll let us know if they hear any more?'

'Of course. You'll be getting an official communication of some sort that will just say the same, but don't let that worry you,' Robert said and explained the kindness of Luke's CO.

'So,' Sam said, 'there's hope, then?'

'Yes,' Robert nodded and repeated what he had said to Alice earlier, 'there's always hope.'

Luke strained his eyes through the darkness, watching and listening. A light drizzle had begun, but beneath the trees, he was sheltered. When the farmer had returned his cows to the field after milking, he had brought a basket of food and a bundle of clothes. There was even a rain cape that Luke now had around his shoulders. The clothes fitted him well enough not to draw attention to him; some old clothes of the farmer's, he guessed, who was just a little taller and broader than Luke was. He'd even thought to bring underwear too, so that now Luke was not wearing anything that was British. The only things he'd kept – which he would have to dispose of quickly, if he faced capture – were his watch, his compass and his dog tag.

'We'll hide your uniform with the parachute. Show me where it is.'

Together they'd pushed Luke's clothes deep into the bushes.

'When you are safely away,' the farmer had said, as they walked back to the edge of the copse, 'I will burn them all.'

'Thank you.'

'Now, you must stay here hidden until dark. Someone – a young man – will come for you. Don't ask him any questions, nor will he ask you any, but you need to tell me where you'd like him to take you, if he can.'

'Can you tell me where we are, because I have no idea?'

'Not far from Dranouter in Flanders.'

'Belgium?' Luke couldn't keep the surprise from his tone.

'That is correct.'

Luke thought quickly, turning over an idea in his mind. 'Could he get me to Ypres, do you think?'

The man shrugged. 'That shouldn't be a problem. It will take about three hours to walk there. Easier, probably, than the normal way to the coast. All the ports are heavily guarded.'

He glanced at Luke but said nothing. Feeling he owed the farmer some kind of explanation, but not wanting to give the man too much information, Luke said carefully, 'I know Ypres. I've been there before.'

'Ah.' The farmer was thoughtful for a moment then shrugged again. 'There will be help there if you need it. You'll just have to find it. But be careful, the Germans are there.'

The farmer had left him then and the long wait until darkness had begun.

It was gone midnight when he heard a rustling through the grass as someone came up the slope towards him. The figure, clothed in black and with a hood hiding much of his face, paused only a few yards from where Luke was standing, still and silent. The figure cupped his hands around his mouth and hooted softly like an owl. Luke gave an answering call. Trained in following the direction of a sound, the man moved closer until they could see each other through the gloom. They shook hands and the guide spoke in English, though he was not as fluent as the farmer and said only a few words. 'We go to Ypres – yes?'

'Yes, please.'

After the farmer had left him for the last time, Luke had pondered whether he should have told him the real place he wanted to go to, but then decided it was safer to say Ypres. He had to trust his life to these strangers – he needed their help – but he didn't want them to learn too much about him. Besides, he could find his own way from Ypres.

'About thirteen kilometres,' his guide was saying. 'Maybe further. No roads, only country.'

'I understand,' Luke said, thankful for the sturdy boots the farmer had brought him. Luckily, they fitted well, otherwise he might get blisters walking that distance.

They set off, his guide walking a few paces in front of Luke, pausing every few minutes to look and to listen. They were fortunate; there was no sound of patrols or of any vehicles. The good people of the district were in their beds and the Germans thought the open countryside hardly worth a look. No doubt, if they were looking for him, it would be near where his aircraft had crashed. As he walked, he thought about those at home and wondered how he could get a message to them that he was alive, if, at the moment, not exactly safe.

Forty-Four

Peggy had made tea for them all and they sat round her kitchen table.

'What's Len Dawson going to say to this?' Peggy whispered.

'I'll tell him in the morning,' Sam said. 'I'll see Mrs Dawson too. You go and see your mother, Peggy. I don't think we should tell anyone else tonight.'

'There might be more news in the morning,' Robert said, but he didn't sound too hopeful. 'We'll let you know at once, of course, if we hear anything.'

'Are you going to tell Daisy?' Peggy asked. 'And I'd better write to Harry.'

'Yes, of course, and I'll also write to Pips. They'll probably both telephone us then.'

It was still an hour or so before dawn by the time they arrived on the outskirts of Ypres, yet already people were about.

'I go no further,' his guide whispered. 'Germans in town.'

They were near the Menin Gate, the huge white memorial dedicated to all those who had lost their lives in the Ypres Salient in the Great War. Strangely, Luke felt comforted. He felt – foolishly or not – as if all those named there were watching over him. He thought back to when he had been here almost fifteen years ago now at the inauguration of the memorial. That time, his grandfather Dawson had allowed Luke to come to Belgium because Pips had promised to take him to see the graves of his father, Harold, and his uncles, Bernard and Roy Dawson. How sad it was that all these thousands of men had given their lives believing that their sacrifice was to bring peace to the world for ever, only for the same foes to be fighting over the same ground just over two decades later.

Luke shook hands with the man who had brought him here. 'Move at night,' his guide warned and then he slipped away into the shadows. As the dawn filtered through the streets and lit the memorial with a rosy glow, Luke walked the length of the towering archway. Still standing beneath its shadow, he looked down the street towards the market square. He could see mounds of rubble and was shocked to think that the city had received yet more damage after it had been so lovingly restored after the devastation of the Great War. But he dared not venture from his current shelter to take a closer look. He pondered what he should do for the day. He didn't want to run into the enemy and yet he didn't want to hide. If he were found doing so, it would be a giveaway that he had reason to conceal himself. If only he could find something to do that would look completely normal. He walked back through the memorial, going up the steps on either side and then up more steps in each direction. He marvelled at the massive construction.

On every surface there were lists of names. So many, Luke thought soberly, and each one with a family left in mourning.

Passing back beneath the archway towards the direction they had come from, Luke now saw in the morning light that a river, which he'd not noticed when they'd arrived in the dark, ran close to the memorial. Further along the bank, he saw a mound of earth with a spade sticking up out of it. There was no one there, so he walked towards it. Reaching it, he looked down to see an oblong had been marked out with tape and about a quarter of it dug to a depth of about two feet. There was still plenty of work to do.

A voice spoke behind him making him jump; surprisingly a voice that spoke in English and with a proper English accent.

'Sent someone else to finish the job, have they? Well, don't just stand there looking daft. Get digging.'

Luke stared at him and shrugged as if he didn't understand. The big, burly man gave an exaggerated sigh and made the motion of digging. Then he spoke again, now in a language that Luke did not understand, but he pretended to, nodded and smiled and picked up the spade. The man looked pleased and spoke again, but luckily also made the motion of eating. Luke presumed he was saying that if he dug the hole he would feed him later.

He nodded, though he wasn't sure he would take up the man's offer. He didn't want to get trapped sitting in a café somewhere. He was puzzled at what the hole could be for in a public place on the river bank, but it wasn't his concern, so he dug slowly trying to eke out the time until nightfall. It would be a long day.

'Daisy! *Daisy!*' Gill rushed into the room where the ferry pilots had congregated, waiting to receive their delivery chits for the day.

The Fox Moth had picked Daisy up early that morning and she had come straight to the office; she had not been home to their digs and so had not seen Gill.

'I'm here. What's the matter?'

Gill, her eyes wide with fear, her hair flying loose, gripped Daisy's arm like a drowning man. 'Luke! It's Luke. He's been posted missing. He didn't come back from a mission yesterday.'

'Sit down and tell me calmly what you know.'

'Calmly?' Gill's voice rose an octave. 'How can you tell me to be calm?' Tears filled her eyes. 'It's Luke, Daisy. *Luke.*'

'Because getting hysterical isn't going to help. Now, who rang here?'

Gill released her grasp on Daisy, flopped into a chair and covered her face with her hands. In a muffled voice she said, 'His friend, Tim.'

'So – what did he say exactly?'

Slowly, Gill pulled her hands away from her face. 'They'd been on a mission to northern France yesterday – that's all he could say, but Luke and three others too, I think, hadn't come back.'

'Did anyone see his aircraft crash or a parachute? Anything?'

Gill bit her lip and shook her head. 'Nothing,' she said hoarsely.

'I'll ring Daddy. Luke's family might have been told more.'

Daisy went into the office and explained swiftly to the Operations Manager what had happened and got permission to telephone home before she set out on her delivery for that day.

'I'm sorry to hear that, but make it quick,' was all Mary said. 'You still have your duty to do.'

'Daddy?' Daisy was saying into the receiver a few moments later. 'Do you know about Luke?'

'Yes, but we don't know much.'

'I know, we're the same. Just that he's been posted missing. Have you told Aunty Pips?'

'No, I'll write to her.'

'Telephone Aunty Milly. She might be able to get a message to her quicker than a letter.'

'That's a good idea. I'll do that.'

Word soon spread both through the village and in the various parts of the country. Pips heard from Paul working at the War Office. Harry heard eventually from his mother by letter and, of course, all the villagers heard via the 'grapevine'.

Henrietta walked down into the village to see Norah. She found Bess there and so was able to speak to both Luke's grandmothers at the same time.

'Peggy's had a telegram now, Mrs Maitland,' Norah told her, 'but I aren't going to believe it until they have proof that he's dead. I mean, it's not the same as last time, is it?' Her sad eyes glanced towards the black-shrouded photographs of Luke's father,

Harold, and his two brothers on the mantelpiece. 'Then it was certain, but with planes and that, you don't really know, do you? I mean, he could have parachuted out, couldn't he?'

'He could indeed, Mrs Dawson,' Henrietta said, keeping her voice bright and optimistic.

Bess, sitting by the range, was unusually quiet. 'I thought I'd feel summat,' she said slowly. 'I mean that I'd have an instinct that he was still alive or – or that he'd gone, but I don't.' Tears shimmered in her eyes as she met Henrietta's gaze.

'I know, Mrs Cooper. I know just what you mean.' She turned to Norah. 'How's Mr Dawson taken it?'

Norah shrugged. 'Hard to tell. He's still mad at Luke for going. Harry too, though he's not so bothered about him. Sorry, Bess, but you know how he is.'

'I do, Norah duck,' Bess said wryly.

'He didn't say owt when Sam came here early before work to tell us both,' Norah went on. 'He just grunted and went to work as usual.'

'He's a hard man to live with, Norah. We can see all that. Will you be all right? I know Luke used to keep an eye on you.'

'I'm fine, Mrs Maitland, honestly. 'Course I have to put up with his moods, but I'm used to that and Bess comes every day without fail. I'd soon tell her if there was real trouble.' She gave a small smile. 'And Len knows that.'

Henrietta got up. 'I'll leave you to it. We'll let you know if we hear anything else, of course. By the way, there's a meeting of the WVS at the hall tomorrow afternoon, but I'll understand if neither of you feel like coming.'

The two women glanced at each other. 'We'll be there, Mrs Maitland,' Norah said. 'We need to keep busy.'

At lunchtime, the man for whom Luke was digging the hole came back carrying a plate of sandwiches and a bottle of water. He spoke to Luke in a language that Luke now thought was French. His own French was very limited. He'd learned a little at the Lincoln Grammar School but certainly not enough to pass as a native speaker. He nodded his thanks and smiled. Hoping that it was enough.

'Don't say much, do you?' the man tried English again, but this time, although he obviously understood him perfectly, Luke did not dare to reply. He was afraid of a trap.

Luke smiled again and bit into a sandwich gratefully.

'Ah well, have it your way, then. But if you do need help of any kind, I've got a café just down the road, though if you decide to disappear' – he paused and pulled out a couple of notes from his pocket – 'here's something for saving me a job.' He pointed to the hole and smiled. 'You've saved me a bad back. Thanks.'

Luke took the proffered money. He didn't know how much it was, but anything might be useful. Again, he nodded his thanks.

He'd finished digging the hole by late afternoon, but it was still several hours until nightfall when he would be able to leave. He'd decided that he would linger around the memorial, pretend he was searching for a name, perhaps, on the many panels. He walked back purposefully towards the Menin Gate. It wouldn't do to appear furtive. He walked through the archway to the centre and took the steps up to the left, which then divided and rose on each side. There were wreaths laid on several steps. He found a vantage point where he could watch the roads if necessary. He sat down behind a wall to wait.

He heard movement through the archway and people's voices, but there didn't seem to be the usual 'Last Post' service at eight o'clock taking place. He wondered why as the hour came and went and the sounds from below grew less instead of more, as he might have expected.

When it was completely dark, he slipped quietly down to the road and began to walk westwards towards Poperinghe, but he took side roads, sometimes across country; anything to avoid coming across a German patrol. He wondered if the signposts had been altered as they had in England to confuse any invaders, but he didn't need them anyway. He was sure he knew the way.

Forty-Five

Luke was not the only one awake. There were several of his family members and loved ones suffering a sleepless night. Daisy had telephoned again in the evening, but there was no more news from anyone. She and Gill tried to comfort each other, talking in low whispers through the night. The next morning, their superior told them, 'No flying for you two today. You look dreadful. You wouldn't be safe. Take a couple of days off, if it would help.'

'I don't think it would, ma'am. It's just that neither of us slept last night. We'll take today off, but I'm sure we'll be better tomorrow,' Daisy told her.

Gill wasn't so sure that the next night, and for several nights to come, would be any better, but she said nothing. Plenty of other ATA pilots received bad news from time to time. They all had to carry on. So must she. But she felt as if her heart were breaking and by the look on Daisy's face, so was hers.

Sam held Peggy in his arms through the second night.

'It's the not knowing that's the worst, Sam,' she murmured against his shoulder. 'I go from feeling hopeful to being plunged into despair.'

'I know, love. I know.'

There was no such comfort for Norah from her husband. Len turned onto his side, his back towards her. They didn't speak, though Norah knew he was awake because he wasn't snoring. She lay on her back staring at the ceiling through the long night.

Luke's other grandmother, Bess, slept fitfully. Beside her, Charlie snored. She even smiled wryly to herself. Not much kept Charlie awake, but tonight his snoring actually comforted her.

At the hall, sleep was difficult for everyone there too. They were all wondering the same thing; asking the same questions that no one could answer.

Where was Luke? Was he still alive? Was he injured? If only they could hear *some* news. Any news, however bad, would be better than this awful not knowing.

In the early hours of the morning, Luke reached the outskirts of Poperinghe. Now he turned to walk in a south-westerly direction, still keeping to the country-side and avoiding main roads. He was sure there would be Germans billeted in the town and soldiers on duty, maybe even some patrols out.

He reached his destination well before dawn and smiled. Farm buildings that he recognized loomed up through the darkness. He stood for a moment near the farm gate, trying to remember if there was a dog that would alert the sleeping occupants of the farm-house. Very quietly, he walked towards the nearest barn, but, just as he'd thought might happen, a dog sleeping in a kennel near the back door began to bark, though it did not come towards him. Perhaps it was chained up; he hoped so. He didn't want to have to deal with a snarling animal, which was only doing its job of protecting the property and the people who lived there.

A pale light flicked on inside the house, then another just beyond the door. There was a rattle of a chain and the door opened. A man stood silhouetted against the light.

'Who's there? Quiet, Jess. Down, girl.'

Luke moved forward slowly. A little nearer he called softly, 'Uncle William. It's me. It's Luke.'

There was a moment's stunned silence and then a torch beam shone in his face. He submitted to the glare with good grace; he knew William had to be sure . . .

'Good Lord!' William said, turning the beam away and coming towards him. 'Whatever's happened? Come in, come in quickly. I must turn the lights off.'

He ushered Luke into the kitchen and led him to a chair near the fire that was still burning low in the grate.

The door leading to the stairs opened and Brigitta peered round it. 'Oh my!' she said, her eyes wide with astonishment. 'Luke.' She came into the room, her arms outstretched. 'What are you doing here?'

'Get him some food, Brigitta. He looks frozen to death and half starved.'

'Of course. At once.' As Brigitta bustled about the kitchen, Luke said, 'I was shot down over Dranouter. I was lucky; a friendly farmer gave me these clothes and found someone to take me to Ypres. I knew I could find my way here from Ypres, but, Uncle

William, I can't stay here. I just thought perhaps you can put me in touch with someone who could get me to the coast – and then home.'

Before William could answer, Brigitta touched his shoulder. 'Of course you must stay here until we can think what to do.'

'But it would put you in the most appalling danger. I can't—'

'Both our boys – Pascal and Waldo – you remember them?'

'Of course.'

'They are both working for the Belgian Resistance. Pascal is away hiding in the Ardennes.' For a moment her face was bleak. 'He doesn't get home at all. It would be too dangerous, but Waldo is not far away and comes at night sometimes.'

'We don't get many patrols out here – thank goodness,' William said.

'I need to get home,' Luke said between mouthfuls. 'Can Waldo put me in touch with an escape route?'

William and Brigitta glanced at each other. 'We can ask him,' William said. 'But in the meantime, you can stay here. You can help me look after the war cemeteries. The Germans don't interfere with us.' He smiled sardonically. 'Particularly if we're looking after their cemetery at Langemark.'

'I just don't want you to be in any danger because of me.'

Brigitta shrugged. 'Don't you think we were in danger in the last war? We don't mind it for ourselves, though we do worry about the boys.'

'Of course.'

'We must think up a story and how to act if they do come looking. Do you think they might be on the lookout for you?'

Luke shook his head. 'Not that I know. I parachuted out and my plane crashed some distance away. If they are looking for me, I think it must be around the crash site.'

'You don't think they saw your parachute, then?'

'I don't think they can have done.'

'Where is it now?'

'The helpful farmer was going to burn it along with my uniform.'

'Now, you must get to bed. You must get some rest. Later, we will think up a cover story.'

'I'll take you up,' Brigitta said. 'You can have Pascal's room. I always keep it ready although I know he won't get home.'

Luke fell asleep at once. The fear and the long walks had exhausted him, but for what was left of the night, William and Brigitta were awake planning.

'Like you said, William, he can work with you on the farm and in the cemeteries. The Germans allow you to do that. He can be my nephew.'

'But he can't speak the language.'

'No, that is a problem.' She was thoughtful for a moment. 'What if he can't speak at all? I mean, *pretends* that he can't speak?'

'That's a bit risky. You know what the Germans are doing with people with – well – problems. They might transport him.'

'But if he's hiding in plain sight, as you say, *and*

373

doing something they'd see as being for *them*, surely they wouldn't.'

William was thoughtful. 'We'll put it to Luke. It's him taking the risk.'

'Just until Waldo can get him onto one of the escape routes. I don't think Luke is going to be content to sit out the rest of war here, do you?'

William gave a short laugh. 'No, I don't think he is.'

Forty-Six

They explained their idea to Luke when he woke up about lunchtime.

'Whatever you think best, but I'm just so concerned about putting you both in danger. And Waldo too.'

'The boys both made their own choices,' Brigitta said, 'and we have to abide by it. Just the same as your family have had to honour your decision.'

Luke glanced at William and grimaced. 'There was one who didn't? I think you can guess who?'

William looked puzzled. 'Your mam? I wouldn't think Peggy would be too happy about it.'

'Well, she isn't. And Harry has joined the RAF too, so she's both of us to worry about, but I think she's proud of us too. No, it was Granddad Dawson. He threatened to disinherit me if I joined up.'

'If you joined up?' William repeated, bemused.

Luke nodded. 'Yes. That's what surprised us all. Exactly the opposite to last time. We think it's all about what he wants at the time. He didn't want me to enlist because he wanted me to carry on his business and an agricultural worker is classed as a reserved occupation. He believes he could have got an exemption for me. But – I didn't give him the chance.'

'And he wanted me to enlist because everyone else was doing it and it shamed him to have a coward in the family.' William paused and then asked, 'What about Harry?'

'Granddad isn't bothered about him. When he was born, he seemed prepared to treat him as one of the family, but now he's always saying Harry's not his blood relative and has no claim on his business.'

'That's a bit unkind,' Brigitta said and then glanced at William. 'Sorry, darling. It's not my place to speak out.'

William touched her arm. 'But you're quite right. So, Luke, are you willing to take the risk of hiding in plain sight, as it were?'

'Of course. And you want me *not* to speak at all?'

William and Brigitta exchanged a glance. 'We think it best, though we can't be absolutely sure that will work. If the patrols get nosy, they may still want to send you to Germany as forced labour.'

'I'm willing to take that chance. It'd be better than opening my mouth and proving I'm English.'

'Can you speak any French or German?' Brigitta asked.

Luke pulled a face. 'A few words of French, but not enough to pass as a Frenchman.' He turned to William. 'Why have the Germans allowed you to stay here? Is it because you're married to Aunt Brigitta?'

Brigitta giggled suddenly. 'It's a long time since I've been called that – I rather like it.' She put her arm round his shoulders. 'Oh Luke, it's so good to see you, even under these difficult circumstances.'

William smiled and answered his question. 'Partly,

I think, but mainly because I look after the military cemetery here and also tend the German graves at Langemark. I'll take you there. If we're seen looking after their graves, perhaps it will help stop any uncomfortable questions. But today, we'll start here. Are you feeling up to a little work?'

'Of course.'

'Still no news?' Henrietta asked. She called every day now to see Norah.

Norah pressed her lips together and shook her head, banging the flat iron down onto the shirt she was ironing in an angry movement. 'You'd think they'd send word, wouldn't you?'

'Well, in this case, Mrs Dawson, I think no news is decidedly good news. It means they haven't heard for definite that he's been killed. You must cling to that.'

Norah sighed. 'I know you're right, Mrs Maitland, and it's so good of you to come each day.' She looked up and tried to smile. 'It does buoy us up. Me and Bess.'

'I just want to know you're all right, my dear. It's a tough time for you all.'

Tactfully, without actually mentioning his name, she included Len. Catching on, Norah said, 'Aye, it is. Len dun't say much – in fact, he won't mention it – but I know he's feeling it. He's working harder than ever to deal with it. Burying hissen in work. I have to say I'm lucky in one way. He hasn't turned to the drink to drown his sorrows. I dun't reckon I could deal with that.'

Henrietta sniffed and thought, not with his temper inflamed by drink, no, you couldn't, but she kept her thoughts to herself. Instead she said, 'Philippa rings almost every night now and Daisy whenever she can. I think she's in contact with Luke's friend on the airfield where they were stationed. They've heard nothing either.'

'Then we'll just have to keep waiting, Mrs Maitland, won't we?'

Henrietta nodded. 'And hoping.'

As she walked back to the hall, she was stopped three times on the way by villagers enquiring after Luke.

William took Luke to the local military cemetery. 'Is this where Uncle George's friend is buried?'

'No, that's near Brandhoek. I go there too sometimes. We'll go and see if we can find it. How is George, by the way?'

Luke stared at him. 'Oh Lor'. Of course, I was totally forgetting. You won't know, will you? George was killed in the London Blitz. His daughter, Rebecca, too. She was visiting him at the time.'

William turned white. Hoarsely, he asked, 'And Pips?'

Luke shook his head. 'She's fine. She wasn't there when it happened. She's working away from London – though none of us know exactly what she's doing. Here, Uncle William, sit down a minute. You've had a shock. It was stupid of me not to realize you haven't heard news from home for months.'

'It's years now. Pips's last letter arrived just before

the occupation and we've had nothing from either Pips or Alice since.'

'I'm not sure what you do know, then.'

'Not much, I'm guessing. Tell me.'

They sat together on a bench at the side of the cemetery whilst Luke told William briefly about what had happened since the beginning of the war; about Dunkirk, the Battle of Britain and then about the Blitz. William knew some of it, but not all. As he talked, Luke gazed out over the sea of white markers and this, he remembered, was only a comparatively small cemetery in this area. So many lives lost and now it was all happening again.

'We're still getting bombed, of course, all over the country now,' he told William, 'but the London Blitz was horrific. Night after night for months. Ironically, poor Uncle George was killed on the very worst night of the whole campaign. After that they eased up a bit for some reason. You see, they were trying to get control of the skies as a prelude to invasion, but they didn't manage it.'

'Because of you RAF boys, I expect.'

Luke grinned and said modestly, 'Well, we did our bit, I suppose. At least Churchill seemed to think so.' Then his face sobered. 'We lost a lot of pilots – all fine men – and aircraft too. You won't know that Daisy has joined the Air Transport Auxiliary and delivers all sorts of different aeroplanes – though mainly Spitfires now – all over the country. She loves the Spitfire. There's a women's section and she's one of the pilots.'

'Good heavens! Little Daisy? Really?'

Luke chuckled. 'Yes, really.'

William lifted his head as he heard the sound of a vehicle approaching. 'I think someone's coming. We'd better get working. Here.' He handed Luke a thin-tined fork. 'Start at the far end of that row and clear any weeds from around the markers.'

'Right.'

'And remember, if it is the Germans, you don't speak.'

Luke nodded.

By the time the German staff car pulled up and the officer alighted from the back seat, they were both hard at work with their heads down.

The officer came towards William. He was tall and straight-backed, but limped a little. As he drew close, he was looking at William intently.

'Are you Wilhelm Dawson?' He spoke very good English, though he used the German form of the name.

William straightened up. 'Yes, sir. I am.'

'The Englishman who married a Belgian nurse after the last war and lives on a farm near here?'

'That's correct, sir.'

'Yes, I have been told about you. You also tend the cemeteries around here and so have been allowed to stay.' This time it was a statement rather than a question.

'Yes, sir.'

The man grunted and nodded. 'Four months ago, I was posted here to Ypres to control this area.'

'Yes, I think I've seen you driving round,' William murmured.

'I cannot be sent on active service. I was wounded in the last war.' He looked about him, his glance coming to rest on Luke. 'Who is he?'

'My wife's cousin's boy.' Because Brigitta had no siblings – which would be an easy fact to check – they had thought to make the relationship a little vaguer. 'He has come to stay with us for a while, so I thought I would make use of him. An extra pair of hands is always welcome.'

'Where is he from?'

This was something that they hadn't thought to plan, so William was obliged to say the first thing that came into his head: the place Luke had mentioned.

'Dranouter, sir.' Mentally, William crossed his fingers, hoping the officer wouldn't have heard of a Spitfire crashing in that area.

'Mm. I don't know where that is,' he murmured, but it didn't seem to require an answer, so William said nothing.

'Why is he not serving in the armed forces?'

'He – has a speech difficulty, sir. I think he failed a medical.'

'Mm.' The officer stared towards Luke for a long moment, then he turned and gazed again at William, frowning slightly.

Then with a sudden movement, a swift nod, he turned away, walked back to his car and was gone. William and Luke carried on working until the car was safely out of sight.

*

Two nights later, Waldo came to the farm, sitting down at the table to wolf down the meal his mother had prepared for him just in case he should appear.

'We never know when he might come,' Brigitta explained to Luke, 'so I am always ready.'

'It's good to see you again,' Waldo said to Luke in perfect English. He and his elder brother had been brought up to be bilingual. 'It's been a long time, though I'm sorry it has to be under these circumstances.'

'Me too.'

When Waldo had finished eating, they sat around the fire and discussed what could be done to help Luke get back to England.

'We could send him down the ordinary escape routes,' Waldo said. 'I'll see what I can do.'

'Is there any way of letting them know back home that I'm OK?'

'I can get one of my pianists to send a message through the usual channels.'

Luke was puzzled. 'Pianist?'

'It's what the resistance call their radio operators.'

'I suppose you send it all in code?'

'Of course.'

'Well, I've got an idea for the message that wouldn't be easily understood unless it gets to the right people.'

When he told them, they all laughed. 'You'd make a very good agent,' Waldo complimented him.

'No, I'm better flying my Spitfire, if I can just get back home.'

Forty-Seven

The messages for the Special Operations Executive, who liaised with their own agents and with Resistance workers in occupied countries, went through the Secret Intelligence Service or MI6 radio station at Bletchley Park, but a move of their operation to another receiving and transmitting station located at Grendon Underwood was planned for early June. On the Sunday morning after Luke had been posted as missing, an SOE decoder, still working at the Park, sought out his superior.

'We had a very strange message come through last night.'

'Who's it from?'

'One of the Resistance people working around Ypres. He organizes the escape of POWs on the run and airmen who've been shot down if they've been able to remain at large. We don't get many escapees in that area, but there are a few. His main job is sabotage.'

'What's it say?'

'"Pips stop Luke fifteen three to ten stop William". Then he signed off with his usual call sign.'

'You don't think his call sign has been compromised?'

'Not with a garbled message like this that doesn't mean anything, even when it's decoded.'

'Has it been done properly?'

'Yes, I've had two different people do it as a check and they both came up with exactly the same message.'

'Take it across to the huts, Tony. See if anyone there has any ideas. It's an odd one, I grant you.'

'Good morning, ladies. I need your help.' Tony stood just inside the door of the first hut, waving the piece of paper. Three heads shot up.

'Anything for a handsome young man.' A blonde girl stood up and sashayed towards him. 'And to get a break,' she muttered as she neared him. 'How can we help, sunshine?'

He handed the message to her.

'Is it legit?'

'I think so. It's from one of our regular pianists.'

She turned to face the rest of the room. 'Listen up, girls.' Then she read the message out.

'The only "pips" I can think of are those at the beginning of a news bulletin.'

'Is there a news reader called Luke? Or William?'

A ripple of laughter went through the room.

'No, it's usually Alvar Liddell.'

'Or Frank Phillips.'

'There's a John somebody.'

'John Snagge. But no Luke or William that we can think of.'

She handed the paper back to him. 'Take it around the other huts. Someone might have a bright idea. Sorry we can't help.'

'Thanks, anyway.'

In the next hut he entered, there was a William, but he could not think why his name would be mentioned. In another building, a man named Luke felt the same.

It was in the fourth building he visited where someone said, 'There's a woman in hut six called Pips.'

'Oh right, thanks. I'll try there.'

Again, he entered another hut and stood just inside the doorway. 'Sorry to trouble you, but is there a lady here called "Pips"?'

Several fingers pointed to a woman sitting in the far corner.

'She's called "Pips", but she's no lady. She didn't even "come out",' said a slightly superior voice, but it was filled with teasing good humour.

Pips rose from her seat and walked down the room, ruffling the hair of the girl who'd spoken as she passed her.

'Ouch!'

'How can I help?'

Yet again, Tony explained.

Pips took the paper into her hands and then began to smile. 'I think it could well be for me.'

'Ho, ho,' the mischievous voice came again. 'A secret assignation. We'll have to put a stop to this, girls.'

Pips turned towards her colleagues. 'I don't suppose any of you have got a bible with you?' She grinned at the girl who had teased her. 'Not you, of course, Polly.'

A shy girl, who hadn't been with them long, put her hand up tentatively. 'I've got one in my cabin.'

'Be a darling and get it for me, would you?'

'Um – yes – all right.'

The girl scuttled out and was gone for ten minutes. She was breathless when she returned, but she was clutching a bible.

'Thanks, Ruth.'

Quickly, Pips turned to the Gospel according to Luke, chapter fifteen, and read swiftly through verses three to ten. 'It's the parable of the lost sheep,' she said. Everyone in the room was listening now. 'A young airman connected to my family was shot down recently. He was posted missing. His name was Luke.' There was a ripple of excitement. 'And he has an uncle, William, who lives not far from Ypres. I'm guessing he's with him.'

'My goodness,' Polly of the superior voice said. Her teasing had stopped now and she came towards Pips. 'Sorry, I didn't mean to be flippant. It's wonderful news for you. For heaven's sake – go and telephone home.'

'Well, that's good.' Tony grinned, as they walked out of the hut together. 'Mystery solved. We'll see what we can do to get him home. I'll get in touch with our HQ in London.'

It was just before lunchtime when the telephone rang at the hall. Robert was still at church with his parents, so it was Alice who answered.

The line was crackly. 'Pips? Is that you? Is something wrong?' It was a strange time of the day for her to ring.

'No – just the opposite. We're pretty sure that Luke is safe and that he's with William.'

'William!'

'Yes. I can't tell you how I know, Alice, you'll just have to take my word.'

'Of course we will. But – but – I mean – is he safe?'

'At the moment, yes, but we must try to get him home if we can. He is in occupied territory after all. I'll keep you posted.'

'Oh Pips, how . . . ?' But the line had gone dead.

Alice rushed through the house, calling out to anyone who could hear her. 'He's safe. Luke is safe.'

Henrietta was just entering through the front door on her way back from church. 'Alice, whatever's the matter?'

'Oh Mother,' Alice clasped her hands together. Tears of joy were shimmering in her eyes. 'He's safe. Luke is safe. Pips has just telephoned.'

'That's wonderful news, but how on earth did Pips find out?'

'I – um – don't know.' Alice hesitated. She knew that Pips was engaged in some sort of secret work that was not to be talked about. 'But I'm so thankful that she did. I must go and tell Peggy at once and Mam and Dad too. Mother, where's Robert?'

'Still at the church talking to the vicar, I believe.'

'If I don't see him, please tell him the wonderful news.'

'Of course I will, but what about—' Henrietta began, but Alice whirled around and was gone. 'Luncheon?' The older woman finished her sentence

387

with a smile on her face. Alice's mission was far more important and urgent than eating.

'Wainwright,' Henrietta turned to the manservant hovering close by. 'Will you please ask Cook to hold back luncheon for half an hour? I think Miss Alice may be a little while.'

Alice ran down the long drive and through the gate into the churchyard.

'Robert! Robert!'

He was emerging from the church door, still talking to the vicar. The other worshippers had already gone home; there were just the two of them discussing church and village business. He looked up with an anxious frown as he heard her voice.

'Robert, he's safe. Luke is safe. I must go and tell Peggy and oh – everyone.'

She turned away and began to run again.

'Alice, let Jake drive you.'

'No, I can't wait. I'll explain everything later . . .'

She reached the lane and began to run even faster, not stopping until she was forced to do so by the sensation that her lungs might burst if she didn't slow down. But still she hurried towards the cottage where Peggy and Sam lived.

'Peggy,' she panted. She banged on the front door, but there was no reply. Hurrying round the side of the cottage and into the back garden, she saw Peggy tying up some tulips that had bent over in the wind. 'Peggy – Peggy. He's safe. Luke is safe.'

Peggy stared at her wide-eyed. 'Are you sure?'

'Pips telephoned. He's with William. That's all I know.'

'William?' Peggy was shocked, but then realization began to flood through her. 'William,' she repeated softly and then added, 'Of course. Luke has visited him before. He'd know William would help him.'

'But it's still in occupied territory. If William is hiding him and is caught . . .' Alice said no more. They all knew the consequences William and indeed his whole family could face if they were caught harbouring or helping an escaped airman.

'Do you know any more?'

Alice shook her head. 'Sorry, no. Just that he's safe.'

Peggy pulled a face. 'If you can call still being in enemy territory "safe".'

'I know what you mean, but I expect they'll try to send him down an escape route. Anyway, I must go. I must let my mam know and Dad will be at home today. I'll leave you to tell Sam.'

When Alice walked in through the back door of her parents' cottage, through the scullery and into the kitchen, she found her mother and father sitting down to their midday meal.

'Luke's safe,' she said at once, without any greeting. 'Pips has somehow found out that he's with William.'

Norah's knife and fork clattered onto her plate and she stared open-mouthed at Alice. 'How . . . ?'

Alice shrugged. 'Sorry, I don't know any details, but Pips wouldn't have told us unless she was sure it was true.'

Len was motionless, staring into space, his knife and fork suspended in mid-air.

Alice sat down. 'Of course, he's still in enemy

territory, but we're sure William will – well – hide him until he can get home – somehow.'

'But won't that put William and all his family in dreadful danger?' Norah asked, her voice trembling.

Alice turned her gaze on her father, who still hadn't moved or said a word. Slowly, she said, 'It very well might, Mam, but then, William is not afraid of danger.'

Forty-Eight

'I must telephone Daisy,' Robert said when Alice had arrived back home. 'We must let her know Luke is alive and comparatively safe. We've got a number to ring in case of emergencies, haven't we?'

'Yes,' Alice said doubtfully. 'But would her superiors class this as "an emergency"?'

'Well, I do,' Robert said shortly. 'Poor Daisy is worried out of her mind, to say nothing of what Gill will be feeling. Their superiors can think what they like.'

Alice smiled. She knew he was right; Daisy wouldn't care if trouble came her way as long as she got the news about Luke.

Robert put on his most persuasive doctor's voice when talking to the Operations Manager. 'We have something of a family emergency and I must speak to Daisy. It's most important.'

'I'm sorry, Daisy is away at the moment. She will be back later today or tomorrow, all being well. I'll leave a message for her.'

'Oh,' Robert was momentarily deflated. He had so hoped to give Daisy the joyous news straightaway. 'I thought she might be there, it being Sunday.'

'The war doesn't stop even for the Lord's Day,' the Operations Manager said a little piously.

'Can you tell me where she is?'

'No, I'm sorry. I can't do that, but I'll leave a message for her to telephone home the moment she arrives back.'

'Then is Gill Portus there?'

'No, she's away too. I am sorry.' The woman seemed to unbend a little, but not enough to offer to do anything more to help.

'Who else can I get hold of?' he asked Alice as he replaced the receiver.

'What about Johnny? He might be keeping tabs on where Daisy is. Being in the services too, he might be able to do that when we can't.'

Robert smiled wryly. 'Isn't he a little jealous of Luke?'

Alice laughed. 'Once upon a time, maybe, but Daisy has convinced him that Luke and she are cousins and the best of friends, but no more. And of course, now that Luke has Gill . . .'

'I expect you're right. You women have an intuition about these things. So, do we have a number for him?'

'No, but we could contact Mitch. He's sure to know how to get in touch with his nephew.'

'We don't have a number for Mitch, do we?'

Alice chuckled. 'We don't – but your mother does.'

'Mother! Mother has a telephone number for Mitch Hammond? I thought she disliked him.'

Alice shook her head. 'Not any more. I think he charmed her when he looked after her and your father at the time of the unveiling of the cenotaph in London.'

Robert was thoughtful. 'Yes, I remember. Well, well, well. Wonders never cease. So, will you ask her for it, or shall I?'

'I'll go, if you like. She'll be in the parlour waiting until we're all ready for lunch. I'll explain to her why we're having to follow such a roundabout route.'

Minutes later, Robert was asking the exchange to connect him to the number for Mitch's flat in London.

'Hammond,' a voice answered at last.

'Mitch – is that you? It's Robert Maitland here.'

'Oh Lord, this isn't about Pips, is it? Is she all right?'

'As far as we know, she's fine, but she's a little difficult to get hold of just now. We have to wait for her to contact us.'

'Ah yes . . .'

Robert could hear the relief in the man's voice and allowed himself a small smile as he felt a moment's sympathy for Mitch; he was obviously still very much in love with Pips.

'What can I do for you, Robert?'

'We're trying to get an urgent message to Daisy. I expect you've heard that Luke was posted missing? Well, I'm delighted to say that Pips has telephoned to tell us that he's safe, but he's with William and that, of course, is in occupied territory.'

'Good Lord!' Mitch thought quickly and then said, 'He must have bailed out and found his way there. He's visited William before, hasn't he?'

'Yes, that's what we thought too.'

'And Daisy doesn't know yet? That he's safe?'

'No. I rang her superior officer, but she wasn't exactly helpful.'

Mitch chuckled. 'They're not allowed to be, Robert. Don't blame her.'

Robert laughed with him. 'No, I understand that. But poor Daisy must be told as soon as possible. We wondered if you could get in touch with Johnny. He might know where she is or be able to contact her more quickly than we can.'

'Ah, I see now why you're ringing me, but there is something else, something that is probably even more important than letting Daisy know. If he's in Belgium, both he and, I'm afraid, William and his family too, if they're harbouring him, are in dreadful danger. Has anything been said about getting him back home?'

'No – we haven't been told anything about that and I don't expect we will be.'

'Leave that with me too. I have one or two contacts . . .'

When he replaced the receiver, Mitch was thoughtful for a moment. Then he dialled a number he knew very well. 'Jeff, I need your help and it's urgent.' He explained swiftly.

'Of course,' Jeff Pointer said at the other end of the line. 'We'd better move as quickly as possible.' He was silent for a moment, thinking. 'Get Johnny to bring Daisy here. We need her.'

Next, Mitch telephoned the airfield where his nephew was stationed. He was in luck; Johnny was not flying and was brought to the telephone.

'This is an emergency, Johnny. Can you get leave?'

'I think so. I'm grounded because I've injured my leg. It's not serious, but they won't let me fly for a few days.'

'Can you still ride your motorcycle?'

'Oh yes, but . . .'

'Now listen carefully. A message has been received that Luke is safe – for the moment – but he is still in grave danger. Johnny, you have to find Daisy and bring her to London as soon as you possibly can. To Sixty-four Baker Street. Have you got that?'

'Yes, Uncle Mitch.'

'Right. I'll be waiting for you whenever you get there. But make it as fast as you can. This is urgent.'

Johnny knew better than to ask for more information, especially over the telephone. He trusted his uncle implicitly and would do whatever he asked.

Within minutes Johnny was standing in front of his commanding officer. His sense of urgency had communicated itself and he'd been admitted to the CO's office at once.

'Sir, I can't tell you details, I'm afraid, mainly because I don't know them myself, but one of our chaps who was reported as missing from Hornchurch last Tuesday has been located as being safe, but only for the moment. Sir, will you trust me when I tell you that there are ways I can help, but I need a few days' leave?'

The CO frowned thoughtfully. Hammond had a good reputation, was known to be not only an exceptional flier, but also trustworthy and honest. He was in line for a promotion very soon, though the young man didn't yet know this himself.

'Of course, Hammond. I will see to it. Off you go.'

'There's one more thing, sir, if I might ask a huge favour. Could you telephone the senior officer at Hamble? I need to get in touch with Daisy Maitland urgently.'

The CO raised his eyebrows. Had he misjudged this young man? 'Isn't she your girlfriend?'

'She is, sir, yes, but my uncle has asked me to take her to Sixty-four Baker Street in London as quickly as possible.'

The older man stared at him. He had little information to go on, but he – unlike Johnny at this moment – knew exactly what was at that address. Without further hesitation, he reached for the telephone.

They were working at the Langemark cemetery the following day when they encountered the German officer again.

'It will be good to be seen tending the German graves,' William had said and so this morning they had come to where the German soldiers from the Great War were buried.

'Hitler came here for a visit in June 1940,' William said. 'Evidently, he served in this area during the Great War.'

'Did you see him?'

'No,' William said shortly. 'I didn't know he'd been until later. If I had—' He turned away quickly and Luke wondered what had been in his mind.

The staff car pulled to a halt outside the cemetery and the officer strolled amongst the graves, reading one or two inscriptions and then pausing for a long moment beside the rectangular box shape that marked the mass grave that contained thousands of dead.

Then, still limping on the uneven ground, he came directly to William.

'Do you get – what is the word – vilified by the locals for tending enemy graves?'

William shrugged. 'No, I remain completely neutral. They know that – and accept it.'

The man gave a curt nod, his gaze still roaming around the sombre place and finally coming to rest upon Luke, who was working a short distance away, his head down.

'Wilhelm,' the officer said softly, 'I have come to talk to you about your – relative.'

A stab of fear shot through William, but he straightened up and faced the officer, keeping his face expressionless.

'First, I will explain why I am about to do something for which I could be shot.' They were standing in the middle of the cemetery. No one could overhear what was being said, not even Luke.

'You will remember the first Christmas of the last war when up and down the lines soldiers from both sides climbed out of their trenches and met in no-man's-land?'

'I do indeed,' William murmured.

'You played football, I believe, with each other.'

'Yes, that's right. We did.'

The officer was silent for a moment before saying,

'I could not play. I was lying very ill in our trench. There was no one available from our lines so one of my friends persuaded one of your doctors to see me.'

William gasped but said nothing, allowing him to continue. 'Your doctor said that if I did not get immediate attention, I would die.' Slowly, he turned to look straight into William's eyes. 'You carried me from our trench across no-man's-land to your first-aid post. Your doctor amputated my foot and your nurses cared for me.'

'My God,' William said hoarsely. 'You're Hans?'

'You remember me?'

'Of course I do. When you were well enough, I took you to the nearest casualty-clearing station, from where, I presume, you were eventually taken to England as a prisoner of war.'

Hans nodded. 'I was, but I was treated well, with courtesy and kindness. You – and your fellow countrymen – saved my life. And now, I owe it to you to save your – relative.'

William frowned. 'I appreciate your sentiment, but – how?'

'Whilst I am here – in charge of this area – he is safe, but I have been recalled to Berlin.' He smiled wryly. 'Perhaps they think I am not doing a good job here. I have been notified that my replacement will arrive this coming Saturday, the sixteenth. I cannot guarantee that my successor will look so kindly on him. You and your family are safe – it is in the notes at our headquarters in Ypres – but there is nothing about him. Wilhelm, you must get him away from here by Friday morning at the latest

– send him home, if you can. For the next four days, you will not be watched. I promise you that, but afterwards . . .' Hans said no more, but William understood.

'We've been lucky that you were posted here.'

'No coincidence, I assure you. I asked for a posting near Ypres. I wanted to come back here, though, of course' – he smiled faintly – 'I didn't know then that I would be able to help one of the men who saved my life.'

'Hans, I would like to shake your hand to thank you properly, but your driver is watching.'

With his back turned towards his driver, Hans smiled. 'It is better not. Just – do what you can, otherwise the young man may be taken prisoner and I cannot say what might happen to him then.'

Inwardly, William shuddered.

'I may not see you again before I leave, so I hope all goes well. *Viel glück.*' He gave a curt nod and, setting his face in a serious expression, he turned and walked back to his vehicle without even glancing in Luke's direction.

Forty-Nine

'Waldo – I'm so glad you've come tonight. We have a problem.'

William, Brigitta and Luke were sitting in the firelight, with the blinds drawn. Swiftly, William related all that had happened between himself and Hans earlier that day.

'Can you trust this German, Father? You don't think it's a trap?'

'I think we have to, Waldo. It's our only chance to get Luke away before Hans leaves this district. His warning was clear. Someone else will not be willing to turn a blind eye to Luke's presence here and we only have three days left. We have to get Luke away by Friday as the German officer's replacement arrives on Saturday.'

Waldo sighed. 'Our escape route overland has been compromised. Two British airmen were caught only recently and have been taken to a prison camp in Germany. Sadly, two of our Resistance workers were shot.'

Brigitta made a little sound and covered her mouth with her hand, her eyes wide with fear. Waldo touched her arm. 'We have to do this work, Mama. You know we do.'

She nodded, but could not prevent the tears from falling. Facing danger herself was one thing; knowing her beloved sons were facing it every day was quite another.

'So,' Waldo turned to Luke, 'we have to get you away from here. We have to get you picked up by an aircraft. I'll send a message to my contact in England tonight.'

'I don't want anyone losing their lives for my sake,' Luke said worriedly. 'I'd sooner hand myself in. I've still got my dog tag. I can prove I'm RAF – not some spy.'

Waldo grinned and slapped his shoulder. 'You leave me to worry about that. It's what we do, Cousin Luke.'

Waldo left soon afterwards to send his message. Despite his father's trust in the German officer, Waldo was not willing to take unnecessary chances.

'Where on earth are you taking me at this time of night?' Daisy said, throwing her trousered leg over the pillion seat of Johnny's motorcycle. Johnny had ridden his motorcycle to Hamble as soon as he had left his CO's office. Luckily, it was to find that Daisy had just arrived back at the ferry pool after a long train ride from the north of England. Fortunately, she had been able to catch a little sleep on the journey. 'You must have worked your charm on Ma'am for her to allow this.'

'I think it was more my CO's charm – God bless him. From the look on his face, I think he knows more about this than we do at this moment. We must get on, but before we go, I have to tell you that this is about Luke. He's been located. He's safe for the moment, but we have to act quickly. Uncle Mitch has told me to take you to an address in London. He'll be there waiting for us.'

'Oh Johnny. Thank God! I must tell Gill at once.'

'No time. We must go.'

'But—'

'No "buts", Daisy. Hang on.'

She wound her arms round his waist and leaned her head against his back as he kick-started his motorcycle and they roared off into the night.

The unfamiliar streets of London were shrouded in complete darkness. The only people abroad were fire-watchers and air-raid wardens. Although the London Blitz was deemed to be over, raids still occurred and the authorities were ever watchful.

They had to stop and ask for directions three times before they turned into the street, but at last they halted outside the number they'd been given. Johnny parked his machine and, as they approached the door, it opened and a figure emerged. 'You made it,' came Mitch's familiar voice out of the darkness. 'Come in quickly.'

Once inside, with the blackout safely back in place, Mitch turned on a light.

'Is it true, Uncle Mitch? Is Luke really safe?'

'For the moment, Daisy, yes, but we haven't long. There's been another message from their contact in that area just come through to us. It's even more urgent than we thought. He has to be got out by Friday.'

Daisy gasped. 'But where is he?'

'He's near Ypres – with your Uncle William.'

Daisy stared at him and then began to smile. 'And you want me to go and fetch him?'

'Certainly not, young lady. The very idea. What we do want from you is for you to brief our pilot on the area, which you know so well.'

'But . . .'

'No "buts", Daisy. This is what the SOE do.'

'Is that where we are?'

'Yes, this is SOE headquarters. And now, there's someone I'd like you both to meet. I think you might remember him.'

He led them along a corridor, up a flight of stairs and along another corridor to an office at the end. Opening a door, he ushered them inside and as the man behind the desk rose, Daisy gasped.

'Jeff!'

Jeff Pointer smiled at her and held out his hand. 'Hello, Daisy. Good to see you again. Do sit down – all of you. I'll have coffee brought in.'

When they were sitting down with a cup of coffee and biscuits, Jeff came straight to the point. 'Daisy, we need your help. We have to get Luke out by Friday morning at the latest. I don't know why, but this is what our contact says and we trust him. His message read "Parcel collection before dawn Friday. Imperative no later." When an operator uses the word "imperative", we know it's desperately urgent.'

'But that's only three days away,' Daisy said.

Jeff nodded. 'That's why we need your help. We've

already managed to get a Special Duties pick-up pilot, even though it's short notice. He's on his way here now from Tangmere, but it's quite a drive in the blackout. We'll need you to brief him because you know the area and can point out William's farm to him on the map.'

'I do wish you'd let me go.'

'Out of the question. For a start, you haven't done any night flying.'

Daisy grinned. 'Not officially, no, but I've been very late back from trips once or twice because of delays that weren't my fault. It was dark for the last hour of the flights. I did get a ticking off each time, mind you. I was told I should have landed somewhere and waited until morning.'

'We'd get more than a ticking off if we let you do this,' Jeff laughed, but Daisy only pulled a face.

Whilst they waited for the airman from the squadron that handled many of the SOE missions, they discussed the logistics of the proposed mission.

'It's a slightly longer trip than we're used to, so we'll make sure they can refuel the Lysander if needed and that they'll be able to light a runway in the field for him to land.'

'A Lysander? Is that what he's taking?'

'Yes, we're using Mitch's aeroplane. It's the most convenient aircraft for this type of operation and his has also got the additional fuel tank underneath. And it's always on standby for us at Brooklands if we need it.'

'You can fit two in the passenger seat if needed,' Mitch said, 'though it's a bit of a squeeze.'

'I've flown several of those,' Daisy said quietly. 'Including Uncle Mitch's before the war.'

Jeff stared at her for a moment. 'Have you really?'

Daisy nodded, whilst Johnny laughed out loud. 'She won't tell you herself because she's too modest, but she's flown most types of aircraft currently in operation.'

'Not quite. I've still to pass the conversion course for Class Five and learn radio procedures. Then I'll be able to fly four-engine aircraft.'

There was a new respect in Jeff's eyes. Then he chuckled. 'I must have taught you well, Daisy.'

Quite seriously, she replied, 'You certainly did, Jeff.'

'And you're enjoying being in the ATA?'

'Absolutely. I think we all are. All the women seem to have a passion for flying. We're like a sisterhood.'

'What is your favourite aircraft?'

'The Spitfire,' Daisy said promptly.

'It's a wonderful machine,' Johnny murmured. 'The Hurricane's good, of course, but there's just something magical about the Spit.'

At that moment the pilot they were expecting arrived and the next hour was spent discussing his mission. When the meeting broke up, Mitch said, 'I expect you two would like to hang around until all this is over. Meet Luke when he gets back.'

Daisy glanced at Johnny. 'Could we?'

'I can, because I'm on sick leave until next week, but what about you?'

Daisy bit her lip. 'I can only ask.'

'Leave it with me,' Jeff said. 'I'll clear it with

Hamble.' He winked. 'We might still need to pick your brains right up until the last minute.'

Daisy grinned. 'Thanks, Jeff.'

'No, thank *you*, Daisy. Your knowledge of the area has been invaluable. I wish we had such detailed information for all our pick-ups.' He turned to Mitch. 'Where will you be staying?'

'At Milly's tonight – well, what's left of the night – and then we'll travel down to my house in Weybridge tomorrow to be near Brooklands. I've already telephoned her and she's delighted to have three unexpected guests. Nothing fazes Milly.' He glanced at Daisy and Johnny. 'I'd take you to my flat, but I'm not really prepared for visitors.' He turned back to Jeff. 'You've got Milly's number in case you need us again, haven't you?'

Jeff nodded. 'So,' he turned to the pilot, Tom Keenes. 'Unfortunately, the weather doesn't look too promising until Thursday night, which is cutting it a bit fine, I know. But maybe it's not such a bad thing. They'll need a bit of time to organize things that end. I'll pick you up from Tangmere and take you to Weybridge to Mitch's place on Thursday morning. All right?'

Tom nodded and shook everyone's hands before setting off for another long drive back to his base through the blackout.

'Right,' Mitch said. 'Let's get to Milly's. We'll be just in time for breakfast.'

'*Dahlings!*' Milly greeted them, throwing her arms wide. 'What a lovely surprise to get Mitch's telephone call. Come in, come in. Breakfast is all ready for you.'

'It's very good of you to put us up at such short notice, Aunty Milly,' Daisy said and then yawned suddenly. 'Oh, sorry. We've been up all night and I was flying yesterday.'

'Oh, you poor thing. You must have some breakfast and then go straight to bed. Your room's all ready.' She turned to Mitch and Johnny. 'You don't mind sharing the other spare room, do you?'

'Of course not, Milly.'

She regarded them with her head on one side. 'You both look worn out. Have you been up all night too?'

They glanced at each other and then nodded.

'Then breakfast and off to bed for all of you.'

'There's just one thing,' Daisy said. 'May I use your telephone, Aunty Milly? I must get a message to Gill about Luke. She should be back at Hamble by now.'

'Don't tell her about what's happening,' Mitch warned.

'Of course not, but she deserves to know that he's alive. No one else will have told her.'

The three of them slept for several hours but dragged themselves out of bed in the afternoon so that they could be sure of sleeping again that night.

'We can't tell you what it's all about, Milly,' Mitch began, but Milly held up her hand, palm outwards.

'I'd rather not know, darling. You know me, I can't keep secrets.'

'Maybe not,' he laughed, 'but you have other

qualities, like looking after three people who've descended on you without warning.'

'It's not a problem. The beds are always ready. Now, come and eat.'

Fifty

Wednesday was a difficult day for everyone; it was just waiting. The three families in Doddington, all worried about Luke, had no idea what was happening. Even Pips didn't know. Messages were now going through the normal channels and she was no longer involved.

In Belgium, William, Brigitta and Luke waited on tenterhooks. They'd learned from Waldo that the pick-up would be during the early hours of Friday morning and that a light aircraft would land in one of William's fields. He and Waldo had chosen the field and Waldo had already organized three other Resistance workers in the area to help lay out a landing strip with three torches on the ends of poles set in an A shape to guide the aircraft in. Aircraft fuel was stowed in William's barn, just in case it was needed. Everything was ready and all they had to do was wait. But waiting was always the hardest part.

'Perhaps we should travel down to Weybridge this evening. There's plenty of room at my house for all of us and my housekeeper keeps everything spick and span,' Mitch said. 'Jeff is bringing the pilot down tomorrow morning. Is that all right with you, Milly?'

'Of course it is, darlings. We'll have dinner early and then you can set off.'

'Perfect.' Mitch grinned and kissed her cheek, making Milly turn pink with pleasure.

'You don't change, Mitch Hammond,' she giggled. 'I'm pleased to say.'

'Too late now, Milly old thing.'

Milly smiled at him, a little wistfully now. She knew there was far more behind those words. Mitch would never change in all sorts of ways and that included his devotion to Pips.

'Have you heard from Pips?' she asked tentatively when they were alone for a moment.

His face was suddenly bleak and, as if not trusting himself to speak, he shook his head.

'Of course, she's very busy. Burying herself in work, I think. That's the best thing she could do, but she rang me last week. I think she's coping very well.' She touched his arm. 'Things will be all right, Mitch, once all this is over.'

He forced a quick smile, patted her hand and turned away.

As Londoners went home at the end of their day to be with their families, perhaps to listen to the latest news and to prepare for the blackout and what they hoped would be an undisturbed night's sleep, Mitch, Johnny and Daisy set off for Weybridge in Mitch's car.

Just as Mitch had predicted, the house felt as if it was waiting for them; the beds were made up and there was even a tray of cups and saucers sitting on the kitchen table just waiting to be used.

'A cup of something and then I'm off to bed,' Mitch said, after he had shown them their rooms.

Left alone at last, Johnny took Daisy in his arms. 'It seems a long time since I was able to hold you and kiss you properly,' he murmured against her lips. 'I wish this damned war would end so that we can be together for always.'

Daisy held him tightly but shuddered inwardly. Somehow, she knew instinctively that there was a long way to go before it was all over and that there was a lot more danger for them all to face before it was. Luke being posted missing had shown her that. She didn't want to say anything to Johnny that sounded pessimistic; she was determined to live for the moment and not to dwell too much on what might happen, but not everyone was like her. Perhaps Johnny needed to be able to cling to plans for the future. It was what kept him going.

They spent a precious hour together before Daisy said reluctantly, 'We should go to bed. We'll have a long day tomorrow and then we'll be up all night waiting for Tom to get back with Luke.'

The following morning, Mitch drove them to Brooklands. Daisy gazed around wistfully. 'It seems an age since we were all here. Aunty Pips racing and then taking me flying for the first time and then, later on, Jeff teaching me to fly.'

Johnny squeezed her hand. 'It's where we met, isn't it?'

For a brief moment, they gazed at each other. For both of them that very first meeting had been special.

'I'm just going to check the aircraft,' Mitch said. 'I sent word to have it ready, but I like to make sure all is well. By the way, Milly's arranged for us to have something to eat at the Vickers works.'

Daisy and Johnny sat close together on Members' Hill, the only visitors now. They held hands and talked quietly. When Mitch came back, they sprang apart hastily.

'Don't mind me.' He grinned. 'Everything's ready. I've put a parachute for Luke in the passenger seat. Now, we just need a pilot.'

Time hung heavily.

'I wonder if my watch has stopped.' Johnny frowned, consulting it for the umpteenth time as they walked outside again after a light lunch. Already, they seemed to have run out of things to talk about and, now, they were all feeling the tension. 'I'm sure Jeff said he'd be bringing him down this morning.'

'He did.' Mitch said shortly and frowned worriedly. 'Let's go and wait in the hanger. There are some seats there.'

After what seemed an age of waiting, they heard a car pull up outside. As they hurried out, they saw Jeff emerging from the driver's seat.

Daisy gasped in surprise – and concern. 'He's on his own. Where's Tom?'

As Jeff slammed the car door behind him, they could already feel his anger and frustration. 'Sorry,' he said. 'The mission's off. Silly bugger fell down stairs this morning and broke his leg. I've done my damnedest to get another pilot, but I can't get one down here quickly enough to be briefed and to set off by the time we decided. And our contact over there was adamant that it had to be tonight or not at all.'

They glanced at each other, disappointment and anxiety on all their faces, apart from Daisy's. Quietly, she said, 'Then I'll go.'

The three men stared at her and all spoke at once.

'Oh no, Daisy.'

'Impossible. I'd be breaking every rule in the book.'

'Pips would kill me if I let you go,' Mitch muttered.

Cheerfully, Daisy said, 'And I'll kill you if you don't.' She glanced round at them and added seriously, 'Just think about it. I'm familiar with the aircraft. I've flown at night and, we're lucky, it's forecast to be bright moonlight tonight. If it's the same over there, I'll have no problem in seeing the ground. I know what to do – I was there at the briefing, don't forget. I know the route I have to take and the corridor over the coast to avoid the worst of the flak and, with the additional tank of fuel you have on your aircraft, Uncle Mitch, I may not even need to refuel.'

'William will have some ready – just in case,' Jeff murmured, glancing uncomfortably at the other two. Daisy could feel that he, at least, was weakening. It was his responsibility to get personnel home from enemy territory and there was no doubt in anyone's mind that Luke's position was dire.

She glanced round at them, her chin set. 'I'll go as a civilian, if you can't back me officially, Jeff.'

413

He shook his head. 'No, you'd be better in your uniform. If you did get captured, remember all the information you give them is name, rank and number . . .' His voice faded away as the other two stared at him.

'I'll go,' Mitch said, but Jeff shook his head. 'I can't let you do that. You haven't got Daisy's knowledge of the area and at least she's a member of the services. I can't let a civilian go.'

Johnny opened his mouth, but Jeff forestalled whatever he had been going to say. 'Nor you, Johnny. You haven't flown Lysanders, have you, and you don't know the area. It's Luke's only chance, Mitch. You know it is. We have to let her go.'

Mitch groaned and Johnny turned pale.

'Right, it's decided. I'm going. Now, let's go over everything one more time and then if we can get something to eat . . .'

'We'll go back to my place. I'd arranged for Mrs Pearson to cook dinner for us anyway before Tom had to leave. We'll just be one short.'

After going over the details once more, they sat down to dinner, but none of them felt much like eating or talking. Daisy couldn't wait to be on her way and the other three were still silently wrestling with their consciences.

Just before midnight they set out for Brooklands once again. 'You should be there and back across the coast before dawn,' Jeff reminded her.

As they all walked out to the aircraft, Johnny squeezed her hand. 'Luke's a lucky bloke,' he murmured. 'Would you do this for me?'

Daisy grinned and squeezed his hand in return. 'In a heartbeat.'

As Daisy trundled the aircraft along the grass and rose into the air, the three men stood watching her. She waggled her wings just once in farewell.

'If anything happens to her, Pips really will kill me,' Mitch murmured.

'She'd have to stand in line, Uncle Mitch,' Johnny said grimly and, for once, he wasn't joking.

They stood watching her until they could no longer see or hear the aircraft.

'Now,' Mitch murmured, 'all we have to do is wait.'

Hans stood at the window of his office in the German headquarters in Ypres and looked down at the silent, moonlit street below. From a back room across the corridor came the sounds of a raucous party. Drink flowed and his men were enjoying themselves. It was just as he had planned. Through the early hours of Friday morning, they would be sleeping off a hangover.

'We will have a leaving party on Thursday night,' he'd told his men. His eyes had twinkled. 'Friday night will be too late. I don't want you bleary eyed for your new commander on Saturday.'

The soldiers had laughed. They loved any kind of party and were very willing to give Hans a good send-off. Although he had only been there a few months, he had been a good senior officer; he had done his job but he had been lenient and as friendly towards his men as his position allowed. They were sorry to see him go.

Hans lifted his gaze above the buildings and watched the night sky. Somewhere up there, only a few miles away, he hoped there was a little aeroplane coming.

Fifty-One

'Do you know what time he's coming?' William whispered to Waldo. Alongside Luke and the three Resistance workers, they were waiting beneath the shadows of a hedge at the side of the field they had chosen.

'I've been told approximately three a.m. GMT. He wants to get back across the coastline before dawn, I think.'

They'd been keeping watch since two o'clock and were beginning to feel stiff and cold. They were listening intently, not only for the sound of an approaching aircraft, but also for any enemy patrols that might be out. But all was silent. Just before three o'clock, Waldo's sharp hearing caught the distant noise of a Lysander. He'd met several on pick-up missions and knew the sound.

'He's coming,' he whispered urgently. 'Light the torches.'

Stealthily, the three Resistance men hurried towards the torches and turned them on. Now everyone was gazing towards the sky as the noise of the aircraft's engines came nearer and nearer . . .

Above them, Daisy saw the lights switched on. Jeff had explained everything that would happen. 'They'll set torches in the shape of an A or an arrowhead, whatever you like to call it, so you follow it and set down as soon after the point as you can. They'll have chosen a field where there'll be plenty of length. Turn the aircraft at the end and wait there for your pick-up. They'll have fuel, if you need it, so be sure to check your gauges just before you land, though I don't think you'll need to. Don't turn off the engine and don't get out. You must leave as soon as possible, just in case a patrol has seen you. They will know to get Luke aboard as quickly as possible . . .'

Daisy flew low over the lights and felt the wheels touch the ground and bump along the grass field. When she knew there was enough length for take-off she turned the aircraft and then stopped to wait . . .

They were all running towards her. Waldo was the first to reach the aircraft. He shone a torch. 'My God! A woman.'

Daisy grinned down at him. 'Hello. Waldo, isn't it?'

He gasped. 'You – you know me?'

Before she could answer, William and Luke arrived beside him, gaping up at her.

'Good Lord,' Luke said. 'Daisy!'

'Sorry, no time for chat. Get in, Luke. We must go.'

As he climbed aboard, Daisy looked down at William. 'Thanks, Uncle William. I hope this doesn't cause you trouble.'

'We're fine, Daisy. Give them all my love at home, won't you? Take care . . .'

As Luke strapped himself into the passenger seat,

Daisy revved the engine and the plane began to move down the field. It gathered speed and lifted into the air. The whole operation had taken only minutes.

For a moment, William, Waldo and their helpers watched the aircraft fly away.

'Come on,' Waldo said, 'we'd better get out of here. Father—' Briefly he gripped William's arm. 'I'm going to disappear for a while – just in case. I'm going to join Pascal in the south. You and Mother take care of yourselves.' And then he and his fellow Resistance workers were gone, melting into the darkness.

In the air, Luke shouted from the passenger seat. 'It's so good to see you, Daisy. But why you?'

'It's a long story,' she shouted back. 'I'll explain when we get home.'

Now Luke fell silent. He knew, more than anyone, how Daisy would need to concentrate to get them both home safely.

As they approached the French coast, in the moonlight they could see shell bursts ahead, black puffs of smoke.

'I didn't get any of this when I came,' Daisy said.

'We're trained to change our course frequently, then their guns can't keep you in their sights.'

'I'll try it,' Daisy said, as a shell burst quite close to the aircraft. After a few seconds, she altered course again, but this time she felt a jolt as a shell burst very close. The aircraft shuddered, but Daisy managed to steady it. It was a frightening few minutes until they were out of the range of the guns.

'Well done, Dais,' Luke said. They both heaved a

sigh of relief as they saw the Channel shining in the moonlight below them. The sky was lightening as they crossed the English coast and Daisy turned towards Brooklands.

Mitch, Johnny and Jeff were outside again now, scanning the sky worriedly.

'They should be back by now, shouldn't they?' Johnny muttered, but the dawn was silent; only the sound of birdsong disturbed the stillness.

'Give it time,' Jeff murmured. 'We're all anxious, I know, but—'

'Listen!' Mitch said suddenly.

They were all still, straining to hear.

'Yes, they're coming. I can hear an aircraft coming in from the south-east.'

'That should be them.'

The noise grew louder and then they could see the Lysander coming in. Wordlessly, the three men grasped each other's shoulders and when Daisy landed the aircraft smoothly, they ran across the grass. As she switched off and she and Luke climbed out, open arms were waiting to catch them as they jumped down.

'Oh Daisy, Daisy.' Johnny held her tightly, his voice breaking with emotion. 'Thank God you're safe. Luke, old chap . . .' He reached out and grasped Luke's hand. 'It's good to see you.'

'Come on, let's get you something to eat,' Mitch said, but they could all hear the relief in his voice.

'I can't believe it was Daisy who came.' Luke shook his head. 'I still haven't heard the whole story.'

'It shouldn't have been her at all and I just hope

she's not going to expect to make a habit of it. I'll probably get a right royal rollicking all round for this,' Jeff said ruefully, 'but it's good to see you safe and sound. And we really had no choice. Our contact over there said you were in imminent danger.'

'Your contact,' Luke said, 'is our cousin, Waldo. He and Pascal are both members of the Resistance. Pascal is in the south of France and Waldo is going down to join him for a while just in case there are any repercussions from this.'

'What about Uncle William and Aunt Brigitta?' Daisy asked as they all climbed into Mitch's car and headed to his home. 'Could they be in trouble?'

'I think they'll be OK, but you're right. If I hadn't got out today, I would probably have been arrested.'

Mitch's housekeeper Mrs Pearson was waiting for them, ready to cook them all a huge breakfast.

'You shouldn't have come this early, Mrs Pearson,' Mitch admonished her gently.

'Oh, you know me, Mr Hammond. I'm always up with the lark and I knew your visitors would want a good breakfast. You sit down and leave it all to me.'

Now the fear and the anxiety were over, they all ate hungrily whilst Luke told them all about what had happened to him since he'd bailed out of his aircraft.

'I was sorry to lose a Spit, but it was on fire. I hadn't any choice.'

'Of course you didn't,' Jeff said. 'Go on.'

He ended his tale by saying, 'I had a helluva lot of luck, really, when you think about it, starting with the fact that the very first farmer who found me was friendly. If he hadn't been, it might have been a very different story. But the Belgians are very helpful towards the Brits. They haven't forgotten the last war yet and then there was the fact of it being Hans who was there.'

'That was a lucky coincidence, wasn't it?'

Luke shook his head. 'Actually, it wasn't a co-incidence at all. Hans can't be on active service because of his injury, but he'd asked for a posting to Ypres. He just wanted to go back, though he hadn't expected to find Uncle William there – or me! Anyway, he's certainly repaid his debt now.'

'Will he be in trouble, do you think?'

'I hope not, but he did take an enormous risk to help us, though I don't think anyone can trace my escape back to him. He would only be in trouble, perhaps, because he wasn't vigilant enough. He'll be leaving today, which is probably for the best. But to be honest, I don't think Daisy's arrival and departure was noticed. I just hope all those who helped me – Waldo and the three Resistance workers – got back to safety all right.'

'Will Waldo let us know?'

Luke shook his head and Jeff agreed. 'I don't think so. They try to keep messages to an absolute minimum.'

'The more radio contact they have,' Jeff explained, 'the more vulnerable they are to being located.'

'Does Gill know about all this?' Luke asked suddenly. 'And what about the folks at home?'

Daisy shook her head. 'They all know you're alive,

but not exactly safe and, no, only we know about tonight. Johnny was on sick leave anyway and Jeff organized with my boss for me to have leave.' She glanced at him. 'How much did you have to tell her?'

'Not much. She understands the need for secrecy.' He grinned. 'She knows what I do.'

'What about Pips?'

They all laughed. 'She was the one who understood what Waldo's first message meant, but she doesn't know what's happened since.'

'I expect she'll find out – eventually,' Mitch said dolefully. 'And then I'd better keep my head down.'

Daisy laughed. 'Don't you worry about Aunty Pips. She'd have done *exactly* what I've done.'

Mitch chuckled. 'I don't doubt it for a minute, but letting *you* do it is a bit different.'

Quite serious now, Jeff said, 'I don't think I need to tell you that you mustn't say a word about this to anyone at home – apart from Pips and maybe Gill – not until the war is finally over. I know it'll be tempting to tell them about Daisy's daring rescue, but it could compromise William's position and certainly Waldo's. Just tell them some vague story. I'm sure you'll think of something plausible.'

They all nodded solemnly and Daisy said, 'My folks are pretty good. They know not to ask for details about anything. I'm not really sure they know exactly what I do and they certainly don't know what Pips is doing. Even I don't.'

'Well, as soon as I've reported back and been debriefed, I'll be asking for some leave to go home,' Luke said and glanced at Daisy. 'Why don't you and

Gill see if you can get some time off and come home too? You too, Johnny, if you can. It'd be wonderful to all be together.'

'That's a great idea. Why don't we get in touch with Harry? See if he can make it too.' Daisy looked at Mitch. 'And why don't you get in touch with Pips and you both come up? Granny would love to have a houseful.'

'Oh, I don't know.' Mitch seemed strangely reticent.

Daisy chuckled. 'You'll have to face her some time. Why not get it over with?'

'It's not just that. I – I haven't seen her since – George's funeral.'

'Then,' Daisy said firmly, 'it's high time you did.'

Fifty-Two

When Daisy first told her what had been happening, Gill was a little put out. 'You might have told me.'

'The fewer people who knew about it, the better. Besides, there were enough people worrying about it.'

'I'm amazed they let you go.'

'They didn't want to, but in the end they had no choice. It was that or leave Luke there.'

'Oh Daisy, how brave you are.'

'You'd have done just the same – for Luke – now wouldn't you?'

'I'd like to think so, but – oh Daisy . . .' She flung her arms round her dearest friend as tears of relief flooded down her face. 'Thank you, thank you, thank you. I can't wait to see him.'

It was then that Daisy told her about her idea for them all to try to get leave at the same time and go to Lincolnshire. 'If only it works.'

Miraculously, it seemed to all of them, it did. They all got leave together for a whole week. Even Pips was able to get leave from Bletchley Park. She went to stay for the first night with Milly from where Mitch picked her up in his car. He was nervous about seeing her and when she opened the door to him and they stood staring at each other for a moment, he found he was holding his breath.

'I don't know whether to slap you or kiss you,' she said with a sudden grin.

'I'd prefer the latter,' he said, still holding her gaze.

As she invited him in, she said, 'I suppose I should be angry with you for allowing such an escapade, and in your Lysander too, but I can't be. She got Luke home – and only just in time, by the sound of it. Oh Mitch, thank goodness they're both safe.'

'And so say all of us,' he said wryly. 'I was so afraid you'd never forgive me, especially if something had gone dreadfully wrong.'

Pips shrugged. 'It's wartime, Mitch. We all do things we shouldn't when push comes to shove.'

He touched her cheek with gentle fingers as he said huskily, 'You certainly did last time. I wouldn't be here now, if it hadn't been for you.'

'Oh phooey,' she said and they both laughed.

'Come on in. Milly's got lunch ready for us before we set off north.'

It was the best way the week could have started for Pips and Mitch. With Milly's delightful manner and constant chatter, they were soon both at ease with each other, and by the time they set off in Mitch's car, it was as if any constraint between them had never happened.

It was an idyllic week for all of them in Doddington. Luke and Harry naturally stayed with Sam and Peggy whilst Pips, Johnny, Mitch and Gill and, of course,

Daisy stayed at the hall, but they met up all the time.

'We must have a party,' Henrietta said happily. 'I'll invite the Dawsons, the Coopers and the Nuttalls, just like we do on Boxing Day. We must take advantage of us all being together.' She did not say the words aloud, but it was in her mind that an occasion like this might never happen again. Whilst they were all safely home just now, the war was still raging over much of the world and Luke being posted missing had shaken them all.

Gill spent a lot of the time at the Nuttalls' house and the more they saw of her, the more Peggy and Sam liked her. They took to Johnny too, but eyed Harry warily to see if he had any problem with the young man who was now so obviously Daisy's boyfriend.

But Harry was his usual self, flirting with the girls in the village and every day sending off a letter addressed to a different WAAF.

'Just how many girlfriends have you got, Harry?' his mother asked.

'Lost count,' he said cheerfully. 'Safety in numbers and all that.'

'Is there no one special?' Peggy persisted.

For a brief moment, a shadow crossed his face but it was gone in a flash. 'They're all special, Mam. Each and every one of them.'

'Kitty Page from the village is always on my door-step, asking after you. She's such a nice girl – and pretty too.'

Harry pretended to give his mother's words serious

thought. 'You're right, Mam, she is. I'll take her out one evening. Make her day.'

'Oh you!' Peggy laughed.

They all went riding, taking it in turns to use the horses in the stables at the hall. Jake was in his element showing Pips and Daisy all that he'd been doing in the grounds to help the war effort.

'I see you've ploughed up the croquet lawn and the front lawn is being used for grazing,' Pips said evenly. Jake glanced at her. 'We'll soon get it right again, Miss Pips, when all this is over.'

'I know,' she said gently. 'I'm just sad to see it, that's all, but it has to be done.'

On the first morning after their arrival, Luke took Gill to the Dawsons' cottage. Norah flung her arms around him and wept against his shoulder. 'Oh Luke, I thought we'd never see you again.'

'Be a good job when all this nonsense is over and you can come back and take up your work again,' Len said gruffly, but as he gripped his grandson's shoulder, there were tears in his eyes. 'You and Harry,' he added, almost as an afterthought.

As they walked home, Luke was unusually quiet until he suddenly burst out, 'Gill, will you marry me?'

Gill gasped and then stopped walking as they turned to face each other. 'Yes, I will, Luke, but not until all this is over.'

'But we can get engaged, can't we?'

'Of course.'

'Ought I to speak to your father?'

428

Gill burst out laughing. 'Only as a matter of courtesy. I'm a grown girl and you don't have to ask his permission.'

Luke grinned. 'I know, but he'd expect it, wouldn't he?'

'I don't know about "expect", but I'm sure he'd like it.'

'We'll go into Lincoln tomorrow and I'll buy you a ring. Then we'll announce it at Aunty Hetty's party on Saturday.'

Gill laughed. 'You certainly know how to sweep a girl off her feet.'

In the quiet stillness of the lane, Luke pulled her towards him to kiss her.

A little later as they walked on, Gill said, 'Of course, there'll be the problem of where we're to live. That's one thing my father will expect; that I go back and help run the farm. One day it will be mine.'

'And one day my grandfather's business will be mine,' Luke murmured. He laughed. 'But let's not worry about all that yet. Let's just enjoy *now*.'

Johnny did not actually propose to Daisy, but there was a tacit understanding between them. It was as if they didn't dare speak about the future in case it tempted fate. They, too, were living – and loving – for the moment.

At Henrietta's party on the Saturday night before they were all due to leave the following morning, Luke tapped a glass to attract everyone's attention. When there was silence, he cleared his throat. 'I have an announcement to make.' He took Gill's hand as he added, 'Gill and I are engaged to be married. I hope you'll be happy for us.'

After a moment's surprised silence, everyone clapped and cheered but Len's harsh voice rose above the excited chatter.

'What on earth d'you want to go and do a damned fool thing like that for?'

Len's outburst had put a dampener on what had been a wonderful occasion for all the families whose young ones were away fighting the war, each in their own way, and Gill was still worrying about it the following morning when they were preparing to leave.

'I'm so sorry your grandfather took it like that.'

Luke didn't seem to be worried. 'When the war started, he told me that if I joined the RAF he would disown me. Now, it seems, he's changed his mind.'

'But . . .'

Luke silenced her with his lips, murmuring, 'No "buts", my darling, it will all work out. You'll see.'

As they all departed in a flurry of 'goodbyes', Mitch took Henrietta's hand and raised it to his lips. 'Thank you for your hospitality, Mrs Maitland.'

Her eyes twinkled mischievously at him. 'It's good to see you again, Mitch. You're welcome here any time.'

'That's very kind of you,' he said. 'I might very well take you up on that.'

'I'm sure you will,' Henrietta said dryly. Their eyes met and they exchanged a look that spoke volumes but neither said another word.

Mitch drove Pips back to London, leaving her at

Milly's apartment to spend the night there before she had to return to Bletchley Park. As they said 'goodbye', Mitch was strangely hesitant. 'When might we meet again?'

Pips wrinkled her forehead, reading nothing more into his question than a casual enquiry between two friends. 'I really can't say, Mitch. We don't get a lot of leave. I've been extraordinarily lucky to get a whole week just now.' She chuckled. 'I'll have to keep my head down for a while. Tell you what, I'll telephone you if I get any time off. That's if you don't mind driving down to meet me.'

He arched his eyebrow and glanced at her as if to say 'that's rather a silly question', but all he said was, 'Of course I don't.'

As she got out of the car and lifted her suitcase out of the back, she said, 'Bye for now. See you soon . . .'

Milly and Pips enjoyed an evening together.

'No Paul?' Pips asked.

Milly sighed. 'I don't see much of him. He works such long hours, but at least he's not away all the time, like a lot of women's husbands are. I'm luckier than most. And I keep myself busy. I help out at the WVS now. There's always plenty to do.'

'Are you going back to your parents?'

Milly shook her head. 'I've managed to persuade Paul to agree to me staying here, for the time being at least.'

And so it was back to life as they'd all known it before Luke had gone missing; Luke and Harry to their squadrons, Daisy and Gill to Hamble and Pips to Bletchley. Life in Doddington settled back into its routine, though the anxiety for those left at home was constant, perhaps even sharper than it had been. Now they knew what could happen.

Fifty-Three

There were no repercussions from Daisy's daring rescue of Luke. If those in high authority had got to hear about it, they had chosen to turn a blind eye. No harm had been done and a serving pilot had been rescued to fight another day.

The weeks passed; Daisy, Gill and their fellow airwomen continued to deliver aircraft to wherever they were needed. Much to her delight, most of Daisy's deliveries were now Spitfires. Luke and Harry continued to fly their aeroplanes and those left at home went on worrying about all of them.

In the middle of November there was, at long last, some good news. Church bells, which had been silent for so long throughout the country – only to be sounded in the event of an invasion – now pealed in glorious celebration at the news of General Montgomery's Eighth Army's victory at El Alamein earlier that month. A few days later, Russian troops near Stalingrad launched a counterblow on the German Sixth Army. German soldiers were dying of starvation and the extreme cold as well as being killed by gunfire.

Another Christmas came and went and none of those in the services could get home this year. 'What a good thing we had that party in May,' Henrietta said. 'But we'll still have the Dawsons, the Coopers and the Nuttalls here on Boxing Day.'

Edwin chuckled. 'That's if they'll come. After Len's little outburst last time, I'm not so sure.'

'Silly man.' Henrietta sniffed. 'When's he going to learn he can't have everything his own way?'

'I don't think he ever will, Hetty, my love.'

In January 1943, Field Marshall von Paulus surrendered to the Russian Army at Stalingrad. The Russian winter, as well as the fierce defence of their country by the Red Army, was slowly defeating the German invasion.

Such news gave the Allies hope and a renewed vigour. In March, the authorities began plans to target German industry, in particular the Ruhr. In the same month, a new squadron was formed at RAF Scampton in Lincolnshire. Its eventual first mission was veiled in secrecy, but the aircrews, who would fly in Lancaster bombers, had to undertake special training in low-level night flying. In April, the Prime Minister decreed that church bells could be rung every Sunday in the normal way. This, perhaps more than anything else, told the people of Britain that the threat of invasion no longer existed.

A few days later, Johnny told Daisy that he was being posted.

'The American Air Force is coming to Duxford,' he said, 'so my squadron are moving out.'

'Where to?'

'We don't know yet, but I think it'll still be in the south somewhere.'

Daisy sighed. 'It was bound to happen.'

In the middle of May, the Operations Manager called Daisy into her office.

'I have a special delivery for you. Since you passed your Class Five, have you flown a Lancaster?'

'Only once, ma'am.'

'I've got one for you today, so be sure to study your pilot's notes again carefully. I've already arranged for a flight engineer to go with you.'

'Where am I going?'

'It's to be picked up from Farnborough and taken to Scampton in Lincolnshire.'

Daisy gasped. 'That's just down the road from where I live.'

The CO was thoughtful. 'I can let you have a seventy-two-hour pass. I'll get the flight engineer picked up from Scampton, but you'll have to make your way back here by train after your leave.'

Daisy nodded, her eyes shining. 'Thank you, ma'am. I haven't been home for almost a year and I'd love some time with my family, even if it's only for a couple of nights.'

'I'm sorry about that.' The CO's mouth twitched. 'I expect it's difficult for you to decide where to go when you do get some leave. Home – or to wherever Flight Lieutenant Hammond is.'

Just before she was due to take off, Daisy inspected the huge aeroplane carefully. 'It looks a bit different.'

'It's been modified, but don't ask me why or what for, because none of us know,' one of the fitters told her. He tapped the side of his nose. 'All shrouded in secrecy, but we're guessing it's for some special mission.'

'Will it affect the flying?' was all Daisy wanted to know.

'Not for you, I don't think. Anyway, take it carefully. You'll be in a lot of trouble if you lose this beauty.'

The flight was uneventful and when she landed on the flat, windswept airfield she was quickly surrounded by several very handsome airmen.

'Good Lord, a girl? Come on, love, let's take you to the mess and get you something to eat.'

'How did she handle?'

'Perfectly.' The men glanced at each other, but no one volunteered any information and Daisy knew better than to ask. It was like a party in the mess, each young man vying for her attention.

'Well, well, well, if it isn't the lovely Daisy Maitland.' A voice she knew very well spoke behind her.

'Good Lord. *You!* Whatever are you doing here, Harry?'

'Can't really say, Dais. You know how it is.' He joined the merry group.

'How are you getting back to Hamble?'

'The Anson's coming to pick the flight engineer up today, but I've been granted a seventy-two. I can go home for a couple of days whilst I'm up this way.'

'Well, keep your eyes peeled,' one of the younger airmen said with a grin. 'We do a lot of low-flying night-time practising. Much to the disgust of the locals.'

Still, Daisy asked nothing.

As she prepared to leave to go to Doddington, the

airmen vied with each other to be the one to give her a lift. To her surprise, Harry declined the opportunity. Just as she was leaving with a fair-haired young airman, he drew her aside.

'Please don't tell them at home that I'm here, Dais. We don't get any leave and it's all very hush-hush. Just for your information – and only yours – I'm with 617 Squadron now and we're obviously being trained for something special, but none of us know what yet.'

'I won't say a word to anyone, Harry.' She kissed him on the cheek. 'Just take care of yourself.'

It had been good to meet them all, but she was saddened to think that whatever their special mission was, the likelihood of every one of them returning was remote. She just prayed that Harry would come back safely.

As always, her bed was ready at the hall and she spent a cosy family dinner with her parents and grandparents, hearing all the village news. Afterwards they sat in the parlour, still talking and reminiscing, but plans for the future were not easy to talk about.

The following day she went riding with her father and visited Norah Dawson and Peggy, though she did not see either Len or Sam, who were busy at the workshop.

That evening, just after they had lingered longer than usual over dinner, Robert said, 'Daisy, come outside a minute.'

They stepped out of the front door and stood side by side at the top of the steps.

'Listen.'

In the stillness of the May night they could hear a faint, continuous low throbbing sound that ebbed and flowed.

'I know that sound. That's Lancasters taking off from Scampton,' Daisy whispered. 'They're on their way to wherever it is they're going.' She said a silent prayer for all those fine young men she had met the previous day. She felt very guilty that she could not share the knowledge that Harry was most likely one of their number, not even with her father. But it was best that way; they all had wartime secrets that must be kept. The sound died away but still, they stood listening to the silence.

'I wonder how many aircraft have gone,' Daisy murmured. 'And where they're going.'

'I expect they'll go in waves and probably take different routes to wherever they're going.' Robert put his arm around her. 'Come on, let's go in. It's getting chilly and you're shivering. Perhaps we'll hear about it tomorrow. If it's a big mission, they'll release information once it's over.'

But Daisy couldn't sleep; through the night she imagined she kept hearing aircraft returning and her thoughts were with the airmen she'd met, their merry faces and teasing banter – and Harry.

The following day the BBC gave the news that during the night nineteen aircraft had left to attack dams in the Ruhr valley, the centre of Germany's industry. Two out of the three major dams attacked had been breached, causing devastating flooding. Power stations and factories had been destroyed or badly damaged, which would interrupt the German production for several months. But then came the sad news as the announcer in a solemn voice ended, 'Eight of our aircraft are missing.'

'Hello, Mam.'

'*Harry!*' Peggy flung her arms around him and pulled him into the house. 'How wonderful to see you. Where have you come from?' Without waiting for his reply, she shouted, 'Sam – Sam! Harry's home.'

Sam came into the kitchen, smiling broadly, and shook his son's hand. 'It's good to see you. Where have you come from?' He now asked the same question as his wife, but he waited for the answer.

Harry's grin widened. 'Just up the road. I'm based at Scampton at the moment.'

'Never! Well, that's good news. You'll be able to get home a bit more often perhaps. When did you arrive?'

Harry chuckled. 'Now I'm going to get a rollicking from Mam. Two months ago.'

Peggy stared at him, her mouth open. 'You've been that close all this time and not been to see us? Not a word?'

'Now, Peggy, love. Maybe he wasn't allowed.'

'Dad's right, Mam. You've all heard about the raid on the dams in Germany . . .'

Before he could say more, Peggy gasped and her hand fluttered to her mouth. 'Oh no. Don't say you were on that.'

Slowly he nodded and now his face was solemn. 'Yes, I was and it was all so hush-hush, none of us were allowed leave until it was all over and the news was out. I'm sorry, Mam, but—'

Peggy rushed to him to hug him hard. 'Don't, Harry. Don't say any more. I'm sorry for saying anything. Sam's always telling me that you and Luke can't get home. And Daisy, why, she's only just been after nearly a year without a visit.'

'I know, I saw her.'

'You – you did?'

'She brought one of the Lancasters to Scampton, one of the planes that were to take part in Operation Chastise.'

'Daisy? Daisy flew one of those huge planes?'

'She did. She flies all sorts.'

'Oh Harry.' Peggy buried her face against his shoulder and he put his arms about her.

Over her shoulder he caught and held his father's gaze. 'Dad, will you do me a favour? Can you ask them at the hall to let Daisy know I'm safe? She's probably gone back by now.'

'Of course I will,' Sam said huskily.

'And now,' Harry said lightly, holding his mother at arm's length. 'I'm off down the road to see little Kitty Page – if she's at home. I want her to know that her four-leafed clover kept me safe.'

Fifty-Four

Through the summer months of 1943, life in Doddington continued. Edwin was still a member of the local Home Guard and enjoying every minute. It had given him a new lease of life, even at eighty-three, and Henrietta still ran the estate with Jake's help.

'Goodness me, we're in the middle of September already and there's still so much to do on the farm and in the orchards. I don't know what I'd do without you, Jake,' she said yet again. 'But I can't say I'll be sorry to hand over the reins to Miss Daisy and you when the war is over.'

'Do – do you think we're going to win, Mrs Maitland?'

Henrietta stared at him in surprise. 'Don't ever doubt it, Jake. Not for a minute. With Churchill leading us, we can't possibly fail.'

Jake smiled. 'He does inspire folk, doesn't he?'

'It's his indomitable spirit that keeps us all going. Now, tell me your ideas for planting for the next year . . .'

Remarkably, the energetic Henrietta – now in her seventy-ninth year – still found time to involve the women of the village in the war effort. At home, the family were still fortunate in having enough staff to keep the hall running as it always had, though Cook sometimes despaired of how to produce appetizing meals with the rations. In the village, the women were all heavily involved in the WVS and in caring for the evacuee children who were still with them. All of them that were still there had settled in very well. Even Len was happy for Bernard to go to his workshop any time he wanted. Little by little he began to show the lad the work and Sam, too, guided the boy through the art of blacksmithing.

As for Florence Everton, she had never been happier. At last – even if it was only temporary – she felt like a real mother. The two little waifs, June and Joan Carter, who had arrived bedraggled and frightened in Doddington, had blossomed into boisterous, merry little girls. And Florence loved them.

'I just don't know what she's going to do when they go back home,' Conrad confided in Robert. 'She'll be heartbroken.'

'Have you ever thought about adoption? I don't necessarily mean those two, but you know that after the war there are going to be plenty of unwanted babies – ones born either out of wedlock or whilst husbands were away. Not all communities will be as forgiving or as supportive as ours was to Peggy over Luke.'

'Yes, perhaps you're right, Robert. I'll talk to Florence about it. Perhaps it would give her something to focus on instead of worrying about when she'll have to part with these two.' He smiled fondly. 'They are adorable, though.'

Betty Cooper had never married, but she loved her

job at the hall as lady's maid to Mrs Maitland and Alice. Peggy, too, still worked part time there except when her boys were home on leave – which, sadly, wasn't very often now.

'Do you know,' she said one morning when she was helping her sister to put away the laundry in Henrietta's bedroom, 'little Kitty Page comes faithfully twice a week to visit me to ask after Harry?'

Betty smiled and shook her head fondly. 'She's a nice little thing.'

Peggy laughed. 'We've always called her "little Kitty", but she must be eighteen or nineteen now. She works hard on the farm and in Mrs Maitland's grounds, but she's forever smiling, bless her.'

'You sound fond of her.'

'I am.'

'Would you like her as a daughter-in-law?'

'I would, but I don't think it's ever going to happen. Harry's such a flirt. Mind you, when he was home the other week, he did go to see her.'

'Is he still just up the road at Scampton?'

Peggy shook her head. 'No, his squadron has moved to Coningsby now.'

'That's still not far away, though, is it? Still in Lincolnshire.' Betty paused and then added, 'But I do hope he doesn't break little Kitty's heart. She obviously idolizes him.'

'Always has done, right from being a little girl.'

Betty sighed. 'War's cruel, isn't it?'

There was silence between the two sisters for a moment as they remembered their own terrible losses in the last war.

'Let's hope it'll all be over soon and the boys will be back home,' Betty murmured, almost afraid to voice such hopes. 'Then we'll see . . .'

It was only two days after this conversation that Peggy arrived at the hall, her face blotchy from crying and tears still coursing down her cheeks.

'Oh, whatever's the matter?' Betty pulled her into the kitchen and pushed her gently into a chair.

'It's – it's Harry.'

'Oh no,' Betty breathed. 'Tell me. Tell me quickly.'

'We had a telegram. He crashed his plane. Down south somewhere.'

'Is he – is he . . . ?'

Peggy shook her head. 'He's still alive, but – but he's terribly injured. That's all I know, Betty. I don't even know where he is. I just wondered if – if Mrs Maitland . . . ?'

'Of course she'll do whatever she can. We both know that. Come on, let's go and see her. She's in the parlour with Cook planning the day's meals.'

Betty knocked on the door and opened it. 'Mrs Maitland, I'm sorry to interrupt, but this is urgent. Harry's been badly hurt in a plane crash. We wondered—'

'Oh come in, Betty. Is Peggy here? Oh yes, I see she is.' Henrietta stood up and held out her arms to the weeping woman. 'Come in and sit down. Cook, please would you ask Sarah to bring us hot, sweet tea. Poor Peggy's had a nasty shock. Now, dear, tell me all you know.'

Peggy hiccupped and dried her tears, but fresh ones soon welled. 'I don't know much, Mrs Maitland. That's the worst.'

'I'll telephone Scampton. He's still based there, isn't he?'

'No, no, he's still with the same squadron, but they're at Coningsby now.' Whilst she drank tea and tried to stop shaking, Henrietta telephoned the RAF base, but when she came back into the room, she had no more news. 'They don't know any more than we do at the moment, but they said his crew will be on their way back. They'll know more when they can debrief them.'

'What – what does that mean?'

'After any mission, they talk to all the crews to find out everything that happened,' Henrietta explained gently. 'Or as much as they can tell them.'

'I just wish I knew where he was,' Peggy whispered. 'And if he – if he . . .'

'As soon as we know, Peggy dear, we'll arrange for you to go to him. I promise you that.'

'Daisy, I have a special job for you today,' the Operations Manager greeted her as the girls arrived at the office to collect their chits. 'A Lancaster crashed last night on Romney Marsh and the crew need to be taken back to Coningsby as quickly as possible. They're on their way here by lorry and you're to take them back in the Anson.' She grimaced sympathetically. 'I know it's fairly near where your folks are, but I can't allow you any time off to visit them this time. Sorry, but we need the Anson – and you – back here.'

Daisy hid her disappointment quickly. 'Of course. I'll be ready when they get here.' She said no more, but silently she was thinking, oh please, don't let it be Harry. Then she shook herself. That would be far too much of a coincidence.

Half an hour later, the covered lorry arrived, bringing six exhausted and shocked crew members. After greeting them, she said, 'Let's get you a quick cuppa before we go.' As she guided them towards the mess, she said, 'I thought a Lancaster had a crew of seven. Who's missing?'

'The pilot. Harry.'

Daisy's heart lurched. 'Not – not Harry Nuttall?'

One of the airmen moved forward. 'Yes, that's him.' He paused and then said, 'You must be Daisy.'

'Yes, yes, I am. How did you . . . ?'

The airman tried to smile through his weariness. 'He was trying to get to you. To Hamble. He said, "If we can get to Daisy somehow, she'll help us".'

Over their tea, the story unfolded. The flight engineer, whose name she discovered was Bob Hudson, explained, though with one or two interruptions from his fellow airmen.

'We were on a low-level mission to the Dortmund-Ems Canal . . .'

'It was the second one. We'd tried the night before and had to abort because of fog.'

'And last night was a bit of a disaster as well. We certainly lost two aircraft that I know of – possibly more. We were hit as we were turning for home and badly damaged. Harry decided to alter the route a bit. He said if he could keep us flying over land and get across the Channel at the narrowest point, we could land at one of the southern airfields.'

'He'd got it all planned out in his mind. If he could get us as near Brenzett as he could, they'd help us get to Hamble and you'd take us home.'

Daisy nodded. 'His brother's at Brenzett at the moment and I'm here.'

'And also he reckoned Romney Marsh would be a good place to let the aircraft crash after he'd bailed out. Only he didn't – bail out, I mean.'

'We were losing height all the time, but he managed to get us across the water,' Bob went on, patiently allowing his colleagues to interrupt now and again. 'I've never been so pleased to hear our navigator say, "we've just crossed the English coast".'

'Then, when we knew we were over land, he told us to bail out, which we did, but he carried on, trying to find an airfield, we thought.'

'But we understand now that he crash-landed on Romney Marsh.'

'Sounds as if his undercarriage wouldn't operate because he belly-landed in a field and smashed into some trees.'

'At least he didn't crash on houses, which is what he wanted to avoid. I bet he picked Romney deliberately.'

'Killed a cow though, by all accounts.'

'So we all started walking towards Brenzett and met up there.'

'Do you know how Harry is and where he is now?'

'The lads at Brenzett saw the aircraft crash and sent an ambulance.'

'He was badly smashed up, we've heard. He might lose his left leg and he's got injuries to his face.'

'He's been taken to the Royal Berkshire Hospital.'

Daisy frowned. 'Why there? I'd've thought there was somewhere nearer.'

'Because there's a fantastic surgeon there who will save Harry, if anyone can.'

'He's a protégé of the man who operated on Douglas Bader.'

'Ah,' Daisy said. 'Then he couldn't be in better hands. Did he see his brother, d'you know?'

Bob shook his head. 'We didn't know anything about his brother. He just mentioned you at Hamble.'

Daisy nodded. She'd have to let Luke know as soon as she could, but first, she must telephone the hall. 'And now, I'll get you back to Coningsby, but can you give me five minutes? I must make a telephone call.'

'To his family, I presume?' Bob said.

Daisy nodded.

'Just tell them where he is and his injuries, but not all the details we've told you.'

'Of course not.'

'Granny?' Daisy was saying a few minutes later. 'Have you heard about Harry?'

'Yes, Daisy, but we know very little.'

'All I can tell you is that he's been taken to the Royal Berkshire Hospital in Reading. His left leg is very badly injured. He might lose it, but there's a splendid surgeon there. I can't tell you any more, but I think you should get Peggy and Sam down there as soon as possible.'

The urgency in her tone spoke volumes to Henrietta. Luckily, Peggy was at the hall, insisting that working would keep her mind occupied and she'd also be on hand if messages came through. Five minutes later, Henrietta was saying, 'Of *course* you must go to him, Peggy. He needs you.'

'But I – I daren't go on my own, Mrs Maitland. I've hardly ever been out of the village. And Sam – well – I dun't reckon Mester Dawson'll let him have time off.'

Betty gave a derisive snort. 'You leave Len Dawson to our mam. She'll sort him out.'

'You can go down by train or we'll get Jake to take you. But first, we must sort out some accommodation for you. I know just the person to help with that. Leave it to me and you go home and pack, Peggy. Betty, you go with her and help her.' Despite the gravity of the news they'd just had, Henrietta's mouth twitched. 'And ask your mother to go to Mr Dawson's workshop and tell Sam.'

Fifty-Five

'Milly? Is that you, dear?'

'Mrs Maitland. Is anything wrong?'

'I'm afraid so. Milly, I need your help.'

'Of course. Anything. You know that. What's happened?'

Swiftly, Henrietta explained. 'Harry's in the Royal Berkshire Hospital in Reading and I need to book a hotel as near to the hospital as possible for Peggy and Sam. Can you recommend anywhere?'

'Nonsense. They must come here. I insist. You put them on a train in Lincoln and tell them to take a taxi here when they arrive and I'll look after them after that. We can easily get to Reading and back from here each day one way or another.'

'Are you sure, Milly? It's rather an imposition . . .'

'I'll be glad to help. I'm rattling around this flat on my own most of the time. Paul works such long hours. I'll be glad of the company, though not, I hasten to add, in these circumstances. Is he – is he very bad?'

'Yes, I'm afraid he is. Even if he survives – and at the moment even that hangs in the balance – he's likely to lose his left leg and the left-hand side of his face will be badly scarred, by all accounts.'

'How dreadful,' Milly murmured, tears in her voice. 'Does Pips know?'

'Not yet. We're trying to get word out to Pips and Luke. Daisy already knows. It was she who telephoned us to let us know where he is, but she didn't go into further detail.'

'Just send Peggy and Sam down. I'll get everything ready.'

'Thank you, Milly. You're a dear.'

Replacing the receiver, Henrietta put on her hat and coat and walked to Peggy's cottage. Since they were so short-staffed these days and Betty had already gone with Peggy, Henrietta must do such errands herself.

When she arrived at the cottage, she found Peggy still in a daze, but Betty had taken charge. 'She hadn't got a suitcase, poor lamb, but I've fetched her mine from home and Mam's gone down to see Sam and Mr Dawson.'

'I'll wait until Sam gets here. I must give him instructions how to get to Mrs Whittaker's flat, or they'll likely get lost in the big city. It's a bit of a daunting place for us country mice. Jake will take them to the station when they're ready and see them onto the train. He knows what to do.'

The village grapevine seemed to work faster than ever. Within an hour everyone knew about Harry's accident and that Peggy and Sam were going to Reading to be with him.

Bess Cooper was the one to go to the workshop to stand outside with her arms folded, ready to do battle if necessary.

'Len – I need a word.'

'What now, woman?' he muttered, but he was honest enough to realize that no one bothered him at his place of work unless it was urgent. So, he dropped his hammer and moved out into the September sunshine.

'I need to speak to Sam. He and Peggy have to go to London and then to Reading straightaway. Harry's been injured in a crash.'

For a brief moment, Len stared at her. 'Bad?'

Bess nodded. "Fraid so. At the moment, they're not sure if he's going to make it.'

They stared at one another and Len could read the anxiety in the woman's eyes. He nodded then turned and shouted, 'Sam. Get yarsen out here.'

A moment later, Sam appeared, wiping his hands on a rag. When he saw his mother-in-law standing there, he stopped, knowing instinctively that something was wrong. Swiftly, Bess explained, adding, 'You're to go to London – right now. Mrs Maitland's arranged everything. You're to stay at Mrs Whittaker's and she'll take you to the hospital.'

'My boy, my poor boy,' Sam began – but when he turned anxiously towards Len, Bess said, 'You need to go, Sam, lad. You need to go to Harry. Now.'

By the time the couple had made the mesmerizing journey to the capital, had been greeted warmly by Milly and given a meal, word had reached Pips and Luke. Luke at once applied for compassionate leave and was granted it. He was coming to the end of a tour of duty anyway and his senior officer saw no reason not to grant his request in the circumstances.

Daisy couldn't get immediate leave, but she had three days due shortly and would hurry to Reading then. Pips too would visit him as soon as she could.

'It's too late for you to go today,' Milly said, 'but we'll set off first thing in the morning. In the meantime, would you like to telephone the hospital for any news of him?'

'Would you do it for us, Mrs Whittaker?' Sam asked. 'I'm not very good with them things.'

Milly telephoned at once, but the only news they would give out was that he had had an operation to remove his left leg and that he was 'comfortable'.

'Well, I doubt that,' Sam said. 'But it's the stock phrase, isn't it?'

'So,' Peggy's voice quavered, 'they – they've taken his leg off.'

'I'm afraid so, my dear.'

Peggy closed her eyes and groaned in anguish.

Peggy paused at the entrance to the ward, her glance scanning the beds down each side.

'This way, Mrs Nuttall.' A softly spoken nurse led them into the long room and to the bed nearest the door. Half of Harry's face was bandaged and the part that they could see glistened with sweat. The mound of bedclothes held up over his left leg was testament to the injury.

Tentatively, Peggy approached the bed. 'Harry?' she whispered, hardly daring to speak.

'It's all right to talk to him, Mrs Nuttall. It's what he needs.'

Peggy pressed her lips together to try to stem the

ready tears, but nodded. A little stronger, she said again, 'Harry?' Sam too moved to the bedside and spoke his name.

Harry's right eye opened, but it was bloodshot and Peggy doubted he could see them. Fresh fear gripped her. Was he blind too?

'Mam?' Harry croaked out of the side of his mouth.

'We're here, Harry,' Peggy said. 'We're both here.'

'How . . . ?'

'Mrs Maitland organized it all.'

The corner of Harry's mouth twitched in an attempt at a smile. 'Aunty Hetty. God bless her.' There was a pause before he said bitterly, 'They've cut my leg off, Mam.'

'I – we – know, but I expect it's to save your life.'

Harry muttered something, but they couldn't quite hear what it was. He closed his eyes and began mumbling words that were unintelligible. The nurse, still hovering nearby, said, 'He's feverish and keeps lapsing into a semi-conscious state.' She paused and glanced at them both before saying quietly, 'There was no way they could save his leg. It was – mangled, is the only word I can use to describe it. Sorry to be quite so graphic, but you need to know the truth.'

'Please don't apologize,' Sam said. 'You're right. We do want the truth.'

They sat beside his bed until nightfall, the ward sister allowing them to stay beyond normal visiting hours. Just as they were getting up to leave to go back to Milly's, Luke slipped quietly into the ward.

'I got here as soon as I could.' He kissed his mother and gripped Sam's hand. 'How is he?'

'We think a little better,' Sam said. 'He's not sweating so much.'

'Sister said I could have five minutes. I've only got a forty-eight-hour pass.'

'Where will you stay?' Peggy asked. 'We're at Mrs Whittaker's. She's been so kind.'

Luke smiled. 'I'm sure if I turn up with you, she'd welcome me, but I don't like to impose upon her good nature. I've already been in touch with Mitch. He's in London at the moment and I can go there. I can kip on his sofa if necessary.' He paused, though his gaze was still on his brother. 'Has Daisy been yet?'

'She can't get leave until next weekend. She'll come then. Mrs Whittaker's already said she must go there.'

'She's a good sort, is Aunty Milly. You get off and I'll stay for as long as Sister will let me.'

As his mother and Sam left, Luke sat down beside the bed. 'Poor old chap,' he murmured, though he doubted Harry could hear him. Luke had faced death many times in his Spitfire and had been lucky to escape from Belgium like he had. He smiled as he thought yet again about Daisy's brave rescue. For some unaccountable reason, he'd never thought that it would be Harry who'd be so badly injured and yet, flying bombers over enemy territory night after night, he'd been lucky to survive until now. But at least it looked as if he was going to live, thanks to the clever doctor. But how would Harry face up to the loss of his leg and of his good looks?

*

Betty answered the tentative knock that came on the back door of the hall. She opened it to find a white-faced Kitty Page standing there, twisting her fingers nervously.

'Is it true about Harry?'

'Come in, duck, and I'll tell you everything I know.'

Half an hour later, after Betty had finished telling Kitty every little detail, the girl said, 'But he will live? You're sure he's going to live?'

'As far as we know at the moment, yes, but he's still very, very poorly.'

'Can I go to see him?'

Betty stared at her open-mouthed. 'You mean – you mean – you'd go all the way to Reading on your own?'

Kitty nodded. 'I'd do anything to help Harry. That's if – that's if you think he'd want to see me.'

'I'm sure he would. He'll need the support of all his friends.'

'I suppose he'll have all his girlfriends round the bed,' Kitty said in a small voice. 'Perhaps he won't want me.'

'Well, that's as may be,' Betty said briskly, 'but I'm sure he'd be glad to see a friendly face from home, that is if the nurses will let you see him. That might be the only problem. When someone is very ill in hospital, you know, they only let close family in to see them at first.'

Kitty nodded. 'I understand.' She paused and then added hesitantly, 'Then you think I should leave it a while till – till we hear how he is?'

'I do, duck, but I promise you I'll keep you posted. How would that be, eh?'

Kitty nodded, but Betty could see the disappointment and the anxiety in the girl's face and so, when Kitty had left, Betty went in search of Henrietta. 'Could I have a word with you, ma'am?'

'Of course, Betty. Come into the parlour. We won't be disturbed there.'

Moments later Betty was recounting Kitty's visit. 'She wants to go to see him, but I don't like the thought of that young lass going all that way on her own. She's never even been on a train.'

'Quite right, Betty.'

'But she's determined – I could see that – once we hear that he's well enough to have visitors other than his immediate family, that is.'

'Mm.' Henrietta was thoughtful for a moment. 'There might be a way. Jake has been asking after Harry constantly. He's always been so fond of all three of them ever since he began taking them riding as children. And, though he's a country boy at heart, he has travelled a little. Perhaps he would agree to take her. Leave it with me, Betty, I'll think about it.'

'She's not looking for charity, ma'am. She says she has enough money to pay for her fare.'

Henrietta's eyes twinkled. 'We'll see about that. I would treat them both to a couple of nights in a modest hotel. You can't do that sort of trip in one day.'

'Do – do you think Harry would want to see her?'

Henrietta's face sobered. 'He's going to need all his friends – his *real* friends – to rally round. I'm very much afraid that many of his so-called girlfriends will fade away. Only the ones truly devoted to him will stay.'

'Won't they regard him as a wounded hero? Those other girls, I mean. Won't they see it as all rather – romantic?'

'For a while – maybe, but it takes a remarkable young woman to last the course. What my Robert would have done without Alice's devotion, I shudder to think.' Henrietta and Betty regarded each other, remembering the tough times Robert had been through.

As if reading each other's thoughts, Henrietta said, 'And now we must see Harry through this.'

Fifty-Six

'Now Milly, dear, I know exactly what you're going to say, but please, this time, will you find a small hotel in Reading for Jake and Kitty?' During the middle of the week following the accident, Sam, in his nightly telephone call to the hall, had said that Harry was now allowed visitors other than his immediate family. Henrietta had felt obliged to tell Milly about Jake and Kitty's plans. 'We really cannot impose on your kindness any more.'

'Oh, do let them come here. *Please.* They'll be lost in London and I can look after them. I have three bedrooms and I'm sure Jake wouldn't mind being gallant and sleeping on the couch.'

Henrietta chuckled. 'He's slept in far worse places in his life, I can assure you, Milly.'

'But, of course, if anyone else wants to come down, I will have to draw a halt.' She giggled. 'I can't put the whole village up, though I'd do it gladly if I had the space.'

'I know you would, dear. Very well, then. Just this time, but no more.'

If it hadn't been for their anxiety over Harry, Kitty and Jake would both have enjoyed the journey.

'It's exciting, isn't it,' she said, as fields and houses

459

flashed by the window, but when they arrived at the huge railway station in the city, she clung to Jake's arm, overwhelmed by the bustling crowds. When they stepped out into the busy, noisy streets, she stared about her in wonderment. 'I thought Lincoln was big, but this . . .'

'Come on, over here. We're to find a taxi and go straight to Mrs Whittaker's.'

Kitty was open-mouthed as the cab weaved its way through the streets. They were lucky in having a chatty driver who, realizing they didn't know his city, proudly pointed out all the landmarks and places of interest.

''Course, 'Itler's trying to do his best to ruin it all, but 'ee won't manage it. We'll build it all again once this lot's all over an' we've beaten 'im. You'll see.' He paused and then asked, 'Where're you from, then?'

'Lincolnshire,' Jake said. 'Near Lincoln itself.'

'Oho, bomber county, eh?'

Jake held his breath, waiting for what he thought was the inevitable question. Are you in the forces? But it didn't come. Perhaps, he thought wryly, the man thought he looked too old.

'We've come to see a – friend of ours. He's a bomber pilot and he crashed. He – he's badly injured.'

'I'm sorry to hear that, mate. In hospital here, is he?'

'No, in Reading, but we're going to a friend's home first. She'll take us to see him.'

'Right you are. We're nearly there.'

A few moments later, the cab drew up outside Milly's apartment, but when Jake tried to pay the driver, the man waved aside his money. 'Have this one on me, mate, and I hope your friend recovers. Where we'd be without the RAF lads, I don't know.'

As they stood on the pavement and watched him drive away Kitty murmured, 'Aren't people nice?'

'They certainly are,' Jake said, picking up their bags. 'And there's none nicer than Mrs Whittaker.'

Moments later, Milly greeted them effusively. 'Now, you must have something to eat and then I'll take you to the hospital, if you're not too tired. You must have caught a very early train to arrive here by lunchtime.'

'We did, but we're fine,' Jake said and Kitty added, 'We want to see him as soon as possible, even if it's only for a few minutes. How is he? Have Mr and Mrs Nuttall said?'

'Yes, they give me a daily report. He's starting to respond to the treatment, but it's very slow. He had a fever for a while and was often delirious, but he's coming out of that now. You mustn't be shocked at his appearance. The left side of his face is injured too. Did you know that?'

Kitty nodded, unable to speak for the lump in her throat.

'Has Daisy been to see him yet?' Jake asked.

'She's coming at the weekend.'

Jake nodded. 'We're only stopping two nights, if that's all right, so we'll be gone by then.'

Milly only shrugged. 'It's no problem. Daisy and Kitty could share the room. There are two single beds in there.'

'Oh, but we couldn't—' Jake began, but Milly

flapped her hand. 'As far as I'm concerned, you can both stay as long as you like. I mean it. We'll manage.' For a moment, her face crumpled. 'I do know how much Harry means to all of you and he needs you.'

'Has he – has he had lots of visitors?' Kitty asked, holding her breath, fearing to hear the answer.

'What she means is,' Jake smiled, 'has he had a lot of girlfriends around the bed?'

Milly stared at her and then realization flooded through her. Kitty wasn't just a friend; she was in love with Harry, but she obviously knew about his bevy of girlfriends.

'As far as I know,' Milly said carefully, 'only his mother, Sam and Luke have visited. The only other person they've mentioned was a visit from his commanding officer, but other than that – no one.'

Kitty smiled.

When Milly took Jake and Kitty to the hospital, the ward sister warned them, 'As he improves, you will have to stick to visiting hours, though I do realize you have all come a long way to see him.' She smiled. 'We can be tartars, but we have our patients' best interests at heart, you see. Constant visitors can be tiring and we have to be fair to the other patients too, of course. Though in this case, I have to say, everyone has been most understanding towards a brave pilot. Here we are . . .'

As she ushered the three of them into the ward, Sam and Peggy rose from their chairs on either side of the bed.

'Hello, Jake – Kitty,' Sam said. 'We'll go and get

a cup of tea and maybe a sandwich whilst you talk to him. And then I think we should all go for a while and come back tomorrow. Sister has been most kind, but I think he needs a rest.'

'I'll just say "hello",' Milly said, 'and then I'll leave you to it.'

Moments later, Peggy, Sam and Milly left. Kitty moved tentatively to the side of the bed and gazed down at the man she had adored for so many years. He was changed, of course, but to her he was still her Harry; her beloved Harry.

'Kitty,' he said in a croaky whisper. 'It's good to see you. Fancy you coming all this way to see me.'

A smile hovered on her lips; she'd walk to the ends of the earth to see him, but she said nothing. As he held out his hand towards her, she took it, feeling its warm clamminess. He still had some fever, she thought, as a quiver of fear ran through her.

'And Jake too.' He turned his head on the pillow but winced as if the movement pained him.

'I couldn't let Kitty come all this way on her own, now could I? Besides, I wanted to make sure you're behaving yarsen.'

'How's things at home? How are all the horses? I've missed our rides out, you know.'

'We'll do it again. Just get yourself better and come home. We'll soon have you riding out again.'

'You think so?' Harry sounded doubtful.

'I know so,' Jake said firmly.

Kitty sat, holding his hand, but she couldn't think of anything to say. All the things she wanted to tell him could not be spoken. He turned his head again slightly to look at her. Half his face was still bandaged and his right eye still looked bruised and sore.

'Can you – see all right?' she asked hesitantly.

'Out of this one, yes, but they're not sure about the other one yet.'

Jake talked softly, telling him all about home and life in the village until Harry drifted off to sleep.

'I think we should go,' Jake whispered. 'Let him rest a while. Sam said we can come back tomorrow.'

Reluctantly, Kitty nodded and eased her hand out of his grasp. Quietly, they left the ward and found their way back to Milly's.

'Dinner's almost ready,' Milly greeted them. 'This is my husband, Paul. I don't think you've met him, have you, Kitty?'

'It's very good of you to have us all,' Jake said, shaking Paul's hand.

'Glad we can help and Milly likes nothing better than having a houseful. Now, can I get you a drink before we eat? Beer? Sherry?'

Jake glanced at Sam, who was standing in front of the fireplace with a beer glass in his hand.

'Beer would be very nice, thank you,' Jake said.

'And Kitty? Sherry, perhaps?'

'Thank you, but I don't drink, Mr Whittaker.'

'Call me "Paul", please. I'll get you a soft drink, then.'

As they all sat down to eat, Kitty was still nervous in such lavish surroundings and anxious not to make a fool of herself.

'I've been thinking . . .' Milly said.

'Oh dear, that's ominous,' Paul said, rolling his

eyes. They all laughed, easing the tension. Kitty suddenly found she was very hungry after the long journey and the emotion of seeing Harry and began to eat the lovely food in front of her.

'I know Jake and Kitty can only stay two days,' Milly said, 'and I expect that you, Sam, will have to get back to work before long.'

Sam nodded. 'Yes, Mr Dawson's getting on a bit now. He can't cope with the work like he used to do. And the two young lads from the village we've got helping us until they're called up aren't exactly the world's finest wheelwright and blacksmith, though they do their best. I have to say that the young evacuee lad, Bernard, is better than the pair of them put together.'

'What about you, Peggy? Could you stay longer? I'm sure your mother – and Betty – would look after Sam.'

'Well, they would, but . . .' She hesitated, glancing at Sam.

'Of course you could stay, love, but we don't like to impose on your kindness, Mrs Whittaker.'

Milly flapped her hand. 'Think nothing of it. I enjoy the company and you'd be here when all the others come visiting. Daisy will be here at the weekend and I know Luke will be back again as soon as he can and then there's Pips. She's sure to come.'

'It'll be like Piccadilly in here,' Paul joked, but all Milly said happily was, 'Yes, won't it?'

Over the next two days whilst Kitty and Jake were still there, Harry slowly improved. On the evening before they were due to leave, Sam said over dinner, 'He's so much better now, Peggy, love, I think I will go back with Jake and Kitty tomorrow afternoon.'

'We'll ring the hall every night to let you all know how he is,' Milly said.

'That's a good idea and then I can let everyone else know,' Sam agreed. 'Our parents are all very anxious. And the Dawsons, too, of course. They've always treated him almost like another grandson.' He laughed wryly, 'At least Mrs Dawson does.'

'Well, if they want to come down . . .' Milly began, but Sam only laughed.

'It's very kind of you, Mrs Whittaker, but I don't think the womenfolk – Mrs Dawson and Mrs Cooper, that is – or my mother – have ever been further than Lincoln in their lives. I really don't think they'd make the journey.'

The following morning, when they had to say goodbye to Harry, Kitty's tears were very close. She managed valiantly to hold them in check in front of him, but on the journey home she could no longer hold them back. Sam held her hand and talked softly to her. 'We know how you feel about Harry, love. We've always known, but we don't want you to get your hopes up. You know what a flirt he is. I don't think he's ever been serious about any of the girls he's taken out. I don't want to hurt you, Kitty, love, but I have to be honest with you.'

Kitty sniffed and wiped her tears. 'I know, Mr Nuttall. I don't have any false hopes about Harry's feelings for me, but I just had to go and see him. I love him so much – I always have – and I just needed to see for myself that he's going to be all right.' She smiled tremulously. 'But please don't worry about me. I know I don't stand a chance with him alongside all those pretty girls, but I hope he sees me as a *friend*. I don't ask for anything more.'

Sam felt a lump in his own throat as he patted her hand, but there was really nothing else he could say. He was very much afraid that what she said was true.

Fifty-Seven

The Maitland family were seated round the table in the Great Hall finishing dinner.

'So, did Jake say how Harry is?' Edwin asked.

'Recovering slowly,' Robert said. 'But it's going to take a while.'

'As soon as he's fit to be moved, we'll see what we can do about getting him brought to Lincoln,' Edwin said. 'If the RAF will agree, of course. He'll still be their responsibility. But it would be so much easier for his family and friends. Poor Milly must feel her apartment has become a hotel.'

'Don't worry about Milly,' Henrietta said. 'I get the impression she's loving it. Oh, not poor Harry being hurt, of course, but to feel she's helping. She loves company and I expect she'll persuade Peggy to stay for as long as she wants. Bess and Clara will look after Sam whilst she's away.'

Edwin's eyes twinkled as he regarded his wife. 'And no doubt, Hetty, my love, you'll be asking if there's anything you can do to help.'

Henrietta smiled at him. 'No doubt I will, Edwin.'

It was several weeks before the doctors deemed Harry fit enough to be moved north. He had had a steady stream of visitors. His mother went every day, often accompanied by Milly. Daisy, Luke, Johnny, Gill, Pips and even Mitch visited him whenever they could. But to everyone's surprise there were no pretty girls queueing along the corridors of the Royal Berkshire to visit the handsome hero, nor any pink, perfumed letters arriving for him. There were only letters from home and one, twice a week, from Kitty. 'A chap whose face is scarred for life and who can no longer take them wining, dining and dancing is not much of a catch,' Harry said philosophically, but strangely there was no bitterness in his tone.

'Kitty will never desert you.'

'Ah yes. The ever-faithful little Kitty.' He frowned lopsidedly. 'Tell me, Mam, did I dream it or did she come to visit me? Those early days are all a bit hazy.'

'She did. Mrs Maitland arranged for Jake to bring her and they stayed with Milly.'

'Good old Aunty Milly. She's a brick, isn't she?' There was a pause before he said, 'Well, Mam, I have some news. Kitty will soon be able to visit me again. The doctors have said I can be moved to Lincoln hospital. They've been in touch with them and they have a bed there for me. I'll be there in time for Christmas.'

The stitches had been taken out after two weeks and Harry had improved rapidly after that. After a month, at the end of October, he could lever himself out of bed and into a wheelchair. And now, six weeks later, even the bandages had been removed and the surgeon had agreed he was well enough to be moved nearer his family.

'They will help in his recovery now, almost as much as nursing care,' he'd remarked. And the RAF had agreed to his removal to Lincoln hospital; it was near where he was based anyway.

'Oh Harry,' Peggy said, tears of thankfulness glistening in her eyes. 'That's wonderful.'

'Of course, I expect I'll have to come back down here when my stump has healed well enough to have a leg fitted, but in the meantime, at least I'll be nearer you all and then soon, I hope, they'll let me come home, though I'll be on crutches for a while.'

'We'll manage,' Peggy said happily. 'You're alive and you'll be out of the war.'

'For a while – yes, but don't forget I'm still officially in the RAF.'

Peggy's face was a picture. 'But – but surely you can't fly again.'

Harry grinned, unable to stop himself teasing her. 'Well, as everyone has been reminding me, look at Douglas Bader – and I've only lost one leg.'

Harry was back on home turf just before Christmas and much of the festivities for the Nuttall family took place in his ward in Lincoln hospital. Now, he had a steady stream of visitors, none more frequent than the faithful Kitty.

'My four-leafed clover didn't work, did it?' she said dismally, when she visited on Boxing Day, Harry's birthday.

''Course it did, Kitty. I'd've been a goner if it hadn't been for that.'

But the girl didn't seem convinced. He reached for

her hand. 'Don't you ever think that, you silly goose. Now, tell me who's coming in later?'

She smiled. 'All of 'em. The Maitlands – though Miss Pips, Daisy and Luke couldn't get home for Christmas this year, so they're not here. All your family, of course, and even Mrs Dawson's coming, though I don't know about Mr Dawson. Sister will have a fit, but I don't think she'll say too much. Not to a hero.'

Harry had the grace to blush. The previous week he had received the news that he had been awarded the Distinguished Flying Medal for saving the lives of his crew by flying his Lancaster until they had all bailed out safely and, in so doing, had risked his own life. And even then, he had continued to fly it until he found an open space in which to crash-land, rather than bail out and let it crash into houses. It had been a wonderful piece of news for Bess to impart proudly to the whole village and beyond.

'Sister won't mind,' Harry said now. 'All the chaps in this ward are walking wounded. We won't be disturbing anyone who's seriously ill. Besides, a lot of 'em whose families live a distance away won't have visitors today. Those who could, came yesterday – so we'll share mine out.'

Just as Harry had predicted, the four members of the Maitland family arrived mid-afternoon and, when they had greeted Harry and loaded his bed with presents, they moved around the ward to sit with the patients who had no visitors. Bess Cooper held court at his bedside with Norah alongside her.

'So, Master Robert,' Harry said, when Robert took

his turn beside him. 'What d'you think's going to happen this year?'

'I'm optimistic, Harry. It was in the papers on Christmas Eve that the American, General Eisenhower, has been appointed as Commander of the Allies. They're planning to get ground troops back onto the mainland of Europe. Montgomery is to be his field commander. But it won't happen for a few months. There'll be an awful lot of preparations and, hopefully, without the enemy knowing where the invasion is going to be.'

'I hope so,' Harry said quietly. 'But I should be there. I should be helping them and now I'm going to miss it all.'

'You're still in the RAF, so I expect once you're fit and have an artificial leg, they'll find you something to do.'

'But it won't be flying, will it?'

'Perhaps not,' Robert agreed. He was always truthful, even with his own seriously ill patients. 'No doubt you could leave the RAF, if you wanted. I would give it some serious thought.'

'I will. Thanks, Master Robert.'

Through the early months of 1944, there was a new feeling of optimism throughout the country and none more so than in Doddington. They read and listened to the news avidly.

'Have you seen this?' Robert said to Alice. 'Hitler has mobilized all children over the age of ten. The man's a monster.'

'He certainly is if all the tales about what's

happening to the Jews are to be believed. It's – it's – well, to be honest, I can't think of a word strong enough to describe him and his cohorts.'

'The sooner we get him stopped, the better,' Robert said grimly.

British and American troops invaded Italy and RAF bombers dropped thousands of tons of bombs on Berlin. The fightback had begun in earnest; Russia too had a momentous victory taking back Leningrad, which had been under siege for two years. But there was also the Japanese to contend with; an Allied campaign began to turn the tide in Burma.

'Something's going to happen before long. The Allies have to get back into Europe,' Robert said.

Harry had come home in February when the doctors declared that the wound had healed really well. Henrietta was soon planning a celebration.

'Last Christmas was a bit odd with so many of the families missing and Boxing Day spent with Harry in hospital. Let's have our traditional party at Easter instead.'

'I wouldn't bank on the others being able to get home then either, Mother,' Robert warned her against disappointment, but Henrietta waved away his worries.

'We'll make the most of whoever can come.'

The week before the planned party, Pips telephoned the hall. 'Mother, would you mind if Mitch came to us for Easter? Johnny can't get leave, so Mitch is going to be on his own.'

'Of course, Philippa. He'll be very welcome.'

Henrietta was smiling smugly as she replaced the receiver.

She had planned the party for lunchtime on Easter Sunday as if it were Boxing Day and had asked all the usual people.

'They can all walk across when they come out of church,' she said.

Daisy, Pips and Mitch arrived on the evening of Good Friday. Luke, like Johnny, could not get leave.

'Pips, have you got a moment?' Robert said the following morning.

'Of course.'

'Let's go into my surgery. I want to talk to you about Harry.'

'Oh, right. What is it?' she asked as they sat down.

Robert frowned. 'Conrad tells me his wound has now healed well enough for him to be fitted with an artificial leg, but nothing seems to be happening.'

'Where will he have to go?'

'Roehampton, I think.'

'In London?'

Robert nodded. 'I think the RAF will sort it all out, so I understand, but it seems that it is Harry himself who is putting it off.'

'Ah,' Pips said with feeling. Then, with a chuckle, she added, 'Being too well looked after by his mother, I shouldn't wonder. Right, I'll see him before I go back, but after tomorrow's party. I wouldn't want to spoil that by getting a little – um – *firm* with him.'

Now it was Robert who chuckled.

Fifty-Eight

Late on Easter Sunday morning, Harry arrived in style for the party, which was really in his honour. Sam had managed to scrounge a battered bath chair from someone he knew in the next village and he pushed him all the way from their cottage and then carried him up the front steps and into the Great Hall. Harry sat in a chair at the end of the room and looked for all the world as if he were holding court. Perhaps he was, for everyone came in turn to sit beside him for a while.

'Now then, old chap,' Robert said, taking the seat next to him. 'How's it going?'

Robert was the one person Harry knew would really understand how he felt when, every so often, his natural ebullience deserted him and he fell into a dark place. But surrounded by family and friends, today was a good day.

'Up and down a bit, if I'm honest.' Robert nodded understandingly, as Harry went on, 'Everyone's been so wonderfully kind and I feel guilty that I sometimes get a bit impatient with them all fussing over me.'

Robert chuckled. 'I understand exactly what you mean, but stick with it. They all mean well.'

Harry sighed. 'I know and I should be grateful. That's why I feel guilty because the opposite would be so very lonely. D'you know, little Kitty still visits every day, even when she's had a long day at work on the farm? It's sometimes gone nine o'clock when she comes, but she never misses.'

'It'll get easier. When you get your undercarriage back and can get about on your own you won't feel so dependent on anyone else. How's the stump healing?'

'Very nicely, Dr Everton says. He thinks I'll soon be ready to go and have a proper leg fitted.' Conrad had been attending Harry since he'd come home. Robert did not tell him that he already knew this; in fact, Conrad had said he was ready now.

Robert nodded. 'It'll be a lengthy process, I'm afraid, but you'll get there, Harry.'

'So, you don't think I'll be well enough to have one last crack at the enemy?'

'Best not, old chap.' Being a doctor, Robert could be blunt as he sought to steer Harry away from thoughts about the RAF. 'Has anything been said about the injury to your face?'

Harry stared at him. 'What do you mean?'

'Have you heard about Archibald McIndoe?'

'Oh, the plastic surgeon fellow? Yes, but he only does burns victims, doesn't he? You know, pilots who've been trapped in their burning aircraft.'

Robert shrugged. 'I think he does anything to do with scarred tissue. It's worth enquiring, if you're interested.'

Harry was thoughtful for a few moments before

saying slowly, 'I think I'll concentrate on getting back on my feet first, but thank you for thinking of it.'

'Let me know if you change your mind. My door is always open, even if you only feel the need for a chat.'

'Shall we go riding tomorrow morning?' Pips suggested to Daisy and Mitch as they helped clear up after the party.

'That'd be nice,' Daisy said. 'I'll warn Jake.'

The following morning, a bright but breezy day, they set off through the fields and lanes.

'My goodness,' Daisy said as she looked about her. 'Granny and Jake have been busy. They've certainly been "digging for victory" in a big way.'

Pips laughed. 'It'll take you a long time to get it back to how it was after the war.'

'We'll probably leave a lot of it as it is now, though it'd be nice to have the croquet lawn and the flower gardens back to how they were.' Daisy chuckled. 'It was amazing to see just how many cabbages the area yielded last autumn. I think we must've kept the whole village in cabbages for weeks.'

'It really is a beautiful part of the world,' Mitch murmured. 'What d'you plan to do after the war, Pips? Shall you stay in London – or come home?'

Pips wrinkled her forehead. 'D'you know, Mitch, I really haven't thought much about it at all? We just seem so engrossed about winning the war that we can't see beyond doing just that. We're in a little world of our own down there.' She paused and then glanced at him as the three of them rode together at a gentle walking pace so that they could talk. 'D'you think they'll ever open Brooklands up again?'

Mitch shrugged. 'I honestly don't know. There's been a lot of damage done. It'll take major repairs to get the track fit for racing again.' He paused and then asked, 'And what about you, Daisy? What are you going to do after the war?'

'Marry Johnny,' she said promptly and they all laughed, but then Pips said quite seriously, 'But what about running the estate? I'm sure Granny's still counting on you to do that. She is getting on, you know.'

'I won't let her down. I promise you that.'

'So, how's it going to work? I mean, what will Johnny do?'

Daisy chuckled and tapped the side of her nose. 'We have plans, Aunty Pips, but they're top secret at the moment and when we're ready to share them, Granny must be the first to know.'

Pips nodded. 'Fair enough. I can respect that. Now, let's give these horses a good gallop before we have to go back for lunch. Come on, race you to the far side of the field and then I have to get back. I have to see a man about a leg and, Daisy, I want you to come with me. I just might need your support.'

Daisy laughed. 'I doubt it, but of course I'll come with you.'

'So, Harry, how are you?'

Pips and Daisy sat facing him as he sat near the fire that burned in the range winter and summer.

'Fed up that I can't fly any more and that I'm out of the war.'

'What makes you so sure? What about Douglas Bader, he . . . ?'

'Now don't you start. Everyone keeps mentioning Bader ever since this happened. One of my RAF chums actually calls me "half Bader" since I've only lost one leg.'

Pips stared at him. He was nothing like the ebullient Harry she remembered. Now he was morose, apathetic and sunk in self-pity. He must have been putting on a bit of a show at the party the previous day. She frowned, pondering how to deal with him. Shooting straight from the hip had always been her method. It had worked with Robert, but would it with Harry?

She took a deep breath and decided to risk it. 'Well, it's high time you got up off your backside and onto your one leg and got on with things. You can get about on crutches, can't you?'

Harry shrugged. 'What's there to get on with? I don't think the RAF are going to let me fly again. Certainly not flying bombers with six other chaps being my responsibility, and that's all I know.'

'If that's the case, then you should start to think about what you *are* going to do. I expect Mr Dawson would have you back. You probably wouldn't be able to shoe a horse, but there's plenty of other work you could do. Now, have you had any word about getting an artificial leg fitted?'

Harry was quiet for a few moments before admitting reluctantly, 'I got a letter a couple of weeks ago. They say I can go down to Roehampton to be assessed.'

'Right. I'll telephone them first thing tomorrow morning and see if it's all right for me to take you down on Wednesday. That's when we're going back. If it is, you're coming with me.'

He stared at her and then suddenly he grinned. 'Yes, *Aunty* Pips. Whatever you say, *Aunty* Pips.'

Pips sighed with relief, but all she said was, 'I'll let you know what they say.'

As Pips and Daisy walked back to the hall, Daisy said, 'Phew! That was a bit of a risk.'

'Wasn't it just? I must admit I was holding my breath.'

'But it did the trick.'

'Yes, I think it did.'

'D'you think he'll go back into the RAF if they'll have him?'

'One step at a time, Daisy. Literally!'

''Lo, Harry.'

'Good Lord, you're not here *again*, are you, Kitty?' But he was grinning as he said it. 'Haven't you got anything better to do than visit an ugly cripple?'

Kitty sat down in front of him and stared at him, taking in every detail of the damaged left-hand side of his face and the stump of his left leg propped up on a stool. She was a gentle soul and found it very difficult to be firm with him like she'd heard Miss Pips had been.

'If it hadn't been for her,' Peggy had whispered to the girl when she'd arrived, 'he'd still be sitting there moping and feeling sorry for himself. As it is, he's agreed to go with Miss Pips on Wednesday to see about his leg. I think that's how we've all got to try and treat him. I find it very hard, but me an' Sam were talking last night and have decided that's what we're going to do. We're going to be firm with him.'

Kitty had sighed. 'I'll try, Mrs Nuttall.'

Now, sitting in front of him and trying to think how to answer his blunt question, Kitty took a deep breath. 'No, I haven't at the moment, actually.'

For a brief moment, Harry glared at her and poor Kitty quivered inside. Had she pushed it too far? He wouldn't expect such a flippant answer from her of all people.

Then, suddenly, Harry burst out laughing. 'I asked for that, didn't I?'

She smiled. 'You did a bit.'

'It's just so boring sitting here all day.'

'So why are you? You can get about now.'

'Mebbe. But there's nowt I can do. I can't stand on one leg to shoe a horse, can I?'

'No, but you ought to be moving a bit more, ready for when you get your proper leg. You won't need crutches or even a walking stick then. You'll really be back on your feet.' Again, she took a deep breath before daring to tease him. 'And chasing after all the girls again, I expect.'

But this time Harry did not smile. 'What about this?' He touched his injured face. 'I'm hardly the good-looking lad I was before, now am I?'

Kitty stared at him. Very softly and completely serious she said, 'Harry Nuttall, if a girl truly loves you, that won't matter a jot. Not your face, not your leg – nothing. You're alive and you're still *you* . . .' She stood up now, her face flushed and her eyes sparkling with an anger that little Kitty Page rarely showed. 'You should be thankful for that because everyone who loves you has been thanking the good Lord every day that you've come back to us. A lot haven't and they've left loved ones who'll grieve the rest of their lives for them.'

She turned and ran from the room, tears running down her face, startling Peggy as she hurried past her in the scullery and out of the back door. Peggy dried her hands and went into the kitchen. 'Whatever have you been saying to Kitty? She rushed past me just now in tears.'

Harry blinked as if slightly mesmerized and stared at his mother. 'I think Kitty must be in love with me.'

Peggy cast her eyes to the ceiling and shook her head. 'Hallelujah! Has it really taken you all this time to realize that? I despair of you, Harry Nuttall. I really do.'

Fifty-Nine

When Pips called for Harry on the Wednesday morning, Peggy greeted her outside the cottage.

'Oh Miss Pips,' she said, clasping her hand. There were tears in Peggy's eyes, but they were tears of gratitude. 'We don't know how to thank you. We didn't know how to deal with him – how to reach him. We're all following your lead now and trying to be a bit firmer with him. It seems to be working.'

'Peggy, dear, I took a bit of a risk, I know, talking to him so bluntly, but sometimes you have to be cruel to be kind, as they say. I'm just thankful it worked. Now, we'd better be off. Is he ready?'

'Yes, I've packed his suitcase. When Betty brought the message from you yesterday that he could go, she said he might have to stay a while.'

Pips nodded. 'Yes, they haven't said how long. I expect at this stage they perhaps don't know themselves.'

'As long as he gets his leg and gets back on his feet, I don't care how long it takes.'

It took two weeks for his leg to fitted and adjusted to be comfortable and for Harry to prove to them that he could do everything they required him to do before they let him come home, complete with new leg.

'Oh Harry, you look normal,' Peggy exclaimed, as he walked into the cottage wearing proper shoes and socks and his half-empty trouser leg no longer flapping.

Then swiftly, she added, 'I'm sorry, that sounds awful.'

Harry chuckled. 'It's the best thing you could have said, Mam.'

By nightfall, the whole village, including everyone at the hall, knew Harry was home, complete with artificial leg.

'He's got a bit of a limp,' Bess told everyone proudly, 'but you wouldn't guess he'd got a false leg if you didn't know.' But all Len Dawson said when he saw him was, 'When are you coming back to work now all this stupidity is over? I could use an experienced pair of hands.'

'I haven't been officially demobbed yet. I've to report back next week and see what they say.'

Len grunted. 'Well, don't do anything damned silly like wanting to stay on in the RAF.'

By the third evening he was back home, Harry said, 'Where's Kitty? She hasn't been to see me since I got back.'

Peggy avoided his gaze. 'Oh – um – I expect she's busy. There's always a lot to do on the farm.'

Harry frowned. 'But she's not working in the evenings, surely. Why hasn't she called in?'

'I really couldn't say,' Peggy said off-handedly.

'Then I'd better go and find out.'

He walked the short distance between where he lived and the Pages' cottage, smiling and waving to anyone who saw him. Kitty opened the door and gasped to see him standing there on two feet and so smart in his RAF uniform. Her gaze swept him up and down.

'Oh Harry, you look wonderful.'

'So, why haven't you been to see me?'

'I – I didn't know you'd come back.'

'Yes, you did, Kitty. Everybody knows. And are you going to keep me standing on the doorstep? It's still a bit painful to stand in one place for long.'

'Sorry – yes – come in.'

He walked through their scullery and into the kitchen where her mother and father were sitting at the table finishing their evening meal.

'Harry,' Ted Page stood up and held out his hand, 'it's good to see you. Sit down. Mother – a cup of tea for the lad.'

Lottie Page bustled about the kitchen and after a few moments set a cup of tea and a buttered scone in front of him.

'Thank you, Mrs Page,' he said, but then he turned to Kitty and asked again, 'So, why haven't you been to see me?'

Kitty blushed and glanced down at her fingers twisting in her lap. 'I – I thought – after I saw you last time and – and then once you were better, all the girls . . .' She gulped and fell silent.

'There's still this.' He touched the scar that still cut deeply into the side of his face, running jaggedly from temple to chin.

'But you can have an operation to make that a lot better, can't you? Your mother told me.'

'Maybe I don't want to,' Harry laughed. 'It's my badge of honour. And it gives me a rather raffish look, don't you think?' He paused and then asked softly, 'Does it make a difference to you, Kitty?'

'You know it doesn't.'

'Perhaps we'd better leave these youngsters to it, Mother,' Ted said, making as if to get up.

'No need, Mr Page. What I have to say to Kitty can be said in front of you both.' He grinned suddenly. 'In fact, perhaps it *ought* to be.' He turned back to Kitty. 'Before the war, I was a bit of a flirt, I know that – just having a bit of fun, I suppose. And then the war came and I became a bomber pilot. I could have been killed at any time – an awful lot of my mates were – and it didn't seem fair to get serious about anyone then, but now that I've survived – well, almost . . .' He took her hand and gently put his fingers under her chin to make her look at him. 'I'm ready to settle down. I'm ready to get married and have a family right here in Doddington and there's no one else I'd rather do that with than you. So – forgive me if I don't get down on one knee – but Kitty Page, will you marry me?'

Kitty blushed furiously and glanced at her mother and father, who both burst out laughing. 'Go on, lass. For goodness' sake tell him "yes" afore he changes his mind. It's what you've allus wanted when all's said and done.'

'So, there's going to be another wedding,' Bess told anyone who was willing to listen. She counted them off on her fingers. 'There's Daisy and Johnny's already being planned for when the war's over, then there'll be Luke and Gill, and now' – she waited a moment, keeping her listeners in suspense before saying dramatically – 'Harry and little Kitty have got engaged.'

'And about time too,' was the consensus in the village. 'He's kept that poor lass waiting long enough.'

It was arranged that as soon as he was released from the RAF, Harry would take up his work with Len Dawson again.

'I don't think I'll be able to shoe horses, Mr Dawson, but I reckon I could tackle most other things.'

'Aye, well, we can work round that,' Len said and almost smiled. 'The young evacuee lad, Bernard, he's shaping up nicely and working here full time now he's left school, though I expect he'll be back off home soon. I'm surprised he hasn't gone already, and I can't see Luke coming back here. He'll want to become a farmer in Yorkshire, I reckon.'

'He's saying nothing at the moment,' Harry told Len. 'Even we don't know what his plans are.'

'More fool him,' was all Len would say.

Sixty

'Right, let's get cracking then,' Daisy said as she and Gill walked towards their Spitfires. 'Deliveries first to White Waltham, then to Lee and finally back to Hamble. I've got to do that twice today. What about you?'

'I'm off up north, but I should be back by tonight.'

They parted with the usual hug they gave each other when they were setting out on deliveries and climbed into their cockpits.

The day went well for Daisy and by late afternoon she was on her way back to Hamble for the second time that day. As she flew over airfields near the south coast, she noticed lines of aircraft with unusual markings – ones she hadn't seen before. There were hundreds of aeroplanes all with black-and-white stripes painted on their wings. As she flew on, she noticed a huge build-up of all sorts of ground forces and armoured craft. Her curiosity heightened, she would have liked to have flown directly over the coast, but, for once, even Daisy did not dare to break the rules. Something big was about to happen and she didn't want to cause trouble by venturing where she shouldn't.

When she landed, the other girls were chattering excitedly about what they too had seen.

'It's the invasion. I bet it's the invasion,' Violet said.

Gill, who had been flying in the opposite direction, had seen nothing. 'Oh, I wish we could take a peek,' she said. 'Anyone up for it?'

'Best not,' Daisy said.

'What? You not taking a dare, Daisy Maitland? I don't believe it.'

Daisy shook her head. 'Not this time. If what Vi says is true, then it's far too important for us to get in the way. Besides,' she added with an impish smile, 'they might think we're spies and shoot us down.'

'I bet you're right, though,' Gill said. 'I had noticed that we're getting a lot more aircraft around here now.'

'They've recruited several more women for the ATA,' Daisy said. 'Half a dozen or so arrived last week.'

Gill sniffed her displeasure. 'And they're going to train them from scratch. *They* haven't had to do the flying hours we had to before they'd even look at us.'

'Southampton is chock-a-block with armoured vehicles of all shapes and sizes,' Violet said. 'And there are all sorts of ships in the Solent.'

'And they're building some sort of jetty.'

During the first days of June, the activity around Hamble increased. The CO received top secret documents marked *Invasion Orders*.

Gill rubbed her hands with glee. 'It must be on.'

'I'm sure it is,' Daisy said. 'Violet said there are hundreds of soldiers camping out in the woods and more motor vehicles are arriving by the minute.'

'And bridge sections are being towed behind ships as if they're going to construct some sort of harbour.'

'Perhaps they are. And have you heard, bombers have been seen towing gliders?'

'Come on, Daisy. We've each got deliveries to Biggin Hill . . .'

'I hope I've got a Spitfire.'

'Of course you have,' Gill teased. 'I don't think our operations manager would dare give you anything else now.'

When they landed back at Hamble, Daisy told everyone, 'The roads around here are jammed with trucks and tanks. No one can get in or out and there's a massive gathering of aircraft, all with those black-and-white stripes I told you about.'

Although the weather wasn't at its best, the invasion armada set off on the night of 5 June. The ATA girls listened to the noise filling the air that went on and on, until, at last, it faded into the distance and all was quiet.

'So, they've gone,' Daisy whispered in a reverent whisper and sent up a silent prayer.

'We're closed down tomorrow. Did you know?' Gill said.

'I suppose there's no more aircraft to take anywhere for a few days.'

'No, it's because we're likely to become a repair unit for damaged aircraft.'

'Makes sense. Oh, but I do wish we knew what was happening over there.'

*

The D-Day landings were successful; the Allies were back in Europe, though at the cost of many lives. The ATA girls were busier than ever, with several different types of aircraft to ferry. Then came a new threat. Hitler's 'secret weapon' was unleashed on London; the evil doodlebugs, pilotless jets launched in France, began to terrorize Londoners. Now the RAF fighter pilots had a different mission: to chase the bombers and steer them off course by tipping their wings.

'I hope Uncle Mitch and Aunty Milly, and Uncle Paul too, of course, will be all right,' Daisy fretted. She did not even dare to voice her concerns about Johnny and Luke.

It would seem like tempting fate.

There was a feeling of optimism in the air; there had been since D-Day. Steadily, the Allies gained ground, driving the enemy out of Normandy. By August, they had regained Paris and General de Gaulle led a triumphant walk the length of the Champs-Élysées. The Germans were in retreat, but now the full extent of the horrors they had inflicted upon their captives were being revealed to a shocked world. Rumours had existed, but now there was proof of the atrocities that had been committed. Yet still, there was resistance; the war was not quite over yet. Nevertheless, Christmas 1944 was a merry one in Doddington.

Not everyone could get home, but Pips and Daisy managed it. Gill went home to her family, but Luke and Johnny could not get leave.

'You have to give way to the chaps who have young families,' Luke told a disappointed Gill. Then he kissed her, murmuring against her lips, 'It'll all soon be over, darling.'

Henrietta invited Mitch, Milly and Paul to spend Christmas at the hall and they were there too to join in the usual Boxing Day party.

Edwin made a short speech and raised a glass to everyone present. 'You've all been so wonderful through these difficult times in helping each other when needed, we want to say "thank you", and that includes our friends from London. Milly, I don't know what we'd have done without you and Paul and Mitch too.'

Milly blushed and Paul and Mitch winked at each other, thinking how shrewd and perceptive the Maitland family were.

'And we'd all like to thank you, Mrs Maitland,' Bess piped up, always the one to take the lead amongst the villagers. 'You and all your family have kept the whole village going through some hard times. God bless you.'

'I couldn't have done it without the support of you all,' Henrietta said, smiling.

'Here's to 1945,' Robert said. 'Let's hope it brings the end of the war.'

Sixty-One

'Robert! Mother! Father!' Alice ran through the house shouting at the top of her voice. 'It's over. The war's over. Churchill's just been on the wireless . . .'

She burst into the parlour where Henrietta was sitting mending socks. Henrietta looked up quickly, her needle suspended in mid-air. 'Really? Is it really over?'

Alice nodded, her face pink with excitement. 'Oh Mother, they'll all be coming home. They'll all be safe now.' She clasped her hands in front of her chest, unable to believe that the war had ended and that her family were safe, if not quite sound. Poor Harry, whom she regarded as a member of the family, would live with the after-effects for ever, just as her darling Robert had done all these years.

She whirled around. 'I must find Robert. He might not have heard.'

She hurried through the house to where the surgeries of both Robert and Conrad were situated. In the small waiting room, there were three patients waiting their turn to see one of the doctors.

'Have you heard?' Alice beamed at them. 'It's over. The war's finally over.'

They glanced at one another and then looked back at Alice. 'A' you sure, Miss Alice?'

Alice nodded, unable to contain her excitement.

At that moment, the door to Robert's consulting room opened.

'Robert – the war's over. Have you heard?'

But Robert was not smiling; he didn't seem to be listening to her. Instead he crossed the room and took her arm gently. He turned briefly towards the waiting patients. 'Please excuse me for a moment. An urgent family matter. Dr Conrad will see all of you.'

'Oh, but Dr Maitland—' one of the women patients began, but Robert ignored her and steered Alice out of the room. As he closed the door, Alice said, 'What is it? Has something happened?'

'I've just had a telephone call from Daisy's CO. She didn't return last night from collecting an aircraft due for maintenance.'

'Oh no,' Alice breathed. All the exhilaration at the news that the war was over drained out of her in an instant. 'What – what are they doing?'

'Looking for her, but – it may take some time.'

Alice gripped his shoulder. 'Robert – we must tell Luke and Johnny. Maybe they can do something.'

'I understand Gill is dealing with that.'

'Oh – yes. She'll know how to get hold of them, won't she?'

'Luke? Luke? Is that you? The line's awfully bad. Can you hear me?'

'Yes, darling, I can,' Luke shouted down the telephone. 'Have you heard? It's all over. We can all go home and you and I can get married. Say you'll marry me, Gill.'

494

'Yes – yes, of course, but listen a minute—'

'Well, that's not quite the response I was hoping for,' he laughed, 'but go on.'

'Daisy's missing. She didn't come back last night from Scotland and we've had no word from her.'

Immediately, Luke's elation died. 'Oh God, not now.'

'Can you do anything? I've been given permission to take the Anson and fly the route she was supposed to take. I'm taking a couple of the girls with me as lookouts, but I just wondered . . .'

'Yes, of course. I'll see the CO straightaway.'

'And Luke – tell Johnny. He might be able to help too.'

'Right. Yes. Tell me her route.'

Gill gave him the details and when he replaced the receiver he jotted them down quickly so that he could relay them to Johnny. He was sure Johnny would help – with or without permission. This was worth risking a court martial for.

But no one demurred; both their superior officers were only too keen to help and soon both Luke and Johnny were taking off from their respective airfields in their Spitfires and rendezvousing by communicating over their radios. They could not get in touch with Gill, but they knew the route. They flew at a safe distance side by side and spoke to each other about how they should search.

'We'll fly as we are now as far as Prestwick. That's where she was coming from. If we see nothing, we'll come back on the same route but fly further apart,'

Luke suggested. 'But we'll need to land to refuel somewhere.'

In the distance they saw the Anson, flying steadily in the same direction, but it was Johnny who spotted the crashed aircraft in a field just north of Carlisle. They flew lower and circled it.

'There are people around it.'

'I can't see anyone still in the aircraft, can you?'

'No, and they don't look as if they're making any attempt to get anyone out.'

'She's either been moved already or she bailed out.'

'Would she have had a parachute?'

'I honestly don't know,' Luke said worriedly.

'Shall we land and talk to the folks down there?'

'Where's Gill?'

'Gone on ahead. I don't think they spotted this. She's flying a bit further over to the left.'

'I'll go down and let you know.'

Luke turned his aircraft to make an approach on the far side of the field away from the crowd who were milling around the aircraft. As he landed on the bumpy grass field and came to a halt, several people came running towards him.

He opened his canopy but did not, at the moment, stop his engine or climb out.

One of the young men clambered onto the wing to speak to him above the noise of the engine.

'Any sign of the pilot?' Luke shouted.

The young man shook his head. 'We're searching . . .' He waved his hands towards the surrounding fields and the wooded side of a mountain to the north. 'It crashed last night and we came straight out to it, but there was no sign of the pilot. He must have bailed out.'

Despite the seriousness of the situation, Luke couldn't suppress a smile. 'Actually, we think the pilot was a young woman.'

The young man gaped. 'Flying a Spitfire?'

'Yes. She's a member of the ATA. They've ferried aircraft around the country throughout most of the war.'

'Blimey!' He held out his hand over the side of Luke's cockpit. 'Name's Dan, by the way. If we should find her, I'll put a white cross on this field with sheets or something.'

Luke shook his hand. 'Thanks, Dan. We'll take a look from the air.' He gestured skywards towards Johnny, who was still circling the field. 'If we see anything, Johnny will circle it and I'll come back here. By the way, where's the nearest airfield? We might need to refuel.'

Luke took off again and once airborne, spoke to Johnny, relating what he'd found out.

They circled the field in ever-widening circles until Johnny said, 'I think we should take a look up that mountainside, Luke. She was coming from the north, wasn't she?'

'Good idea. Let's go.'

'But, Robert, where can she be? Wouldn't she land somewhere for the night when it started to get dark? They're not supposed to fly at night, are they?'

'Alice, darling, you know Daisy. She can be a bit of a rule breaker. With all her experience, she probably thinks she can get away with night flying now.'

Alice shuddered. 'But what's happening? What are they doing?'

'They'll be looking for her. Don't worry.'

'Of course I'm worrying.' Alice had tears in her eyes. 'We've had years of worrying about them all and for this to happen now – just when the war's ended – is just so cruel.'

Robert put his arm round her and pulled her close. 'Come on, love, hold up. Don't give in now. We must go and find Mother and Father. We need to tell them.'

Betty was the one who took the news to her sister and subsequently to the rest of the village. 'You can't believe it happening now, of all days, can you? Poor Miss Alice is in pieces.'

'I don't wonder. I know just how she feels,' Peggy said. 'When Luke was missing, it was hell on earth waiting for news. How I wish we knew what was happening. It's the not knowing that's almost the worst thing to bear.'

'I'll just go and tell our mam. She'll spread the word.'

As soon as she heard, Bess hurried to Norah's cottage. 'Daisy's missing. You couldn't make it up, could you? We get to the end of the war with all of 'em all right – well, more or less,' she added, thinking of Harry. 'And then this happens. Our Betty's just been down to tell me so I could come and tell you, Norah, duck. They're all in a right tizzy at the hall, I can tell you.'

Norah sat down suddenly, as if her legs gave way

beneath her. 'Oh, what will Len say? Our only grand-daughter.'

'I'll go and tell him, duck.'

'I know exactly what he'll say,' Norah said flatly. 'She had no need to go. She should have stayed here and helped Mrs Maitland. They all should.'

Norah was right; that was exactly what Len said when Bess told him.

Sixty-Two

They scoured the side of the mountain until Johnny suddenly shouted excitedly. 'There, look. Isn't that a parachute draped over the top of the trees?'

They flew down lower and circled the spot where white silk, entangled with the branches of a tree, was flapping in the breeze.

'Johnny, stay here circling it. I'll go back and tell the searchers on the ground.'

'Tell them to hurry. If she's been down there all night, she could be suffering from hypothermia if nothing else.'

Luke flew back to the field, landed quickly and told the men in the field what they had found. He pointed up the mountain. 'The parachute is about half a mile up on this side.'

'We'll organize the search party to go up there,' Dan said. 'Could you see anyone?'

Luke shook his head.

'I'm guessing she might be injured, otherwise she would have walked down.' At once Dan took charge and began issuing orders.

One of the other men now spoke to Luke. 'I'm Terry. Dan heads up the local rescue team. He'll soon have us organized now we know where to look.' He turned to a woman standing beside him. 'Meg, love, will you notify the police and then the ambulance service so they're on standby? I reckon we're going to have a casualty.'

The rescue party, now properly organized and carrying all the equipment they might need, were soon climbing the mountainside to where the parachute still hung in the trees. Luke had radioed Johnny and told him he was staying on the ground and going with the rescue team.

'Keep circling for as long as you can. It's a really good guide.'

Every so often the team stopped to shout her name, then kept silent whilst they listened for a response. Then they set off again.

The fourth time they did this, Luke was sure he heard a faint call. 'Listen,' he said urgently. Everyone stood still, straining their ears.

'There! Did you hear it?'

But no one else could hear what Luke was sure he'd heard.

'Come on,' he said, with added urgency. 'Johnny's still circling a bit higher up. Let's go.'

Now it was Luke urging the rescuers on rather than Dan, but no one complained. Again, they stopped to call out and to listen. This time Luke heard it clearly and now Dan nodded. 'Yes, I heard that. I think we need to be over to the left a little.'

Practised in rescues in this part of the country, Dan was better at gauging which direction the sound was coming from. Now, each time they stopped to shout and then to listen, her voice was nearer until at last they could all hear it plainly, 'I'm here.'

'I can see the parachute,' Terry said. 'She must be underneath it.' Luke almost ran up the last few yards to where Daisy was lying propped against the tree from which the parachute still dangled. He dropped to his knees beside her. 'Daisy, oh Daisy.'

Swiftly, the team went into their practised routine; wrapping her in blankets and checking what injuries she had whilst Daisy leaned against Luke. 'I'm so cold,' she murmured. 'And I think I've broken my ankle. That's why I couldn't walk down.'

'You're safe now. We'll get you down and an ambulance will take you to the nearest hospital straightaway.'

'Where's the Spit? It didn't land on houses, did it?'

'No, it's in a field just below here.'

'Oh Luke, I've lost a Spitfire. I'll never forgive myself.'

Luke held her close. 'It doesn't matter, Dais. Not now. It was unserviceable anyway and besides, the war's over. It ended this morning.'

'Really?' Her voice was growing weaker. She leaned against him and closed her eyes. 'I'm so tired, Luke. So very – tired . . .'

'Alice! *Alice!*' Robert's urgent tone echoed through the house so that not only Alice came hurrying to him, but also Henrietta and Edwin.

'She's safe. She's in hospital with a broken ankle and suffering from hypothermia, but she's safe and will be fine.'

'Oh thank God.' Tears of relief ran down Alice's face as she buried her face against Robert's chest.

Even Henrietta, who hardly ever cried, surreptitiously wiped tears from her eyes. 'How did they find her?'

Robert, now relieved of the heart-wrenching anxiety, chuckled. 'Luke and Johnny each took a Spitfire and followed the route she was supposed to take. I believe Gill went out in the Anson too, but she went on ahead and must have missed seeing her. I expect she'll eventually catch up with the news that Daisy's been found.'

Robert repeated the story of how they'd actually found her that Luke had told him over the telephone.

'Enterprising young men,' Edwin murmured. 'Thank goodness it worked. I hope they won't be in trouble.'

'I think they both had permission from their superior officers. Mind you, if the war hadn't just ended, it might have been trickier, but knowing those two, they'd have gone anyway.'

'They both love her dearly – in different ways, of course, but – well, you know what I mean.'

'We do, Father. Now, I'm in need of a drink – and I don't mean coffee, Mother.'

Luke and Johnny flew their aircraft to the nearest airfield and then hitched a lift to the hospital where Daisy was being cared for. They'd telephoned their bases and asked for the news to be relayed to Gill as soon as possible. When they walked into the ward, it was to find Daisy sitting up in bed drinking tea and looking none the worse for her night on the mountainside. The only legacy of her adventure was the mound of a cage beneath the bedclothes where her ankle had been put in plaster.

Johnny rushed to her bedside and kissed her. Luke grinned at her and then said, 'I'd better leave you two lovebirds alone.'

'No – don't go, Luke. I want to thank you both for coming to look for me. I don't think I could have lasted another night out there. I couldn't even wrap myself in the parachute. I couldn't disentangle it.'

'Perhaps it was a good job you didn't because that's how we found you,' Johnny said. 'And now, tell me, just how long are you going to be laid up?'

Daisy grimaced. 'I can go home in a few days, but the plaster won't come off for six weeks.'

'Perfect.' Johnny grinned. 'I'll take you home and you and your mother will have plenty of time to organize a wedding. How does September sound?'

Daisy gaped at him and Luke laughed.

'Well, if that isn't the most unromantic proposal I ever heard.' She laughed and the happy sound echoed around the long room. 'But yes, September sounds perfect.'

Johnny turned to Luke. 'And will you be my Best Man?'

Luke grinned. 'I'd be honoured, old chap. I'd ask you to be mine, but I really must ask my brother. Hope you understand.'

'Good Lord, yes. I wouldn't expect anything else.'

As Johnny bent his head to kiss Daisy again, Luke added, 'And now I really will go . . .'

Sixty-Three

'Gill, I don't suppose you want to have a double wedding, do you?' Daisy had been home at the hall for two weeks and plans for her wedding to Johnny in September were gathering speed. Gill was staying for a long weekend on her way home for a week's leave. 'I know we're still at war with Japan, but the feeling seems to be that it won't last much longer.'

Gill shook her head. 'It's sweet of you to ask, Daisy, but I must get married at home. Luke understands.'

'Of course. Have you fixed a date?'

'Not exactly. There are a few things to sort out first – especially with his grandfather. We still don't know if the old man meant what he said when Luke joined up against his wishes.'

Daisy sighed. 'No, I can't guess either. All I know is that he is very good at harbouring a grudge for years.' She paused and then said, 'But you'll need to go home, won't you? You're the only one to take over your family's farm.'

Gill nodded. 'Yes, there's a lot of thinking to be done and talking to my folks – and Luke's.' She stood up. 'But now I'm going to walk down the lane and see that reprobate Harry Nuttall.'

'Give him my love and ask him to come and see me.'

As Gill left, Daisy was thoughtful. She was sitting in the parlour, on her own for the moment, gazing out of the window, but her conversation with Gill had left her pondering. Slowly, she reached for the writing pad and pen on a small table beside her. She had been writing to a few of her ATA colleagues to hear the latest news and what they all planned to do now that the ATA would be disbanding before long. Rumour had it that it would be about November. But now, she chewed the end of her pen, a little uncertain as to how to word a very important letter. And then she began to write.

After several attempts she finished her missive, put it in an envelope and sealed it. Unable to get to a post office herself, she would have to entrust it to someone. But who? Of course, she thought – Gill! She would keep Daisy's secret.

As Daisy hobbled into the Great Hall for dinner with the family that evening, Henrietta had an announcement to make. 'Philippa is coming home tomorrow morning. Just for the weekend.'

'She should be finishing soon, shouldn't she?' Robert said, as he held the chair out for Daisy to sit down at the table.

Henrietta laughed. 'Well, if I knew exactly what she was doing, then perhaps I'd be able to tell you. But as I don't, I can't.'

They all laughed and sat down as Wainwright began to serve the meal. Inevitably, the conversation turned to wedding plans.

'Your dress is coming along quite nicely,' Alice said, 'but just as when I made Pips's dress, no one else is to see it until the day. What about your bridesmaid's dress, Gill?'

'I'm very happy for you to make it, Mrs Maitland, if you've time. I'm going to pick two or three patterns for your approval whilst I'm at home this week. If I find anything I like, I'll post them to you.'

'What about fabric?'

'I'll leave that to you.' Gill pulled a face. 'It all depends what's available and what we can get on our coupons.'

'Several of the villagers have already offered clothes coupons for Daisy and you. Mrs Cooper, Mrs Dawson and Peggy, as you might expect, but there have been others too.'

'Everyone's so kind,' Daisy murmured.

'It's something wonderful for them to look forward to, Daisy,' Henrietta said and chuckled as she added, 'But of course, the whole village will expect to attend the wedding.'

'Oh Granny, we can't fit everyone in here,' Daisy said, waving her hand to encompass the huge room where they were sitting. 'I know it's big, but not *that* big.'

'We could have a marquee on the front lawn. The croquet lawn would have been more suitable but since that's been ploughed up to grow cabbages . . .' She sighed, wistful for the loss of her lovely lawn.

'Don't worry, Granny, we'll soon have it back to how it was,' Daisy said.

Henrietta glanced at her. Daisy still hadn't told

any of them what she intended to do after her marriage, or, indeed, what Johnny was going to do after he was eventually demobbed from the RAF, though that might not be for some time yet. Neither he nor Luke had any idea when they might be able to leave.

'We didn't plough up the front lawns because we let the horses graze there, though the grass is a bit of a mess now.'

'Jake will sort that out and we won't need it to look pristine if we're going to site a marquee there,' Daisy said reasonably.

'What are you going to do after you're married?' Robert asked bluntly.

'In the short term, we'll both be going back to what we do now. There are rumours that the ATA will be disbanded towards the end of the year, but we've no idea when Johnny – or Luke, for that matter – might be demobbed. I think it might take some time.'

'But what about after that?'

Daisy grinned at him and tapped the side of her nose. 'All top secret, Daddy. We're still talking about things. All I can say is that you've no need to worry and I think you'll all be happy with what we decide.'

'There's always a home here for you both,' Henrietta said, 'but I think you already know that, don't you, Daisy?'

'I do, Granny, but thank you.'

'But if you do come to live here to help your granny run the estate,' Robert persisted, 'what's Johnny going to do?'

Daisy chuckled. 'That's what we're discussing, but don't try to wheedle it out of me, Daddy, because you're not going to.'

The family all laughed and then settled down to enjoy their meal together.

All the evacuee children who had come to Doddington had returned home except for three: Bernard, who was still living with Peggy and Sam, and now Harry too, and the twin girls staying with Conrad and Florence Everton.

Florence was tearful most of the time, though she tried to hide it in front of the girls. Every day took her closer to the day she dreaded; when she must say goodbye to the children who had become her life. She couldn't have loved them more than she did if she had given birth to them.

But the days passed and no word came about the twins.

'I suppose,' Conrad said reluctantly, 'we ought to make some enquiries. We can't just leave things hanging.'

'Can't we?' For a moment, there was hope in Florence's tone and then it died. 'No, you're right,' she said reasonably. 'It's not fair on their family.'

'I'll have a word with Mrs Maitland since she was in charge of the billeting.'

Only a week later, Henrietta received a letter from the authorities in London. In the late afternoon, when she knew Conrad would have finished his house calls for the day, she asked Jake to drive her to their cottage. 'It's just that bit too far to walk when it's raining. I don't think I'll keep you waiting too long.'

'It's no problem.'

'I'm conscious of the fact that you have been out with Robert on his rounds all afternoon and you still have the horses to tend, but this is important for Florence and Conrad – indeed for all of them.'

Answering her knock, Florence led her into the small front parlour. She could hear the girls laughing and shouting in the bedroom upstairs.

'Conrad's playing with them. A noisy game of Snap, I think. I'll just call him down.'

Moments later, holding the letter in her hand, Henrietta said, 'The authorities in charge of the placement of evacuee children have written to me enclosing a letter from the girls' maternal grandmother, a Mrs Wright . . .'

Florence bit her lip and clutched Conrad's hand.

'It seems,' Henrietta went on, 'that their father was reported missing, presumed killed, during the D-Day landings and now, it appears no trace can be found of their mother either. Mrs Wright says that the last of the V2 rockets fell where her daughter was living at the time and it has had to be concluded that she died in the attack, even though no trace of her has ever been found.'

'Oh poor little mites,' Florence whispered. 'They're orphans.' She turned towards her husband with wide eyes. 'Oh Conrad, could we . . . ?'

Conrad touched his wife's arm. 'Let Mrs Maitland finish, darling.'

'Mrs Wright says,' Henrietta said, referring to the

letter again, 'that she lives on her own and is too frail to care for two lively youngsters. There is an aunt – their mother's sister – but she has four children of her own, has been widowed by the war and feels she cannot undertake to care for any more children. The family have all agreed that the twins should be adopted, rather than be sent to an orphanage, though they do ask that the adoptive parents should take the children to see them once in a while. They don't want to lose touch entirely.' Henrietta looked up. 'Do you want to apply to adopt them?'

'Yes!' Florence and Conrad almost shouted the word simultaneously without even deferring to the other. Then they glanced at one another and burst out laughing.

Henrietta chuckled and handed the letter to Conrad. 'Well, that seems perfectly clear. You'd better take this and contact the person who's sent Mrs Wright's letter on and see how you should proceed.'

Tears flooded down Florence's face, but now they were tears of joy. 'Thank you, Mrs Maitland, thank you so much. You don't know what this means to us.'

Henrietta stood up to leave. 'Oh, I think I do, my dear. I think I do.'

Daisy was now well enough to return to Hamble and planned to see her superior officer about leaving the ATA.

'I'll see her as well,' Gill said over the telephone. 'I can't wait to get back and help my dad. I expect it's the same for you, isn't it? I think they'll release us, don't you?'

Each day during her time at home, Daisy had watched out for the postman. The family surmised she was waiting for letters from Johnny, but they were wrong. She was anxious to receive a reply to the letter she had written some weeks earlier when she'd first arrived home; a letter she didn't want any of her family to see.

Two days before her departure, it came. She slipped it into her pocket and then gave the rest of the mail to Wainwright. There were always quite a lot of letters received at the hall for various members of the family.

When she read the letter in the privacy of her bedroom, she smiled. It was the answer she'd hoped for.

Sixty-Four

The CO at Hamble was very understanding towards both girls' requests, when they asked to see her together. 'Officially, the ATA isn't disbanding until November,' she told them, 'but I see no reason to keep the two of you any longer. You both have such good reasons for wanting to get home.' She smiled at Daisy. 'And you have such an exciting event to plan, so I will put the necessary paperwork through as quickly as possible and you should both be able to leave by the end of August at the latest. This ferry pool will probably close in August anyway.'

As it turned out, they were on their way home in the middle of August on the very day that Japan finally surrendered.

'It's over. It's really over,' Daisy said as the clattering train carried them home.

'We're back for good,' she announced as she and Gill arrived at the hall. Gill was to stay for a few days so that Alice could fit her bridesmaid's dress and then travel home to Yorkshire. 'And Johnny and Luke are coming for the weekend, so we'll all be together.'

'My dears,' Henrietta greeted them. 'You are all most welcome. We'll have a party on Sunday to celebrate' – she laughed – 'well, everything.'

'You really shouldn't do so much, Granny. There's my wedding coming in just over a month . . .'

'Of course I should. Besides, it's really our wonderful staff who do all the work and it'll only be a small get-together – like our Boxing Day gatherings. Just us, the Dawsons, Coopers and the Nuttalls. Oh, and Philippa will be home too, so it will be just perfect.'

'Is she coming home for good?'

'My dear Daisy, I have no idea *what* your aunt plans to do either now or in the future.'

'Is Uncle Mitch coming too?'

Henrietta blinked. 'I really have no idea. Philippa hasn't said.'

'He'll be coming to the wedding, of course. He's the only relative that Johnny will have there.'

Henrietta chuckled. 'He's a rapscallion, but I'm really quite fond of Mitch Hammond, though don't tell him I said so.'

The weekend was a glorious celebration for them all. The weather was perfect and their guests spilled out onto the front lawn.

'Jake has been working so hard to remove the traces the horses left behind. They've gone back to grazing in the pastures now. Daisy, we must sit down together tomorrow and start planning the future of the estate. Once the wedding and your honeymoon are over, I want you to take over more responsibility.'

'I'm looking forward to it, Granny.'

'Where are you going to live?' Bess, overhearing the conversation, asked. 'Here, at the hall?'

'They'd be welcome too, but I don't believe young married couples should live with in-laws, even though there's plenty of room. There's a nice house on the far side of the village I want Daisy and Johnny to take a look at. If they like it, we can have it refurbished for them.'

'You're very lucky, Daisy. Not all young couples get such a good start. I expect Harry and Kitty will have to live with Peggy and Sam for a while. Or with the Pages.'

'Actually, Bess . . .' For once, Henrietta couldn't hide her smile. 'They don't need to. There's a cottage two doors away from you becoming vacant in a few weeks' time. They're welcome to have that, if they'd like it.'

Bess's eyes widened and her mouth formed a round 'o'.

'Goodness me, Bess,' Henrietta said impishly. 'Don't tell me that bit of news had escaped your notice.'

Bess roared loudly with laughter. 'It had, Mrs Maitland. I must be losing me touch.' Then she sobered. 'You know, you're so good to the folks in this village. I don't know what we'd do without you.'

'You'll have to one day, Bess. We're all only human, but I have every confidence that Daisy will carry on the tradition. She will care for the estate and everyone on it, just as I have done.'

They both turned towards Daisy, who, as if making a solemn promise, said, 'Of course I will.'

Two days before the wedding, one of the guests arrived at the hall earlier than expected.

'I'm sorry to arrive unannounced, Mrs Maitland.'

'You're always welcome, Mitch. There's nothing wrong, is there?'

Mitch grinned. 'I hope not, but I am hoping you will help me in springing a little surprise on Pips on Daisy's wedding day, and I really should ask for Daisy's blessing too, seeing as it is *her* day.'

Henrietta and Daisy were delighted to join in the intrigue. 'You can hide it in the stables,' Henrietta said. 'Jake will make room for it.'

'What a wonderful surprise, Mitch,' Daisy said. 'She'll be thrilled.'

'I'm bringing her up in my car the night before the wedding, so I don't think she'll go riding the next morning and see it by accident, do you?'

Daisy chuckled. 'I'll make sure she's kept busy helping me all morning so that she doesn't have time.'

Sixty-Five

The day before the wedding was a flurry of activity. Gill, as Daisy's only bridesmaid, arrived to stay at the hall whilst Johnny was to stay overnight with Peggy, Sam, Luke and Harry.

'We don't want you running into the bride on the landing on the morning of the wedding,' Henrietta told him.

Pips and Mitch arrived in Mitch's car with their suitcases piled on the back seat.

Just after dinner, as they all retired to the parlour, Daisy drew Henrietta to one side. 'Granny, can I have a word?'

'Of course, Daisy, what is it?'

'I know you've worked very hard on the seating plan in the marquee, but could you squeeze in four more without too much trouble?'

'I expect so, my dear. Who are they?'

'Top secret, Granny. Please don't ask, because I'm not telling anyone. Even my husband-to-be doesn't know. Just – trust me, will you?'

'Of course, but—'

Daisy kissed her cheek. 'You're a darling . . .' And then she hurried away.

With a smile and a fond shake of her head,

517

Henrietta went to tell Cook that there would be four more guests the next day.

'That'll not be a problem, Mrs Maitland,' said a beaming cook, who was in her element. 'There's enough food to feed the whole village and half of Skellingthorpe as well. Everyone's been very generous with their coupons.'

Excitement reached fever pitch at the hall on the morning of the wedding. The only calm person amongst them all appeared to be the bride. Even the normally placid Alice was in a fluster just in case one of the dresses she had made so lovingly over the past few months didn't fit. Only she, Pips and Gill were allowed into Daisy's bedroom to help her dress. Even Henrietta could be seen hurrying between the house and the marquee on the lawn and back again, checking that everything was as she had arranged.

'At least the weather's fine. Oh here, let me do your tie for you, Robert. Alice *is* rather busy. Oh, there's the front door bell. Who can that be?'

'Wainwright will answer it, Mother.'

'I'm not sure he will. I've never seen Wainwright in such a flap as he is this morning.'

But even as she spoke, Wainwright hurried past them and opened the front door.

'Good morning, Mr Wainwright. I hope we're not too early.'

Henrietta and Robert stared at each other.

'I know that voice,' Robert began. 'Surely . . .'

Henrietta began to laugh as they both turned

towards the front door to greet the new arrivals. 'So, that's who Daisy's surprise guests are.'

As she reached the front door, she held out her hands. '*William!* How wonderful to see you. Come in, come in, do. And this must be Brigitta – oh and your sons too. How perfectly marvellous.'

'I hope we're not imposing, Mrs Maitland, but Daisy said we were to come here this morning.'

'Of course, of course. We must get some bedrooms ready . . .'

'That's very kind of you, but we're staying in Lincoln for a week.'

'Well, if you decide you want to stay longer, you must come here when all the excitement has died down a little.' Henrietta smiled. 'It's so lovely to meet you all. You must certainly come to dinner one evening whilst you're here. Please say you'll at least do that?'

'That would be grand, thank you.'

'Now come into the parlour. Edwin is already there. Trying to get a bit of peace, I shouldn't wonder, but we'll soon put a stop to that. He'll be so glad to see you all. Wainwright, please would you ask Sarah to bring us coffee?'

Robert now shook hands with William, Brigitta, Pascal and Waldo. 'It's good to see you all again. My, you two have grown a bit since I last saw you and I'm glad you've all survived the war.'

There was so much to say to one another that it was soon time for them all to leave for the church – all except Robert and Daisy.

'It's so nice that she'll be able to walk to the

church,' Henrietta said, as she put on her hat. 'We were all so afraid it would rain, but the weather is just perfect. Now, we must go. William, you must all sit with us.'

The church was already crowded, but the sidesmen had valiantly kept the front pews vacant for the family. Moments before the bride was due, Alice slipped into her place and Pips took a seat next to Mitch, who had Milly, Paul and Jeff Pointer sitting with him. William sat beside Henrietta, grateful for her staunch support, and kept his gaze firmly fixed on the altar. He did not turn around even when the bridal march began and several heads turned to see Daisy walk up the aisle on her father's arm.

Johnny stood, tall and proud, at the altar steps with a smiling Luke beside him. They both turned to watch Daisy floating towards them. As she reached Johnny's side, he took her hand and kissed it. 'You look beautiful,' he whispered.

The service proceeded, the vows were made, the register signed and they were man and wife, walking triumphantly out of the church to the marquee where they stood to welcome all their guests. Robert, Alice, Henrietta and Edwin stood alongside them.

'Mitch,' Henrietta beckoned him as he entered the marquee, 'you must stand with us as Johnny's closest relative.'

'His only relative here,' Mitch murmured. 'How my sister-in-law would have loved today. I did everything I could to try to persuade her to make the trip, but . . .' He shrugged, signifying that his efforts had failed.

Henrietta squeezed his hand. 'Stand next to me and I will introduce you to everyone.'

'I'll never remember all the names,' he laughed as the family, followed by all the residents of Doddington village, filed into the marquee.

'No matter. They'll remember you.'

'That's what I'm afraid of,' he chuckled.

Henrietta had spent a week sorting out the seating plan only to have it thrown into disarray by the arrival of William and his family. Luckily, she had been able to move the places on one side of the long tables placed at right angles to the top table down four places and to slot the new arrivals in. She had also tactfully avoided putting William anywhere near his parents, though she couldn't help noticing, whilst they were all eating, that Norah's gaze hardly ever left William and his family.

As Johnny ended his bridegroom's speech, he said, 'There is just one other thing we'd like to tell you today.' He glanced down at Daisy and took her hand. 'As you know, Daisy is coming back to help her grandmother run the estate, as she always promised . . .'

'Thank goodness for that,' Robert said, and everyone laughed.

'What you are perhaps all wondering about is what I am going to do. Well, in the immediate future, I shall still be in the RAF. Originally, I signed on for six years, but, of course, that became longer because of the war. I've no intention of staying on any longer than I have to now, but I don't want to give up flying and nor does Daisy, so' – a broad grin lit his face – 'with my uncle Mitch's help and guidance, we're going to set up a flying school here in Lincolnshire. I'm sure that before long there will be quite a few disused airfields in the county that could be put to good use.'

There was a ripple of surprise around the gathering, but approval too. Henrietta was beaming. 'What a wonderful idea,' she said.

Luke's Best Man's speech was littered with funny anecdotes from Johnny's experiences in the RAF, and then, suddenly, his voice became less light-hearted.

'I would just crave your indulgence to tell you a little story. I do have Daisy's permission.' He glanced down at her and then, taking a deep breath, went on, 'Most of you probably know – or have guessed by now – that when my Spitfire was damaged, I bailed out over enemy territory near a place called Dranouter, just inside the Belgian border. I was very lucky to meet a sympathetic farmer, who arranged for a fellow member of the local Resistance to take me to Ypres, where I made my way to my Uncle William's farm, nearby. He and Aunt Brigitta hid me . . .' He glanced at his grandfather, Len, as he said quietly, 'They – and their son, Waldo, a member of the Resistance – saved my life at great risk to their own.'

Len's face displayed no emotion. Only Norah dabbed at her eyes with her handkerchief.

'But luck was with us,' Luke went on. 'The German officer in charge of patrolling the area was called Hans. Aunty Alice – Uncle Robert – do you remember treating a young German boy at Christmas in 1914 during the unofficial truce? When both sides climbed out of their trenches and played football?'

Alice and Robert glanced at each other and then nodded.

'He was that officer and he remembered that it had been William who'd carried him from the trenches to your first-aid post where his foot had to be amputated to save his life. Of course, he then became a prisoner-of-war and was taken to the coast – by William again – and brought to England where, I'm happy to say, he said he was treated with great kindness, even though he was a POW.

'He never forgot that you' – Luke waved his hand towards William, Pips, Robert and Alice – 'saved his life, and in return, he helped to save mine. He told William that I had to get away by a certain date when he was to be replaced by someone who would most certainly not be as lenient. Waldo, through his Resistance contacts, sent a coded message to England.' He grinned suddenly. 'One that I devised.' He glanced at Pips again. 'I knew from what Waldo told me about how the system worked that there was a good chance it would reach someone who would understand it. Luckily, it found its way to Aunty Pips and she knew at once that I was safe and, better still, exactly where I was. Arrangements were then made for me to be picked up by a member of the team who picked up our escapees or agents from enemy-occupied territory. Everything was in place and then the pilot who was coming broke his leg. At such short notice, there was no other official pilot available. There was only one person who could carry out such a dangerous mission; the one person who had advised them on the layout of Uncle William's farm and had helped to plot the course.' He turned to Daisy and his voice broke a little as he said, 'My wonderful, courageous cousin, Daisy.'

Daisy dropped her gaze and began to blush as a gasp of surprise flowed around the marquee.

'Daisy?' Henrietta said. 'Daisy flew across to Belgium in the dead of night? Was she allowed to do that?'

Luke smiled again. 'Officially, Aunty Hetty, no, but you know Daisy. Everyone's always said she's just like her Aunty Pips and that is *exactly* what Pips would have done.' He turned to her. 'Isn't it, Aunty Pips?'

Pips wriggled her shoulders. 'Well, yes, I suppose it is.'

Robert laughed. 'No "suppose" about it. Of course she would have done and I would expect no less from Daisy. I'm very proud of you, my darling. Did you ever have to undertake another such rescue mission?'

'No, but I would have done if I'd been asked.'

'Would you have come to rescue me, Daisy?' Harry piped up.

Daisy chuckled. 'Ah well, now, I'd've had to think about that one.'

There was laughter around the marquee. As it died away Luke went on, 'Flying Uncle Mitch's Lysander, she defied all the rules and regulations, put herself in obvious danger from flak and enemy aircraft as well as landing in enemy-occupied territory. But she came. She came and picked me up and flew me back home.' His voice broke again as he ended, 'I owe my life to William and his family and to Daisy, and I can never repay them.'

As he sat down, the applause was thunderous, but as it faded away, there was a murmur of surprise as Daisy stood up. 'I know it's not usual for the bride to say anything, but then I'm not usual, am I?'

'Most definitely not,' Robert said and laughter rippled again.

Daisy turned to Luke. 'You have repaid me, Luke. You and Johnny – and Gill – came to look for me when I bailed out of my unserviceable Spitfire on the last day of the war. But for the three of you, I would have died on that mountainside if I'd stayed there another night. So,' she held out her hand towards him, 'debt repaid in full.'

Luke rose and came to her, but instead of taking her hand he kissed her on both cheeks.

There was more applause, but now there were several folk wiping tears from their eyes. They had known very little of the danger their loved ones had been in – they could only guess at it at the time – but now they were hearing about it, they realized how close they had come to losing them.

As the speeches ended, everyone rose from the tables and left the marquee, spilling onto the lawn and gathering in small groups.

Len and Norah were standing on their own, a little to one side, though Norah's gaze constantly followed William and his family. Bess stood in front of them.

'Len Dawson, I want a word with you.'

Len sighed and said heavily, 'Aye, I thought you might. Get on with it then, woman.'

'High time you put an end to this nonsense for Norah's sake, if not ya own. Get yarsen across there and shake your son's hand and meet your grandsons.'

'Oh Bess . . .' Norah murmured, but there was a yearning in her tone.

Slowly Len began to move. Norah clutched Bess's arm as they watched him cross the grass to stand in front of William. Bess and Norah moved closer to see Len hold out a hand that trembled visibly.

Not caring now who heard, Len said, 'William, thank you for what you did to save Luke. I've been a stubborn old fool for far too long and I'm truly sorry for the hurt I've caused.'

William stood for a moment, staring at the man that he had not seen for over fifteen years. Len was changed. He was thinner and more stooped and his face was ravaged by time. Instead of taking his proffered hand, William put his arms about his father and drew him close. No more words were spoken, but the years of bitterness and heartache fell away.

'Well said, Len,' Bess Cooper now spoke up. 'I never thought I'd see the day, but I'm glad it's come. Norah, duck, go and give your grandsons a hug.'

Amidst the laughter and the tears, Mitch slipped away from the guests milling about the lawn and went in search of Betty.

'Is everything ready?' he asked her.

'Yes, Mr Hammond. Me and Jake have done everything you asked.'

'Thank you,' he said and kissed a startled Betty on both cheeks before returning to the wedding party with a grin that seemed to stretch from ear to ear. The bride and groom, indeed all the Maitland family, were still chatting and laughing and not wanting this glorious day to end. After an hour, Mitch went in search of Pips. He found her talking to Luke and Gill, arriving beside her to hear her say, 'So, another wedding next spring, is it? What are you going to do then, Luke?'

Luke glanced at Gill. 'We've talked it over with Gill's parents and my granddad and it's all agreed. Once I'm out of the RAF, I'll set up a branch of Granddad's wheelwright and blacksmithing business on Gill's farm. Her dad's already given us a piece of land. And Granddad has agreed that, in time, Sam and Harry will run this end. And it sounds now as if young Bernard wants to stay here. He's taken to the country life.'

'What a splendid idea, don't you think so, Mitch?'

'It is.' He smiled. 'So, everyone's going to be perfectly settled.'

Pips pulled a face. 'All except me. I've no idea what on earth I'm going to do with myself now.'

'Ah, I have an idea about that. Just come with me. Excuse us . . .'

Mitch took her hand and led her through the throng.

'Where are you taking me?'

'You'll see.'

He led her round the side of the house to where a car, gleaming in the sunshine, was parked.

'Oh, Mitch. A Bugatti.' She paused, her glance roaming over it and coming to rest on the number plate. 'Oh. *Oh!* It's *my* Bugatti. Wherever did you find it?'

'In my garage at Brooklands. It's been there ever since you sold it.'

Pips gasped as she stared at him. 'You – you bought it?'

He nodded. 'Jeff repaired it after your crash and has kept it in good order ever since.'

'Oh Mitch. I don't know what to say.'

'Don't say anything. Just get in. We're going for a spin. I'll have to drive, though, as it's licensed to me at the moment.'

He helped her to climb in.

'But we can't just go for a drive. This is Daisy's wedding day . . .'

'And you really think those two lovebirds are going to miss us?'

'Well, perhaps not, but—'

He started the engine and drove carefully down the drive. One or two guests watched them go but only Henrietta and Daisy, hand in hand with Johnny, came to the edge of the lawn and waved, their faces wreathed in smiles.

As Mitch guided the car through the gate, Pips said, 'Where are we going?'

Above the noisy engine, he shouted, 'Gretna Green. Philippa Allender, will you marry me?'

As he gathered speed, the wind whipped through her hair and she gasped. Life with Mitch Hammond would be a roller-coaster; there would never be a dull moment. But it was exactly what she wanted.

Pips threw back her head and laughed aloud, the merry sound bouncing on the breeze. 'Yes!' she shouted back. 'Yes, I will.'